On Dancing Hill

Sarah Challis

review

First published in hardback in 2004
by REVIEW
An imprint of Headline Book Publishing

First published in paperback in 2005
by REVIEW

10 9 8 7 6 5 4 3 2 1

ISBN 0 7553 2574 5 (A format)
ISBN 0 7553 0039 4 (B format)

Typeset in Meridien by
Letterpart Limited, Reigate, Surrey

Printed and bound in Great Britain by
Mackays of Chatham plc, Chatham, Kent

HEADLINE BOOK PUBLISHING
A division of Hodder Headline
338 Euston Road
London NW1 3BH

www.reviewbooks.co.uk
www.hodderheadline.com

Sarah Challis, whose father is the distinguished cinematographer Christopher Challis, travelled widely with film units as a child. She has since lived in Scotland and California but is now happily settled in a Dorset village with three rescued dogs and three chickens. She is married with four sons.

Also by Sarah Challis

Killing Helen
Turning for Home
Blackthorn Winter

In happy memory of my lovely sister-in-law,
Michele

Chapter One

Long before she even got to Waterloo, the excitement Kate Hutchins had felt as she planned for her holiday had all but dissipated. For a while, as the Exeter train rattled through the wet green countryside carrying her to London on the first stage of her journey, she had still been fired by the nervy determination that had built up as the day of departure drew near. It took this stiffening of resolve to leave at all, and not to throw her bags down on the chair in the kitchen and say, 'Right, that's it! You've won! I won't go. I hope you're satisfied.'

But when she had settled back in her seat, the presence of her passport and Eurostar ticket checked and double-checked, her small suitcase in the rack above her head, just when she should have been feeling liberated and carefree, leaving it all behind her – the muddy lanes, the dripping trees, the sodden sheep, the gloomy husband – she felt instead a nasty clutch of remorse and guilt.

They knew what they were doing, the whole lot of them. They had played the guilt card for all it was worth: Josh, her husband; George, her father; Len, their farmworker. Even the dogs had followed her about with gloomy, preoccupied expressions, determined that she should know the extent of their suffering as they sensed her betrayal.

1

Josh had been all right about it to begin with. Back at Christmas when their three grown-up children, Ben, Anna and Edward, had clubbed together and bought her the week's painting holiday in France, he had seemed pleased for her. 'You deserve it, Mum!' Anna had said, hugging her round the middle. 'You'll never get Dad to take you away anywhere, so you've got to go on your own. That's all right by you, Dad, isn't it?' and Kate had looked over at Josh, who was wearing a jaunty paper hat from a cracker, his long, fair face flushed from drinking port, and he had said, 'Fine, by me. Lets me off the hook!' and they had all laughed.

Then as the weeks and months rolled by, Kate had felt an unspoken resentment developing. 'When is this thing you're off on?' Josh asked, and by not giving it its proper name, not saying 'your painting holiday' or 'the holiday the children gave you', he managed to convey his disapproval. A heavy, laden atmosphere began to settle about the forthcoming trip, so that Kate came to dread the subject being raised at all.

Then his campaign moved up a gear and a week before her departure he announced at the breakfast table, as he buttered his toast, 'I might need to be in London while you're away. You'd better find someone to look after things here.' Kate looked up in dismay. She nearly protested before she remembered how this had to be played.

'OK,' she said casually, but was moved at the same time by a quick boil of anger. She got up and began to clear plates.

She knew this passive response would not satisfy him. As if on cue, he put down the toast and said in the tone of a weary reprimand, 'You can't ask Len to see to the dogs and chickens. He's got enough to do. I'm going to want him for the silage if the weather improves.'

'No. All right.' Keep calm, she told herself, her heart thumping as she bent forward to load the dishwasher. 'I'll find someone. When are you likely to be away?'

'Well, I don't know yet. I just might need to, that's all. I might have to go up to see Jarvis.' Jarvis was their solicitor who, as far as Kate could remember, Josh had met in person three times in their thirty years of married life. 'I mean, I can't be tied here while you go gadding off,' he went on in a self-righteous tone.

'No, of course not. I wouldn't expect you to.' She swept across the table with a cloth. 'Have you finished?' she asked, indicating his plate.

He glanced up at her face. He had expected an outburst by now. She could have accused him of being deliberately unhelpful, making things difficult, being obstructive. Then he would have been ready with his big guns – oh, excuse me, who is being selfish here? Who is shelving all responsibilities, apparently without a second thought? Who is being left to cope alone? But her acquiescence spoiled this chance to occupy the moral high ground and denied him the opportunity to point out that going away on this holiday at all was reprehensible.

Grudgingly, he gave up his plate. He sat a moment longer, watching her back as she kept it resolutely turned to him, busying herself at the sink. She was wearing her faded jeans with the splodge of white paint on the seat. Josh remembered the sunny afternoon last summer when she had brought mugs of tea out to him and Len and had sat on a freshly painted ledge in the milking parlour. He knew why he felt so affronted. It wasn't that he wanted to stop her going exactly. More that he was offended that she wanted to go. It seemed to him like a rejection. A rejection of him, the farm, everything.

The place was not the same when she was not there. Damn it, it wasn't just a matter of his convenience, that he would have to fend for himself for a week. He was quite capable of doing that. It was that without her, without the small domestic clatter drifting through the open kitchen window as she cooked to Classic FM, without the sight of her walking across the fields with the collies running in front, or her head bobbing about above the garden wall as she gardened in the afternoons, without these common-place things, Josh felt lonely and adrift. It was only right that she should be made to feel guilty. Which clearly she did not. Maintaining a huffy silence, he got up and went out of the back door without saying goodbye.

As soon as he had gone, Kate sat back down at the table and allowed a stream of angry thoughts to fill her head. He's doing it deliberately, she thought. He wants me to know the cost of this bit of freedom. He wants to make sure I pay the price. Of course he won't have to go to London, but by making this point, by behaving like this, he is spoiling everything. Taking the pleasure away. Why doesn't he come out with it and say he doesn't want me to go? Because if he did, it would show him for what he is – selfish and self-centred – and the children would get at him. He can't stop me but he wants me to feel guilty.

There was an easy way round the practical difficulties he had raised, round the obstacle course he always set when he disapproved of something she wanted to do. She knew a reliable girl in the next village who would come and feed the dogs and the hens on her way to work. It would only take a telephone call to arrange, but of course what had taken place between herself and her husband over the breakfast table was not about any of that. Rather, it was an

4

elaborate emotional skirmish over familiar battle-strewn ground which lay between them. It was about pride and control and self-determination, and it was a battle Kate felt she could not afford to lose. Although she knew this was the case, she still had to make the necessary practical arrangements as if it really were a matter of the care of her animals while she was away.

'It's just in case,' Kate explained to the girl when she got her on the telephone. 'I don't think for a minute that Josh will need to go to London, but just in case.' Anyway, it was as well to have this back-up.

Then Josh managed to get a heavy, noisy cold. He trumpeted round the house, carrying a box of tissues, blowing his nose in great booming blasts. Whenever he answered the telephone and the caller commented on how bad he sounded he would adopt a stoical attitude. 'No, no. I'm OK,' she heard him say through a blocked nose. 'A bit more than a cold, though. Actually more like flu.'

'Poor old thing,' said Kate, realising that he was upping the stakes. You'll get pneumonia, if you can, she thought. Anything to stop me.

Later Len came in for his coffee, sitting at the kitchen table with his grey hair flattened by the lie of his old tweed cap which he had taken off and now turned in his hands. His normally cheerful, weatherbeaten face was cast down. 'You are going, then,' he said in a doom-laden voice.

'That's right, Len. I can't wait. A week in France!' Kate slid a spatula around a bowl of cake mixture and dolloped golden mounds into waiting tins.

'I don't know what you want to go there for. I can't abide them French,' he said indignantly. 'Rob us British farmers, they do, in that EU. Still won't touch our beef, the buggers.'

5

He made her holiday sound a treasonable offence, she thought as she put the tins into the Aga. She closed the door and said lightly, 'I promise I won't eat theirs either, Len. It's for the sunshine, you see. That's why I'm going. To paint in the sunshine.' As she spoke, she imagined a field of yellow sunflowers under a hot blue sky.

'Sunshine!' Len gave a dismissive snort. The truth was he didn't like her going either. He knew from experience that Josh would be short-tempered while she was away and working with him was not something he looked forward to. More than that, Len didn't hold with women going off on their own. Not decent married women like Kate. Especially not abroad. In his view it could only lead to trouble. When he and his wife, Rita, wanted a holiday, they took a caravan down at Weymouth, and that was far enough. He couldn't see how you could do better than Weymouth. It had it all, as far as he was concerned.

Sunshine, indeed. Why did she need to paint in the sunshine? Painters just painted what was there, didn't they? Sun or not. Lovely pictures, he'd seen, of sheep in a snowstorm. He finished his coffee in silence, put his mug in the sink and stomped off, back to the muck-spreading.

George, her father, was the next one to express his disapproval. The day before she left, Kate delivered his week's shopping to his bungalow at the foot of the con-crete farm drive. As she unpacked the plastic bags onto the table she heard the lavatory flush and then the shuffle of his feet as he came through to the kitchen.

'Hello, Dad. I've got your things here. I'm just going to put this ham in the fridge.'

'Friday's your usual day,' he said, standing watching, resting on his stick, dressed in his check country shirt and corduroy trousers. Once a tall man, he was now stooped

6

by age, his thick bushy hair a snowy white.

'I'm away tomorrow, remember. Off to France.'

'Ah, yes. France. I forgot. How long is it you're going for?'

'Only a week, Dad. I'll be home next Saturday. You'll hardly know I've been away.'

'I've got that doctor's appointment on Wednesday. What am I going to do about that?'

'Dad! I told you. Susie's taking you.' Kate knew this was not popular. Her sister-in-law, Susie, was as much use as a wet hen-pheasant as far as her father was concerned.

'Hmm. I don't like going with her. You know that. I think I'll cancel it. Wait till you get back.'

'You can't do that, Dad. You need to have your check-up. You're getting your ears syringed, too.'

'Well, I don't know.' He sat down at the table and sighed. 'She'll bang on about the farm, like she always does. I'll be at her mercy.' Susie never lost the opportunity to complain how hard her husband, Kate's brother Tom, had to work on their neighbouring farm.

'You'll have to put up with it. Pretend you're more deaf than you really are. Keep saying, "What?" '

'What?'

'Yes, like that. Look, I'm putting this lasagne in the freezer.'

'Do I like lasagne?'

'Yes, you do. Dad, why haven't you eaten this melon? It's past it now. I'll have to throw it out.'

'I didn't know what to do with it,' he said gloomily. 'All those bloody pips. France, eh?'

'Yes. Only for a week, and you *must* go to the doctor. It's all arranged. Susie will come for you at ten fifteen.' Kate looked at her watch. Outside her little car was loaded with trays of homemade cakes and pies which she sold to local shops and restaurants. 'Now, I must go. I've got my deliveries to make yet.'

'Won't you stop for a coffee?'

'No, I have to get on.' Kate kissed the top of her father's head. 'Take care, old thing. I'll see you when I get back.'

George shrugged and pulled a face, indicating that this would involve a measure of luck or chance. He's really making it hard, thought Kate, with a pang.

'Well, I hope you enjoy yourself,' he said. 'You know I'll miss you.'

He came to the door as she got into the car and reversed into the lane. She could hardly bear to glance in the mirror and see him standing there looking dejected, the droop of his shoulders eloquent with unspoken reproach, his large, red, farmer's hands hanging helpless by his sides.

When it finally came to leaving, it was Tom who took her to the station. Josh had a lorry of calves to take to Taunton and had left with them soon after milking. There was a last-minute fuss over the paperwork and Kate had been glad that they had had something to distract them. She had checked and double-checked that the passports for the beasts were correct and in the cab of the lorry, but at the last moment Josh decided to hold some back and send others in their place. When they had everything finally sorted out and the calves loaded, there was only time for him to turn to her and say, 'Well, have a good time.' He held her briefly and at the last moment managed to mutter, 'I'll miss you,' and Kate was overwhelmed by compassion and affection and hugged him back.

'I will, I will,' she said. 'I'll miss you, too,' and she meant it.

'That's it then,' he said. He could not bear what he called 'scenes'. 'I'd better be off. Telephone to let me know you're there safely.' As he climbed into the lorry, he turned back and added with a half-smile, 'Mind you paint an effing masterpiece.'

Standing in the yard in her old dressing gown, she waved until he was out of sight, the lorry rattling down the drive to the bottom of the hill where she knew her father would look out of his kitchen window and take note of its passing. It was a beautiful morning. Everything seemed to be conspiring to make it hard to leave. Dancing Hill Farm, a name which always brought a catch to Kate's throat, was a plain post-war farmhouse with a serviceable yard and set of buildings tucked into the side of the hill, with Hanging Wood behind. In front, like a canvas, a wide landscape rolled round the farm. The view over the valley was all green and shimmering now in the early sunshine and silvery with dew. The small grass fields, some pale where the silage or hay had already been cut, some dark with long, lush grass, each known to Kate by name, Berry Close, Boar Close, Goodly Hill, John's Field, Meslams, New Leaze, Ropers Ground, sloped like a lumpy bedspread down into the dark trees where the stream ran through, and up again the other side to meet the blue line of the distant hills. From high above, a lark sang and swallows swooped in and out of the barns where they had nests and young to feed.

Kate's black and white collies, Patch and Sly and old grey-chinned Bonnie, hovered round her knees, nudging at her hands with cold muzzles. She stooped to caress them and they pressed their soft, long-furred bodies against her legs. These dogs were special to Kate for all sorts of reasons. She loved them because they were so clever and quick and sensitive and loyal, but they were more than that. Patch and Sly still worked the remaining small flock of sheep with her father, and brought the cows in for milking, and all three were descendants of a long line of Dancing Hill sheepdogs, stretching back to when Kate was a child. God's Little Heaven, her father called this place then and Kate thought he was right, in those uncomplicated days when farming hadn't changed much for generations.

There was a clarity to the morning and a glassy brightness in the sky which suggested the early sunshine might not last, and sure enough, rumpled purple clouds threatened and rain was blowing in from the west by the time Tom sounded his horn to collect Kate for her train. She was ready, watching for him, and ran out, throwing her case in the back.

'Lovely morning!' said Tom, not getting out. His tall frame, which had become bulky in middle age, was folded into the driver's seat. His cosy-looking rounded tummy which strained at the buttons of his work shirt rested comfortably on his lap. Her junior by three years, his hair was still dark and boyish looking, only going grey around his temples and was cropped short in a modern style that Susie liked. His round, freshly shaved face smiled across at his sister. 'English summer! I reckon you're going to the right place!' He looked at her and added, 'You look nice. New hair-style?' It was typical of Tom to notice and comment. He was extraordinary like that, taking a genuine interest in what Susie wore and often choosing her clothes himself. Kate had once found him reading a copy of *Vogue* at the kitchen table, which for a farmer was the equivalent of being caught wearing suspenders and stockings and a French maid's outfit.

10

'I had it cut yesterday. Do you like it?'

'Yes. Makes you look younger.' Kate smiled at him gratefully.

'Got everything?' he asked. 'Kissed the dogs goodbye?'

'Of course. They've been sulking all the morning. They wouldn't speak to me when I left!'

'Funny, isn't it, how they know. What about Josh? Is he sulking too?'

'Naturally!' Kate grinned. 'And Len and Dad.'

'Don't you worry about any of them,' said Tom, turning round in the yard. 'Do them good to manage on their own. Susie says she'll ask Josh and Dad for lunch on Sunday.'

'That's kind of her.' Kate imagined the elaborate meal, the daintily set table and knew how little they would enjoy it. They were spoiled, that was the trouble.

George was up and dressed when the lorry went by. He'd had his early cup of tea and rinsed out the cup and set it upside down on the draining board. Later on he'd have a piece of toast and marmalade. It didn't do to have his breakfast too early. Kate had pointed out that if he got the whole lot over and done with by seven o'clock, it made for a long, empty morning. The days were well in the past when he had a cooked breakfast, a farmer's breakfast. When his wife, Pat, had been alive she had always laid a proper plate in front of him when he got in from the milking. Bacon, eggs, fried bread and sausage. Sometimes mushrooms and tomatoes, too. She used to grow tomatoes all along the south wall of the old farmhouse. He could smell them now, the smell of heat and sunshine. Sometimes he found big creamy-capped horse mushrooms out in the cow field when he went to bring in the herd for milking. He used to tuck them into his shirtfront and put

11

them on the kitchen table as a surprise. Chocolate brown and fleshy, they were, the gills almost black when they'd been in the pan with a bit of butter and a dash of Worcestershire sauce.

Although he was going deaf he heard the cattle lorry come banging down the drive. Not that Josh drove too fast. No, he was always careful when he'd got stock on board. It was a disgrace how some loaded trucks were driven, with the poor beasts thrown about at every bend and piled in a heap to the front when the brakes were slammed on. He watched the lorry turn into the lane and as it went past his window, Josh looked across and raised his hand. George did not wave back. He didn't like to be caught watching. It was undignified, somehow. It served as a reminder of how his life was reduced. Just an old man, watching out of a window. A back number, that was what he was, left to shuffle about indoors, making cups of tea, no use to man nor beast.

He went through to his sitting room where the French windows opened onto the garden and beyond to his favourite view across the valley. It was a bright morning – bright too early, he'd guess. There'd be rain later. They wouldn't be haymaking today. Josh had only managed to get a couple of fields cut in June, down at the bottom, along the stream. Lovely hay, that was. Crisp and dry and fragrant. It filled the Dutch barn with the smell of summer. After that, it had rained near on every day and it was getting to the point where if they didn't get the rest cut soon, it would all be wasted, the goodness gone out of it.

He'd have liked to put his sheep down in the meadows from where they had taken the hay. Those fields were never sprayed and were full of herbs and old grasses; there was nowhere like it for grazing. It had been a good three years since he'd been able to walk down there. Through the gate across the lane, down the slope to the hunting gate in the corner of the big field they called Goodly Hill, then along the blackthorn hedge to the gate at the bottom. It was a fine old hedge, that one, properly cut and laid so that it was thick and black and a good four foot wide. Under it, at intervals, were the badger runs, where the earth was scuffed and bare, and through all its spiny branches twined sweet-smelling dog roses, honeysuckle and traveller's joy. This time of the year it would be grown all along the edge with the cream plumes of meadowsweet and tangled purple vetch.

That gate at the bottom was off its hinges and had to be lifted open. George could remember the feel of the silvery old wood under his hand and the rusty chain that went round the gatepost, the two ends joined by sliding a T hook through a link. Just the other side of the gateway was a flat, smooth rock, resting in the grass by the old gatepost. George could see it now in his mind. It was a bleached cream colour, as big as the seat of a dining chair, domed slightly at one end. It was a bugger, really, catching the tyres of vehicles that cut the corner through the gateway, but they'd never thought of getting it shifted. It was part of what made the place particular. When he was down there with his dogs they'd wait eagerly by his side for him to get the clumsy old gate open and they would crowd up on that rock, jostling for position as if it was a vantage point.

Open that gate and you were in Ropers Ground, a long field that ran along the stream where there was a line of thickly growing trees, hazel, willow, thorn and wild plum, which made a dark tunnel over the water. You could walk along the line of them and not know that there was water running down below in the dark deep pools, hidden from the light. It was a favourite place for the roe deer to lie up during the day, secretive and undisturbed. At the far end the trees thinned out and there was a sloping bank down to a wide shallow pool where the cattle could drink and the dogs, on a hot day, rushed down into the brown water and tossed it about in silver showers. A little gated foot-bridge crossed the water there, leading to another low meadow on the other side, before the land started to climb upwards. These were the two best hay fields on the farm. The grass grew lush and green, even when the season was dry. It flooded in the winter and the ground held the moisture deep down and never became parched or cracked open in a thirsty mosaic.

He used to summer his cattle down along the stream after the hay had been taken off, but that was nearly twenty years ago when he still had his Red Devons. The sitting room in which he stood held many reminders of those days, photographs taken at cattle shows and silver cups on the mantelpiece – but that was another story. No, he'd have liked to run his ewes and lambs down there but he had to face the fact that he couldn't make it that far to check on them every day. For the last three years the sheep had been up behind him on Dancing Hill, near the farm, a five-minute walk up the concrete drive. Even that felt a bit of a haul some days, but the surface was smooth underfoot with nothing to trip on, and he could always stop and rest to catch his breath and he was never out of sight of the house and Kate's watchful eye. He was a liability, these days. It was no good harking back to when he had been young and strong, a broad-shouldered man, well over six feet with a thatch of dark hair. He'd even lost the strength in his hands, crooked as they had become with arthritis. He'd had a pot of jam on the table for two days last week, unable to turn the screw-top lid. In the end, Kate, without saying anything, had picked it up and loosened the lid with a quick turn of the wrist and put it back in the cupboard.

Failing eyesight and growing deafness meant that since last year he had had to give up driving. That was his independence gone in one fell swoop. Kate was good about carting him here and there, and she had come to an arrangement with Wilf, his retired stockman, and ten years his junior, to drive him to market or to occasional cattle shows, or to follow the hounds in the winter. Wilf was good company. They had the same interests and he remembered how things were in the past. Sometimes Josh took him round the fields in the Land Rover and he liked that, but it wasn't the same, jolting about as a passenger, looking out of the window like a bloody tourist. If you weren't working the land, you lost contact with it and it began to change, the mark of your hand fading away. Josh was a tidier farmer than ever he had been. In his day there had been stands of nettles behind the barns where the butterflies used to feed and where old machinery lay rusting. There had been rough edges everywhere, gates tied with baler twine, mud two foot deep in the gateways, old baths serving as water troughs, pigs rooting under the apple trees in the orchard. All that was gone. Everything businesslike and in good order now and slowly he had relinquished his hold over the place.

That was the way it should be. When he'd got back from the war, back from the desert, his father had moved over for him and he'd made his own changes to the way things were done. You had to let go and stop dwelling on the past. Josh and Tom had to survive in different times and the fact that they spent more hours filling in forms and doing paperwork than they did out farming meant that he didn't envy them the job. He was too old to keep up with it all. Farmers were just the pawns of politicians, it seemed to him. He could understand what Josh told him about efficiency and having to expand to survive. That stood to reason, but the way of life he had known and loved had gone forever.

He didn't like to think of the economies of keeping his sheep. The bottom line, as he was forever hearing Josh call it. Although his poll Dorsets fetched good money at market because they produced lean meat that the modern house-wife wanted, he suspected that Josh looked upon them as an old man's hobby. He could imagine Kate saying, 'They're all Dad's got left, you can't get rid of them.' He wouldn't be telling Josh that he'd paid out forty-eight pounds to the gang of shearers three weeks back and he'd got a cheque yesterday for twenty-two pounds for the fleeces. That didn't add up for a start. Lovely fleeces they were too, clean and soft.

He went through to the kitchen and got the loaf out of the breadbin and set it on the board. He carved two neat slices and as he was putting them in the toaster, caught sight of Tom's car going past. George glanced at the kitchen clock. He'd be on time to collect Kate, so he didn't know what the hurry was. She would be ready and waiting for him, bags packed. She was well organised. Never one for a last-minute rush like a lot of women. Watching the car fly up the drive, he noticed that the bright promise of the morning had given way to the rain he had predicted and that congested grey clouds loomed from the west. There would be no hay cut today.

He was still standing at the window when the car came

back with Kate. Tom sounded the horn and she waved and then she must have said something to Tom because he pulled over and stopped in the lane and she jumped out and came running back to the front door. It took George a moment to go through to the hall and get the door open, the new lock Josh had fitted was tricky, and there she was, sheltering in the porch from the rain. She gave him a hug and reached up to kiss his cheek. 'Bye, Dad,' she said, laughing. 'Take care, you old codger! See you in a week!'

When she'd gone, still waving, he went back through to the kitchen. His toast looked unappetising, two pale slices on the plate next to the tub of spreadable butter or whatever it was that Kate bought him. He disliked eating alone. There was no ceremony to it somehow. Often he forgot whether he'd had his breakfast and had to check to see if his plate had been used and was washed clean in his rack on the draining board. He'd miss Kate, no doubt of that. Seven days seemed a long time. He couldn't fathom why she wanted to go off like this. Not when she had a husband and family and the farm. It didn't seem natural, somehow. All this nonsense about wanting to paint. It was a mystery to him.

After breakfast he would put on his waterproofs and get up to the sheep. With Josh out of the way, he would take his time, have a chat to Len, look the heifers over, cast his eye over the new bull, make a morning of it. The dogs would be glad to see him. They would be downcast with Kate away. When he got back from all of that, it would be time for Wilf to collect him for their weekly visit to the White Hart in the village. That would be his day taken care of.

Despite her brother's cheerful assurances Kate fell silent and anxious on the way to the station. Had she remembered everything? Frozen meals were labelled and stacked in the freezer, telephone numbers on a list in the kitchen, instructions for Joyce who would be in on Tuesday and Thursday to clean, her father's appointment taken care of, all the loose ends of her busy life neatly tied. Now was the moment to sit back and enjoy the sensation of doing something for herself for once. She knew this, but she still had to battle with waves of apprehension. Somewhere in her head she could hear a voice asking, what was she thinking of, setting off on her own, going where she knew no one, leaving everything familiar and everything that she loved behind?

On the train, she tried to relax but her nerves were stretched so taut that the passenger announcements made her jump and she could hardly swallow the coffee she bought from the refreshment trolley. This is absurd, she told herself sternly. I am a woman of fifty-two, not a nervous teenager. Looking out of the window, she thought of Josh, driving home with the empty lorry, and of the pattern his day would take. The rain would halt the silage-making and he would be frustrated and bad-tempered. She imagined the still, tidy kitchen where she had left him bread and cheese and homemade pickle in the larder for his lunch. She pictured the scene in her mind like a Dutch painting – a room which looked as if someone had just that moment walked out and closed the door, yet leaving something of themselves in the arrangement of the furniture, the objects on the table, the apron over the back of a chair. She wondered in what way Josh would miss her. Just by not being there, she supposed, as you miss anything that is suddenly removed.

The dogs would be lying in their shed in the yard, watchful, ears pricked at the slightest noise and after a moment's listening, laying their noses back on their paws, dejected that she had left them. At the bottom of the drive her father would be reading the newspaper, waiting for the rain to stop before he slowly climbed the hill to look at his sheep. Tom was right. Life would go on without her.

Through the train window the lines of terraced houses thickened and then a congestion of factories and ware-houses flashed past. She checked her watch and found there was only twenty minutes left before Waterloo. Soon they would be passing Clapham where Anna shared a flat with two young male lawyers, an arrangement Kate had found extraordinary to begin with but could now see was successful. Domestic chores were strictly divided and Anna never did more than her share – in fact, Kate suspected she was rather idle. She had arrived once to find Anna lying on the sofa reading a novel while Jeremy vacuumed round her, wearing a T-shirt and boxer shorts. 'Here, Jems, make us a cuppa,' she had said, and he had obediently switched the Hoover off, neatly coiled the flex, and gone to fill the kettle. Where does she get it from, Kate had thought, this freedom from any feelings of obligation towards men? She thought of her own mother who would not allow her father to so much as pick up a tea towel, and of Josh, who although willing to clear the table and stack the dish-washer, would never consider tackling dirty saucepans or brushing a floor. Anna was, Kate thought fondly, a new breed.

She had telephoned the night before. 'You'll have a fab time, Mum. The place looks so beautiful – just think, the chance to paint all day, every day. Delicious French food and buckets of vino. Sunshine. Good company. You'll come back a new woman! For heaven's sake, don't worry about home. They'll all be fine. I'll ring Dad in the week and check up on him, and Tom will keep an eye on Grandpa.'

The thing is, thought Kate, it's not as easy as that. Married as long as Josh and I have been – since childhood, practically – hardly spending a day apart, it feels so odd to strike out alone, as if part of me is missing.

This mutual dependency was the norm amongst older, traditional farming couples, and it was lovely in some ways, like snuggling under a security blanket of seamless coexistence, but it could also feel constricting and binding – more like a straitjacket than a comforter. Farmers and their wives worked alongside, bickered and bullied and loved and supported one another until before they knew it the years went by and they had grown together like the dog rose and the blackthorn in the hedges, the one shaped and formed by the other and impossible to pull apart.

This is what I have to resist, she told herself as the train drew into Clapham Junction. Before it's too late. Before I lose all sense of who I am. Mother, daughter, wife, all those responsibilities, and to be fair, all those rewards, but somewhere there's still me, I hope. A tiny kernel of something original that's not been shaped by other people's expectations. There's got to be more in my life – or at least different things than Josh wants in his. This holiday for a start.

Arriving at Waterloo took her mind off home. Although she had plenty of time, Kate found herself hurrying as she made her way to the Eurostar terminal. On her infrequent trips to London she had seen the elegant silver trains sliding in and out but had never used the service before. As she went down the escalator to the ticket check and passport control, she already felt removed from the commonplace travellers in the station above. The Eurostar passengers looked different – more sophisticated, perhaps, more stylish. Some were obviously foreign, not just European but

American, Japanese and Australian. Gaggles of young people with enormous backpacks looked as if they were embarking on long, carefree trips and there was already, Kate felt, a sense of endless glamorous possibilities.

She noticed that the staff wore smart uniforms with gold braid, more like an airline than a railway, and the handsome young man who came forward to show her how to feed her ticket into the machine at the barrier and wait for it to be stamped and to re-emerge, spoke with a charming French accent. He smiled as he handed her back her passport. ''Ave a good trip,' he said. Kate smiled and thanked him and felt her spirits lift.

On the other side of the security checkpoint, a steel and glass space opened out where people strolled or sat on low seats waiting for the departure screens to indicate that their train to Brussels or Lille or Paris was about to board. The atmosphere was relaxed, unhurried, and utterly unlike the frenzy of an airport. Kate felt as if she had passed some sort of test and had been permitted to enter a different world, like playing an adult game of snakes and ladders where she had managed to avoid sliding back down the snakes.

Somewhere amongst these people was a Mrs Elspeth Hunter who would be joining her on the painting course. Up until now Kate had been too preoccupied with other things to wonder what this unknown woman would be like. Now she began to speculate as she joined a queue to buy a cup of coffee. Anna had pointed out that it didn't much matter, that apart from the train journey when she may be glad of company, she could be as independent as she liked once they arrived. She and Mrs Hunter did not have to be friends, but of course it would be pleasant if they hit it off. For some reason Kate had formed a mental picture of someone like Miss Bell, her old art teacher from her schooldays, who was as thin as a rake and wore ankle socks and T-bar shoes and had wild frizzy grey hair.

Not far away, in a taxi crawling over Westminster Bridge, Elspeth Hunter was applying lipstick, a sophisticated plum colour called Cool Claret. Checking her face and finding everything in order, she snapped shut the small square of her silver compact mirror and consulted her watch. She was cutting it fine, but that was hardly her fault. Her Portuguese cleaner, Maria, who was supposed to have called round in the morning to collect a door key, had telephoned to say that she was sick, forcing Elspeth to trek over to her flat to drop it off. She had nipped down the Fulham Road to change a pair of white linen trousers for a size larger – always depressing, but at sixty one couldn't go in for that sliced bottom effect. Then she had rung Archie to say goodbye and he'd been quite upset, poor old thing. She had had to be brisk on the telephone. 'Now don't be silly, darling,' she had told him. 'It's only for a week and I will ring you the minute I get back.' At eighty-two, for the first time since she had known him, he was getting sentimental.

She checked her bag for her new copy of *Vogue* and her sunglasses. Both there. She sat back in her seat. In a short time she would arrive at Waterloo and from then on she could switch off and enjoy the fun of being out of London for a week in the summer. After Ascot and Wimbledon were over, there was a lull with nothing much to entertain until August, when, in the old days, she and Archie would have gone north for a bit of golf and then the grouse. He was past all that now, but my goodness, they had had fun and he had his memories. At least she had given him that.

She wondered what this other woman, this Kate someone or other, would be like. It was rather annoying to have someone foisted on her when she much preferred travelling alone. Still, there was no need to talk. Good manners did not demand an endless conversation and a sharing of life histories all the way from London to St Raphael. Elspeth hoped that her companion wouldn't be a retired teacher or something dull like that. Women holidaying alone were always rather suspect in her experience. Sad spinsters or lonely widows, as a rule. Of course, one shouldn't generalise. She herself was a widow, but you could hardly call her lonely.

Ah, they had arrived. Collecting her things, she stepped elegantly from the cab and, after paying the driver, coolly trundled her wheeled case into the station with a mere ten minutes to spare. She swept straight through the Eurostar departure lounge and up the escalator to the platform. The hustle of boarding the train was all but over and she congratulated herself on her good timing. Counting the carriages, she found coach 12 and suggested to a young man struggling with a backpack that he might like to lift in her suitcase. This safely stored, she entered the grey and yellow carriage and looked for her seat number. Thank goodness, no babies or young children, just the usual businessmen already poring over their laptops and four burly Frenchmen at a table, who had lost no time in opening a bottle of red wine.

Now where was this woman she was travelling with? Halfway down the carriage she spotted what must be her, sitting by the window. With relief Elspeth thought, well, she looks all right. Middle-aged, rather a nice face, dressed in a pair of jeans and a pale blue long-sleeved T-shirt. No gold sandals or ankle chains, she was relieved to see, just plain brown loafers and rather a pretty silver bracelet. Where she had pushed up her sleeves her forearms were tanned, and altogether she had a nutty brownness about her. A neglected complexion – the rosy broken-veined cheeks of a countrywoman, shockingly unmanicured hands, but pretty, curly, glossy hazel-coloured hair. Elspeth was expecting brown eyes, but when Kate turned from the window and looked up at her, she saw they were a bright blue and fringed with dark lashes.

'Hello,' she said, extending a hand. 'I'm Elspeth Hunter. We're travelling companions, I think.'

Kate, seeing a good-looking woman, older than herself, sixty perhaps, half rose and took her hand. 'Hello,' she said. 'I'm Kate Hutchins. I was terrified that you had missed the train or that I had got on the wrong one.' She laughed nervously. The slim, elegant woman who slid into the seat opposite her was not what she had been expecting at all and the image of Miss Bell faded abruptly. At that moment, the whistle blew and the train slid soundlessly from the station. Kate and Elspeth smiled across the table as they glided past graffiti-daubed walls and jumbled house backs, junk-filled balconies of tenement blocks and rubbish-strewn yards. 'Amazing, isn't it? The detritus of human life,' said Elspeth, turning to look out of the window, 'and I expect it all appears quite tidy from the other side.'

Across the river in another part of London, Anna Hutchins swivelled round on her desk chair and glanced out of the window. Her office was fourteen storeys up and the view was magnificent. Even after eleven months of sitting in the same seat, she was still riveted by the city spread below. The uniform pale grey of the buildings was broken by the vivid green of parks and squares and gardens and the shining, luminous ribbon of the Thames which wound through its heart, past famous landmarks like the Houses of Parliament and the Tower of London that from here looked matchbox-sized. Traffic moved steadily along the grid of streets, the red double-decker buses like little scarlet cubes. The sense of order was what Anna found fascinating. From up here it was like looking at the inner workings of an intricate machine where each little cog moved in a precise and preordained pattern. It was hard to believe that it was human lives in all their infinite variety, with their ups and downs and unpredictable turns and mood swings, their broken relationships and lack of judgement, which kept the whole thing ticking. The orderliness was an illusion. Down there on the streets anything could happen.

Anna's eye was caught by a small silver arrow moving through the clouds above St Paul's Cathedral – an aeroplane recently taken off from Heathrow. This made her think of her mother, setting out this morning from Waterloo. She looked at her watch. Her train should have just left. The holiday had been Anna's idea and she so wanted it to be a success. She had suggested it to her brothers as a special Christmas present for their mother. Ben and Edward, though good-natured young men, were too engrossed in their own lives to consider anyone else's with much imagination and it would never have occurred to them that their mother might enjoy a break from the farm and a chance to start painting again. They would not understand that it was something she might love to do but would never consider spending the money on herself. That sort of self-denial was not within their experience. 'Going without' was a woman thing, thought Anna. Or at least, a woman of her mother's generation. Her father spent what money there was on farm machinery or livestock. If he wanted or needed something and they could afford it, he bought it. It was quite simple and there wasn't this element of female martyrdom to complicate matters.

It wasn't as if her mother did not contribute to the family income. Quite apart from all the unpaid work she did around the place, she also ran her own little business. What she earned went on household expenses and what she called 'extras', like running her own small car, buying clothes and make-up, Christmas and birthday presents, things for the house and garden, the odd day out. Anna knew she felt guilty spending on what she called 'fripperies' and often concealed them from Josh who would have thought them a waste of money.

The Protestant work ethic ran strong in her father. Anna always thought he had the look of an eighteenth-century Puritan preacher. She could imagine him in a white collar and a black frock coat denouncing dancing as the work of the devil. This was unjust, she knew, because he enjoyed a party as much as the next man, but there was something of the sobersides about him. Not joyless, but inclined to be sombre. Rarely exuberant; always cautious and restrained. Mum's not like that, thought Anna, watching the plane disappear into the grey sky. She's got a different sort of spirit. I want this holiday to allow her to be herself for once.

She had seen the advertisement for Arc en Ciel in a Sunday paper, alongside an article written by a woman journalist who had been on such a holiday in France. She wrote so lyrically of the peace and tranquillity of the Provençal landscape, describing how she slowly unwound in the sunshine and, restored by excellent food and wine and the chance to develop a dormant longing to paint, came home refreshed and invigorated.

That's what would do Mum good, Anna had thought. Their mother deserved a long-service medal and she and her brothers could well afford it. They were all on London salaries, spending what they earned on high-octane life-styles, and if they gave the holiday to her as a present, she could not resist. She needs a push, thought Anna. She's lost all sense of adventure. She needs to be reminded that there's another world out there.

Her telephone started to ring and she swung her chair back to pick it up. 'Anna Hutchins. European desk. Oh, hi, Rich. Yeah, busy as usual. This weekend?' Anna stared out of the window again. 'Actually I thought I might go home. Haven't been back for ages and Mum's gone off to France today so Dad's on his own. Why don't you come too?' On the other end of the telephone, Richard Lovegrove, a few miles away and at a similar desk in a similar office, tried not to sound annoyed. He had wanted Anna to himself this weekend and he didn't much enjoy the country.

'I thought you wanted to see the new Russian film everyone's raving about.'

'Well, I do, but I'm not sure I feel up to grainy black and white vodkaholics living in one-room apartments, facing the challenge of post-Soviet society. I think I'd rather loll about at home and watch a repeat of the *Two Ronnies*. You know, a bit less demanding.'

'I see,' said Richard, his voice huffy.

'Don't be like that. I've asked you to come too. Come on. It will be a change. Dancing Hill is lovely in the summer.' As she spoke, a blast of wind flung raindrops like a shower of pebbles at the window. 'Better than London, anyway,' she added.

'OK. Well, I'll think about it. I'll see you this evening.

27

Six o'clock?' Richard felt resigned. Once Anna had made up her mind she was generally unmoveable.

'Yeah, great. I can smell the gin, hear the ice clinking already. See you then.'

Anna was glad she was busy. She did not want to think too much about Rich. He was great. Lovely. She loved him. Funny, bright, handsome. She was bloody lucky to have found him. Why then did she always want to challenge him, to set him up in situations where he might possibly show himself in a less than flattering light? Why was she always testing him? She knew he wasn't that keen on the farm. Really, he had no interest in the country, so why did the idea of going home come into her head the minute he made a suggestion about what they might do at the weekend? I'm a bloody contrary woman, that's what, she told herself sternly. And I don't deserve him.

Chapter Two

At about the time in the afternoon when George, the better for three pints of Badger beer with Wilf, was dozing in his armchair, and Josh was hosing down the lorry to comply with the government's foot and mouth regulations on moving livestock, Kate and Elspeth were sitting outside a Paris pavement café, on the corner of Rue Hector Malot. The sun was hot and strong and the ugly paved square across from the Gare de Lyon was carved by young skateboarders and rollerbladers and mothers escorting neatly dressed children from school. It had been Elspeth's idea that they leave the station and find somewhere to sit and have a drink. Kate would not have had the confidence, nor would she have coped so well at Paris Nord, with its confusion of signs and exits, but Elspeth knew the ropes, whisking her onto a double-decker RER train for the two swift stops.

'Now what shall we have?' said Elspeth, pushing back her dark glasses onto the top of her head. Kate was about to say, 'A coffee would be lovely,' but Elspeth had already called the waiter and was asking about wine. She turned to Kate as the man, impossibly French-looking, with a small black moustache and a wide white apron, hovered with his pad and pencil.

'White, I think, don't you? It's too hot for red. How about a nice Sancerre?'

'Lovely,' murmured Kate.

'And some olives, please. What on earth are olives in French?'

'Olives?' suggested Kate in a French accent and giggled. It was a relief that Elspeth, despite her confidence, spoke no better French than she did.

Kate gave a deep sigh of happiness, looking about her appreciatively. It was all so different; so, well, French. The tall grey buildings opposite with their shutters and balconies and grey tiled roofs out of which romantic-looking attic windows opened; the extraordinary old woman who was tottering past in a nylon fur coat, her sparse hair dyed apricot to match her ancient poodle and with a baguette under her arm; this café itself, with its little round tables set on the pavement, its elaborate lunch menu chalked on a board under the reassurance of '*boeuf français seulement*', and one or two lone men dining with a sort of concentration that you would never find in England. Certainly not at half past four in the afternoon.

The wine arrived and the label was elaborately displayed to them both, with the bottle wrapped in a white napkin. A mere inch was poured into Elspeth's glass. She tasted it with a critical and serious expression while the waiter paused. Kate found it hard not to smile at the ceremony and then Elspeth looked up and nodded and the waiter filled their glasses. The wine was delicious, a good choice, cold and clean-tasting. It reminded her of the taste of rusty metal from when she and Tom used to swing on gates as children.

'Well,' said Elspeth, leaning back in her chair, lifting her face to the sun and readjusting her sunglasses, 'this is more like it!' A pleasant-looking middle-aged man walked past with a large boxer dog on a chain. He gave the two women a frank, assessing stare, before sitting down at a table two away from them and adjusting the position of his chair to continue his appraisal. His dog sat on its haunches and, lifting one hind leg, began a thorough licking of its very conspicuous organs.

'My God!' said Elspeth, pulling a face at Kate. 'Have you got dogs? That one should really wear a pair of pants, don't you think?'

'Yes, I do,' said Kate, glancing over at the man who raised his eyebrows suggestively, 'but then the dog is just an advertisement for his master, isn't he? Poor thing. A bit like a walking billboard saying, 'See my dog! Wait till you see me!'

Elspeth burst out laughing. 'Absolutely right! Here, let me fill your glass.'

'Am I being crude? Sorry. Remember I'm a farmer's wife. I'm used to these male displays. We have three dogs. Collies. Working dogs, not pets.'

'Ah, yes. I'll have to hear all about this farm of yours. I love Dorset. Archie used to have a cottage near Lyme Regis; not that I went there often. It was very much the preserve of his wife. Off limits to me.'

'Oh, I see,' said Kate, who didn't at all. From their conversation on the train she had gathered that Elspeth was widowed; who Archie was she could only guess. Elspeth seemed to assume some previous knowledge on her part and she felt it was prying to ask. They lapsed into a companionable silence and Kate was grateful that Elspeth was not the sort of woman who felt the need to chatter. It was such a pleasure to sit and drink in the sunshine and feel anonymous and free of obligations or responsibilities towards anybody.

After ten minutes or so, Elspeth consulted her watch and said, 'We should drink up, I suppose. Half an hour before the TGV leaves, but there's no rush, the seats are all pre-booked. Trains in France are so much more civilised than ours.' She leaned across and refilled Kate's glass. Kate was already hot from the sun and now she began to feel slightly tight as well. It was funny, she thought, that it should be called tight, when in fact the general feeling was the opposite, one of loose-limbed relaxation.

'Here,' she said, reaching for the slip of white paper placed on a saucer. 'I'll do this.'

'Thank you. That's very kind,' said Elspeth, taking her compact out of a cosmetic bag and studying her face.

Kate struggled with the bill, which seemed to be in both euros and francs and included some sort of tax and service charge and came to a huge amount when she tried to convert it back into pounds sterling. Surely a bottle of wine couldn't cost eighteen pounds in such an ordinary café. Never, ever, would she spend that amount on a bottle at home, where she and Josh cheerfully quaffed supermarket plonk. Carefully, she counted notes onto the saucer while Elspeth reapplied lipstick and smoothed her brows with a finger. Then the waiter swept past and whisked away her money and for a moment, as he studied the bill, she thought she had made a mistake with the decimal point and that she was going to get handed back a sheaf of notes, but no such luck. Only a few unimportant-looking coins were returned to her.

'Ready?' said Elspeth, putting away her lipstick. 'Shall we go?'

As they crossed the hot concrete plaza back to the station, Kate still felt rattled. She couldn't believe that she had just parted with so much money, so carelessly. It had quite spoiled the pleasure of the café. Had she known Elspeth better, she would have exclaimed at how expensive the wine had been, but having offered to pay, it would now seem churlish to draw attention to it. Oh, damn it! she thought, impatiently. Josh wasn't with her, so why should she feel the weight of his imagined disapproval? A spark of rebellion ignited and she thought of Anna who had so much wanted her to have a good time. She wasn't going to let a little thing like an expensive bottle of wine upset her day. She could put it down to experience and save on other things, and after all, it had been delicious.

Together the two women hurried along, but Kate's little suitcase felt heavy and her bags were awkward, bumping into her legs while Elspeth, unencumbered, wheeled her suitcase smoothly at her heels like an obedient dog. When they reached the station, Kate stopped to change hands and Elspeth disappeared into the crowd gathered round the departure board. When Kate caught up with her she was standing waiting by a ticket-stamping machine. 'There you are,' she said. 'Look, you have to put your ticket through here. Platform ten. This way.'

Is she going to be bossy? thought Kate. Bossy and managing? I can't really blame her for the wine. That was my fault, I should have found out the price. Still, she's a bit like a prefect, herding the juniors along on a school trip. Kate followed Elspeth's neat white linen back along the busy platform. The train was going to be crowded by the look of it. Elspeth's low-heeled shoes clicked along in a businesslike way and Kate wondered how her slim grey trousers managed to remain uncreased. She felt rumpled and untidy by comparison. She saw that, like Susie, her sister-in-law, Elspeth was the sort of woman who was always immaculate and Kate allowed herself to wonder whether this wasn't in some way a failing – an indication of a shallow, self-centred character.

Elspeth counted the carriages and when she found the right one, commandeered a young man to lift her suitcase into the train. He spoke no English but she made her request perfectly clear by hand signals and a pleasant smile. Kate bundled on behind her and when they found their seats, facing each other across a table, Elspeth settled herself neatly by the window, with her back to the engine. How would she have managed without me? she thought as she watched Kate stowing her bags in the overhead rack and dropping her sweater on the floor. She's really rather gormless. All that pondering over the bill, for instance, as if she had never had to handle foreign currency before. I hope I won't get stuck with her when we arrive. I don't want her round my neck the whole week, pleasant though she is.

Kate, sliding into the seat opposite, got a novel out of her bag and laid it on the table. Watching her, Elspeth recognised the inevitable stab of hostility that she routinely felt towards a younger, attractive woman. Years of looking after herself had made her wary. Still, this was a holiday and not the workplace, where she had grown to dislike the fluffy young PAs with their short skirts and kitten heels and languorous looks. Closing her eyes, Elspeth determined to snooze for most of the long journey ahead.

Kate opened her book. She could see that Elspeth wanted to sleep and it was a relief not to have to make conversation. Two stout, grey-haired men were negotiating their way into the two adjacent seats at the table, stowing plastic bags and jackets on the rack and talking loudly in a torrent of excited French as the train drew out of the station and slid smoothly through Paris suburbs. Kate glanced at them. Tieless, and wearing checked shirts with the sleeves rolled up, they did not look like Parisians. With their ruddy complexions and air of prosperity they could be a pair of horse butchers, she decided, up from the country. The one sitting opposite caught her eye and smiled and said something to his companion which made him turn to look at her. She smiled back.

'English? he said.

'Yes,' she replied. '*Oui*, rather.'

'Marseilles?'

'*Non*, St Raphael,' said Kate, showing him her ticket.

'Ah! Very good!' He looked pleased and indicated from his own ticket that he and his friend were also going there. 'I no speak English,' he added, shrugging happily.

Good, thought Kate, keeping up the smile. That makes things easier. More smiling, and then she was able to drop her eyes to the page.

The carriage was warm and she must have fallen asleep because what seemed like only a minute or two later she was woken by a jolt. Opposite her, Elspeth was awake too, her head up in a questioning attitude. The train was slowing down and the whole carriage seemed unsettled and anxious. The level of talk grew and heads turned to peer out of the windows at the green rolling countryside dotted with fat white cattle, in which they were gradually coming to a halt.

'Has something happened?' said Elspeth. 'Why are we stopping?'

No one seemed to know, to judge by the air of puzzlement. Then came a lengthy passenger announcement, after which there was a hubbub of voices, impatient exchanges, a consulting of watches and reaching for mobile telephones.

'What is it? Did you get any of that?' asked Elspeth. 'I didn't catch a word.'

People were starting to get to their feet and the two horse butchers began to collect their bags and indicated that they were getting off the train.

A well-dressed young man who had been working on a laptop computer on the other side of the aisle leaned across. 'I am afraid there has been an incident,' he explained in precise English. 'A stone has been thrown through the window of the driver's cab. It is necessary that the train stop at the next station and that we disembark. Another train will arrive to convey us further.' He shut his computer with a snap and began to stow it in its case.

'A stone?' said Elspeth incredulously.

The young man shrugged. 'Vandalism, I am afraid. No doubt the work of children.'

'Goodness!' said Kate. 'How like home! It's quite heartening to hear you have that sort of thing in France. That it's not just us.'

'But where are we?' said Elspeth, looking out of the window. 'Back of beyond, it looks like.' She glanced at her watch. 'Only just over an hour from Paris. Oh dear, this is not a good start.'

The train drew slowly into a long, empty platform and stopped, upon which there was a terrific surge as people, already on their feet, jostled one another to get out, the horse butchers among them.

'Really! Just look at this stampede!' said Elspeth, disapprovingly. 'What on earth is the rush? We'll be very British, shall we, and just sit here and wait. Let them get on with it.'

Kate watched the muddle of passengers disentangling themselves on the platform. Mothers struggled with folded baby buggies, an elderly lady with a Yorkshire terrier under her arm heaved along a suitcase, and two vast black women in brightly flowered robes and turbans seemed to have all their worldly goods stacked at their feet. There were no trolleys in evidence and no porters; in fact, no station staff at all that Kate could see.

'Shall we go?' she said, getting to her feet as the carriage emptied. 'That seems to be the rush over.' She was frightened that the train might leave with them still on board.

As they stepped down from the carriage the first thing she noticed was the smell. They've been haymaking, she thought, looking about her. The long platform did not seem to be attached to a station of any size. At the far end she could make out only one small building, like a sort of modern bus shelter, and that was it. On all sides the tranquil countryside basked in the evening sunlight. In fact, it was still hot in the sun. The few benches were already taken and people were heading off to sit on the ground in the strip of shade provided by the bank which edged the platform. Above the swell of voices Kate could hear birds singing.

She recognised this sort of country, which was mostly grass. Stock country. The large cream-coloured cows were Limousin, she guessed, and they grazed in small hedged fields bordered with trees. In the distance she could see a church spire and the roofs of a large village. All looked prosperous and well kept. Familiar, but unmistakably foreign. The scale was wrong for England – everything too wide, too spaced apart, and the quality of light was different, harder and brighter.

Elspeth, who had nabbed one of the horse butchers to retrieve her case, came to stand beside her. 'Really,' she said, 'isn't this infuriating. Look, there are no seats, either. I gather from that young computer man that we have forty minutes to wait for the next train. I'm parched and hungry, aren't you? I'd love a cup of tea and something to eat.'

'I've got a bottle of water and some sandwiches in my bag,' offered Kate. 'We could find somewhere to sit and have them.'

Elspeth warmed to her. 'Wonderful,' she exclaimed. A countrified, practical sort of person came into their own in these situations.

Together they walked up the platform to where the people thinned out and found a cleanish place to sit on the glittering asphalt next to a group of American girls who had rolled up their jeans, pulled up their T-shirts and were sunbathing propped against their backpacks.

Kate unpacked her sandwiches and offered them to Elspeth. Despite the long journey and the heat, the home-made brown bread travelled well and she had tucked baby tomatoes and radishes along the edge of the old ice-cream carton. She had wondered if it was silly, old-maidish, to bring her own food, being just something else to carry, but because she was cutting sandwiches for Josh to take in the lorry she had made a few extra for herself.

'But these are delicious,' said Elspeth appreciatively. 'Don't tell me you make your own bread?'

Kate nodded. 'Eggs from my own chickens and cheese from the next door farm. It's my business, food. I supply some local shops with homemade cakes and pies, and do a bit of outside catering.'

'That's very enterprising,' said Elspeth, 'but then one is

always hearing about the plight of farmers and how they have to diversify.'

'It's true. Farmers' wives traditionally had their jobs on the farm, working alongside their husbands, but we all need a second income these days. My brother, who farms next door to where we are – where I grew up, in fact – his wife does very smart B&B. They don't have children, so they have plenty of room. I thought about doing the same but we don't live in a rambling old farmhouse like they do, and we couldn't put in en suite bathrooms, which, of course, everybody expects these days.'

Elspeth helped herself to another sandwich. 'May I? I can't believe the colour of these egg yolks.'

'Very free range, my chickens. That's what makes the difference. They forage for themselves and aren't fed much in the way of concentrates.' Kate felt pleased by Elspeth's compliments. It was satisfying when people appreciated proper food.

'It must be hard work, doing B&B,' said Elspeth, considering. 'The awful necessity of having to keep everything tidy all the time and being forced to share one's home with people one perhaps doesn't like.'

'Do you work?' Kate asked her, imagining that she didn't have to. There was something about Elspeth which suggested a life of ease.

'I certainly do,' she replied emphatically, 'and always have. I was married, you see, to a much older man. An American. It wasn't a happy marriage for all sorts of reasons and I left him when our son was three, came back to London and had to get a job. I was a PA for years. That's how I met Archie. I worked for him for twenty years when he was an MP. Then he retired and I couldn't bear to go on without him, so we left Westminster together. I wanted a change and a friend of Archie's asked if I would like a job as a rather upmarket tour guide and I jumped at it. I escort small groups, mostly Americans, round London. I take them to private viewings, tea with grandees, drinks on the terrace at the House of Commons, that sort of thing. A snob's tour, really. It pays quite well and I can pick and choose when I work to a certain extent.'

Ah, thought Kate, that explains the bossiness. She's used to marshalling people.

'It sounds interesting,' she said. 'I hardly know London. I've only done that open-top bus tour a couple of times when we've had friends over from abroad.'

'Well, frankly, that's just about the best way to see London.'

'Do you get the chance to paint much? I wondered why you were on this particular holiday.'

'Hardly ever. My flat's too small for all the paraphernalia. You know, it's very discouraging when you have to put everything away each time. I used to have to stand my wet canvas in the bath. I do enjoy it though and went to evening classes for a couple of years. Then they changed the evening and for one reason or another I gave up. When I saw this course advertised, the idea of being able to paint all day in a lovely climate and enjoy good food and wine was very attractive. I like having something to do on holiday. I'm not a beach person. What about you? Do farmers' wives have time for hobbies?'

'Hardly,' said Kate. 'There's always something else that seems more important. I did an art foundation course before I married, then Josh appeared on the scene and I never went on with it. He came to work with my father as a farm student, you see. After we married I helped on the farm and then had babies. I didn't think of doing anything else. Not that I regret it for a moment,' she added hastily.

'I know,' said Elspeth. 'We were in much more of a hurry in those days to get married and start breeding. People rather pitied you if you had got to about twenty-five and weren't at least engaged.'

'My daughter, Anna, is nearly twenty-six and doesn't seem to feel any urgency to settle down. It worries me sometimes because for the last three years she has been going out with a really nice young man, a few years older than she is, who I think would like to get married, but it's Anna who won't make a commitment. I don't say so to her, obviously, but I think that either they should get on with it, or break up. It doesn't seem fair on him to keep him hanging about if she doesn't intend to marry him. They have split up from time to time, but then she seems miserable without him, and they get back together.'

'I fail to understand young people. They appear to make more of a hash of things than we did – if that's possible. Especially girls, to judge from all the Bridget Jones wailing we never hear the end of.' Elspeth glanced across at the young Americans, oblivious in the evening sun. They looked happy enough.

The two women sat in silence for a while and then a high-speed train roared southwards through the station, making the platform tremble.

'I wonder how late this is going to make us the other end,' said Kate anxiously. 'I suppose there will be someone to meet us.'

'Of course. Whoever it is will have found out what has happened to our train,' said Elspeth confidently. 'They'll make inquiries when it's late. One might have hoped for a bit more information ourselves. And apologies. We haven't heard much of "*Nous sommes désolées*", have we? Oh, listen, here's something now.'

A disembodied voice had begun another lengthy announcement which was the signal for resting groups of passengers to come to life and start to organise themselves up and down the platform.

'What's happening now?' asked Elspeth crossly, to the world at large. The American girls shrugged, but started to get to their feet and hauled their backpacks onto their shoulders. They were all tall and broad, Kate noticed; healthy, well-fed young women with mouthfuls of strong-looking white teeth.

'I think we've got to get ourselves into certain parts of the train depending on our destinations,' she said. 'Look, there are our men.' She pointed to the horse butchers who were walking purposefully down the platform. 'They were going to Saint Raphael. I think we should follow them.'

'Right you are,' said Elspeth.

They got up and collected their things and went to stand behind the men, who turned and smiled and shrugged their shoulders in a gesture of despair at the situation in which they found themselves.

After a few minutes a second train appeared in the distance and slowed to a crawl as it drew into the platform. They could see that it was already full of passengers, their faces peering out of the windows, annoyed at the disruption to their journey.

'Would you believe it?' exclaimed Elspeth. 'It's full! Do you suppose we have to fight for a seat? I think it's going to be every man for himself, by the look of it.'

As the train stopped, there was a rush for the nearest door and when it sighed open Elspeth was in in a flash, followed by the butchers with her suitcase. She turned to look for Kate, who had lost her place in the rush, and called, 'I'll find seats!'

Kate could see that it was hopeless. When she eventually got into the carriage it appeared to be completely full and there were people crowding in from the other direction. She saw the top of Elspeth's head. She had managed to get a seat and was turning to signal that there was another place further down. When Kate reached it an elderly woman grudgingly moved her belongings and, looking affronted, allowed her to sit. She plonked down gratefully. The woman, sighing, managed to wrestle her bag beneath the table and onto Kate's feet. Kate didn't care.

In fact, this whole fiasco brought home to her yet again the wonderful freedom of travelling on her own. Josh would have been thoroughly worked up by now, complaining and cross, and she, stupid though it was, would have felt somehow responsible. The journey would have become a personal issue. For the second time that day Kate was glad that Josh was not with her.

As she watched through the window, the country became more rugged and dry and the light began to fade until the last glimmer was gone and darkness fell.

Josh was eating bread and cheese in the farm kitchen. When it came to it, he couldn't be bothered to get one of Kate's frozen meals from the freezer and sit and wait for forty minutes for it to heat up. It was easier to get the loaf out and hack away at the lump of cheese she had left him. He opened a bottle of beer and sat at the kitchen table reading the paper and then washed his plate and knife and put the food away. There wasn't anything worth watching on the television but he supposed that later he would go

43

and see the news. The evening seemed to be dwindling and shapeless without the rigmarole of a proper meal on the table and the customary ebb and flow of conversation. Maybe he would have a whisky and doze off in the armchair, but he felt unusually awake and when he went into the sitting room he couldn't decide where to sit. Not having Kate there somehow threw the arrangement of chairs off balance and the room looked unwelcoming, so he went back through to the kitchen and sat at the table again. He had some paperwork he could do, a few letters to write, but he didn't feel inclined. The house was so quiet that he jumped when the telephone rang. Ah! That would be Kate to say that she had arrived, but when he picked up the receiver it was Anna's voice he heard.

'Dad, hi. It's me. I'm on the train. Hope you don't mind. I thought I'd come for the weekend.' The line crackled and faded before Josh could answer. His immediate response was to feel his heart lift. He put down the telephone and waited for her to try again. Anna would fill the house with her laughter and chatter, dispel the gloom that always seemed to settle round him when he was alone.

The telephone rang again. 'Hello, Anna? No, that's fine. Lovely, in fact. I'll meet you. Which train? What about Rich? Is he with you?'

'Just me, Dad. I'm on the seven thirty-five. Sorry it's so late but I only decided to come at the last minute. See you at the station. Bye.'

Feeling in altogether better spirits, Josh went and stood at the kitchen window, looking across the valley. The light was going but he could still see the dark shapes of trees and the lines of hedges. Between them the fields gleamed pale and silvery under the pewter-coloured sky. The banked clouds were lit by the last light of the invisible sun going down behind the hills. The rain had persisted until early evening but now there was a pale violet line on the horizon which suggested that the sky would clear and that tomorrow the weather would be fine. With any luck they would be able to start on the hay.

Down below, at the foot of the hill, he could see two yellow squares of light. George was still up and about. Thinking of how pleased he was at the prospect of Anna's company, Josh wondered what it was like for George, always on his own in the evenings. He supposed that you got used to a solitary life, that when it was a permanent state you adapted to it, but his conscience had been jogged. He ought to have more time for the old man, he knew that. George loved to hear about the farm, to be kept informed, for his advice to be sought, and he was, after all, still a partner, but Josh was irritated by him more often than not. He could see that his father-in-law made an effort to be tactful, prefacing remarks with something like, 'I know I'm old fashioned', or 'Not that I'm criticising', and yet Josh always felt annoyed. He knew it, and disliked it in himself, this lack of patience and forbearance.

Part of it was Kate's fault. She and her father were so close that he felt excluded. She was always in and out of the bungalow, looking after the old man, and there were times when Josh felt his resentment was justified. She might say she had had a busy day and there was nothing for supper, that she'd make him an omelette, when he knew damn well that she'd been down at her father's for an hour or two, ironing his shirts or mowing his grass. Josh didn't see that it was necessary, fussing over George like that. He could pay someone to do his ironing, for goodness sake, pay a gardener to cut the lawn. He could afford it. When he said this to Kate she would look at him coldly and say, 'It's not what I'm *doing* when I'm there. Don't you understand that? It's the time I spend with him that counts,' and he would feel a stab of jealousy. How much time does she give me? he thought. Kate liked to wear the devoted daughter badge, that was it, while she couldn't care less about him.

Standing at the window, he knew this wasn't true. It was an unworthy thought that he had allowed to insinuate itself into his mind because of Kate's current defection. He expelled it at once, but as he turned away to find the timetable and check the arrival of Anna's train, he was conscious of a residue of resentment, the merest suggestion of being ill-used.

Kate, of course, might telephone while he was out collecting Anna from the station. She would wonder where he was at this time of night, maybe think there had been an emergency. Josh felt a moment of satisfaction. A little bit of anxiety was no more than she deserved.

Long after they should have arrived, Kate and Elspeth stood on a dark platform waiting for a small local train to take them to St Raphael. The lights of Marseilles strung out beyond the railway sidings and behind them low hills clung to the dark horizon. The station was almost empty, the long platform dimly lit. Large, soft- bodied insects battered against the yellow lamp under which they stood. Now they were in the south the night air was hot and humid and Kate could feel her hair damp against her neck and her T-shirt sticking to her back. When they had discovered that the train which had rescued them terminated at Marseilles and that from there they would have to wait for a local connection, it had seemed the last straw. They were both exhausted by the endless, disrupted journey and stood in silence but glad of each other's company. When at last the little train drew in, nearly empty, they got on gratefully and sat side by side and watched the lights of the city disappear.

They had lost the horse butchers who had apparently decided enough was enough and had opted to stay in Marseilles. 'They're probably sitting down to a bloody good meal right now,' said Elspeth. 'I'm starving, aren't you? Thank goodness you had the sense to bring those sandwiches.'

'They'll have something waiting for us,' said Kate, 'something Provençal and delicious.'

'After a long cool shower, and a drink of very cold white wine. Bliss!'

'Do you know anything about this outfit? Do you think there will be other people staying? From the brochure, I got the impression it was run by a husband and wife team. There was a lot of emphasis on "family", wasn't there?' asked Kate.

'Rather off-putting, in a way. I mean, as a rule, it's family one wants to get away from on holiday.'

Kate laughed. 'It's certainly my family that makes painting an impossibility at home. That's why my daughter thought of this wonderful Christmas present.'

Elspeth peered out at the lowering black hillsides between which the little train was moving. 'Must be nice to have a daughter,' she said to the glass, without turning her head. 'More thoughtful than sons, I should think.'

'Oh, yes, in some ways, although sons are more affectionate, I find. Less critical, less tricky. But now she's grown up, Anna is a wonderful friend. I suppose it boils down to sharing a feminine perspective.'

'Hmm.'

47

'And your son?' Kate asked.

'Harry? Not much love lost, I'm afraid. He's forty this year. An overweight oil executive in Houston. Twice divorced and now living with some bimboesque creature, barely more than a teenager. He has four children from his two marriages, who live with their mothers, neither of whom consider a far-off English grandmother any kind of priority.'

This barren view of family life, or lack of it, made Kate feel a pang of compassion for Elspeth. 'I'm sorry,' she murmured.

'No need,' said Elspeth cheerfully, turning away from the dark window. 'Suits me, frankly. I'm far too selfish to want to be a doting granny. Now how much longer do you think we've got on this bloody train?'

'At least an hour,' said Kate. 'I said I'd ring Josh when I arrived. He will be getting worried by now.'

'Well, he can ring them, can't he? At Arc en Ciel, or whatever it's called. You must have left the number.'

'Yes, I suppose so,' said Kate, although she didn't think he would. If she had said she would telephone he would doggedly wait for her call.

They lapsed back into silence as the train trundled through the dark night. The carriage was nearly empty, apart from a Chinese woman who sat opposite them, sleeping soundly, and a young couple further up who appeared to be engaged in advanced and vigorous love-making. That's one way to pass the journey, thought Kate. She glanced at Elspeth who also seemed to have fallen asleep. What a strange day it had been, the length of the disrupted journey adding to the sensation of having trav-elled very far from home. She began to feel light-headed with tiredness – she had been up since six o'clock – and her own reflection eerily looking back at her from the dark window was dreamlike and surreal. The little train moving through the night seemed suspended in time, disconnected from the rest of the world, certainly from anything with which she was familiar, and Kate felt as if she was being spirited away into a different dimension. The face that stared back at her from the window was a pale, floating orb with features she barely recognised. Is that me? she thought in a panic, glancing over her shoulder to check that a stranger hadn't taken her place in the reflection. She closed her eyes, too tired to think.

An hour passed in this strange trance-like state between sleep and wakefulness until the lights outside the window became strung together and Kate guessed that they were approaching a town. The Chinese woman stood and put on a coat and the young couple disentangled, the girl getting up and pulling her T-shirt down over a smooth brown stomach and the young man dragging his dishevelled hair back into a pony tail.

Kate touched Elspeth's arm. 'I think we're arriving,' she said.

Elspeth opened her eyes and groaned. 'Thank God for that. About bloody time, too.'

The train drew into a platform and wearily they collected their belongings and trailed after the few other passengers towards the station building. They blinked in the bright light by the ticket barrier, where a group of taxi drivers spilled out of a station bar and stood smoking and chatting, paying no attention to the arriving passengers. The hot night air pressed about them and Kate found her legs heavy and tired as if she was walking uphill. She paused, shifting her suitcase from hand to hand as Elspeth scanned the group, searching for someone who was

49

looking for them. One of the men threw a cigarette to the ground and stepped on it before coming towards them. He was short and thickset with a nylon football shirt stretched over a hefty paunch.

'Arc en Ciel?' he asked, with no smile of welcome. 'English ladies?'

'Yes, yes. Thank God! We've had a terrible journey!'

Without responding, the man reached for their cases and led them out to where a silver car was drawn up at the taxi rank. Opposite, a few men loitered outside a shabby kebab house from which Turkish-sounding music spilled, but otherwise the street, under its line of palm trees was quiet and empty. Their driver put their luggage in the boot and then opened the rear door and gestured for them to get in. He got into the driver's seat and slammed the door.

'How far?' asked Kate.

The man glanced at her in his mirror and held up his hand, fingers outstretched in a gesture he repeated four times.

'Twenty?' said Elspeth. 'Twenty what? Kilometres, minutes?'

'Kilometres,' said the man. His face was unresponsive in the mirror.

'Definitely not a charm school graduate, is he?' said Elspeth, glaring back.

'I suppose he's fed up with waiting,' said Kate.

'Too bloody bad. It's his job. He'll get paid. What about us?'

The taxi drove fast through the sleeping town, round an important-looking deserted square with an empty bandstand and stacked chairs outside pavement cafés. Kate was too tired to take in much except the unfamiliar cascades of bougainvillea tumbling from balconies and baskets and palm trees reaching up into the night sky. After a stretch on what seemed like a ring road, the car took a turning out into the dark hills and Kate wound down her window. The air was hot and smelled of dry earth and something pungent, like thyme. Above the noise of the engine she could hear the insistent thrumming of cicadas. Oh, this is lovely, she thought, rushing through this beautiful, hot night to somewhere unknown where people are expecting us. The road climbed steeply, between tall, dark trees, twisting and turning up the side of the hill with what looked like a pitch-black drop on the other side.

After a while the driver came to a halt at a junction, turned sharply to the right, left the tarmac road and jolted upwards on a dirt track, the headlights picking out the rutted stony surface and the dry banks on either side, grown with bleached brown grasses and thorny shrubs. The track wound on and up until, turning a last bend, Kate could see lights ahead and then the shapes of dark buildings against the sky. The car bumped between stone gateposts and drew up in a courtyard beside an old van. A dog began to bark from a barn and a male voice shouted, and then a door opened and became a square of yellow light. Kate saw a figure standing on the threshold and when the driver turned off the engine she could hear the faint noise of guitar music above the cicadas.

'It looks as though we have arrived,' said Elspeth.

The driver got out and their luggage was unceremoniously dumped on the ground. The figure in the doorway had vanished but a moment later a girl appeared, about eighteen with short dark hair and glasses. She hurried over and shook their hands.

'Welcome,' she said. 'Welcome to Arc en Ciel. You have had a terrible journey, yes?' She indicated that they should enter and then turned to the taxi driver, whereupon there began a loud argument over the fare.

Pointedly leaving her case where it was, Elspeth led the way. The room they stepped into was a large stone-walled kitchen with a flagged floor. A country dresser took up most of one wall, heavily laden with bright pottery, and on the opposite wall was a long wooden table laid for dinner.

'Pretty, isn't it?' said Elspeth, looking around. 'Very rustic. Just what I'd imagined.'

The girl, having dealt with the taxi, followed them in and now introduced herself. 'I am Monique,' she said. 'I show you your rooms. Perhaps you like to wash and then have your dinner?'

She opened a heavy wooden door that led into a passage and then up a flight of stone stairs. On the landing at the top she said, 'All this area is for our guests. Here we have one room,' and she opened a door and snapped on the light. Inside was a plain whitewashed room with shuttered windows and a double bed covered in a white cotton bedspread. The furniture was simple – two chairs and table by the window, a line of brass hooks in a curtained recess for clothes, and a chest of drawers. A pottery jug of wild flowers stood on the bedside table. The girl moved across and opened the shutters and the warm night air flooded the room. 'The view here is of the garden,' she explained. 'The bathroom is here,' and she indicated a door in the corner.

'The other room is here,' and she went back out into the passage and opened a door on the other side. 'Almost the same, but the view is of the valley and also the sea.'

She turned on the light to reveal a similar room, this time with twin beds.

Elspeth and Kate looked at each other and shrugged. 'I really don't mind,' said Kate. 'They're both lovely. You choose.'

'I don't mind either. Shall we toss?' Elspeth took a coin from her purse. 'How shall we do this?' She peered at the coin. 'Heads, you get the sea view?' She threw the coin into the air and when it hit the ground it rolled under the chest of drawers. Monique went down on her hands and knees to retrieve it and Kate wanted to laugh. For a French girl she had an ample backside.

'Ah!' she reported from the floor. 'It is not the head.'

'That's fine,' said Kate, laughing. 'I'm just as happy with the other one.'

'Now you like to wash? Then eat?' asked Monique.

'A drink, first, please,' said Elspeth firmly. 'We'd both like a very large glass of very cold white wine. In fact, bring the whole bottle.'

'Very well,' said Monique. 'I will bring it to your rooms. Dinner will be ready in half an hour. That is good?'

Heaven, thought Kate, twenty minutes later as she unpacked, a glass by her side. She had had a quick cool shower in the little whitewashed bathroom and noted with pleasure the handmade square of lavender soap and the huge rough bath towel. She had changed into a clean shirt and loose pair of cotton trousers and her hair was wet and sleek on her head. She found her scent and gave herself a generous squirt and ran a dark pencil round her eyes. A slick of lipstick and she was ready.

'I'll be down in a sec,' shouted Elspeth when Kate went along the passage to call for her. 'Don't wait.'

It was therefore on her own that Kate lifted the heavy

latch on the door and went back into the kitchen. There was no sign of Monique, but there was the steamy smell of boiling potatoes and standing by the old-fashioned range, a saucepan lid in his hand, was a tall, grey-haired man who turned when he heard Kate enter.

Chapter Three

The man was very tanned and was wearing a loose pale shirt with the sleeves rolled up, and a pair of battered jeans. His feet were bare and brown on the stone floor. As he paused and looked at her, she saw a hollow-cheeked face with heavy-lidded, deep-set, lazy eyes and a large, bony, hawkish nose. It was the face of a pirate or a Velasquez nobleman. The mouth was wide and unsmiling and his expression seemed almost fierce. He stood, holding the saucepan lid in one hand, a knife in the other, and looked at her for a moment longer than was comfortable and she realised that she was blushing. His bare feet and the untidy kitchen made her feel as if she had intruded into a private domain.

Then he smiled and as he did so he moved his head back and sideways into his lifted right shoulder and raised both hands in an attitude of openness, appreciation, welcome, she didn't know what. It was a winning gesture, wholly foreign, very Gallic.

He moved across the room with a torrent of French, and in her agitation Kate understood nothing and shrugged helplessly.

'You speak no French?' he asked. His voice was very deep, very masculine and his physical presence was so considerable that she could take in nothing else. She found him so attractive that before she could stop herself, she was rewarding him with a coquettish smile and lowered lashes.

'Not really, I'm afraid. Just schoolgirl French.'

'Ah,' he said, reaching for her hand and kissing it. 'English schoolgirl! How charming. I am Patrice. Your teacher. Which of the ladies are you?' She looked down at his hand which continued to hold her own. It felt warm and dry and the fingers were long and brown. A beautiful hand.

'Kate. Kate Hutchins.'

'Ah, Kate. I hope not a little bit of the shrew?'

Kate felt lost for a moment before she understood his allusion. 'You know your Shakespeare,' she said with a laugh, taking her hand away and trying to return to normal.

'Of course. *Alors!* Your dinner is nearly ready. You are very hungry, I think, after this terrible journey. Please, sit,' and he indicated the table where two places had been set, before turning back to the pan. As he poked at the potatoes he reached for a cigarette which was smouldering on the edge of the counter and continued to talk with it stuck to his bottom lip.

Kate hovered behind him. 'Actually,' she said, 'could I possibly just make a telephone call to let my husband know that I've arrived?'

'Ah. The husband.' Patrice threw up his hands in mock despair. 'But of course. The telephone is here.' He indicated a door which Kate opened into a lofty whitewashed room – it had once been a barn, she imagined – where canvases were stacked against the wall and shelves were crowded with paints and brushes. The telephone was on a tidy work table just inside the door.

Trying to concentrate but unsettled by the man she had just met in the kitchen, she dialled the number and as soon as Josh answered rushed into an explanation for the lateness of her call, the train, the long journey, the remoteness of her destination, and as she talked, just his presence on the other end of the telephone had a sobering and dispiriting effect. She could feel the vivacity drain from her voice until finally she asked him if all was well and how his day had been and then, as if acknowledging defeat, laying down her arms, said, 'Are you sure everything is all right? You sound tired.' That was the cue he had been waiting for, the opportunity to sigh and say in a long-suffering tone that he had had a long day and to remind her of his cold.

She knew what was expected of her, that she should sympathise and reflect that she was wrong to go away, that she should be there, at home, when he needed support. Instead, she heard herself adopt a brisk, games mistress tone. 'Has it got worse then, your cold? If it has you should go to the doctor. Maybe you need antibiotics.'

'No, no. I'll be all right,' Josh countered, satisfied to hear that he had needled her. 'Anyway I've got Anna here to look after me.'

'Anna? She didn't say she was coming home.'

'A last-minute decision. She rang from the train.'

'Not Richard, too?'

'No. Just Anna.'

'Oh well, that's nice for you. Tell her how lovely everything is here, won't you?'

'I will.'

'And tell her that there's a little shoulder of lamb in the freezer if she wants to cook it for Saturday, but remember

57

you're invited to Susie and Tom's for Sunday lunch.'

The conversation drifted on pleasantly enough but when Kate pressed the button to terminate the call, she felt disheartened. Why did she let Josh do it to her, even after all these years? Why did she go on expecting anything different from him? I want him to conform to some sort of idea I have of him, which, truthfully, he has never been, she thought as she put down the receiver. I want him to be generous and open-hearted and it is asking too much when I am doing something which he disapproves of.

She felt the fun had gone out of the evening when she returned to the kitchen where Patrice was still busy at the stove. There was no sign of Monique or Elspeth and she wondered if she should offer to help.

'You got through OK?' he asked, indicating that she should sit at the table. 'All is well at your home?'

'Yes, yes, thank you,' she said, smiling brightly, not wanting to betray her feelings.

She went to sit down and he came across with a bottle of wine and filled a glass for her. Their eyes met again and once more she felt unsettled by the frankness of his look and found that she had to avert her attention and fiddle with the stem of the glass. He stood watching her for a moment in his strange, unsmiling way and she had the acute sensation of being judged, that Patrice was weighing her up, assessing her, and that she very much wanted his impression of her to be favourable. The next moment there was a clacking of heels outside in the passage and Elspeth entered in a cloud of expensive scent. She had changed into a narrow cream linen shift which skimmed her slender body and Kate thought she looked lovely with her dead straight silvery hair and a slash of dark lipstick.

The atmosphere in the kitchen altered immediately. Patrice put down his cigarette and went through an identical welcoming ceremony. Even the gesture with the tilted head was reproduced. Kate watched in amusement. This man was a professional charmer. Elspeth sparkled in response as he held and kissed her hand and assured her that he was enchanted to meet her.

'Now, ladies, please allow me to serve your dinner,' he said, cutting up a baguette and piling the pieces on the table. Elspeth took her seat and shook out her napkin on her lap.

'At last,' she said to Kate. 'I'm starving, aren't you? Did you make your telephone call? Everything all right?'

Kate nodded but further conversation was interrupted by Patrice, who with a flourish set a plate before each of them. They both stared in dismay. A slab of what looked like a floor tile, a mosaic of pink and white squares, nestled against an undressed lettuce leaf and a quarter of tomato.

'Bloody hell,' said Elspeth under her breath, poking at it with her fork, 'this looks grim.'

'Yuk,' murmured Kate. 'The white bits are fat, I think.' She reached for a piece of bread while Elspeth energetically ground black pepper over her plate before cutting off a very small sliver and putting it into her mouth.

'Yes,' she informed Kate under her breath. 'As I thought. Utterly repellent. Sort of cold and slippery and slightly spongy. It's probably made from bits of pig best forgotten. You know, ears and snout and other extremities.'

Kate found it terribly hard not to laugh. 'Pig, if you're lucky!'

Patrice had his back to them, sloshing about with saucepans in the sink, and giggling together behind his back annulled the powerful and disturbing effect he had had on

Kate. Fuelled by tiredness and wine, she felt increasingly out of control and silly.

'I've got a tissue up my sleeve,' she suggested in a whisper. She pointed at her plate. 'Do you think we could wrap it up and smuggle it out?'

'Brilliant! I'll mess it about a bit first to leave some traces on the plate.'

This done, like two naughty schoolgirls they dumped the offending slices of terrine onto the tissue on Kate's lap. Hastily she wrapped the parcel and shoved it up her sleeve.

'Just don't blow your nose,' warned Elspeth and Kate had to stuff bread in her mouth to stop herself laughing.

With a serious face and obviously taxed by his efforts, Patrice came back to the table to collect the plates and pour some rosé. Elspeth managed to pull herself together to look at the label and talk with him about local vineyards. He filled their glasses and Kate took a gulp of wine to steady herself before the next course which was now placed before them.

Kate had to bite her hand very hard not to explode with laughter. Swimming in a watery red pool of stewed tomatoes was a soggy breadcrumbed escalope of something or other, which Patrice, coming back with the pan of potatoes, informed them was turkey. The vegetables were what Kate thought of as nasty overcooked Scottish veg – tiny cubes of turnip, swede and tinned peas and slices of grey potato. Elspeth shot a look of gagging horror over the table and Kate actually snorted out loud and had to turn it into a throat-clearing noise instead. Her agony was increased when Elspeth, who had more control, asked innocently, 'Now tell me, Patrice, do you always do the cooking?'

He came back to the table and refilled his own glass, a cigarette still stuck to his bottom lip. 'But no,' he said with a nonchalant gesture. 'It is Julie who cooks, but unfortunately she is not here. She comes tomorrow. Your meal, it is fine? My cooking is not so good, I think.'

'Oh yes,' said Kate weakly, 'but in actual fact I'm not terribly hungry. I'm so sorry when you have gone to so much bother.' She cut into the escalope and found it was made of greyish minced meat and particles of white gristle.

Elspeth who was wolfing the boiled potatoes said pointedly, 'These are delicious.'

It came as a relief when Patrice removed the plates, grimacing over the largely untouched meat. 'The dogs, they will be happy,' he observed wryly, putting a platter of goat's cheese and a bowl of fresh figs on the table. Both were delicious and while they were eating he piled dirty dishes in the sink and then asked them if they would like to sit outside to have coffee and a cognac.

Kate made an attempt to clear the table but he waved her away and shepherded them out to seats under a vine where the warm night air was scented with something exotic which smelled of oranges. Exhausted, they sat in silence, listening to the wind sighing through the pines and watching the brilliant stars which spangled the dark sky.

Kate felt very slow-witted and tired after all the suppressed hysteria of the meal and she had drunk enough to achieve a pleasant sense of drugged stupor. I can't believe I'm here, she thought, sitting under Mediterranean stars, after probably one of the worst meals I have ever eaten. Her unsatisfactory conversation with Josh did not seem to matter any more. Dancing Hill seemed very far away. Too far off to worry about.

Through the open door and windows they could see Patrice moving about making the coffee. The telephone rang twice, the first a short conversation, the second longer and noisier, then another man's voice could be heard in the kitchen speaking in French and Patrice answering.

Elspeth glanced into the softly lit room. 'He's very attractive,' she remarked. 'In that rather derelict and louche French way. He has wonderful manners, hasn't he? Stopping just short of being openly flirtatious. I wonder what his marital status is. Do you think Julie is his wife? He's so charming that one can forgive him the appalling food, but not for long. Julie had bloody well better turn up tomorrow. I couldn't live through another meal like that.'

'I think he's one of those rare men who actually like women,' said Kate, thoughtfully. 'Rare in England anyway,' she added. 'The cooking might have overstretched him but he was quite at ease entertaining us on his own. Most men I know wouldn't be left to cope with two strange women to save their lives.'

'It's not having had the public school experience, I suppose,' agreed Elspeth. 'My brother used to talk about having a dance *against* St Mary's, or whatever neighbouring girls' school, as though it was a rugby fixture. Most Englishmen never quite throw off that attitude, do they? As if women were an opposing team. Is your husband like that?'

'Hmm.' Kate considered, looking up at the stars. 'Probably. He hasn't any women friends that I can think of. Lots he likes, of course, but not real friends. He'd certainly always rather talk to men at parties.'

'There you are. Talking of your husband, did you say everything was all right at home?'

'Yes, fine,' said Kate, not wanting to think about it. 'He was a bit grumpy, that's all. End of a long day.'

'Oh, how typically male. Sulking, of course, because

you're away. Archie was the same. I hope you took no notice.'

'Well . . .' Kate tailed off, not wanting to talk about Josh or the effect he had had on her. 'Oh, look. Here comes our coffee.'

Patrice arrived with a tray of cups and a bottle of cognac. He pulled a chair out to join them and they chatted easily about the weather, the region, the painting course. Kate was interested to discover that he was a professional artist and that there was also a potter and a sculptor on hand. The coffee was strong and dark and the cognac burned the back of Kate's throat as she sipped. I'll never sleep after this, she thought, but after a while she felt that she couldn't keep awake a moment longer. 'I'm sorry but I'm going to have to go to bed,' she said with a yawn when there was a lull in the conversation.

'Me too,' said Elspeth and Kate found that she was secretly relieved that she was not intending to sit on, alone with Patrice. It would have seemed like allowing her a sort of advantage.

They both got up and stretched and said goodnight and Patrice stood and kissed their hands in a courtly ritual, before returning to his seat and refilling his glass from the bottle. He looked as if he was set in for the night.

Kate followed Elspeth up the stone stairs to their rooms and they said goodnight outside her door, too tired for further conversation. Sitting on her bed she pulled off her shirt and the gruesome, damp package fell from her sleeve. Opening the shutters, she threw the bits of vile terrine as far as she could into the dark bushes and then after a quick wipe at her face and hands climbed gratefully into bed and turned out the light. She was asleep within seconds.

When Anna woke on Saturday morning she turned over and lay on her back and watched the sunshine stream through the open window. The instant wide-awake edginess that accompanied the start of a working day took a few moments to expel before she could luxuriate in the knowledge that she could stay where she was and doze for as long as she felt like. There was no need to grope for the alarm clock to check the time, no need to engage her brain with what awaited her in the office, no need to consider what to wear. Later she would shuffle downstairs and cook herself and her father a giant breakfast. Bacon and eggs. Just thinking of the smell of frying bacon made her hungry.

From outside she could hear her father and Len busy in the yard. She knew that if the weather held they would be haymaking by lunchtime. That was another reason to be glad to be at home on Dancing Hill. An afternoon of sunshine and fresh air, driving the little old Ferguson tractor, would be a good antidote to London life. Rich would enjoy it, too, she was sure, but he had stubbornly refused her invitation to come to Dorset with her. He had been grumpy that she had changed her plans for the weekend and only had time for a quick drink with him on Friday, before chasing off to catch the train.

She could see his point, but then, he did not have the same sort of draw to go home. The flat in Roehampton where his father and mother were busily retired was hardly an attraction and the Suffolk cottage held no memories for him and had never been his home. Not like the farm, which she sometimes missed with a physical ache.

Recently, perhaps walking along a London street or in a crowded pub or waiting on a station platform, Anna had felt seized by such a powerful rush of longing for the country that it was almost like a panic attack. She yearned for an open window and a draught of cool, clean air carrying the smell of earth and grass, and if she closed her eyes to shut out the concrete and dirt, she saw the soft green contours of the hills and an empty landscape. Then she imagined herself, a bit like the corny scene from the start of *The Sound of Music*, as a small, solitary figure moving freely, running across the green hillside instead of being jostled and crowded by strangers who stood so close that she could smell their sweat.

It was hard to explain this to Rich who had no yearning for places, other than an urge for a pint which might make him impatient to find a pub. She smiled, thinking of him. Later on she would give him a ring to see if he had relented. If she could persuade him to leave London at lunchtime he could be in Dorset for tea. Now she was at home she wanted to see him. She knew that this seemed contrary, but it would make things perfect to have him here.

Her father had sounded surprised but pleased when she telephoned from the train to say that she was on her way. He had come to meet her at the station and, driving home, was more talkative than usual. She supposed it was not having Mum around that made him pleased to have company. He had opened a bottle of wine when they got back and they had drunk it at the kitchen table while she made herself cheese on toast for a late supper. They had chatted about her job and the farm, how much he had paid for the new bull, milk prices, the future, the sense of despair at dealing with an urban government totally out of sympathy with the countryside. 'We don't want bloody subsidies,' Josh had said, his face flushed from the wine.

'We're only asking for a level playing field.'

Anna had heard it all before. She often argued it out with Rich who took a pragmatic, unemotional view. 'Why should farming consider itself a special case?' he said, 'Shipbuilding has gone, coal mining has finished – whole communities have been wiped out in the north-east. Why do farmers think they should go on being supported?'

'We're not saying they should!' she always cried. 'We can produce safe, healthy food with animals reared to the highest standards demanded by every lobby out there – the environmentalists, the animal welfare brigade, the ramblers association, the tourist board, the whole bloody lot, but we need protection from cutprice stuff from everywhere else which is produced just anyhow. Don't you see that?'

'No. People want cheap food. Why should they be made to pay more?'

Anna gave up then. She was wasting her breath. Richard was a committed townie and enjoyed being deliberately provocative.

As she lay in the bed in which she had slept all through her childhood she thought fondly of the man who sometimes shared it with her, creeping along the corridor at night from where he lodged in her brother's old room, to slip in beside her. Saturday morning sex would have been nice. She felt like it right now, with the same sort of whetted appetite that she looked forward to a cooked breakfast. Sadly, she would have to wait.

Suddenly fired with energy, or frustration, she didn't know which, she no longer wanted to lie in bed. She got up and went to the window, wrapping her naked body in the curtain. The yard below was empty but she could hear Len hosing out the milking parlour and see the last of the cows swaying in a sedate single file along the track to graze on Dancing Hill. She used to know most of them by name but now she could only pick out one or two that she recognised. The herd had trebled in size since she was a child.

Glancing the other way, down the drive, she saw a familiar figure climbing upwards: Grandpa, stick in hand, head down, wearing his old tweed cap. Below her window, the sharp-eared dogs had heard him and started to bark and jump up at the wire door of their run. Watching the stiff old figure resolutely plodding along, Anna felt her heart move with love. She grabbed her old towelling dressing gown from behind her bedroom door, pulled it on and, still tying the belt, ran down the stairs and through the kitchen to the back door. No time to find shoes, she trod carefully and painfully over the stones of the path and when she reached the grass, flew down to meet him, her bare legs flashing pale and youthful in the morning sun.

Josh saw her from the Land Rover. He had driven down the hill and over the lane to check on the hayfields. The early sun would dry off the grass and they should be cutting by lunchtime. In an hour or two when there was some heat in the sun he would start turning the mown grass in the few fields they had managed to cut earlier in the week. With any luck they could get some of that baled up by the evening. It was going to be a busy weekend.

He watched his daughter reach her grandfather and the old man stop and lean on his stick as she kissed him. Then the pair of them, Anna with her arm tucked through his, and treading carefully in her bare feet, started to walk on. She looks like Kate when she was young, he thought. The same rangy figure, the same shiny brown hair. Of course when Kate was her age she already had two children, the boys, and she wouldn't have been racing about like that, like a teenager. You had to grow up when you were a parent.

He considered his daughter. She was a funny mixture, more worldly and experienced than Kate would ever be, and yet still strangely child-like and – he couldn't think of the word, liberated seemed wrong – unfettered, perhaps. She held down a very responsible and grown-up job and it made Josh faint to think of the sums of money she dealt with on a day-to-day basis, and yet she still listened to pop music and went out clubbing with girlfriends in a way that he found quite extraordinary in a woman of her age. She talked about getting legless, having a blast, as if life was a series of marathon fun events. Josh couldn't understand her lack of – again, he groped for the word, and had to make do with 'weight'. She seemed such a flyweight. A flibbertigibbet, his father would have called her.

As Josh got out of the Land Rover to shut a gate, he wondered how Rich put up with it. He was a solid sort of chap who Josh suspected would like to settle down and get on with the serious business of life. Perhaps all girls were like Anna these days. London girls, anyway, because he knew of several of Anna's schoolfriends still living locally who had married and already started families.

He got back into the cab and thought of Kate. Last night her telephone call had come very late and she had gone on about having had a terrible journey. She had sounded excited, and spoke fast with a laugh in her voice as she relayed some story about the train breaking down. She had said the place was lovely, that there appeared to be only two people on the course, her and another English woman she had travelled out with. He had listened to it all and then she had paused and asked him if everything was all right, said he sounded a bit flat. What did she expect, he thought now, after a fourteen-hour day? He said he was just tired, reminded her that he was getting over a cold.

He wished now that he had been more generous, been more glad that the place was nice and that she was having a good time. She did that to him, though, made him feel disgruntled when he could tell from her tone that she was asking him for his blessing, or seeking his approval. After all, she was doing what she wanted to do, why did she need him to put in his two pennyworth and say something on the lines of how much she deserved this holiday? That's what she wanted, and he wasn't going to do it. The excitement in her voice had evaporated by the end of their conversation and he felt bad about that now. He made up his mind that when she got back he would be more amenable, take an interest in her photographs or whatever. Admire her paintings. He would make it up to her for being a grumpy old sod. She had been married to him long enough to know he didn't mean it, know that he didn't really begrudge her the holiday.

When he drew into the yard the kitchen window was wide open and he could smell bacon cooking and hear Anna chatting to her grandfather. His vow to be less churlish, the better weather and the prospect of a cooked breakfast conspired to make him feel positively high-spirited. He got out of the Land Rover and with a jaunty step went inside to wash his hands.

Kate woke early as usual, so early that the light creeping into the room was still pale and milky with none of the intensity it would acquire later in the day. She got up and opened the shutters and looked out. Now she could see that Arc en Ciel was a traditional old stone farmhouse with a red tiled roof, built into the side of the hill. Her room at the back had a view over a neat vegetable garden where she could see onions, beans and tomatoes with a line of hosepipe running between the rows. A range of ram-shackle cart sheds covered with tumbling bougainvillea and clematis crowded the side of a roughly fenced, sloping corral of smooth, bare earth where five or six glossy brown goats lay beneath a tree and a group of golden-coloured chickens scratched busily in the dirt. Above, the hill climbed steeply upwards in a series of broken terraces which disappeared into the trees at the top and, far beyond, the rounded, heavily wooded mountains crept in a dark line to meet the primrose-coloured light along the horizon. Nothing moved. Then Kate's eye was drawn to a far-off wheeling in the sky and she saw a pair of buzzards lazily skimming the trees.

There did not appear to be anybody else about and below her window, where there was a stone terrace shaded by a vine, the coffee cups and bottles and glasses of the previous evening still littered the table. The air was pleasantly cool but with a promise of warmth to come. It smells hot, thought Kate, not like the damp earth smell of England. Turning from the window, she got back into bed to enjoy the luxury of not having to get up and also to think about the night before.

I'm not going to let Josh spoil everything, she told the ceiling sternly. Or, at least, not let myself spoil being here by worrying about him. It's sort of instinctive behaviour on his part. Probably most men are the same. It's an old trick, playing the guilt card. It must be on page one of the Husbands' Handbook, and they go on using it because wives allow it to work every time. The next generation won't, though, she thought. Not Anna's lot. They'll do what they damn well like, in the same sort of way that

70

men do. It will be a different story with them.

The truth was that although she tried to bolster her resistance, thinking about Josh had managed to hook her back from the edge of enjoying being away from home. Small stabs of anxiety began to needle at her. What if something happened to him while she was away? What if he was really unwell? Men of his age were prone to unexpected heart attacks and he did work so hard. Perhaps she should telephone again this morning just to check he was all right and to confess that she was worried about him.

She felt now as if she had something to atone for – her unforgiving thoughts towards him, for one thing. It was an unpleasant sensation to harbour ill will towards someone you loved but who was out of reach. Minor disagreements, in the ordinary run of things, could be settled between breakfast and lunch, forgotten by suppertime, but in this case she would carry around the uncomfortable weight of discord unless she did something to relieve it. Yes, she would telephone again after breakfast.

She glanced at her watch. It was getting-up time in the country. The alarm went at four o'clock when Josh was doing the milking, which admittedly wasn't often these days, and six on other mornings, but no one seemed astir here even though it was an hour later. Last night's drinking had left her with a slight headache – no more than I deserve, she thought – and she longed for a cup of tea. She had put some tea bags in her case in the English belief that a proper cup of tea was not to be found abroad and wondered whether she dare creep downstairs to the kitchen and make a cup.

She got out of bed, found the tea bags and opened her bedroom door silently. She stuck her head out and listened. Nothing. She felt perfectly decent in her pyjamas and so on bare feet she crept down the stone stairs and gently opened the kitchen door at the bottom. The room was empty and she slipped in, shutting the door behind her.

Patrice had made some attempt to put things straight from the night before. He had cleared the table but the dirty plates were still piled in the sink. There was no kettle to be seen so Kate filled a pan with water and put it on the stove while she searched for a mug, which she found amongst the china on the dresser. Then the milk had to be located but there did not appear to be a fridge. Opening what she thought was a cupboard door she found a further room – an old dairy, she imagined – with no windows, which was cold and dark. Shelves filled with jars and bottles ran along two walls and a large fridge and a deep freeze hummed at the back. When she opened the fridge she found it filled with yoghurt pots and little rounds of cheese – which explained the goats – bearing an Arc en Ciel label, and a claim to be biodynamic and organic. In the door of the fridge was a glass bottle of milk and as she returned with it to the kitchen, she heard someone open the door from the hall and Patrice entered. He looked particularly dishevelled in the daylight, his thick hair on end and the bags under his eyes heavy and dark. He was wearing the same clothes, which from their crumpled state looked as if he had slept in them. His feet were bare.

He looked startled to see Kate and evidently the early hour and the unexpectedness of her appearance found his good manners wanting. He ran a hand over his face and peered at her, nonplussed.

'I wanted some tea,' she explained, feeling awkward and acutely conscious of being in her pyjamas and alone with him. 'I hope that's all right. I've put the water on to boil.'

'Ah,' he said gruffly, going over to the dresser and searching for his cigarettes. 'Of course, but you are up very early. I had not expected . . .' His voice was thick from sleep and he coughed.

'I'll take it back to my room,' she said hastily and turned to watch the pan of water, hoping that it would quickly boil and she could make her escape. Out of the corner of her eye she saw him go to the back door and open it, and stand in the doorway, smoking, looking out at the morning.

The water started to bubble and Kate made her tea and put the milk back in the fridge. Patrice was still standing in the door with his back to her. Taking up her mug she crept across the kitchen. He turned as she opened the door to the stairs.

'Stay if you wish,' he said, unsmiling. 'I make coffee now.'

'Um, well, thank you, but I think I'll go upstairs,' she gabbled, anxious to escape.

In her room she got back into bed to warm her feet which had grown cold on the stone floor. The awkward atmosphere in the kitchen disconcerted her. Everything had been so friendly and easy the night before when she had foolishly imagined that Patrice had particularly liked her. Of course, she thought, suddenly appearing out of the cupboard like that had taken him by surprise.

As she thought about it, the cup of tea and the pleasure of a room filled with sunshine made the incident seem silly, funny even. Later she would make Elspeth laugh when she described it.

'This is the life!' said Elspeth as she and Kate sat on the terrace eating croissants and drinking coffee. The sun was hot and the shade of the vine was welcome. The croissants were warm, flaky and golden on the outside but pulled apart into soft tender layers within. A pot of homemade apricot jam stood on the table between the large pottery cups filled with café au lait.

'The French do breakfast so well, don't they? Think of a great greasy plate of bacon and eggs and fried bread – ugh! But I expect that's what you farmers sit down to every morning.'

'With a pint of cider and wearing smocks?' laughed Kate. 'Not quite. Although Josh would probably like to. My father had a cooked breakfast every day of his working life. He'd done a hard day's work by half past eight in the morning.'

Monique appeared to refill their cups. She wore steel-rimmed glasses and her wiry black hair was tucked behind each ear and the wings which framed her face were held in position with rows of hair clips. Her short sleeveless red dress revealed skin which was very white and doughy looking and brushed over with fine dark hairs. Rather short, stumpy legs finished in flat, heavy sandals. 'Not the epitome of French chic,' Elspeth observed, surveying her critically as she returned to the kitchen.

'I'm glad to see her, though,' said Kate. 'I don't know what sort of breakfast Patrice would have produced.'

'There's also a sort of cleaning person who is scouring the kitchen,' said Elspeth, turning to look into the house. 'A rather dear old thing with no teeth who I met on our landing. Anyway, let's hope Julie turns up before lunch.'

Kate swatted a wasp away from the jam. Since she had emerged at nine o'clock for breakfast there had been no further sign of Patrice. She had told Elspeth of her early encounter and had been taken aback when she observed, in a matter of fact tone, 'Of course he will have imagined that you went down early in the hope of a close encounter. A happily married woman is probably a delightful challenge to a man like that!'

'Don't be ridiculous!' she had replied with a laugh and changed the subject hastily but the remark had shaken her. If it was true, she could not remember the last time a man seemed interested in her and the very suggestion that she crept around in her old pyjamas hoping to bump into him was absurd.

They had been told by Monique that their teaching would begin each day at ten o'clock and that Patrice would be ready for them in the studio. The plan was that they would work until noon, then there would be a two-hour break for lunch, after which they were free to paint or sleep, read or walk in the hills. Classes would start again at four o'clock. Dinner would be at eight and there was an opportunity to sightsee or shop whenever they wished. The last night of their visit they would be taken to a firework display in St Raphael and afterwards to have dinner in a well-known fish restaurant in the town.

'Wonderful!' they had both exclaimed.

Fortified by the coffee and the sunshine, when Kate had finished breakfast she went inside to telephone home. Josh was sure to be out but maybe she could speak to Anna and leave him a message. If she put things on a better footing, she would be able to stop feeling anxious and start to really enjoy herself.

When Anna told him that Kate had telephoned, worried about him, Josh grunted and said something about an unnecessary fuss. He had to admit that he had not given her a thought all morning. Frankly, he was too busy. He and Len had been cutting and turning the hay, only stopping for a break when Anna appeared at lunchtime with tea and sandwiches. They'd stopped then, down by the stream in the shade of the willows, while the dogs ran down the bank and splashed in the water. It was hot, hotter than forecast, the sky a hard bright blue. Perfect haymaking weather. With any luck they would get at least two fields baled up and into the barns by nightfall and if necessary they would work on after dark.

Anna lay on the ground in the sun wearing an old pair of jeans and a strappy vest top, her hair tied up in an untidy knot. Her mobile telephone rang twice and each time she got to her feet and walked off, away from the stream out into the field, talking with her head bowed, kicking at the ground with her toe. It was Richard, Josh gathered. Some sort of argument. After the second call, just as he and Len were about to get started again, she came back to where they sat, her face lit up by a broad smile.

'Rich is coming down,' she said. 'Leaving now. He'll be here about four. He'll give us a hand, Dad. Help move this lot off the field.'

'Good,' said Josh, getting to his feet and wiping his hands on his backside. 'We could do with another man, eh, Len?'

Len was already on his way back to his tractor, anxious to get started on the baling. Anna collected the plastic mugs and put them back into the basket. She whistled up the dogs who were hunting a rabbit along the hedge. 'Phew! It's hot,' she said, squinting up at the white sun. 'I'll take this lot back and come down with the trailer.

You'll be ready to start loading, won't you?'

'Len should have the bottom field baled by the time you get back. You can begin shifting that. When Rich gets here, he can help you stack the other end. It will save a lot of time. The Ferguson's hitched to the trailer in the yard.'

'Yes, I saw. I won't be long.' She opened the back of the Land Rover for the dogs to jump in. With a cheerful wave she hopped in and drove away across the field. There was an air of relief about her, even Josh could see that. Whatever had just passed between her and Richard had evidently put her in a good mood.

Why on earth don't they just get on with it? he thought as he started the tractor. Make a decision, stop all this mucking about like teenagers.

George could see that they had started haymaking again. From his seat in the garden where he had taken the newspaper to read, he had spotted the tractors working in the hay fields along the bottom of the valley. He had thought the forecast was wrong when yesterday's rain gave way to a fine evening and a soft rosy sunset. A settled spell now was just what was needed. He brushed a fly away from the brim of his straw hat. It was really too hot outside. In a moment he would go in and sit in the sitting room, but he couldn't see so well from there and he liked to keep an eye on how they were doing. He had seen Anna taking down the lunch and knew that Josh would be impatient, not wanting to stop. He could understand that. When you were haymaking or harvesting and the weather was right, you worked all the hours God gave and forgot everything else.

Now he could see the Land Rover coming back up the

hill, Anna driving. No doubt she would give him a wave when she went by. Stop, maybe, for a chat. She was a grand girl. Like Kate in some ways, but with more of a will of her own, more independent, more courageous. She was braver than her brothers when it came to riding. She used to go across country on Merrylegs, her little grey pony, like a bat out of hell. He'd gone out hunting with her, back in the old days when he still kept a horse, and he'd been proud of her, his fearless little granddaughter. He could see her now, her hair in plaits, her face splattered with mud, looking up at him and grinning a gap-toothed grin. 'Shall we try the hedge, Grandpa?' she'd asked, pointing at a great black bugger of a place to jump, and then without waiting for permission she had wheeled the little pony and, gallant little chap that he was, he'd flown over where many a big horse would have stopped.

George wondered if that was a problem to her now, whether that streak of recklessness didn't make life diffi-cult. She wouldn't be an easy woman to live with, he knew that. As a child she had not been given to rages or temper tantrums, but she had cared too much about things, minded too much. They'd had the devil of a time with her when a bottle-fed lamb went to the slaughter house or when a calf she was rearing died. Farmers' children had to be tough. There was no room for senti-mentality when you looked after stock. She knew that, but she took it hard. She was a funny old mixture, physically tough but with a soft heart.

Any minute now the Land Rover should appear in the gateway opposite before crossing the lane to go up the drive to Dancing Hill. He could see the top of the cab approaching over the hedge. The gate was open so she wouldn't have to stop but it would be nice if she did.

George watched as the vehicle slowed to pass through the gate. Anna looked across and saw him standing there. She slid an arm through the open window and waved, before revving away up the hill, the collies swaying in the back. Disappointed, he picked up his newspaper and went inside out of the sun. It was too hot to sit out there any longer.

Chapter Four

By eleven o'clock, Elspeth, too, was finding it uncomfortable in the sun. Despite her large straw hat, the fierce white light hurt her eyes and her skin started to prickle uncomfortably. She was not prepared to suffer for the sake of art, particularly not to damage her complexion, so she got up and, treading carefully through the dry, prickly grasses, relocated her canvas seat and easel under a tree where the dappled shade offered protection.

Looking up, she wondered what sort of tree it was – not a Mediterranean pine, at any rate. A cork oak, perhaps, with its deeply creviced bark and contorted branches. The ground beneath the tree was stony and rough and so dry that the toes of her sandals were already powdered with dust. It sloped uphill and it was not easy to find a flat place to park her easel and just when she was satisfactorily settled she noticed that she was in the path of a line of enormous ants, marching in a single determined file from beneath a rock. Damn, she would have to move again. Up in the branches of the tree a large black bird started a raucous cawing noise, objecting to her presence, she supposed.

Having relocated herself for the second time, she looked at her canvas critically. So far she had only sketched the shapes of the trees, hills, and distant mountains, but now she had moved her position they were all wrong and she would have to start again. She wondered where to begin and sat vacantly for a while, listening to the din going on all around her. The brown grasses and the thorny, dead-looking shrubs positively thrummed with the activity of bees, cicadas, crickets and goodness knows what else tumultuous insect life.

From somewhere distant she could hear the tinkling of bells and, looking down the path she had climbed from the house, she saw the figure of Monique shooing the brown goats out of their enclosure and turning them away up the hill. Did she do everything, that girl? Elspeth watched her go into one of the sheds and a moment later the hose in the vegetable garden sprang to life in a hundred sparkling fountains of water.

Elspeth glanced at her watch. It was nearly half past eleven and at midday she could pack in the attempt at painting and walk back down to the farmhouse. A glass of cold wine would be nice before lunch. She wondered how Kate was getting on. She knew that she had chosen to walk in the opposite direction, down the hill, wanting to paint the farmhouse and the jumbled buildings from below. She had seemed very keen, a real eager beaver, when Patrice was giving them some suggestions in the studio and helping them to select paints and brushes.

Of course, she was terribly smitten by Patrice, that much was obvious. Elspeth had seen it so many times before – the fate of the middle-aged woman abroad on her own for the first time. Sad, really. She supposed it was the exotic situation, the freedom from all the restrictions of home, the sunshine, the drink – a whole range of things which stirred something long hidden or suppressed in the female English breast.

Not that she didn't understand the attraction. No, Elspeth was only too conscious of the charm of Patrice. She admired his tall, powerful, broad-shouldered body, his tanned skin, his penetrating grey eyes. When he had been demonstrating painting techniques to them in the studio she had noticed the beauty of his forearms where his shirt sleeves were rolled up. The lines of sinew and tendon ran prominently beneath the fine pale skin of his inner arm, tapering into the strong wrists. The outer skin was deeply tanned and furred with fine dark hair. His hands were broad and wide with long, spatula-tipped fingers. She had watched how he used them in gestures to express what he meant, bunching the tips of the fingers together or splaying them wide, palms uppermost.

She imagined those hands making love, stroking, coaxing, teasing, probing. It was an intoxicating thought. The point was, though, that one had to keep these things under control, in perspective. She hoped that Kate wasn't set to go off the rails, do something stupid and regrettable. It would be tiresome if the week were to be taken up with some sort of silly drama like that.

Over the many years since her marriage ended, Elspeth had experienced a great many men, some good, some bad, few that she regretted, and she had learned the hard way to keep any affair that she embarked upon strictly within certain limits. The men she slept with had to be financially secure – she had no intention of supporting any failures or drop-outs. They had to be amusing and well mannered. They must have no vices and be considerate and proficient lovers. She never took them back to her flat and she never gossiped.

What it amounted to, she realised, was that having had

to look after herself for so many years, she knew the price of things. She had learned through the cost of her mistakes. It wasn't exactly being tough or hard-nosed, it was more a clear-eyed understanding of the consequences of certain behaviour and a realistic set of expectations.

That was what was dangerous about an ingénue like Kate. Someone like her could create endless havoc, upset her own life and cause distress and unhappiness to others if she didn't understand the score with a man like Patrice.

Of course she could be wrong about Kate. She was probably sensible and level-headed. In fact, she would have to be, leading the sort of life she described with such a close-knit family. She wasn't a spoiled, bored wife looking for excitement. A little flirtation would probably do her good. Elspeth yawned and looked at her watch. Only five minutes had passed. Where had Patrice got to, anyway? She could do with a bit of help with this bloody drawing and he had promised to come and see how they were both getting on. She hoped that Kate was not going to monopolise him, being teacher's pet and all that sort of thing. That would not be fair and while prepared to allow her a clear run at Patrice – she herself was not interested in a man like that, not now, not at her age – she was not going to be ignored or sidelined.

Elspeth's objectives on this holiday were quite clear. She wanted a week in the sun, away from her poky London flat and her job. A change of scenery and a change of pace. Good French food was part of the deal and if that was not forthcoming today then she would complain. The painting was secondary but on the other hand it was the reason for coming here and she wanted to feel that she had had value for money. She started to rub away at her charcoal drawing.

From further down the hill she heard someone approaching, the scattering of small stones on the path, and looking down she saw that it was Patrice. He was wearing a battered straw hat and a red handkerchief knotted round his neck. He stopped on the path and shaded his eyes, looking up.

'Patrice! Over here. Under the tree!'

It did not take him long to reach her. The straw hat was of the sort obligatory for all French painters. With the brim pulled low and the cigarette in the corner of his mouth, it enhanced his rakish air. She smiled up at him as he stood beside her easel, looking down at her. 'I'm glad to see you. I moved out of the sun and then everything went wrong with what I had done already.'

Before commenting on her painting, he swung a canvas bag from his shoulder and produced two glasses and proceeded to pour some homemade lemonade from a bottle.

'A little refreshment,' he said. 'It is very hot, no? You are wise to move out of the sun. Now let us see.' He leaned across her shoulder and Elspeth felt acutely aware of his physical proximity. Faintly she could smell a mixture of sweat and tobacco which was not at all unpleasant.

Taking up her charcoal, he began to sketch, pointing out the angle of perspective, the deep shadow, the shape of the distant mountains reflected in the shape of the hills and then the round trees. Suddenly the landscape became manageable and Elspeth saw what the underlying structure of her painting was to be.

'Yes, yes!' she cried. 'I've got it now. I know what I want to do.'

'Good. That's good. Change things, exaggerate – this is not an imitation of nature. Put how you feel about this

85

landscape into your painting.' He handed the charcoal back to Elspeth. 'I think you should start painting. Stop fiddling with this drawing. Start to paint!' He patted her shoulder encouragingly. 'After lunch I show you the work of Cézanne and Van Gogh, which I am sure you know already. I will explain what they do with colour and form.'

'Talking about lunch,' said Elspeth in a determined tone, 'is Julie back?'

'Yes, yes, Julie, she is here,' he assured her. 'Do not worry. Today you will be well fed.'

'Good,' said Elspeth, smiling. 'I just wanted to get that straight. Who exactly *is* Julie, by the way? Kate and I were wondering.'

Patrice looked surprised. 'Julie?' he said. 'Julie is my mistress.'

Ah, thought Elspeth. Just as well, maybe. That will put a dampener on things.

Of course, it wasn't really a disappointment to Kate when Elspeth told her about Julie as they tucked into a delicious tomato salad, scented with garlic and basil. In a way it was a relief. It put everything on a proper footing, or an improper one, whichever way you chose to look at it. She had not really entertained any lustful thoughts about Patrice, merely responded to him as any woman would to an attractive man who appeared to find her attractive too. She had no designs on him, as Elspeth seemed to imply. For goodness sake, she was a happily married woman. Kate told herself all this as they sat under the vine with the table prettily laid with a checked cloth. A small pottery jug of marigolds had been put in the centre and a loaf of warm crusty bread and a dish of black olives accompanied the salad.

The fact that Julie was about was further evident from the delicious smell wafting out of the kitchen – hot oil and garlic, the smell of frying.

'It's awful to be hungry again,' said Elspeth, 'but I have to admit that I am.' She leaned across and filled Kate's glass from the carafe of rosé.

'Me too,' said Kate, 'and wasn't it heavenly to be able to get on with painting in the sunshine and not have to think about food – the buying of it, the lugging it home, putting it away or finally cooking it.' She rested her forearms on the table. Already she had started to acquire a deeper tan. She only had to be in the sun for two minutes before she went brown. When she was washing before lunch she noticed the freckles creeping across the bridge of her nose. OK in a teenager, she thought. Not so attractive in a woman of my age.

She had still not managed to get a glimpse of Julie and had to admit to a certain curiosity. She would be glamorous, obviously. Patrice would go for the glamorous type. Younger too, perhaps. She guessed that Patrice had probably been married at some stage. There would most likely be an older cast-off wife somewhere in the background.

Kate reflected on how she had spent the morning. She had felt so happy. Not thrilled sort of happiness but a deep contentment at being able to paint undisturbed. She had chosen a place to sit below the farmhouse where she could look up and see it against the skyline and paint its solid shape and the planes of its roof. She liked the tumbledown farm buildings, the henhouse, the bench under the oak tree, the old washtub slung out in the long grass. Humble, homely things which gave the place its air of rest and tranquillity. That was how she wanted to paint it.

When Patrice came to see how she was getting on, he

had stood watching her paint, standing behind her, saying nothing.

'You do not need my help, eh?' he commented finally. 'You know what you are doing, I think.'

'I know what I want to do,' she said, 'but I do need your help. I am very rusty.'

He lit a cigarette and took a draw on it before saying, 'Rusty? What is this?' The smoke drifted towards her and Kate noticed how different it smelled from English tobacco. Foreign, masculine, sexy.

'It means out of practice. I haven't painted for ages. I've forgotten anything I was taught.'

He continued to stand silently. 'I do not think so,' he said finally, unpacking the bottle and handing her a glass of cold lemonade. 'Perhaps you prefer tea?' he asked, with a twinkle.

She turned to look at him and his face was gently mocking. 'No, no,' she said in confusion. 'This is lovely. I only wanted a cup of tea this morning, because . . .' but he was laughing, bending down to put the bottle away in his canvas bag.

'I am going now to find Elspeth,' he said and touched her elbow. A light touch, hardly more than a tap.

After he had gone she had smoothed the place with her fingers and noticed that the skin was rough, puckered and sandpapery and she wished that this had not been so.

'I thought we might have all eaten together, didn't you?' asked Elspeth. 'All that emphasis on living as family led me to envisage a long table and animated conversation passing back and forth.'

'Perhaps we will tonight,' said Kate. 'Everything seems a bit disorganised, doesn't it? Patrice went off in an old car just before lunch. I saw him as I came downstairs from my room. Something about seeing builders. They're converting one of the barns into a self-catering apartment apparently. Monique told me. Her father is knocking around here as well, it seems. He's Patrice's brother and an architect. His name is Jean-Luc, I think.'

'You have found out a lot,' said Elspeth. 'I'm glad. We could do with more company. It's a bit sad, two English ladies sitting here on our own.'

Kate laughed. 'Yes. I know what you mean. Not that I'm not loving every moment of the peace and quiet.'

Monique appeared with a plate of crisply fried calamari and tiny, crusty golden flat fish, decorated with lemon wedges and a dish of perfect pommes frites. Kate sighed. Really, she couldn't be happier. Drinking wine at lunchtime was having a predictable effect. She felt sleepy and content.

Anna had carted the second load of bales up to the yard when Richard arrived. He had had a slow journey out of London and had felt aggravated by what he reasonably saw as the time wasted on the drive. He was inclined to blame this on Anna. If it hadn't been for her suddenly changing their plans for the weekend, he would have avoided the crawling queues on the A303 at any price. The last half an hour, though, had been lovely, even he had to admit that. Turning off the busy main road he took to the lanes, opened his window and stuck his elbow out. Round one particular bend on the brow of a hill the Blackmore Vale lay spread before him, the sun turning the patchwork of small fields deep green and gold, criss-crossed by hedges and trees which cast deep purple shadows. The hills shimmered in the blue distance. The lane wound down into a village of golden stone cottages and past a farm gate where black and white dairy cows queued patiently to be milked.

Richard drove noticing what was pretty, picturesque, quaint, but not observing the real details of life lived along these lanes. He did not sense the urgency that the turn in the weather had brought about, he did not notice the activity in the fields where farmers and contractors were cutting or turning hay. He did not see that the wheat and barley was slow to ripen this summer, that more maize crops were being grown for silage, that the clamps were already half full of winter feed.

The country was just the country to him. Of course, physical features struck him as they would any intelligent person. He observed landscapes, understood physical features, geology, differences in soil or climate but did not comprehend what went on there. A cow was a cow, a sheep a sheep, a field of grass just that. Milk, beef, mutton, wool, wheat, potatoes, eggs; what went into their production did not interest him. He had shocked Anna to the core when she had learned that he did not know that a cow had to have had a calf in order to produce milk. 'How can you not know that?' she had demanded, genuinely astonished. 'You've drunk milk nearly every day of your life but you haven't understood that simple, basic fact!'

'Why should I?' he had laughed. 'You've driven in a car all your life but you don't know how an engine works!'

Anna's country, as he thought of it, was old-fashioned farming country, even he saw that. The farms were mostly small, the stone farmhouses picturesque, long and low, standing in orchards with chickens scratching under the trees. There were animals everywhere, fields full of sheep, yards full of cows, even a bull here and there. He could tell the difference between cows and bulls. That much was obvious.

It was messy, untidy country with muck on the road, and the smell of manure in the air. Gateways, even in July, were deep in mud, farm buildings ancient and patched up. To his tidy, orderly eye it all looked haphazard and inefficient. Richard thought of Suffolk where his parents had a cottage where the fields were huge and uniformly manicured and trips he had made to Holland where animals were kept in factory-like conditions and every aspect of their husbandry was computerised. That was surely the future, he thought, not this bumbling, traditional way to which these backward-looking west country farmers were so deeply attached.

He was nearly there now, threading his way down the lanes which were only a car wide, between the giant blackthorn hedges which spilled the scent of dog roses and honeysuckle through his window. Meet a vehicle head on and one or other had to give way and reverse into the nearest gateway in order to pass. He had to stop twice, once for a giant milk tanker and then for a tractor and trailer. It was impossible, ridiculous, inconvenient, to be buried away like this but trying to run a business in the twenty-first century. Why couldn't people like Anna and Josh get that into their heads, that this sort of British farming was doomed?

The last crossroads led him into the lane which wound along the valley below Dancing Hill which soared up on his right. Anna's family owned the land on both sides and it was beautiful. Richard appreciated that. If building permission were to be granted it would be a fantastic site for development. He imagined the sort of millionaires' homes which could be built along the side of the hill, perhaps with golf courses and other sports and leisure facilities as they went in for in the wealthy playgrounds of the United States.

That was the sort of thing that Anna's family should be fighting for, not clinging on to an archaic way of life and an income which fell year after year. Round the next bend, he turned off the lane onto the long concrete drive up the hill. Out of the corner of his eye he saw Anna's grandfather in his garden by the lane. The old man raised a stick at him, either in greeting or as an admonishment to slow down, Richard didn't know which.

He pulled up in the yard as Anna appeared from the hay barn, driving the old tractor with the prongs on the front for lifting the great round bales off the trailer which was parked in the middle. She waved at him and, turning off the engine, jumped down and ran to meet him as he got out of the car.

'Rich! Hi, darling!' He caught her in his arms and they hugged affectionately before he lifted her face with one hand and kissed her mouth. Her body felt hot and damp. She had been working hard, he could tell, and the hair round her face and neck was dark with sweat. The dogs came trotting over wagging their tails in a friendly welcome, nosing at his legs.

'Get off!' he said, pushing them away. 'Get your noses out of my bollocks.' Anna laughed and linked her arm through his.

'How was your journey? No, don't tell me! You should have come down on the train last night with me. Come on, come in and have a drink. I'm gasping. We've been hard at this for hours. Dad's desperate to get as much off the fields as possible while the weather holds.'

Taking his hand she led him into the farm kitchen and

92

filled a jug with elderflower lemonade made each year by Kate. She plopped ice cubes in two large glasses and got a fruitcake out of a tin from the larder.

'Shall we go outside?' she asked. 'It's hot in here with the Aga.'

'Where's your father?'

'Like I said, down in the hay fields.'

'Then let's go to bed!'

'Rich! I'm filthy, hot and sweaty.'

'That sounds like a very exciting porn film!' Grabbing her arm he pulled her to him and lowered the straps of her top off her shoulders. Her strong body was still very warm, the skin damp. He reached behind and undid her bra, pulling down the top and running his hands over her naked breasts. 'Come on. I need a reward for ploughing through all that effing traffic!'

'Have this first,' said Anna, reaching behind her and handing him a glass of lemonade.

Richard took it from her and put it back on the table. 'I can wait for that,' he said.

When they came back down to the kitchen later, the ice had long since melted.

Susie Butler was making a trifle. It was not something she would choose to eat herself but she knew that George liked it and she was anxious to please him. Quite why this was so, she did not know. She had been married to Tom long enough to understand that as far as the Hutchins were concerned, there was family and everyone else, and marriage itself did not provide one with membership of the elite. She could do her very, very best to fit in and she would be no closer to being truly accepted than when she had walked down the aisle with Tom fifteen years ago.

93

Not actually down the aisle of course because they had married in a register office. That in itself was a major black mark, the fact that she had been married before and precious Tom-Tom had got himself involved with an unsuitable older woman.

When she and Tom had met she was working as a secretary at the local boys' public school, her five-year marriage to Andrew having bitten the dust. It was hardly her fault that she had been ditched for a young woman sales rep of the pharmaceutical firm he worked for. After the divorce she had sold the Birmingham house and moved to Dorset, to what seemed like the other end of the country to a girl brought up in the Midlands. She had met Tom the second week after she had moved in, in the library where she was filling in an application for a ticket.

'Where have you moved from?' he had asked as he queued up behind her to return a video, and she took in his height and wide, cheerful face and floppy brown hair. He spoke well – a gentleman's voice her mother would have said, and indeed it turned out he was an old boy of the school where she was working for the headmaster.

That was it. They were married within the year, but she had never got over what she felt was the hostility of his family. They were never less than kind, she had to admit that, but George and Kate in particular were like a sort of secret society, they were so close, and she always felt that they were judging her and finding her lacking. She had never pretended that she knew anything about the country although she was willing to learn if they let her, but they kept her excluded, changing the subject if she tried to join in, prefacing remarks with, 'This wouldn't mean anything to you, Susie', or, 'We're just talking farm, you wouldn't be interested . . .'

Josh wasn't so bad because although he farmed and in every other way was one of them, like her he had married into the clan, and therefore didn't strictly belong. When she and Tom moved into the old farmhouse, of course there was every expectation that they would have a family, that the house would soon be full of children. When that didn't happen, Susie felt it like a humiliation and as if she did not deserve to live there with all the empty bedrooms as a reminder of her failure.

Later, when farm incomes started to plummet, she had turned her hand to bed and breakfast and had worked hard to make a successful business, putting in en suite bathrooms and striving to achieve the highest recommendations in the tourist brochures. She stopped pretending to be interested in farming then and more and more called on Tom to help her with what was proving to be a more profitable occupation. They let half the farm back to Josh who was grateful for more acreage to grow some cereals and kept a beef herd on the remainder.

Susie went to the fridge for a pot of supermarket custard to spoon over the sponge cakes in the fluted glass bowl, and the cream to whip for the top. She was also planning to make a chocolate mousse or maybe a cheesecake. She felt it was important to offer a choice. Kate, although she was a good cook, just slapped a fruit crumble or a pie on the table and that was that. She was usually throwing it together when you arrived for lunch. She was like that, slap happy, take it or leave it, while Susie liked to have everything prepared well in advance. The pork and apricot casserole for Sunday was already cooked and in the fridge and the potatoes peeled and ready in a plastic bag in the vegetable drawer.

She glanced at her watch. She wanted Tom to rehang

the curtains in one of the bedrooms and hoped he would be back soon. He had taken the new tractor to help with the haymaking on the other farm and it was this sort of thing which annoyed her. Although Tom explained that that was how the partnership worked, that in return they had the hay to feed their cattle, it always seemed to be on Josh's terms, at his beck and call. Susie resented her husband being used like this, especially when she felt she had a prior claim.

They had guests arriving this evening and she must have the curtains back up before then. She had taken them down to restitch the hem and they were too heavy for her to lift. She was as slender as when she was a young girl and her appearance had hardly changed except for a trace of fine lines around her mouth and eyes. She still wore her fine, naturally blonde hair in a neat chin-length bob, the fringe emphasising her large, pale blue eyes. If there was sadness or disappointment at the lack of children, it did not show. To all outward appearances Susie seemed self-contained and happy with her lot.

She finished the trifle with some toasted almonds on the top. No one could accuse her of not making an effort for George, she thought, as she washed her hands. Thinking of her father-in-law made her wonder how Kate was getting on. She could not imagine either wanting or finding herself able to go away on holiday on her own. She would not dream of leaving Tom, for one thing, and she would not have the confidence to go abroad alone for another.

She felt quite sorry for Josh. She knew that Kate was a good wife, capable and strong, a good worker, but there was more to marriage than that. Susie wondered how well she treated Josh in other ways, whether he wasn't made to feel an outsider by the unholy alliance between George and his daughter. Josh was not sweet-natured like Tom, who was the easiest and kindest of men, but perhaps some of the short temper, the grumpiness, was the result of always feeling left out or second best. She would make a special fuss of him tomorrow.

She glanced at the clock again. If Tom wasn't back in half an hour she would ring him on his mobile and tell him she needed him.

George watched the comings and goings of the afternoon. He was glad to see that Tom came to lend a hand with the new tractor and baler. That would hurry things along. He'd seen Anna and her boyfriend emerge eventually, goodness knows what they were up to half the afternoon, and take the trailer back down to the hay fields for another load.

He liked young Richard. A straightforward sort of chap with a good head on his shoulders. He didn't know why they didn't get married. He supposed they were sleeping together – why not, everyone seemed to these days. There was no disgrace attached to it any more but he didn't think this freedom gave girls the advantage that they used to have. In his day a young man couldn't sleep with a girl without making promises first.

He made himself a cup of tea and a ham sandwich and sat out in the garden where he had a view over the valley. Len had come back up to do the afternoon milking and he saw Tom going off home before the job was done. Typical! he thought. It would be Susie rounding him up. She wouldn't let him off the place without her say-so. She was always after him, fussing about this or that, wondering where he was. In the last ten years George couldn't think of a single occasion when he and Tom had been able to enjoy a quiet pint together down in the pub in the village.

She wouldn't allow him five minutes to himself. If she came along as well it was no use. Tapping her fingers against a beer mat, looking at her watch, saying she only wanted a tonic, she made a misery of it. He had given up in the end. Didn't bother to ask Tom any more.

The sun was still bright but the heat had gone out of it now and the shadows were creeping outwards from beneath the trees and hedges in the valley. The heifers which had been lying in the shade all day were up on their feet and grazing again. From behind him, up the hill, he heard Len shouting to the cows, keeping them moving out of the milking parlour.

George stood up and took his plate and mug inside and rinsed them under the kitchen tap. He fetched his stick and cap and let himself out of the back door. If he took his time he reckoned he could get himself down to the wicket gate at the bottom of the hill and get a closer look at the work in progress. He whistled to the dogs who were loose in the yard up at the farm. They heard him and came to the top of the drive, anxious for permission to run down and join him. He called again and the three of them flew down to him, young Patch and Sly racing ahead of old Bonnie. They twisted ecstatically round his legs, nudging his hands with their cold noses. Bonnie arrived then, pink tongue lolling, pressing her body against him. He bent down to caress her broad black and white head. She was a good dog. All three of them were good dogs. Just seeing their bright and happy faces looking up at him made his heart lift. Calling them to follow, he crossed the lane to the gate on the other side and set off down the edge of the field.

It was the most beautiful of summer evenings, the scented air soft and warm and the light a gentle blue across the flanks of the hills. It was a pity Kate was missing it.

She'd have been down there helping, driving one of the tractors, and there would have been a proper supper, a hot meal, waiting for Josh when he came in, stiff and tired after a long day. That's what a wife should be about. Painting, indeed! Still, he hoped she was enjoying herself. She'd only been gone just over a day but it seemed longer.

Taking his time, he reached the wicket gate at the bottom of the field and rested on it for a moment. He could see now what they were up to. Anna was driving the old tractor, side-raking the hay into neat lines, while Josh came along behind with the new baler. They were making big Heston bales, which would be used for the beef cattle and the sheep and for the wintering heifers. It wouldn't be the best hay – that was what they made in June – but if they got it in tonight with no more rain on it, it would be good enough.

Richard was driving the second tractor, lifting the bales onto the trailer. If they kept it up at this rate they should get the whole lot in tonight and they could start on the silage tomorrow. It was all different from his day when everything took longer and the machinery was always breaking down. He remembered the old baler, what a bugger it had been, spewing out broken bales, tangling the twine. They'd been small bales in those days, which you shifted by hand and that was back-breaking work, stacking them in eights for lifting onto the trailer and then restacking them in the yard. Hundreds and hundreds of bales they moved by hand. Six thousand he counted one year. That was real work.

While George stood watching, old Bonnie came to lie panting at his feet while the two youngsters raced about. It was always a grand sight, getting the hay in, but these days it lacked some of the romance. The huge machinery was too efficient. Sitting up there in the closed-in cab Josh wouldn't feel the sun on his back or smell the mown grass. The old Ferguson was more his idea of a tractor, although it was slow and cumbersome. Anna drove it well. She was the sort of girl who could back a trailer, always a high recommendation in George's eyes. Susie, now, she'd be no use at all. Couldn't even reverse her car straight if she met another vehicle in the lane.

Lunch tomorrow would be quite an affair. He would really rather not go at all, have a sandwich at home, but he couldn't get out of it now. Josh wouldn't be going, that was for sure, not with the weather looking to hold. He would want to spend every moment on the silage. That was the sort of thing, even after all these years, Susie didn't understand. She'd take the huff, he expected.

Much later, long after he returned home, he saw the lights of the tractors still moving down in the valley and heard the loaded trailer going up to the yard and rattling back down again empty. Ten o'clock, he reckoned, before they finished. Then Josh would have to walk round the animals. There were two heifers due to calve and when he had looked them over in the morning George reckoned it wouldn't be long, and he had meant to tell Josh that the new bull, penned in one of the yards, looked restless, hadn't settled, and that old Frank, the Angus, had caught sight of him and was stomping up and down the fence bellowing his challenge. He must remember to tell Josh to get one or other shifted, drive Frank and his harem further up the hill. The newcomer was only two – a baby still. He needed an eye kept on him.

Up at the farmhouse, Anna, now wearing an old sweater, but still in her work clothes, pulled the roast lamb out of the oven. It was after ten – too late to eat, really, but she knew they would all be hungry and had put the meat in the oven early in the afternoon, cooked it very slowly, with garlic and onions and potatoes and rosemary from beside the back door. Now it scented the kitchen and fell off the bone in succulent chunks. Rich, his shirt out of his jeans, his hair on end and in bare feet, opened a bottle of wine and handed her a glass. They sat either end of the kitchen table in companionable silence, eating ravenously.

'This is delicious,' complimented Richard. 'Like that fantastic lamb we had in that taverna in Greece.' He got up to help himself to more. 'Where's your dad got to? We'd better make sure we leave enough for him.'

'He's out with a heifer – a difficult calving. I'll go and see how he's getting on in a minute.'

'Couldn't he have had his supper first? He must be starving. He said he'd been on the go since six. Why can't it wait until morning?'

'Rich! Of course it can't! The calf would probably die and he might lose the cow as well. It's a big calf, apparently, facing the wrong way.'

'God! It's one drama after another, isn't it? I thought you told me that calves aren't worth anything, anyway.'

'I never said that! A heifer calf is worth a lot. We produce our replacement dairy cows and sell what we don't need. A Friesian bull calf isn't so important. A couple of years ago they were fetching fifty pence at market and most of them were destroyed on the farm. That was terrible. Can you imagine? A perfect baby but not worth rearing. Life down the drain. It's a bit better now. Dad can get something for them in the market, even if it's only for dog food.'

'There's something obscene about that. Half the world

101

starving and the other half chucking food away.'

'It's world economics, isn't it? That's what fucks up everything.' She stood up and took their plates to the dishwasher. 'Come on, let's go and see how he's getting on.'

Richard slumped at the table. 'Can't I stay here? I'm not that keen on this animal husbandry malarkey. Your dad will probably have his arm up the cow's bum. It's not really my scene.'

'Don't be such a big girlie. Come on.'

Anna pulled him up, still protesting. Finding shoes and a torch, they went out into the dark yard and through the buildings to a low shed where under a strip light they saw Josh kneeling beside a black and white cow lying on her side in the straw. Her flanks were heaving and her head was flat out, eyes rolling. He looked up when he saw them coming. His arms were covered in blood and mucus and as Richard had feared he was reaching up inside the cow with considerable effort.

'It's touch and go,' he said. 'Calf's still alive and I've got it half turned. I think I'll have to use the winch.'

Richard looked horrified. 'I don't think I'll stay for this, Anna,' he said, but she was already down on the straw beside the cow, rubbing her neck and talking softly to her and took no notice when he backed away.

He went outside and lit a cigarette and listened to the enraged bellows of Frank, and then the sounds of further grunting and straining from within the shed and quick instructions being given to Anna by Josh. He finished his cigarette and ground it out and turned back to see a wet, dark shape on the straw behind the cow, and a mass of blood and mess from her rear end. She had lifted her head and was turning to look with an expression of mild surprise at what had been delivered. Anna began to work away with a handful of straw and then Rich saw a flash of black and white and a large dark head on a fragile neck and the next moment a calf had risen on spindly, rocking legs and the cow was struggling to her feet and nudging at it in wonder.

'A great big heifer calf,' said Anna, helping it to find the udder and expressing a squirt of colostrum into its mouth. 'Clever girl. A beautiful baby for you.'

Watching, Richard felt a rush of admiration but also a sense of exclusion. This was a world he had no interest in and far from wondering at the miracle of life, he felt instead a sort of revulsion. Thank goodness that he had eaten supper before witnessing this revolting scene. It was enough to put you off animal products for life and he would keep Anna firmly at arm's length until she had washed off all that horrible gore.

Up on the hillside at Arc en Ciel, candles flickered along the length of the long table under the vine and voices and laughter competed with the rhythmic thrumming of the cicadas. Kate, sitting between Patrice and Jean-Luc, supposed that this was what Elspeth had in mind when she said she hoped for more company. It was certainly lively and noisy, but looking down the table she felt as if she was merely an onlooker, or an extra on a film set. This was partly because she could not engage in much of the conversation, only when Patrice or Monique explained something in English, and partly because the atmosphere and setting were so different from anything that she had experienced at home. Opposite her Julie sat impassively, occasionally rising to move plates or get something from the kitchen.

She had been a surprise, not the least what Kate had expected, altogether older, less glamorous, more ordinary. She had a pleasant face, but lined and slightly battered-looking, and short hair dyed an unflattering chestnut. She had a soft, shapeless body and wore a loose white shirt and wide cotton trousers. She was rather quiet and gentle with a long-suffering air, replying to Patrice in a low tone while he grew louder and more extrovert, laughing and talking across the table, one arm thrown along the back of his chair, or cracking walnuts on the table with his fist. He hardly seemed to notice Julie, thought Kate, except for one moment when she reached across him to remove a bowl of apricots and absent-mindedly he kissed her bare arm.

This tiny gesture unsettled Kate. It was so un-English, so unexpected. She watched Julie across the table and wondered what it would be like to be her, to live with this man, to share his bed, to be the object of his affections.

Julie for her part took very little notice of either Kate or Elspeth. She spoke no English and merely nodded, smiled and shook their hands when they were introduced. When they turned to thank her in clumsy French for the delicious food she had prepared, she dipped her head and smiled, perfectly pleasantly, but with so little engagement or reciprocal interest that it was almost like a snub. She had the sort of smile, Kate noticed, that was more like a grimace, with compressed lips and the corners of her mouth actually turning down.

Next to her, on the other side, Jean-Luc was also a surprise, so little was he like his brother. Short, balding, bespectacled, he made up for his lack of looks by being loud and cheerful. He and Patrice argued vociferously, occasionally turning to explain in English that they had different views about the new building, and then broke into hearty laughter which was taken up by the two men at Elspeth's end of the table. These two had been introduced as the next-door farmer and the builder, both cheerful, red-faced country men with big appetites and large girths. Surprisingly, Elspeth was getting on with them like a house on fire, laughing and clinking glasses, and they were both turning to her in admiration, clearly captivated by her grace and elegance.

Kate felt increasingly solid and dull. Monique got up and down helping Julie, occasionally stopping to talk in English to her, but otherwise all she could do was to sit and smile and try to look pleasant and as if she was enjoying it all. Which she was, in a way, but not in the sparkling, animated style of Elspeth who appeared to be having much more fun. It's because I'm not used to these sort of people, she thought. I'm not really at home amongst them. I'm not used to men shouting and arguing and expressing themselves so extravagantly, for one thing. When Patrice turned to talk to her she felt little of the earlier resonance because of Julie across the table, watching her with an impassive expression, and because of that dropped kiss which had so clearly marked his territory. She felt warned off, and suddenly foolish and rather homesick.

Chapter Five

When Anna woke the following morning she found herself pressed uncomfortably against the wall, with Rich taking up most of her bed. His gentle snores warned her that he was still fast asleep and she moved her head slightly so that she could look at him. His fair hair, which he grew longish on the top, was tousled on the pillow, his lips just parted, his golden eyelashes fluttering very slightly as he breathed.

She could feel his breath on her cheek, mingling with her own, and his arm was thrown across her. They could not have been physically closer and she lay for a while wondering if this was what she wanted for the rest of her life, to lie within the circle of Richard's arms. It was both comforting and comfortable, but even as she lay there she began to feel weighed down, suffocated by the hot bulk of his body, and found herself wanting to escape the soft breath which fanned her face, very slightly smelling of garlic.

Not wanting to wake him, she wriggled free of his arm and worked her way down the bed until she could climb out at the bottom. She sat for a moment looking back at him. His naked body was sprawled sideways, his back and shoulders visible where the sheet had fallen away. He had a good body, kept fit and trim by visits to the gym, and she felt aroused looking at him lying there, unconscious and vulnerable.

I do love him, she thought. I really do, and sex is great and all that, but why do I always want to move away, have more space, shy away from allowing him to feel we belong to each other? Last night was typical. Richard had not enjoyed the calving. He was tired and wanted to go and sit down, pour himself a whisky and watch the late film. She knew that, and it was wholly reasonable, but she allowed it to count against him, as if he had lost points by not being someone different. Out in the yard she had been deliberately slow, telling her father that she would check on the other heifer yet to calve, dragging the whole thing out in order to make some point, show Rich up in some way. She hated this meanness in herself and felt ashamed because he was a nice and good man. Much nicer than she was.

Almost as if he was aware of her thoughts, he stirred in his sleep, stretched his outflung arm further as if he was reaching for her and finding only the empty bed, roused himself into consciousness. Lifting his head, he blinked at her, and then smiled sleepily and held out his arms. Anna smiled back and crawled up the bed to him on all fours, her long hair hanging over her shoulder. He caught hold of it and pulled her down on top of him.

'How's the midwife?' he asked.

'Sssh.' Anna put her finger on his lips. She didn't want to be reminded of how she had been last night. She would make up for it now. Show Rich how much she loved him, show him she was sorry.

Across the landing, her parents' bed was empty. Josh had been up and out for an hour or two, already started on the day's work. It was only when he had come in from feeding the calves that he thought to listen to the answering machine and picked up his father-in-law's message about the bull. After a nervous pause, always mistrustful of technology, George spoke too loudly and in a strange, formal voice, cutting himself off abruptly at the end. The silly old buffer, thought Josh, quite kindly. He still thinks he has to tell me how to do things. The new bull was all right where he was. He had looked at him this morning and although he was restless and hadn't eaten much, that was because he had arrived a few days ago and was unused to his surroundings. He was only young and had never before been away from the farm where he was born and reared. Probably never been on his own. As soon as the silage was finished, he would move him in with some of the dry cows and he would settle all right then. Whatever George thought, Frank was fine where he was. It was all bluff with the little black bull, all noise and bravado. Josh had been around stock all his life, he didn't need an old man to tell him what to do.

George hasn't got enough to worry about, that's what it is, he thought as he put the kettle on the Aga to make tea. Kate mollycoddles him, that's the trouble, and because he gets everything done for him, he has too much time on his hands.

Old age was an unattractive prospect. Even at fifty-five, it seemed a long way off, but God forbid I should get like that, thought Josh. Let me have snuffed it by then, although he had to admit that George was pretty much on the ball in most respects. Pouring out the tea, he thought of himself growing old and felt an uncomfortable and recurring anxiety about the future. There would be no one left for him to bore. He had no idea who would be running the farm when he was George's age. Would there even be a farm?

He sat down at the table and looked out of the back window through which he could see the yards and barns, several of them put up in his own time. Basic, functional buildings designed to do a job and nothing more. From the window on the other side of the kitchen he could see across the valley, a landscape unaltered by his tenancy, unchanged, probably, for hundreds of years.

Dancing Hill was just about the most beautiful place he knew. Ever since he had first come here to work as a farm student he had loved it, and later, through his marriage to Kate, it had become their own. True, the farmhouse wasn't old or picturesque, but it was comfortable and well built, and it was the position that was so wonderful. The old farm, Lower Holtham, where Kate had been born and which was now the home of Susie and Tom, was a lovely old place, but right down in the valley, tucked away among the trees, whereas up here was like being on top of the world. They were sheltered from the worst of the winter winds which roared through Hanging Wood behind them and in front their land lay spread out like a map. On this bright morning with the valley filled with golden light, he could see Tom's cattle, like miniatures, moving down to the stream to drink, and a girl on a grey horse opening the gate onto the bridlepath that crossed the foot of the hill. He could see two deer stand frozen, watching from the side of the covert known as Pipers Wood, and then turn to slip between the trees.

It was not entirely with a sense of satisfied ownership that Josh sat watching, because he felt more like a care-taker, a trustee of this beautiful valley. What nagged at him was that Tom was childless and his own two sons showed

110

no interest in carrying on farming, and who could blame them, the future was so bleak. When he and Tom could no longer farm – and he had wondered recently if Tom, under Susie's influence, wasn't reaching that point sooner rather than later – then what? He couldn't afford to buy Tom out, and the one farm would no longer be a viable economic unit on its own. Lower Holtham would go to some City type as a country estate. Dancing Hill was not attractive enough as a building to encourage that sort of buyer; maybe it would be parcelled off with the farm buildings and a bit of land as an equestrian holding, or the yard demolished and built on. The remaining acreage would be sold off in lots, bought up by the big landowners to increase their estates, and two more small family farms would go the way of so many others.

It was a depressing thought, that your life's work would come to nothing, that the inevitable end was the dismantling of what you loved, but the reality was that the farm had no future. They were lucky, he knew, that the land would always be worth something and that he and Kate would come out the other end with a bit to retire on, after the bank had been repaid, of course. They could live anywhere then, their ties to this particular piece of country dissolved, the continuity broken.

When George died, that would be the first link sundered. He had been born down at Lower Holtham, just after the First World War, his father the only survivor of the three Butler brothers who had gone to fight in France. Their names were on the war memorial in the little stone church in the village, although their bodies lay scattered in fragments over French fields. They had been tenant farmers then, only buying the place between the wars.

Years ago Kate had taken George to the graveyards in

northern France, the silent acres of white crosses, and what had struck them both was how wrong the landscape seemed as the resting place of those Dorset lads, the fields too flat and wide and featureless, the sky too low and grey and oppressive. 'How they must have missed home,' said Kate sadly to Josh when they got back, for the brothers had all been born in the valley and spent their boyhoods on the farm.

But Josh wouldn't get drawn into that sort of sentiment. He maintained that one place was much like another, that a sense of belonging to somewhere was a sort of superstition or a matter of habit. He liked to think that his approach to the farm was modern and practical. Farming was a business like any other and he would never admit to Kate or George that he loved the place or that there was an inevitable deep attachment to the land he worked.

But how could it be otherwise? he thought. When every working day you trod the fields, you trimmed and felled the trees, cleared the streams, cleaned the ditches and drains, tilled and furrowed, harrowed and sowed, reaped and harvested, every part of the farm became known to you and special in a way that he could not explain or articulate. It was just an acreage, for heaven's sake, yet there were places where the curves of the hills were as rounded and sensual and tender as a woman's breast, places where the hedges ran down into the valley with such exuberance that when they were white with black-thorn in the spring they made his heart lift.

But when Kate went on about the future, dreading the loss of the place, he was always brisk and unsympathetic. The facts had to be faced and it was up to him to be hard-headed. Clinging to romantic, indulgent notions about farming and farmers did the modern industry no good at all in his opinion.

He drained his tea, picked up his cap and went out of the back door to check the hydraulics on the new tractor. Today they would be making silage, blowing the chopped grass up into the trailer and bringing it to the farm to put into the clamps for winter feed. As soon as Len had finished the milking and had his breakfast they would make a start. They had a long day in front of them.

Down in Lower Holtham farmhouse, Susie was squeezing fresh orange juice for her guests. She had some of Kate's homemade rolls ready to warm and local bacon and sausages to grill if they wanted a full English breakfast. The table was set in the dining room with a crisp, white cloth and napkins and sweet peas from the garden in a glass jug. Homemade marmalade and jam and Dorset honey were ready in matching pottery jars, and the butter prepared in delicate dewy curls.

Susie liked to do things nicely and the trouble she went to to make her guests comfortable had earned her quite a reputation. This morning, however, she felt agitated and upset. It seemed that neither Josh nor Tom would be in for lunch, after all, which meant that she and George would have to keep each other company and there would be far too much food. Silage-making was the excuse but Susie had argued that they could well have afforded an hour's break in the middle of the day. They had to eat, after all. Now she wondered whether to call the whole thing off. She could telephone George and suggest that she took him up his lunch, like meals on wheels, but she knew in her heart that it was the company that was important. Getting him out of his own

113

house, giving him an outing as she had promised Kate.

Perhaps she could think of someone else to invite with him, even though it was so last-minute. That would relieve the strain of sitting there on her own, trying to make conversation. She cast in her mind for who would fit the bill and then thought of old Colonel Tucker, a widower of many years who lived alone in a cold, dirty cottage on the Corlett estate next door. She knew he went to church every Sunday morning but he could come on afterwards. He and George were old friends. They had been in the same Dorset regiment in the war and droned on endlessly about the past. He was a nice old man, a gentleman, and by inviting him she was killing two birds with one stone, so to speak – spreading her good works to beyond just the family. It would be a treat for them both.

Pleased with her idea she looked up the colonel's telephone number. He answered on the second ring and clearly wasn't wearing his hearing aid.

'Who?' he boomed. 'What did you say your name was?'

'It's Susie Butler,' she shouted back. 'Tom's wife. I wondered whether you would like to come to lunch today?'

'Is WHO back yet?' He had misheard. 'You must have a wrong number.'

'NO. This is Susie Butler,' she yelled this time, just as she heard the door of the dining room open and her guests nervously approach the breakfast table. The shouting startled them and they looked about to bolt. From the kitchen, she gesticulated to them to sit down and made a face at the telephone to show that she was dealing with a mental defective. The shouted conversation went on for several more excruciating minutes before she got the message across, or hoped she had, and the colonel had agreed that he would like very much to accept her invitation. However, as she put down the telephone she could hear him saying to himself in a normal voice, 'Well I never! Who? Who did she say she was?'

Her guests, a pale, tidy couple from Guildford wearing matching sweaters and with neatly combed hair, watched anxiously. More than anything else in life they wanted not to be a nuisance and so even to attempt staying in a private house was a brave venture. They could hardly bear to agree to the suggestion that they had cooked breakfasts and the wife kept saying, 'If you're sure it's not too much trouble.' They were nice people, Susie thought. The very best sort of guests and she knew that they would write a lot of superlatives in her visitors' book in careful handwriting. Not like the dirty young couple from Newcastle, who left the sheets in a heap on the floor and wrote 'Good bonking. Crap toast' in the comments section. It had made Tom laugh but she had to tear out two whole pages, which spoiled the book.

Tom was already gone, but he would be back and forth all day, the tractor and trailer bouncing down the lane, stacking the silage in the winter yards behind the house. At least it wasn't as bad as muck-spreading when great dollops of the stuff spread across the lane and everything smelled for days. She would make sure that he came in at lunchtime, if only for a bite. What Josh did was up to him, but she wasn't having her own husband go without.

As she stacked plates in the dishwasher she wondered, as she often did, about Kate. Kate had confided in her that Josh was against her going away to France and yet she still went through with it. They had joked about men being like children and Susie had said, 'You go. He won't come to any harm,' and yet she knew this was not really what

115

she felt. Men *did* come to harm if left on their own. Her father, a dentist, had run off with one of his patients. It seemed odd to think of a romance blossoming under those circumstances – Sonia, her future stepmother, lying back in the dentist's chair with her mouth open, having her cavities probed. But that just went to prove her point that all sorts of unexpected things got men stirred up, and then they were capable of untold treachery.

Her own ex-husband had devised a whole set of deceits to earn him time to conduct his affair with Marilyn, the south-east rep for Saniproducts. Susie blamed herself for allowing him the scope for all those covert meetings in service stations along the M25, because unless you kept an eye on things, kept up the vigilance, men were dangerous, swerving creatures, in her view. Even dear Tom, so faithful and gentle, just because of his niceness was vulnerable. She saw how other women were drawn to him, trusted him instinctively and wanted to confide in him, flirted with him, even, given half the chance. It was always happening, wherever they went, at parties, on holiday, in shops, everywhere, and she made sure that she was always there to give him a gentle nudge every now and then, a little reminder.

She knew that Tom thought it was great that Kate should go off to France. 'It's only a week, for God's sake,' he had said when she mentioned it to him.

'Well, you know I wouldn't do it,' she had retorted and he smiled and held out a hand, and said, 'I know that,' and she felt superior to Kate for a moment before he added, 'But you're different. It's important for Kate to do something on her own every now and then.' This insight into his sister had annoyed her and she had said, 'Selfishness, I'd call it!' Which it was, in her view.

If you were happily married, why did you need to be doing things on your own? That was the whole point, wasn't it, that you had found a life partner to share things with. Susie liked the term 'soul mate', which she felt summed up her relationship with Tom, with its suggestion of togetherness on a higher plane than the everyday. She couldn't understand these women who saw marriage as a long struggle to escape, to get under the wire, to break out, to do their own thing. No wonder so many relationships broke down with that sort of attitude prevailing.

Yet there was something tough about Kate and Josh which she envied, a robustness that lent itself to teasing and fond put-downs, to joking at one another's expense. This could have seemed unkind or critical but in fact reflected a warmth and matiness that she knew did not exist between her and Tom. She had gone round to Dancing Hill once to return a cake tin that she had borrowed, and had stood outside the open door on the brink of knocking and going in. In that moment she heard a snatch of conversation between Josh and Kate, she couldn't remember what about, that wasn't important, but what she did remember, what had stuck in her mind and, if she confessed, made her jealous, was the animation she heard in their voices, the engagement, the pleasure in discussing something. Kate made a remark and Josh laughed and answered, and Kate laughed back at him. Susie had knocked then and pushed the door open and saw Kate cooking at the stove, an old apron tied round her jeans and sweater, and Josh at the table, the newspaper propped up on a jug of cow parsley. They each had a can of beer to hand and there was something about their closeness that made Susie shudder because she knew that it did not exist in that way between her and Tom.

Since then she had nursed this little scene like a grievance and sought to find cracks in their marriage, to show that it was not the solid, durable, bedrock thing that she believed she had witnessed. She burrowed away, undermining, and fanning discontent without ever intending to be malicious or unkind. She did it for herself, for her and Tom, to highlight, by contrast, their devotion to one another. Each time she demonstrated that Josh and Kate were less than co-operative with each other, less than supportive and caring, she strengthened the view that hers was the better marriage, she and Tom the more devoted couple.

She fed these little observations to Tom, and when she could she slipped them into conversations with her father-in-law, and even sometimes with Kate and Josh themselves, like giggling with Kate over Josh's grumpiness, saying she didn't know how she put up with it, or last week sympathising with Josh when she had called for something and Kate appeared to be out. She had found him in the yard and he had said, 'God knows where she is! She's always out!' and she had said. 'She is, isn't she? Tom would hate it if I was never at home.'

There were other things about Kate she was jealous of, she knew that. The children, of course, her closeness to Tom, her superior position in the family, her assurance. She dealt with things around the farm with such ease because she was born to it. She drove a tractor, herded the cattle, delivered calves, worked alongside the men and yet she wasn't tough or unfeminine. She was an attractive woman whom men liked and she was natural with them, teasing, chatting, not lost for words like Susie often felt.

It didn't make it any easier that Kate was nice to her and always had been. She had gone out of her way to welcome her into the family and had never shown any resentment that Susie and Tom rattled about on their own in the lovely old farmhouse while she and Josh and the children had been on top of one another at Dancing Hill. Kate's generosity made Susie feel worse about being jealous and peevish, but she couldn't help it. Anyone could appreciate that her situation was difficult, marrying into a closeknit farming family like the Butlers, and Kate's efforts towards her seemed to emphasise their differences.

Whenever Kate said something like, 'Oh, Susie, how nice you look! Is that a new skirt?' Susie felt it was more a comment on her extravagance than a compliment. Kate wore dreadful old clothes around the farm, as if scruffiness was a virtue. When she said recently, 'You've done so well with the B&B. I really take my hat off to you for getting it going. It can't always be easy, having people in your home and keeping everything immaculate all the time,' Susie instantly sensed implied criticism. 'Immaculate' was such a loaded word. Didn't it suggest that Lower Holtham Farm was not a proper home, unlike Dancing Hill where the kitchen was always a terrible tip and Susie often spotted the tea towel, fallen off the rail in front of the Aga, in the dog basket?

She imagined Kate in France, tanned and relaxed, laughing and drinking wine, surrounded by other attractive people. She imagined men admiring her, flirting with her, and the ease with which she would deal with it, secure in the knowledge that she was loved and wanted at home. Thinking about Kate like this made Susie's own life seem depleted by comparison.

'You're not in Kate's shadow!' Tom had once said to her, after she'd had one of her bouts of depression. 'I don't know why you always go on about Kate. She's not so specially wonderful!' It was comforting at the time but didn't really cheer her up, because it wasn't true. She *did* feel in Kate's shadow and always would, as long as they lived at Lower Holtham Farm.

George was cheered up by the colonel's telephone call.

'George?' the colonel had bellowed. 'Tony here. Got a bit of a poser for you.'

'A poser? What do you mean, Tony?'

'What I mean is, I was asked out to lunch today by a woman on the telephone. No idea who she was. I accepted of course. Never turn down a square meal, as you know. Anyway, my only clue is that she said you would be there!'

George stood puzzled, unsure for a moment of the day of the week, before it dawned on him that it was Sunday and he was going to Susie and Tom's for lunch.

'It would have been Susie. Tom's wife. Kate's away, so I'm going there.'

'Ah! That's it then. Mystery solved. Very kind of her to ask me.'

'I'm glad you'll be going, Tony. She's a good cook but she's one of those girls who's forever wiping up round you and giving you mats to put things on. I generally spill the gravy because of all the fussing about. You're a messy old bugger so she'll have her work cut out keeping an eye on you. Give me a bit of peace.'

'Better not take Roger, then? Wouldn't get much of a welcome?' Roger was a very elderly and stout black Labrador, the producer of frequent and smelly farts.

'Best not, I'd say,' said George. 'She's got the old place done up like bloody Trust House Forte.' George's only experience of such a hotel was stopping on the North Circular thirty years ago on the way to Smithfield, but it had made a lasting and unfavourable impression. 'There's a bunch of flowers in the lav, Tony,' he confided.

'Good Lord! Still I'm very grateful to be asked and so should you be, you miserable old so-and-so. I'll come round and collect you, shall I? After church? Twelve-ish? Have a snifter first, shall we, at your place?'

Putting down the receiver, George felt much perkier. He enjoyed seeing Tony and they could have a good old grumble about the government and a bit of a reminisce about the past. It was kind of Susie to have thought of asking his old friend, and now George felt a pang of guilt at being disloyal to her. Trouble was, she made him uneasy and even after all these years he didn't feel he knew her any better. That was probably his fault, he admitted. Earlier on it was true that he had thought she was unsuitable for Tom, but as the years went by he had come to admire her willingness to get on with things, get her business going, not sit on her backside. She was a good wife to Tom, he accepted that, and perhaps, after all, he needed all that rounding up and hen-pecking, for the honest truth was that he could be an idle sort of man, a bit of a dreamer.

George glanced at the clock in the kitchen. Half nine. It was another lovely morning. The sun was already hot through the kitchen window. He'd left the tub of butter on the counter and it had melted into a greasy yellow soup in five minutes.

George reckoned Josh and Len had been cutting for an hour. They'd hope to get the bulk of it done today and tomorrow. He'd seen Tom driving the trailer, taking the chopped grass down to Lower Holtham to put in the silage clamps in the cattle yards.

There was no sign of Anna or her boyfriend. Young

people were no good at getting up in the morning, he knew that. Always said they were knackered or some such expression. He'd get his stick and go up to the sheep before it got too hot. He wanted to check whether Josh had heeded his advice about the bull. He'd hesitated before telephoning, knowing how his son-in-law was pressed for time, and disliking to use the blooming answering machine. He couldn't stand that woman telling him what to do after the tone, but he steeled himself and got the message across, he hoped.

It would be a strange Sunday without Kate around. She'd have picked him up for church as a rule and then taken him home for lunch. A proper roast, she always had, and all the trimmings. After lunch they took the dogs for a walk round the farm and then he went home for a cup of tea and a snooze. Susie would do something fancy, he was sure of that, whereas he was a meat and two veg man. Still, he couldn't complain. It was kind of her to ask him. He collected his stick from by the back door and set off up towards Dancing Hill.

Kate and Elspeth had been promised a trip into the hills for Sunday lunch, to a small village renowned for its beauty and its cooking. They did not feel completely confident of when or with whom this excursion would take place. Partly it was a question of not understanding the language sufficiently well, so that when Patrice and Julie began a lengthy discussion of the plans at breakfast they could not follow the drift. It seemed controversial, at least, on the part of Patrice, who talked loudly and threw his arms about. Julie merely shrugged slightly and looked away with a long-suffering expression and an air of being put-upon, before replying in a low stream of French, too difficult to grasp but which suggested an overwhelming lack of enthusiasm.

Their confusion was also due to the casual nature of arrangements at the farmhouse. 'You are on holiday!' Patrice had exclaimed when they asked him the day before when they should come down from their rooms after their afternoon siesta. 'You do not need to be ruled by the clock. Come when you are ready!'

'That's all very well,' said Elspeth afterwards, 'but one does need some guidance and we are, after all, paying for a painting course. The teaching is the whole point. I'm not a great one for all this hanging about waiting for things to happen. It isn't professional, in my view.'

'Oh, I love it like this!' said Kate fervently. 'It's such a wonderful change from all the organising I have to do at home. I think the relaxed atmosphere is the best part of the place. We should just go with the flow, chill out. All that stuff my children talk about.'

Should we, indeed? thought Elspeth, giving her a sharp look. She did not appreciate being advised upon how she should behave and had a shrewd notion that Kate would love anything to do with Patrice. She had noticed with irritation how she softened every time he spoke and gazed into his face with adoring looks. She was clearly completely smitten and Elspeth knew well enough how good sense and judgement were the first casualties when middle-aged women embarked on that sort of foolishness.

Now this morning they had been waiting for the party to depart for over forty minutes. Not that it mattered one bit, in Kate's view, but she could sense Elspeth's growing irritation and it spoiled her own enjoyment of the sunshine and the pleasure of not being responsible for anything herself. She thought of the ritual of Sunday lunch at home. After the usual rounds of the stock there were the potatoes to peel and vegetables to prepare with an eye on the kitchen clock, allowing herself enough time to change and collect her father for church in the village. It was the same, winter and summer, and had been since she was a child when it was her mother who manhandled the sizzling joint in and out of the oven. Just the smell of roasting meat meant Sunday lunch and a routine that was an inescapable part of her past and which she still felt obliged to honour today. Would I bother if it wasn't for Dad, she wondered. Now the children were gone, it hardly seemed worth the effort and she expected Josh could be trained to accept something like a salad in the summer.

As they waited, Monique brought them out a dish of olives and a carafe of wine but Elspeth was still fretful. 'It's very irritating,' she said, pouring out two glasses, 'that nothing seems to happen on time.' She moved crossly in her seat and plucked at the legs of her black linen trousers. 'Really, it's not good enough, keeping us hanging about like this!'

Glancing at her, Kate wished she was less tetchy. Elspeth seemed to find it hard to switch off, to relax. She was obviously used to schedules and timetables and preferred things to happen as planned. Kate also sensed that she disliked sharing the attentions of Patrice. She made it seem as if she and Kate were in competition for his favours, which was nonsense. If anything, Patrice was more admiring of Elspeth, and Kate could understand why. She looked very striking this morning in a plain white T-shirt with a caramel-coloured scarf worn bandeau fashion round her head. She had terrific style, Kate thought enviously, which she had noticed was not lost on their host. Patrice ran his eyes over her like a farmer eyeing a cow at a fat stock market and then made an appreciative noise in his throat. Kate could not think of a single Englishman who would manage that sort of compliment without turning it into a Benny Hill type of gesture. She said this now to Elspeth, to cheer her up and take her mind off the delay but Elspeth merely shrugged dismissively.

'Yes, but then Patrice is a typical Frenchman – best at seduction and smoking too much, as far as I can see. Archie, though, is a dear about that sort of thing. He always notices if I wear anything new although he's terribly old fashioned, the darling, and calls everything a "frock".' She made no attempt to return the compliment and say that Kate, too, earned a second look. She's used to being admired, thought Kate. She accepts it as her due. I don't merit that sort of attention, she thought, even though, over the last two days she had begun to make a special effort with her appearance. She didn't have the right clothes, for one thing, and even if she had, she didn't have the flair. She had to satisfy herself that her faded jeans were quite a good fit and that her T-shirt, tucked into her old leather belt, showed off her athletic figure. That was the best she could hope for.

She looked well, though, she allowed herself that. The two days of sunshine had turned her skin a rosy brown and put golden highlights in her hair, which seemed suited to the soft water and was glossy and well behaved. She had had a lovely morning of painting and felt pleased with the results, and now, despite Elspeth, the wine made her feel light-headed and happy.

It was nearly two o'clock before a car arrived in the courtyard which was evidently the signal for them to leave. 'Ladies, you are ready?' called Patrice from the door, in a marshalling sort of voice. Obediently Elspeth and Kate got up from where they were sitting under the vine and collected their bags and sunglasses. It seemed that the occupants of the car, a man and a woman, who did not get out and were not introduced, were to be part of their party.

After a bit of loud organising, Monique and Jean-Luc climbed into the second car which led the way down the track in a cloud of dust. Julie, who had trailed out of the farmhouse, got into the front passenger seat of the old Peugeot and Patrice opened the rear doors for Elspeth and Kate.

'Now where exactly are we going, Patrice?' asked Elspeth, in a firm tone. 'And who are these people who have joined us?'

'Ah!' said Patrice. 'I have told you I think?'

'No, indeed you haven't,' she retorted. 'And one does like to know.'

'We go to a hilltop village. Very ancient and very beautiful, with chateau and church from the Middle Ages. It is perhaps half an hour from here, but you will enjoy the drive. We have lunch in a restaurant very well known to me, where I think you will enjoy the food and the atmosphere.

'This couple in the car, they are my friends. Robert is a sculptor and Brigitte is a doctor. You will like them very much. They also live nearby and they are busy with their goats, so, Kate, they are also farmers like you!' He laughed heartily, as if at a joke, and Kate felt obliged to join in. What was so funny about being a farmer? she wondered. Through the car windows she had got the impression of a very tall man with an outstanding nose sitting in the front passenger seat, being driven by a little woman with a strong face and cropped grey hair, who could almost have been a small man herself.

Kate and Elspeth sat side by side, bounced around by the rough road, both craning their necks to take in the scenery. They wound down the hill through the pine forest, catching a glimpse of the wide valley beyond and the sparkling deep blue of the distant sea. On the slopes of the wooded hills closest to the coast there was the glitter of glass and the red tiled roofs of villas, but up here the houses were few and far between and most appeared to be traditional small farms with tumbledown cart sheds and little patches of cultivation.

In front of Elspeth sat Julie, the seat belt slicing across her puffy bosom like a line across a hot cross bun. And she *is* cross, in her sighing, reproachful way, thought Elspeth. Our Lady of Infinite Sorrows; it really must be a bit down-getting day after day. She wondered how Patrice put up with it. Julie's head was turned away from him to look out of the window. She had drawn black kohl lines round her eyes and slapped on a bit of lipstick in a haphazard way, but Elspeth judged that she didn't take much care of herself. The hair, for a start. That particular shade of maroon, the colour of a nasty school uniform, suited only the very young and the very punk. It was well cut but in an unforgiving style which did not flatter a face which, although pretty, was collapsing into soft pouches and folds.

And the clothes, thought Elspeth, who had over the years learned how to be chic on a budget. What on earth induced a Frenchwoman of all people to wear that sort of baggy, sleeveless tunic top over shapeless trousers? It was all too depressing and so odd when this woman had a man to dress for, an extremely sexy man. What was the matter with her? Why the style bypass? It somehow all went with the suffering attitude. She wore the modern equivalent of a hair shirt. These were clothes to *suffer* in.

127

Glancing at Patrice, she could detect no intention to suffer on his part. He wore a lovely old cambric shirt in a heavenly blue with sleeves rolled up to reveal the beautiful brown forearms, and a pair of well-fitting jeans. Around his neck was knotted a bright little red handkerchief. One fantastically sexy hand rested on the steering wheel, whirling it this way and that along the twisting road, the other on the gear stick, changing up and down as required, yet he managed to keep an eye to right and left and point out interesting features to his passengers as they went past. He exuded bonhomie and high spirits. This was an outing which he intended to enjoy.

Kate, too, seemed livelier, having been a bit subdued, Elspeth noticed, the night before. That was the trouble with married women, they found it hard to adapt to socialising on their own. Husbands and families provided a sort of social crash barrier around them and when this was removed they often floundered. They either went quiet and were leaden company, or worse, drank too much and became laddish. Elspeth had witnessed with distaste the groups of middle-aged women let loose from home and husbands, getting noisily pissed in London with a gang of girlfriends.

Elspeth had had to make her own way for so much of her life that she had developed a strategy for dealing with social situations as a single woman. Don't talk about oneself and be fascinated by the dullest man in the room, were just two of the rules which she stuck to, and which meant that she never became the anxiety to her hosts that some lone women were, standing trembling on their own in corners or skulking about the fringes of a party searching for other dull women to attach to, like drowning persons at sea without a lifebelt.

She had enjoyed last night, liked the company of the two Frenchmen. The builder, Bernard, was a charming man, and despite his fractured English they had managed to communicate very well. He had put his large, hard hand on her knee at intervals, and to be admired was, of course, the greatest boost. Apparently he was a grandfather himself, but full of vigour and enjoying life. With age, he had told her, through Patrice, the pleasures are sweeter and the mistakes fewer. They had both drunk to that. In fact, she had drunk more than usual and this morning approached the mirror in her bathroom with some trepidation. However, there was no sign of what she called 'drinker's eye' and no trace of a headache, so all was well.

She was slightly annoyed to see that Kate was looking well. Although she had no idea at all about clothes, she wore what suited her. Her long legs looked good in jeans and the plain white shirt showed off her attractive colouring and emphasised her fine English skin and her glossy hair. Elspeth could not deny that she was a nice-looking woman. She wondered why her husband let her go off on her own, or rather, what led to her wanting to and him agreeing. She did not have about her the air of being much cherished. That was it. Elspeth was pleased with herself for having put her finger on it. That was the difference between them. Elspeth, for all her single status, was a woman who knew what it was to be valued. She had been lucky like that. Dearest Archie, who even now wanted to marry her.

On Dancing Hill they had done a good morning's work. When eventually Anna and Rich had emerged, looking shagged out, thought Josh, which didn't totally surprise him, they had taken over the job of driving the trailer, which freed him to take the new tractor and begin rolling the silage they had already got in the clamps, squashing the chopped grass, breaking it down and compressing it into a solid mass. This was a tricky job done by driving the tractor up and down the heap and he preferred to do it himself. Once finished, they could get the plastic sheets on and weigh them down with hundreds of old tyres to keep them in place and the rain out. This was hard work and it would be useful to have extra pairs of hands.

He'd met the colonel in the lane, going like the clappers, with his father-in-law in the front seat. He'd had to smile at the pair of them, both spruced up for lunch at Susie's, the colonel very dapper in a matching tie and handkerchief. Despite the fact that Josh was driving the tractor, it was he who backed up into a gateway to let them pass. It was safer and quicker in the long run. The colonel wound down his window to bellow 'Good morning!' and George waved his hand. It was good of Susie to have them both. Of course, she would understand why he couldn't spare the time to join them. Hay and silage making was always in the lap of the gods. You just had to snatch the opportunity when it came.

Driving the tractor to a halt in the yard, he turned off the engine and jumped down from the cab. He'd go indoors and grab something to drink and some bread and cheese. Anna had said that she and Rich had had a big breakfast and would carry on working for the time being. Rich seemed to enjoy the driving part of farming, thought Josh. He liked handling the big machinery and got the knack of it quickly.

As he crossed the yard to the house, he heard Frank bellowing and remembered George's telephone message. Perhaps he would just check on the bulls before going inside. They couldn't come to any harm, but it would put his mind at rest.

The new bull, whom they had christened Charlie, was standing at the back of his pen, up against the metal railings, shaking his head and trembling in agitation, with his back turned to Frank, who was trotting up and down the fence on the other side of the farm track, swinging his great head and flicking his tail in the air.

'You silly bugger,' Josh yelled at him. 'Pack it in, will you. Leave him alone!'

Whether the sound of Josh's voice enraged him further it was hard to say, but with a roar Frank turned and charged at the wire. He hit the three strands with his head and the two adjacent fence posts were lifted clear out of the ground as if they were matchsticks. The wire bowed, the top strand snapped and Frank was through, gathering speed to charge at the metal gate of the bull pen. Josh began to run to head him off, but it was a futile gesture. Nothing was going to deter Frank now, as with lowered head and furious eye, he gathered himself to do battle with the eight-bar obstacle that stood between him and the object of his fury.

Josh reached the gate at the same time as Frank hit it. The metal bars buckled and the bottom hinge was lifted clear of its post. Frank turned to come at it again and Josh, shouting and waving his arms, tried to deflect him. This time the gate gave way and Josh was caught by Frank's shoulder and catapulted into the air, over the broken gate and into the concrete pen. The last thing he remembered thinking as he saw Frank climbing in after him was, 'Bugger! George was right!'

Chapter Six

George poked suspiciously at the pork casserole Susie had spooned onto his plate. It qualified as mucked-about food in his view and why she couldn't produce a perfectly ordinary piece of roast pork was beyond him. Still, the mashed potatoes looked safe enough although he had seen her in the kitchen putting them into a machine and whizzing them about, when his late wife, Pat, or Kate come to that, never needed to use anything other than a potato masher. But that was Susie all over, always looking to bring things up to date and introduce new gadgets.

Across the table, old Tony was tucking in all right. They had had a couple of stiff whiskies at the bungalow and another one when they arrived at Lower Holtham and his face was as red as a turkey cock's. It was a hot day to be wearing a three-piece tweed suit and the collar of his shirt looked too tight. He was shovelling up the pork and potatoes enthusiastically, smacking his lips, and wiping his mouth on the lacy napkin. Of course, he never got a square meal unless he was invited out. George occasionally shared a steak pie with him down at the pub, but home cooking was a treat he did not often enjoy. Old age on one's own could be a miserable, comfortless thing and George knew how lucky he was to have Tom and Kate next door. He was spoiled, he realised that.

Susie was up and down from her place every few minutes, going to the window on the look-out for Tom. She was listening for the tractor and trailer on its way into the yard with the grass for the silage clamp. She had told them she wanted him to come in for lunch, and George wondered, given the pressure of getting the job done, why a grown man couldn't make up his own mind when he wanted to eat, to come in when he was ready. He wouldn't have put up with it himself, but he said nothing and old Tony made one of his flattering remarks on the lines of if he had a wife as charming as Susie who produced such delicious food, there would be no need to call him in to lunch; he would be there waiting.

It was hot in the dining room. Susie and Tom had added a conservatory to the front of the old house and the heat was intensified by all the glass, even though the windows were open and the blinds pulled down. It's like eating in an oven, thought George, wiping his forehead, remembering the old days when the room was dark and cool. Cautiously he tasted the pork and had to admit it was delicious. Strange, but delicious. It seemed to have orange in it, which was something he had never heard of before. Tony was already passing his plate for a second helping.

Susie, wearing a pretty, feminine cotton dress which she had made herself from a *Vogue* pattern, flirted gently with Tony, touching his arm as she passed, and laughing a tinkly laugh. She piled mashed potatoes on his plate. At least he appreciated the effort she had made, unlike her father-in-law, but as she turned to check how George was getting on, she was gratified to see that he had finished as well and willingly accepted a second helping.

'I have to say it tastes better than it looks,' he said,

paying her a clumsy compliment.

'Thanks!' laughed Susie. 'I know what you're thinking, though, that you prefer a plain roast.'

'No, no. It's very good. Very tasty.' George did not want to seem ungracious, especially not in front of Tony.

'My dear girl,' said Tony, 'you're a genius. Delicious. Best thing I've eaten for years. What a lucky man your husband is. I hope he realises his good fortune.'

Steady on, thought George, don't overdo it, but Tony was like that with the ladies. He was so much on his own, or in the company of other miserable old codgers, that he went overboard in mixed company.

'Yes, he does,' said Susie. 'Dear Tom. He's always appreciative. Unlike some!' and she tapped her father-in-law's hand playfully. 'Josh, too. I never hear him tell Kate what a good cook she is.'

Well, of course, you don't carry on like that when you're married, thought George. It's not normal. Josh would tell anyone who asked that Kate was a good cook, but he didn't have to keep telling her.

Tony started on one of his stories which George had heard many times before. 'Did you know Roland Cahill?' he asked Susie. 'He was vicar here straight after the war.' Of course she didn't, thought George. She was hardly born then, but her reply didn't matter because Tony was well away on his story.

'George will tell you, he was a fine chap, very well liked amongst the farmers. A proper countryman, not like our present specimen, but I won't go into that now . . .' Tony's disapproval of the current incumbent, a pale, well-meaning young man from an urban background, was a well-aired topic. 'Anyway, old Roland was a great one for visiting round his parish – always out and about he was.

Drove an old black Riley, didn't he, George? Wherever he went he was always invited to take tea and cakes, biscuits, scones, pancakes. It was always, "Have a piece of sponge cake, vicar. Have a slice of homecured ham, vicar. Have a glass of cider." It was hard to refuse, he said, and he did his best to do justice to his parishioners' hospitality.'

George could see that Susie wasn't listening. She was up out of her chair again, having heard the tractor on the lane. Tony ploughed on, enjoying his role as raconteur.

'One day he was out at old Harrison's farm, right on the edge of the parish – nearly into Cattistock country, eh, George? Old Mother Harrison had passed away. Great mountain of a woman she was. Legs like tree trunks. I can see her now up a ladder, picking apples, like the Colossus of Rhodes. Anyway, Roland had gone to pay his respects and offer comfort to Harrison and as usual was asked to stay and have a cup of tea. "Come on, vicar," said Harrison, "have a slice of cake. It's the deceased's own baking!" ' Tony wheezed with laughter. 'The deceased's own baking!' he repeated. 'Poor Roland!'

George laughed too. He enjoyed the story, however often he heard it. It reminded him of the past, when the vicar, the doctor, the local policeman were important figures in the locality.

Susie had not heard the end of the story. She was in the kitchen, calling to Tom in the yard, and then George heard him coming in. A few moments later Tom put his head round the door of the dining room and raised a hand in salute to the two old men. His face was flushed from the sun and his hair was flattened to his head.

'All right, Colonel? All right, Dad? I'll be through to join you when I've had a wash.'

She's got her way, then, thought George. Got him well under her thumb.

Susie came back carrying a heavy glass bowl of trifle and a cheesecake decorated with mandarin orange segments. Tony looked up eagerly, almost quivering with anticipation like a dog expecting a titbit, and then Tom reappeared, washed and spruced up, with his hair combed. He took his place at the end of the table and Susie darted back to the kitchen to bring him his plate which she set in front of him.

'You get well looked after, lad,' said George, 'that's one thing I will say.' Tom smiled in acknowledgement and Susie, lowering her eyes to cut the cheesecake, felt a rush of pleasure. What was Josh sitting down to now, she wondered, if he was sitting down to anything at all?

Anna and Rich had stopped work to have a swig of water in the shade down by the stream. Their two tractors, Anna's with the mower and Rich's with the forage harvester, were drawn up side by side. Until Tom came back with the trailer, work was at a standstill and Anna was fuming. 'Where the hell is he?' she demanded, pushing wet strands of hair away from her face. 'He's been gone for forty minutes at least.'

'Come and sit down and stop getting so worked up,' said Rich, lying full length on the grass.

'It just makes me mad,' she said, flopping down beside him. 'If he was going to take a break, he might have told us. You could have towed the other trailer behind the harvester. We wouldn't have had to stop then.'

'What difference does an hour make?' asked Rich.

'It can make all the difference. If this lot gets rained on . . .'

137

'It's not going to rain. Look at the sky.' Richard squinted upwards, but Anna was not to be pacified.

'It's typical of Uncle Tom. It's just not fair on Dad. He doesn't pull his weight. He never has.'

'Come on. What is it with your family? No one else is ever good enough.' Richard spoke lightly but he had touched a nerve. Anna swung round on him.

'What do you mean by that?'

'What do you mean, what do I mean? Nothing.'

'Yes, you did. You said it as if you meant it.'

'Oh, come on! Lighten up!'

'Well, tell me.'

'For God's sake, Anna. Let it go, will you!'

Anna lapsed into moody silence, furiously chewing at a grass stem. What Rich had said reminded her of last night and how she had behaved towards him. He was right. The Hutchins did think they were bloody perfect. She was angry with him, all the same. Offended. It wasn't up to him to point out their deficiencies.

Richard had another swig of water. The hot sun and Anna's bare shoulders and low-cut top had started to make him feel horny again. He watched her sitting beside him, hunched forward, her knees drawn up and loosely apart, pulling at the grass angrily. Her long hair was tied up in a knot and the back of her neck was slender and vulnerable looking.

He plucked a long stem of grass and leaning forward let it tickle her neck. She slapped at it with her hand before realising it wasn't an insect. He ran the grass down her neck and shoulder and then pulled her backwards until she collapsed onto his lap.

'Don't be so cross,' he said to her and bent down to kiss her mouth. 'Mrs Grumpy of Dorset.'

Anna squinted up at him. The sun was blinding and his face loomed dark over her with a halo of bright, spiky hair. He looked odd, upside down, and she did not respond, just lay with her head in his lap, staring up at him, thinking, I don't recognise him like this. He looks like a stranger. Gently he moved her damp hair off her face and they fell silent, letting the peace of the place wash over them.

'I want to be buried here,' she said eventually in a different, reflective voice. 'Or have my ashes scattered or something. Whichever I decide. It's my favourite place. I'd be going back to the land that made me.'

'Yeah?' Rich's voice was noncommittal. Anna was such a drama queen. She thought that talking about dying gave her some kind of edge, and he felt that he was being asked for an emotional response. She sat up to look at him better.

'You know, since September the eleventh all things which seemed certain can't be taken for granted any more. Us two, working in London, for multinational companies in multi-storey buildings, on the Tube every day, we could be wiped out, just like that!' She snapped her fingers. 'Who knows? It could happen tomorrow.'

This was an opinion which had been aired frequently amongst their friends suddenly forced to consider their own mortality. It was not an original thought and Richard merely shrugged. He was about to start on the 'any of us could be run over by a bus tomorrow' rebuttal, but Anna cut him short.

'What I think I mean is, I sometimes feel so insignificant. What I do day after day is sometimes interesting, sometimes quite exciting and I get paid bloody well, but what *difference* do I make to *anything*? If anything happened to me, some other little cloned person would pop up to take my place, and if the whole company got wiped out – well, no great loss to the scheme of things.' She waved her arms in the air theatrically. 'Whereas, all this,' and she indicated the fields, the valley, 'is enduring. It's been like this since man first herded animals and tended the land. What Dad does, the result of his work, is all around us. You can see the difference he makes. He gets out of bed every morning with a clear idea of what needs to be done – feeding the animals, caring for the land, whatever. You can see the results of his good husbandry. It is so satisfying and honest and *right*.'

'You could say the same about a dustman,' said Rich, 'or anyone who does hands-on work.'

'Yes, I know. What I'm saying applies to all of that sort of thing. Doctors and nurses especially.'

'But you can't un-sophisticate the civilised world or wind development back. We can't all be making mud pots or be hewers of wood and drawers of water. What we do – our highly specialised financial stuff – is what props up everything else in the developed world.'

'Then it's upside down,' said Anna obstinately. 'All it is is rearranging the deck chairs on the *Titanic*. It's this, this honest toil, that should be the bedrock. Simple stuff like keeping this stream clean and healthy, or producing safe food in a humane way is what should be most important. You and I are just pimples on the face of the earth, we're just on the surface of things, we could all be wiped out and what would still matter? What Dad does here.'

She's really quite childish, thought Richard, getting worked up about the complexities of modern life, like a left over from the hippie generation or the disciple of a green guru. He couldn't be bothered to refute her half-baked argument and so gently changed the subject. 'So what's all this about your burial arrangements? I suppose you want a handwoven biodegradable willow coffin.'

'Yeah, that would be great. Lined with moss. And I want you to be *very deeply* grieving, OK?'

'I'll do that for you. For a day or two, anyway. How about some black horses and plumes and stuff?'

'Oh, yes. That's a wonderful idea. You can walk behind my coffin all the way from the farm, down Dancing Hill, following the horses. And a hunting horn! I'd like to be marked to ground by a hunting horn.'

'You don't want much, do you? You'd better write all this down in case I forget.' Satisfied that he had altered the mood, changed the atmosphere between them, he pulled Anna on top of him. With any luck Tom would be some time yet.

Parking was difficult in the hilltop village of Seillans. The tiny, gridlike cobbled streets, only one vehicle wide, opened out unexpectedly into little squares where the houses leaned forward haphazardly, hung with balconies overflowing with geraniums. Everywhere was clogged with cars drawn up in any available space, obstructing pavements, hard against the walls of houses, pushing against the trunks of lime trees, across gateways.

Kate stuck her elbow out of her open window and felt the heat like a solid block against the side of the car. Her head swam with the onslaught of heat and noise and colour as she squinted against the sun which glittered off the parked cars. The town was crowded with cafés and restaurants and the pavements outside congested with people eating at tables beneath sunshades. She saw harassed-looking, white-aproned waiters hurling in and out, balancing plates on one hand above their heads, and a delicious smell of sizzling garlic wafted through the car window as they drove slowly past.

It was only later, after Patrice had parked at a rakish angle across the kerb and in front of a fire hydrant and they were walking back through the town, that she realised this wasn't an ordinary village at all. Many of the tiny, crooked houses were artfully restored and rebuilt with roof terraces sprouting satellite dishes, and open-plan steel kitchens. The menus posted outside the cafés were sophisticated and expensive and the shops, apart from the boulanger and the boucher and épicier, all properly closed on a Sunday, were boutiques selling Hermès scarves and Chanel T-shirts.

They paused outside a crowded restaurant to wait for Patrice to buy cigarettes and she got a closer look at a big family group at a table under the awning. The grandmother sitting with a baby on her sharp brown knees was not a cosy old dear, but an elegantly dressed woman with golden candyfloss hair in which her dark glasses perched. Her deeply bronzed face had the reptile look of the handbag at her feet. There seemed to be as much German and Dutch being spoken as French and Kate guessed that these people were not locals but international holidaymakers from the yachts and villas along the coast. It wasn't a real village at all and surely not Patrice's sort of place.

Of course it wasn't. They walked swiftly through the town, Patrice cupping his hands beneath their elbows to hurry them across roads, Julie having disappeared to buy some bread. There was no sign of the other car or its occupants. They began to climb a steep street, grateful for the slice of deep shade on one side, the other half burning white under the sun. Ahead, between the houses, the sky was a shimmering block of cobalt blue. They trudged on, away from the congested centre, past a little whitewashed stone church and shabbier, less renovated houses, even a workshop on a corner where a black cat, lying flat in the sun, raised its head and twitched the tip of its tail as they passed. Through the shutters closed against the heat of the day came the smell of cooking, onions, garlic, hot oil, and the sound of voices and the clink of cutlery on china.

Elspeth paused to fan her face. 'How much further, Patrice?' she complained. 'It's too hot to go on a route march like this.'

'We are nearly there,' he cried encouragingly and turning a blind corner the street suddenly opened into a little triangle shaded by a few plane trees in the centre and opposite them was an unpretentious café with tables outside on the pavement.

'Here we are,' said Patrice. 'Chez Didier.'

He hurried them across the road and into the busy café and Kate saw immediately that this was a different clientele, seriously French, a mixture of ages, dressed with casual disregard for the fashion dictats which ruled lower down in the town. There were three or four burly men propped at the bar, wearing jeans and thick cotton shirts and involved in a noisy card game, refilling their wine glasses from a range of bottles in front of them. They and the other men sitting on stools along the bar had strong faces of two types, either beaky-nosed and craggy, or red and meaty, with sausage noses the texture of cork. Without exception they looked as if a good part of their lives had been sacrificed to eating and drinking well.

Patrice only had to stand in the doorway for a moment to create a stir. One of the card players glanced up and there was an instant cry of recognition and pleasure. The cards were abandoned as the group of men came to shake him by the hand and kiss him on both cheeks. Several of the diners also looked up and shouted greetings and even the hatchet-faced woman behind the bar managed a nod in his direction.

'Goodness,' said Elspeth to Kate. 'Does everyone know Patrice?'

They were introduced to the friends at the bar and there was more hand-kissing and then Didier appeared from the kitchen, dressed in a linen smocked shirt and apron: a stout, middle-aged man with slicked-down dark hair and a moustache. He gripped Patrice's arm above the elbow and, laughing and cracking jokes, called for another bottle to be opened. The other diners looked across, interested and smiling, and some even raised glasses to the newcomers.

Didier indicated that a place was reserved for them and when Elspeth looked across she saw that Monique and Jean-Luc and their friends were already seated at a table along the wall. Leaving Patrice to continue the rigmarole of greeting his friends, she and Kate wound through the close-packed diners. Jean-Luc stood up politely and moved to one side so that Elspeth could slide onto the banquette against the wall and sit next to him but she noticed that Kate was hanging back, looking over her shoulder at Patrice. She's trying to arrange it so that she sits next to him, she thought, and a little twitch of annoyance tightened her mouth. She recognised the stalling manoeuvre because she had used it herself on countless occasions when she had not wanted to get trapped at the dull end of a table of diners.

Robert, the sculptor, stood as best he could as she slipped in beside him. He was very tall with thin, round shoulders and receding grey hair. She could not imagine him wielding a chisel and hammer. He looked more like a mathematics professor with his long, mournful, intelligent face, in which the features seemed drawn towards the craggy beak of nose.

On the other side was Brigitte, his wife, who looked as tiny as a child needing a cushion to sit at the grown-ups' table. Elspeth looked her over as she always did another woman, and found her determinedly plain and unadorned in the defiant way of some clever French women. But there was something attractive about her mobile, lively little face and she looked shrewd as well as intelligent. Elspeth settled herself in her seat and shook out her napkin, and across the table, Brigitte smiled and extended a small brown hand.

As she chatted, Elspeth kept an eye on Kate who stayed where she was, half perching on a chair at the other end of the table before Patrice disentangled himself from his friends round the bar. He came over and suggested that Kate slide along the banquette next to Robert and then he folded himself to sit next to her.

Elspeth saw Kate's happy smile of compliance and thought, how tiresome. She's got what she wanted. Now let's see what happens when Julie arrives.

They had chosen their first courses from the blackboard on the wall above the bar before Julie appeared, looking hot and flustered, with two baguettes under her arm. She wound her way to the table and stood beside Patrice's elbow, taking in the seating plan. Elspeth watched, interested, as Patrice stood up politely but did not offer her his seat. Instead, with a wave of his arm, he told Jean-Luc to move up so that an extra chair could be added at the opposite end. Elspeth saw Julie shoot a telling look at Kate before obediently taking her place. Once seated, she fanned herself with a paper napkin and then folded it carefully into a small square to dab at her hot forehead.

Kate, too, had registered the look and felt a moment's discomfort. Honestly, she told herself, Julie thinks this has been arranged so that I can be next to Patrice, when really that isn't true at all. I didn't like to sit down until I knew where Patrice wanted us. He is our host, after all. She did not think she had ever made another woman jealous and felt unsettled by it. She could not imagine being in the sort of relationship where there was so much anxiety and such a lack of trust.

Their food arrived and Kate, who was unsure what she had ordered, found herself looking at a plate of green leaves and some very small, budgerigar-sized wings. They were delicious, only a bony mouthful each, but as she ate them she could not avoid thinking of peanut holders and her bird table in the garden at home. On her right-hand side, Robert was engaged in an animated conversation with Elspeth and so Kate turned to Patrice who filled her glass for the second time and smiled at her in that special, intimate way of his. As she smiled back, and whether because of the heat, the wine, the strangeness of the food, Kate felt an inner confusion, an intense dissolving sensation, which she had not experienced for years and years. Not since she was a teenager.

Elspeth was glad to find Robert good company but glancing down the table at Kate, she saw her sitting close, almost leaning against Patrice, who had his arm stretched along the back of the banquette behind her. She was listening to something he was saying to her, something intimate, it seemed, and inclining her head so that he was speaking close to her ear. Elspeth felt another nip of irritation.

Later, however, while the waiters were clearing plates and she stood up to find the Ladies and was directed to a steep set of stairs going down into a basement, two middle-aged Frenchmen dining alone looked her over appreciatively. That was just the confidence booster she needed, she thought, and she rewarded them with a dazzling smile. What a pleasure it was to be in a civilised country which did not subscribe to the dreadful cult of youth worship. That was another thing to blame America for. In France, a beautiful woman of any age was appreciated and being considered sexy was not the preserve of the under-thirties with their orthopaedic-looking trainers and naked midriffs. She swept down the stairs in style. The lavatory, in an evil-smelling cubby-hole, left a lot to be desired, but in the light of everything else she was prepared to forgive the French their sanitation.

The second courses had started to arrive when she re-emerged, freshly lipsticked and powdered. As she passed to her place she was aware that Kate was trying to attract her attention, but she refused to notice; she still felt annoyed that she had worked her way into what Elspeth considered was the prime position next to the most attractive man, and for the moment she was going to ignore her.

Kate's second course had been chosen for her by Patrice. She listened to his enthusiastic description of each dish and thought of Josh, who regarded meals as opportunities for refuelling and little else. He would sit with the newspaper and eat his way through a loaf of bread if there was a moment's delay in getting the lunch on the table.

Patrice suggested *andouillette de porc* but when Kate saw the opaque, glistening, greyish coil, she was dismayed. Worse, when she slit the skin and the contents spilled out, she found coarsely minced pieces of intestine and a pale, triangular flap of something which looked like a bit of an ear. She tried to catch Elspeth's eye on her way back from the Ladies, but it seemed to Kate that she pointedly looked away. She might have stopped to consider why, had she not had more to drink than usual. She felt as if her cheeks were burning and she was acutely conscious of the closeness of Patrice, of his thigh alongside her thigh under the table and his bare forearm touching her own when he reached for the bottle of wine.

Very slightly, she allowed her leg to relax a little so that it rested warmly against his, but when his foot brushed against hers beneath the table, she felt obliged to silently withdraw her own, searching with her toe for her sandal which she had kicked off to benefit from the cool of the tiled floor.

'You enjoy your meal?' he asked slowly. His height meant that he looked down when he spoke to her and his sleepy hooded eyes had a lazy charm. The intensity of his look made Kate feel that it was as if they were alone at the table.

'Oh, yes,' she lied with a feigned sigh of pleasure. 'Delicious. It's all delicious.'

'Then I am happy,' said Patrice and slid a hand across her back to squeeze her shoulder. Instantly, Kate glanced guiltily down the table at Julie and was relieved that she was in conversation with Brigitte and had not noticed.

The waiter brought two more bottles of wine and as Patrice turned away and she concentrated on trying to disperse the sausage round her plate, there was a sudden clamour across the room and she saw an extraordinary woman working her way between the tables in their direction. A moment later she appeared at Patrice's elbow, uttering theatrical cries and throwing both hands into the air. He stood up at once and embraced her while she shrieked greetings round the table in a cigarette-thickened voice, but it was Patrice whom she wanted. She grasped his arm with a hand covered in huge rings and pulled his head towards her so that she could kiss him on the mouth.

Kate thought that she must have been seventy, with a battered, once beautiful face and ancient-looking, sparse auburn hair with a badger stripe of white along the parting. Her face was heavily made up, but in a haphazard manner, so that the slash of dark lipstick veered off one side of her mouth and the kohl round her eyes was smudged. Despite the heat she was wearing a purple corduroy skirt and laced-up black boots and a strange triangular mustard-coloured top. She had a dim, antique look as if she had emerged from a dusty attic.

Kate watched, fascinated. In a moment the eccentric interloper had moved everybody up so that she could squeeze onto the bench next to him. With a hand on his thigh she took him over, demanding his full attention, only breaking off from gazing into his eyes to call the waiter and order several items from the menu.

When he had the opportunity, Patrice, always good-mannered, contrived to introduce her to Kate and Elspeth. She was Dolly, an old friend, and apparently also some sort of artist. The others seemed to know her well but Dolly was not interested in anyone but Patrice. She angled herself towards him, possessively touching his arm, brushing his hair from his brow, excluding the rest of the table and commanding his full attention.

Kate, left out, felt suddenly subdued and aware that the special connection she had imagined between herself and Patrice was broken. She caught Julie watching her and then looking away with a faintly amused expression, and had the uneasy feeling that she was being falsely accused of something and that a sort of score was being kept.

With Dolly holding sway at the end of the table, Kate managed to get rid of her plate to a waiter. She gave up trying to follow the conversation, which raced along in French, interspersed with loud laughter, until Robert, on her right, turned and addressed her in excellent English. 'So, Kate, you are enjoying your stay here?'

'Oh, yes,' she said fervently. 'It's such a beautiful place and Patrice is a wonderful teacher.' She hesitated, as Robert raised his eyebrows and gave her a quizzical, amused look. She glanced down and began to pull apart a piece of bread between her fingers.

'You are a farmer's wife, your friend, Elspeth, tells me.'

'Yes, that's right.' She tried to make her voice bright, but was conscious that being called a farmer's wife made her sound dull and provincial, like Mrs Dobbin, the apple-cheeked farmer's wife from Happy Families, fat and comfortable with a basket of eggs over her arm. 'We farm together, my husband and I, and I also run a small catering business.' That was better. She did not want to get written off as a doormat and a bumpkin.

'Ah,' he said. 'Forgive me. A business woman,' and she realised that he had been teasing her. 'And your husband is happy for his pretty wife to come away on her own?' It was another tease. She recognised it this time and answered lightly.

'We've been married for over thirty years. I expect he's glad to have a break.'

'A break. Yes. It is good in every marriage, I think.' Again Kate felt wrong-footed. She hadn't meant anything by her flippant remark. It was not supposed to be taken seriously and it certainly wasn't a comment on her marriage.

'I only mean a few days away seem like a great treat,' she felt obliged to explain. 'Being farmers, we're more or less together all the time, you see, but because of all the work, the pressure, we often hardly speak. Well, I don't mean we don't *speak*, more that we don't seem to have time to *talk*. Life seems so much more fraught than it used to be.'

'Yes, of course, we read in our newspapers of the English farmer, the foot and mouth, the mad cows. It is a terrible time for you.'

'Yes, but I am not on holiday to get away from any of that,' said Kate. 'We were lucky enough not to have either disease on Dancing Hill, and don't get me wrong, I love farming. I love the way of life. It's all I've ever known. My family has farmed for generations.'

'Then what is it you get away from?' asked Robert gently. Kate cast around in her mind. She didn't know how she had talked herself into this corner. She hated this sort of probing, personal talk. Robert was watching her, a pleasant, interested look on his intelligent horse face.

'Oh,' she shrugged, 'it's lovely to have a change of scenery, you know, and the chance to paint, for one thing.' Deliberately, she avoided answering his question.

'You cannot paint your beautiful English countryside?'

Kate laughed. 'There's no time! I'm far too busy. Farming is seven days a week, you know.'

'No time to talk with your husband. No time to paint. This life is not the rural idyll.'

'Well, no, not an idyll, exactly, but we have had a good life, raised three great kids, been relatively well off until recently, and lived in one of the most beautiful parts of

England. I can hardly complain.' Robert inclined his head, but somehow suggested that that was only one way of looking at it. Kate changed the subject and took charge of the conversation by asking, 'Do you have children?'

'None of our own, but we each have three from our first marriages.'

'Oh, I see.' How many marriages? Kate wondered.

'Brigitte and I have been together for eight years but we have known one another since we were students,' volunteered Robert. 'We each married other people but we were young, we grew up, changed a little, found we could no longer be happy with those we married and now we are together.'

'Oh, I see,' said Kate again, thinking that in one sentence Robert had tidily dealt with broken marriages, fractured families, maintenance payments, a division of spoils – all the things that paralysed so many people she knew.

'Patrice, too. We knew Patrice when we were all students in Paris.'

'You're old friends, then,' said Kate, interested. 'And Patrice's wife, or ex-wife? Was she a student at the same time?'

'His wife?' asked Robert, again amused. 'No, no. Patrice has never married. Patrice is not a marrying man.'

'Oh,' said Kate, confused. 'I thought . . .' Somehow Patrice not having married seemed very important.

'No, no,' laughed Robert. 'It is something of a joke between us that Patrice has avoided marriage.'

'Has he run the painting school for long?' This was safer ground.

'No. At first it was hoped that the farm could be self-sufficient. There were many goats to begin with and a co-operative with some other farmers on the hill – making

152

organic cheese – but it was not a big success. Last year was the first time that he and Jean-Luc had visitors here. The winter before, they renovated the farm and put in the rooms in which you and your friend sleep.'

'I see. So how many painting courses are there each year?'

Robert shrugged. 'It depends. Last year there were three groups of painters, but there are also guests for what you call bed and breakfast, who come to stay during the spring and summer.'

'My brother, who is a farmer, has to do the same – take in guests, I mean.' But you could not compare the farming, thought Kate. One highly efficient and modern and the other a scratching-about sort of hobby, an excuse to paint in a beautiful place and enjoy the sunshine. No wonder it did not make a living.

There was a slight lull in their conversation and their attention was suddenly caught by Dolly's penetrating, rasping voice asking Patrice, with a laugh, which of the English ladies he was sleeping with. Kate was pretty sure that was what she said although later, when she thought about it, she wondered how, with her shaky grasp of French, she had understood so clearly. She felt a blush creep up her neck and determinedly blocked out the answer, which was, of course, some sort of amused denial. What a horrible, coarse old woman, she thought. How dare she! She took a long drink of water and then asked, 'Who exactly is this Dolly person? She seems very fond of Patrice.'

'Ah, yes. Dolly. You must forgive her. She is something of a character. It is no secret that she seduced Patrice when he was a student in Paris. She was the wife of one of our professors and a beauty in those days. They have been friends ever since. She and her husband, after he retired, ran a gallery here in this little town for years. It was through them that Patrice got to know the area, so in a sense it was Dolly and her husband who brought us all here. Now, sadly, she is a widow. Dear Charles died last year.'

'Oh,' said Kate, thinking, I hate all this. I hate this ramshackle, rackety way of living – lovers and broken marriages and people breaking the rules and talking about it all as if it were quite normal and acceptable.

Plates of pudding started to arrive and Kate looked at hers in wonder: tiny crème caramel, a midget profiterole filled with cream, a tiny wedge of pale sponge and pineapple cream, covered with a teaspoon of thick, dark, chocolate sauce and a slice of solid, almost black, chocolate mousse. The waiter interrupted Dolly which gave Patrice the opportunity to notice Kate gazing at her plate in awe. He laughed happily. The meal was a success with his visitors and to show how pleased that made him, he put his arm round her and drawing her to him, kissed the top of her head.

At the other end of the table, Elspeth and Brigitte glanced at each other. They had both seen Kate's flushed face, noted her girlish confusion and drawn the same conclusion.

'He's a very attractive man, Patrice,' observed Elspeth. 'He's certainly working his spell on Kate.'

'That is just Patrice's way. He loves women but he is a good man, you know. We have been friends since we were all students in Paris together, a very long time ago. He was at the École des Beaux Arts with Robert. You see, it is not just by chance that we end up side by side in the south of France with our bloody goats! First Patrice and

Jean-Luc buy Arc en Ciel and then we follow them here. A community.'

'Do you work here? I thought Patrice said you were a doctor.'

'I am a paediatrician. I work in St Tropez, three days a week. A good arrangement for me. Robert has his studio at home – you must come and visit – and we lead what you call the good life, surrounded by nature.' Their conversation was interrupted by a cackle of laughter from Dolly and Elspeth looked at her curiously.

What an extraordinary old woman she was. Brigitte had said she had once been beautiful. A woman who had captivated the young Patrice. How old would she be? A badly worn sixty-five? Seventy? Not that much older than she was herself. The prospect of such decay was frightening, that slippery slope that awaited her, when she could no longer rely on her physical assets, her good bones, her long legs, her carefully maintained body, to make life pleasurable. A horrid little chill set in. She thought of the depressing talk she had had about pensions with a dismal man from the bank and how she had secretly felt that she would rather go for the euthanasia option, if only there was one. Still, this would not do. She had not come away on holiday to be gloomy about the future.

She dropped her voice to ask, 'What about Julie? How does she fit in? She doesn't seem Patrice's type, somehow.'

'Julie? Julie came to Arc en Ciel first as a guest and then to help with the cooking for the painting course. The rest of the year she lives with her mother outside Paris. Julie is a teacher. Patrice, I think, is an antidote to a dull life!'

That explained the air of exhaustion, thought Elspeth. How clever of Patrice to secure her services each year by offering her sunshine and sex. She supposed he had developed a need in Julie which kept her coming back for more. It all added up.

It was George who found Josh.

After lunch with Susie he had been dropped off home by Tony, who, well over the limit, drove very slowly and with a determination not to budge from the middle of the road. They had enjoyed themselves, he was ready to admit it, and he had felt a sincere affection for his daughter-in-law as he kissed her goodbye. Tom had seemed in no hurry to get back to work, he noticed, and he had said, 'Well, you'll be back to the silage, then, Tom!' as they left, but Susie looked annoyed and Tom had laughed and said, 'OK, Dad. I get the message.'

Tony had ticked him off about it in the car. 'You shouldn't interfere, George. It's not your business any more.'

'It is my business,' he'd retorted. 'I'm still a partner.'

'That may well be, but you're not a working partner. You should let the youngsters get on with it in their own way. You can't tell Tom what to do any more. He's not a boy.'

'What do you know about it?' he'd snapped and then lapsed into grumpy silence and slammed the door when he got out. Tony had not looked round but sounded his horn in a cheery farewell and driven off.

George went into the kitchen which felt hot and stuffy and hitched his jacket over the back of a chair. Tony didn't understand because he had never been a farmer. You didn't just give up and hand over your interest in the land. It was part of you when you had worked it all your life. You might be old and past it but you still knew the right and wrong way of going about things. He opened the windows and swatted at the flies gathered on the glass. In the sitting room he opened the doors onto the garden and stood listening, trying to hear if they were still working along the valley. They'd be getting on with it, he was sure, with or without Tom. Trouble was, he was too deaf and couldn't hear a thing. His head felt heavy with a longing for sleep. That was lunchtime drinking for you. It was a temptation to sit down and have a little nap in the armchair but he always walked off Sunday lunch and he didn't intend to give way now. Particularly not after his comment to Tom. He'd go up the hill, although he didn't feel like it, and let the dogs out and have a look at the heifer that still hadn't calved.

It was a walk he would have done with Kate, only the other way round, starting at the top of the hill by the farm and ending up at the bungalow. He liked this time with his daughter, talking about the farm, looking over the herd. In the old days, after Pat had died and he was on his own and Kate's children were younger, they'd have come too, running along in front, the boys laughing and ragging and Anna often riding whatever was her current pony.

Even these days Kate still asked him his opinion, listened to what he had to say, because she valued his advice as a first-rate stockman. He knew his cattle and his sheep. He spent enough hours looking over farm gates, letting the animals fill his eye, to notice the smallest changes in condition or behaviour. You could divert a lot of trouble and expense by taking the time and the trouble to know your beasts. He didn't think that Josh really appreciated that. He was always in too much of a hurry.

Kate. He wondered where she was now. He couldn't work out what the time difference would be between here and France, but not a lot, he knew that much. She'd have had her lunch, though goodness knows what. Beef? Lamb? It would be French meat, anyway. The French farmers were a belligerent lot and defended their own interests, which he didn't blame them for. They had more political clout than English farmers, fought their corner better.

It seemed a long climb up the hill this afternoon. The sun was hot on his back and the sky was a hard, bright blue. The edges of the drive were thick with flowers. Ox-eyed daisies and corn marigolds grew along the fence and the grass between the tracks was a mass of pink and white restharrow and purple vetch. He checked his watch. Len would be starting the afternoon milking soon. He could see the dairy cows bunched round the top gate waiting for him to let them through. As he got closer, he could see the dogs going up and down the netting of their run. He would let them out as he went by the yard. Then he saw the new tractor parked up against the house. That was odd. He would have thought that they would have been using it this afternoon. Perhaps Josh was about the place somewhere. He stopped and listened. Not a thing. It was a bugger not being able to hear any more. He let the dogs out and they capered about him, Sly nearly bringing him down by banging joyfully against his legs.

Going round the corner, down to the yard where the little heifer was waiting to calve, he was unprepared to come face to face with Frank. It took him a moment to take in the situation, to see that the black bull was standing with sides caked with muck and sweat, and that his head was bleeding from a cut above his eye and that his forehead was puffed and swollen. George knew instantly that he had been in one hell of a fight, and a glance told him that the fence to the field was down where he had forced his way through. He had cuts on his chest and his knees from the wire.

All the rage had gone out of him and it took only a prod or two of his walking stick for George to get him to move over to see what had happened in the bull pen. The heavy metal gate had been knocked clean off its hinges and was three-quarters flat on the ground and in the corner stood the new bull, equally battered about the head, looking cowed and shell-shocked. Despite his size he had taken a bashing from Frank, who had got him in the corner and gone for his belly as well, by the looks of it. George felt a surge of anger. The poor beast was bleeding and bruised and it would all have been avoidable if anyone had taken the trouble to listen to him and heed his advice.

He'd have to get Frank moved. You couldn't leave a bull loose about the place and he wondered where he should put him. The fence would need repairing or all the dry cows would be out – were out already, for all he knew – and the new bull would need attention and would have to be shifted out of the pen while the gate was put back. It was too much for him to manage on his own and for a moment he stood, flustered, unsure of where to start. He supposed that with the help of the dogs he could get Frank back through the fence and then put up a bit of wire as a temporary measure. He'd have to get a hammer and some tacks and find a bit of sheep netting from the back of the cart shed. Len would be about soon to do the milking. He would get him to help sort out this mess. Where the hell was Josh? It was his bloody fault.

He was turning to go and look for the materials he

needed when he saw him, flat out on the concrete of the
bull pen, behind the ring feeder to the left of the battered
gate. George's old heart lurched with dread. From where
he stood his son-in-law had every appearance of being
stone dead.

Chapter Seven

George leaned over Josh and saw to his horror that his eyes were closed and that he did not appear to be breathing.

'Josh!' he cried, patting frantically at a limp hand. 'Josh! For God's sake!'

Josh's eyes remained closed and George got creakily down on his knees to feel for a pulse. As he did so, he saw the almost imperceptible rise and fall of his chest. 'Thank God! Thank God, you're alive. I thought you were done for, lying there like that! Terrible turn you gave me!' Josh did not respond and George put out a hand to steady himself against the side of the feeder. He must be injured, badly injured. Unconscious anyway, that much was clear. He couldn't see any blood or quite make out what had happened until he realised that Josh was imprisoned beneath the heavy metal feeder which was on its side and seemed to have rolled on top of him.

Now George could see that his son-in-law's left leg was pinned from the thigh and that, even if conscious, he could not move from his prone position on his back. The dogs gathered round him in an excited circle, thinking it was some kind of game, Bonnie trying to lick his face. George pushed her away and grappled to weigh up the situation.

Unsteadily, he got to his feet and put his shoulder to the metal frame, testing the weight of it, and gave an experimental push but it was on a slight uphill slope and his eyes bulged with the strain. He gave up the effort and rubbed a hand over his chin.

'Josh!' he said. 'Are you listening? Can you hear me?' Josh's eyes remained closed and George felt a wave of rising panic. 'I'm going to have to leave you. I'm going to see if I can find Len. He should be around soon to do the milking. I could try to shift this on my own, but the thing is, I don't want this bugger rolling back on you, in case you've broken that leg. I'll be as quick as I can.' He felt the need to talk to Josh as if he could hear. It was one way of keeping a hold, dealing with the situation, which if he allowed his worst fears to take over could take on the aspect of a nightmare.

Was there anything he could do to make him more comfortable? It seemed wrong to leave him flat on his back on the dirty concrete in the full glare of the sun. Taking off his cap, George thought to place it gently over his face. It gave him a start then, an awful jab of fear, to see Josh lying there with his face covered. A recollection of the war, the desert, of young men laid out in rows, swam across his mind.

He got slowly to his feet again, his knees protesting, and picked up his stick. He hurried away, his legs bowed with age, his back stooped. He must take care over the fallen gate, he thought, or there would be another accident. Oh, the frustration of being old and slow when speed was all that mattered. Rounding the corner to the yard he could see that it was still and empty. Stock doves feeding on some fallen grain in the corner whirred noisily into the air when they saw him, otherwise there was no sign of life.

162

He must find Len, and together they could move the feeder and see what the damage was, and then ring the doctor. Maybe he should do that first? He stopped mid-way across the yard, fraught with indecision, and then faintly heard the sound of a metal gate clanking in the dairy. He would go and get Len. That was best. Together they could decide what to do.

The milking parlour was cool and dark as he entered and it took a moment or two for his eyes to adjust. The stalls were filling from the bottom end with a line of the black and white dairy cows who moved slowly, their swollen, large-veined udders swaying ponderously. They stared curiously at George with expressions of mild surprise. Len was shouting from the other end for them to get a move on, slapping a rump or two to keep them going forward as George pushed his way through them. He smelled the sweet summer grass on their breath as he worked his way between their sleek and shiny flanks, conscious of their bony hips, their bright yellow ear tags, and all the time fearful of the slippery, wet concrete beneath his feet.

'Len!' he cried as soon as he could get his breath. 'Len! Quick! There's been an accident!' His voice seemed frail and cracked and the cows ducked away, mooing anxiously, their hooves clattering and skidding on the floor while the milking machines sucked and wheezed in the background.

Len saw him then. Saw his shock of white hair moving among the cows, saw the look on his face, and knew that something had happened. He stopped what he was doing and made his way towards the old man, hurrying through the milling cows.

'What is it? Whatever are you doing? You shouldn't be in here. You could have got knocked over, right and proper!' he shouted over the noise.

'It's Josh!' said George, gesticulating with his stick. 'Josh has had an accident. Out in the bull pen.'

'What sort of accident?' Len was alarmed to see a vein throbbing in the old man's forehead and the anxiety and fear on his face which was red from exertion and the heat of the afternoon.

'Knocked out. I don't know how. He's out cold. You must come and help.'

'What about the milking? I'm halfway through the milking.' Even as he spoke, Len was off, hurrying towards the door of the parlour where swallows looped in and out, threading through the blue square of sky.

'Leave it, leave it. You go on!' cried George to his departing back. 'I'll make my own way. He's in the bull pen. For God's sake hurry!'

Breaking into a run, Len disappeared round the corner. He saw the broken fence and the flattened gate. Bloody hell, how did that happen? he thought as he clambered over and into the yard. There was the new young bull in the corner against the wall, his sides heaving, the tip of his tail twitching nervously. A flock of sparrows took off to perch in a chattering row in the gutter of the calf shed. He saw Josh then, lying stiff as a board, his face covered like a corpse, and Len's heart contracted with dread.

George reappeared behind him, picking his way over the gate, his air of agitation and the white of his hair against the blue sky making him look like an enraged Old Testament prophet. He was shouting, 'Don't move him, Len. Don't move him. He may have internal injuries. Let's just get this bugger off his leg. We can shift it between us.'

He was right, thought Len. He knew that much. Farms were terrible places for accidents. Fatal accidents, a lot of them. Falling bales, tractors turning over, accidents with stock and machinery. He never would have thought it could happen to Josh, though. Tough, he was. Hard as nails and seemed invincible.

Together he and George put their shoulders to the ring feeder and slowly pushed it back up the slight slope until it rested against the metal railings of the pen. Then they both hurried back to Josh and knelt beside him, George carefully removing his cap to look at his face. His eyes were still closed but he was breathing all right. Small shallow breaths. Len thought he'd never seen him looking peaceful like that, his face smooth and not creased with irritation or etched with effort.

'What do you think?' asked George. 'One of us should stay here with him while the other telephones the doctor.'

'You stay,' said Len, imagining the search for spectacles, the fumbling with the telephone list on the board in the farm kitchen, the stiff old fingers tapping the wrong numbers into the telephone. 'I'll go. I know where the telephone numbers are. Then I'll go on down and fetch Anna. Bring her back. I'll be as quick as I can.'

George nodded. It was best he stayed. He could see that. Leaning on his stick he stood guard over his son-in-law as Len ran off. Lying so straight and stiff, Josh looked like a carved knight on an old tomb, he thought, and then regretted that such a thing had occurred to him. It seemed like tempting providence, while he felt in his bones that Josh would be all right. Anything else would be unthinkable.

He looked at his watch. Only a few minutes had passed since Len had left. He should have told him to call 999 and get an ambulance and not go through the duty doctor, who might be slow to respond. It was too late now. He concentrated, trying to listen for the sound of the old Land

Rover, but all he could hear were the cows bellowing from the milking shed. He went back to watching Josh. He was still breathing all right and George could swear he had moved his hand a little. It now lay cupped around a clump of mayweed which had managed to root in a crack in the concrete. It looked as if he was holding a little bunch of the pretty, daisy-like flowers. As if he ever would, thought George. Spray them with weedkiller, more like. He consulted his watch again but when he looked back at Josh he saw with a shock that he was jerking his arm in an alarming fashion and an ooze of saliva had collected at the corner of his mouth and was dribbling down his chin.

Were these good or bad signs? George did not know.

'They'll be here in a minute, Josh,' he said. 'Don't you worry, son. Help will be here in a minute.' Bending forward he wiped away the spittle with his handkerchief. Kate, he thought. It was Kate who should be here.

Lunch was drawing to a close at Seillans. Slowly Didier's restaurant emptied until only two tables were still occupied and Madame polished her final glass and went through to the kitchen to fetch a plate of steak for her own lunch which she ate in solitary splendour, sitting on a stool at the end of the bar, as unapproachable as a dog with a bone.

Bearing a bottle of wine and the bill, Didier came to sit a moment with the party from Arc en Ciel and Elspeth moved to make room for him. The bill was passed to Patrice and at the same moment Dolly got up from the table. The next time Kate looked round, she had disappeared.

Patrice went to settle the bill and Madame pushed her plate away to process the details from his credit card, and then they all got up and began saying goodbye, embracing Didier, kissing cheeks, promising to see one another very soon. Outside, the afternoon sun was still hot, bouncing off the pavement in suffocating waves. Julie took the opportunity to ferret her way back to Patrice's side and take his arm and Kate leaned against the wall and felt distinctly the worse for wear, rather depressed and muddled.

Dolly suddenly reappeared, trotting from round the corner with lipstick freshly applied and, inexplicably, a string bag of bruised peaches which she insisted on presenting to Patrice. Lengthy farewells started up again until Kate felt she had had enough. Elspeth was right about all the hanging around, the lack of urgency, the complicated and lengthy social manoeuvring. Too much of it was quite exhausting. Didn't these people have anything to *do* with the afternoon?

She was aware that Elspeth was still being rather cool towards her. As lunch finished and they stood up, she had expected that, having sat apart, they would gravitate towards one another, but Elspeth evidently preferred talking to Brigitte and Robert, and when the time came for the party to divide, she heard her say to Brigitte, 'If your car is parked nearby, may I go with you? I can't face another long walk in this heat.'

This set off more discussion and Monique finally attached herself to Patrice and Julie for the drive home. At last they shook off Dolly, who collapsed on a seat outside Didier's and called for a brandy. She was still shouting remarks to Patrice as they set out down the steep hill to find the car. Julie kept her place at his side, even though this meant hopping on and off the kerb and dodging awkwardly round parked cars, the bag of bruised peaches swinging against her legs, the bread sticking out from her elbow.

Behind them, Monique and Kate bumped along together on the narrow pavements and winding streets which were quieter now. The cafés and restaurants had emptied and were shutting up for the afternoon, waiters busy pulling down shutters and stacking chairs. The smart crowds had dispersed, back to the villas to sleep off lunch, and without them the village looked more ordinary, closed in on itself, simmering in the heat.

At last they found the car and there followed another discussion about who should drive. For heaven's sake, get on with it, thought Kate, who longed to be back in her cool room and to lie on the white bed with the shutters closed. Eventually it was Julie who took the keys and got behind the wheel. So the same rule applies as at home, she thought. What men think of as a fair division. They drive to the party, women drive home.

Julie wound down her window, complaining the car was too hot and then shunted backwards and forwards trying to get out of the tight place that Patrice had shoehorned into. She's an awful driver, thought Kate irritably as Patrice darted from front to back giving directions and hand signals. At last the car was out in the road and Julie leaned to unlock the back door and Kate climbed in. It was like a furnace. Monique and Patrice dodged about on the other side and then Monique got into the front seat and Patrice opened the rear door and climbed in beside Kate. He looked at her and smiled and in the driver's mirror Kate could see Julie watching, but she was too hot and sleepy to care.

As the old car left the village and zigzagged down the mountain, Kate shut her eyes. Patrice slumped beside her, also with his eyes closed and head tilted back in an attitude of semi-comatose inertia. Between them the net of peaches rolled back and forth, scenting the car with a sweet, fruity perfume. Kate put out a hand to stop them cascading on the floor as Julie braked on a corner, and at the same moment Patrice slid his hand across the seat towards her.

Later, after the ambulance had arrived and he had shown the driver where to go and helped shift the broken gate out of the way so that they could get Josh on to a stretcher, Len went back to finish the milking. The cows were restless and upset. They did not like their routine disrupted. Old Ruby took a sideways kick and caught him on the knee and he swore and rubbed at the place, knowing he had been careless. His mind was taken up with images of Josh behind an oxygen mask, his neck cradled in a brace, and of Anna's white, shocked face as the doors of the ambulance closed.

Leaving the last of the cows to make their way back to their pasture, Len hosed down and then went to look at the bulls who seemed to have been the cause of all the trouble. Charlie still stood in the corner of the pen, rolling shudders raking his massive shoulders. His head was lowered and he eyed Len nervously as he approached, shifting his weight from foot to foot and whickering anxiously. His huge cream forehead was battered, with dried blood caking the blond curls, and one eye was swollen and nearly closed. Even from a distance, Len could see he would need the eye bathed and the cuts dressed and a shot of antibiotic in case of infection.

It had been a fight between the bulls, George reckoned. Frank must have gone at the fence like a tank, snapping the wire clean through and lifting out the fence posts. He had battered his way over the gate somehow or other, and then the two of them must have had a terrible ding-dong. As he got closer, Len could see that despite being larger and heavier, Charlie had come off badly. He'd been rammed under the belly and behind his foreleg there was considerable swelling. Dried blood streaked his leg and he was plastered with muck on his nearside where he had slipped and gone down on the concrete. It must have been one hell of a fight.

Len knew he would have to get him penned in the cattle crush to deal with his injuries but he didn't know how he'd take to being handled after what he'd been through. He wasn't naturally an aggressive animal, he didn't think, but he was new, there was no mutual trust between them and fear could make him difficult to handle and extremely dangerous.

Len considered the situation and shook his head gloomily. He'd need some help but he wasn't going to ask George. It wasn't suitable for an old man, especially after the shock he had experienced, finding Josh like that. You had to be steady on your pins and quick on your feet to yard up a big, nervous bull and although there was no doubt that George was an expert with stock, Len didn't want to put him at risk. Kate would never forgive him if anything happened to her dad as well. He'd have to wait until he could get hold of Tom, which was always difficult.

He struggled with the broken metal gate and managed to drag it across the gateway and secure it with baler twine. That would keep Charlie in for the time being. Frank had gone back into his field of his own accord and was grazing peacefully amongst the cows. Bugger it, he'd have to get that fence mended as well. There was too much to do at the best of times and Len couldn't see how they would manage now without Josh. This was the last straw, this was.

If Kate had been at home they could have shared the work between them. In fact, if Kate had been at home, the accident probably wouldn't have happened at all. It just went to show that no good came of this gadding about. It was what he'd said to Rita from the beginning.

It was late by the time George got up the hill to his sheep. He had hung around at the farmhouse after Anna had gone to hospital with Josh, sick with anxiety and deeply disturbed by the sequence of events. It had been terrible to see his son-in-law loaded into the ambulance on a stretcher, his eyes still closed, his face as white as paper. George wondered whether he might make himself a cup of tea but the farm kitchen was in a mess with cupboard doors and drawers left open, the bread still out on the bread board and circled by lazy flies, the butter melting in its packet on the table. Someone had stacked plates in the sink and left them there, unwashed. It upset George to see it left in this state. It served as a reminder of Kate's absence and it worried him that she was not here to deal with the crisis.

He wanted to wait to hear news of Josh but he couldn't see what practical use he was going to be. If only he could still drive, he could have run errands or driven the tractor and trailer and helped with the silage. Now, goodness only knew what would happen. Tom couldn't manage on his own and Len had his hands full with the dairy herd and the calves. They'd got more due to calve this week, too. He'd have liked to help out with that, but the sad fact was that aiding a difficult calving took a lot of strength and he

171

didn't know that he was up to it, with his back and his knees gone. He was a useless old man, that was the trouble.

He supposed he could make a start on tidying the kitchen. He didn't feel like doing it, cleaning up other people's mess was not something he was used to. He couldn't remember which way plates went into the dishwasher but he slotted them in any old how. Then he began to clear the table. He put the bread away and got halfway to the fridge with the butter and then couldn't remember if Kate left it in the larder, so he changed tack and put it in there instead. The milk could go in the fridge but then he saw a fat black fly swimming in the jug, so he emptied it out in the sink which was stupid because he could have given it to the dogs, if he had thought.

The dogs were one thing he could take on. They would need feeding and he could do that all right; and Kate's hens. He was better off lending a hand outside. He never had been much use in the kitchen. Perhaps, by the time he had finished, Anna would have telephoned and he would learn the worst.

Although it had been a terrible shock, being the one to find Josh was satisfying, in a way. It showed that even though he was old and mostly good for nothing, he still had his uses. Just keeping an eye on things often paid off, which brought him back to the bulls. Josh was a damn fool not to heed his advice and now look what had happened.

He rehearsed his version of the events as he would tell it to Wilf. 'I'd told him that very morning,' he'd say. 'Would he listen? No, he would not!' He relived the drama of coming round the corner and finding himself face to face with Frank, which was enough of a shock in itself, and then the awful sight of Josh motionless on the ground.

If only Kate was here. It should have been Kate who had gone in the ambulance, not Anna. He wondered where Richard and Tom had got to. Probably still cutting silage. Work had to go on on a farm. You couldn't just down tools when there were animals to be looked after.

Meanwhile, he could take a look at the fence Frank had knocked down. Although his hands were crooked with arthritis, he could still do a neat job with hammer and staples and it only took him half an hour or so to bang in the old posts and put up two new strands of barbed wire. It was still a botched job but it would do until the winter when they would have time to put in a couple of new posts. He stood back, satisfied with his work, and wiped his brow. It was still very warm and the dogs who had been racing about were lying flat on their sides in the long grass, their flanks heaving. Frank had herded his cows to the top end of the field and was grazing peacefully.

George still had to walk up to the sheep, but he would leave the tools and the loop of wire he had been using beside the track and collect it on his way. Picking up his stick, he set off again, the dogs springing to their feet and dashing ahead. He glanced at his watch. It was half past four and the sky was still a metallic blue. The dung on the track had dried to crisp brown pancakes which gave a hollow sound when he knocked them with his stick. He could see his sheep now, gathered at the top end of their field, hard up against Hanging Wood under the stand of old oaks. A great bough had come down last winter and lay like the remains of a prehistoric monster crouched in the grass, and the flock had crept amongst its forks and branches, the ewes and their lambs lying together in the shade.

Pausing to undo the gate, he sent the dogs on up the

173

field to bring the sheep down quietly and steadily. He didn't want them rushed in this heat, but he needed to look them over. He was always careful about fly strike and foot rot. It was true what they said about sheep, that they had two main aims in life. To get out and to die.

He watched the old ewes getting to their knees, bored and unhurried, while the lambs skittered down the hill, skipping and bouncing into one another. They looked fine, all of them, recently sheared and their fleeces clean and white. Then he noticed that one old ewe bringing up the rear was lame, limping along behind the others. He'd have to go and see what the trouble was. He whistled to Sly and Bonnie who cut her out of the main flock and held her against the fence, while he made his way up the hill.

When he got closer he saw that she was one of his oldest ewes, a long-toothed granny he called Marge. She stood up against the netting, her sides heaving, rolling her eyes nervously while her latest lamb cried piteously. George reached her, talking quietly, and she let him catch her by the neck and back and heave her on her side, where she lay with her sticks of legs pointing to the sky, her belly huge. He took out his paring knife and examined each of her neat little black hooves in turn but could find nothing wrong. No heat or smell of rot. She had probably stepped on something or recently had a sharp stone trapped between her toes. Nothing serious anyway.

He was about to let her scramble to her feet when he noticed her face, and for the second time that day his heart missed a beat. Her white nose and pinkish lips twitched in anxiety and very faintly George could make out a few small lesions, little areas of blistered skin around her mouth.

He bent to look more closely, his heart thumping in his

chest, making it hard to breathe. A sweat broke out on his forehead as he saw, quite distinctly, what he dreaded most. He straightened up, letting Marge sit on her fat woolly bottom and then stumble to her feet. She tripped unevenly away, calling to her lamb who ran forward to butt under her belly for her udder. George watched closely as she stood patiently, letting him suck vigorously.

With one hand on a fence post George surveyed the rest of his flock, his mind racing. He'd have to take them down to the bottom and pen them and examine each one in turn. As it was, he didn't know what to think. There was one dread question he could not even ask himself.

Standing there, an old man who had kept sheep all his life, he went through the options, but he still could not be sure. Not after last year. He thought of the terror of the funeral pyres, the dark acrid smoke billowing into the sky, the empty fields, the mountains of carcasses, the blood-clogged drains, the countryside under siege. It could not be. Not again. Not here. Not on Dancing Hill.

They had had the disease in 1967. He would never forget it, but that was long ago and had little of the horror of what had happened since. Last year they had escaped. They had lived with the restrictions, the fear, the disinfectant-soaked barriers, the misinformation, the bungling, the rumours, the horror of the nightly television news. It couldn't happen again. Not here. Not his sheep.

He must keep calm and think things through. For a start there had been no recent movement. He hadn't bought sheep in since last year when he had purchased a new ram, so an infection could not have been introduced from outside.

Deer. The woods were full of deer who roamed freely across the farm. Up here on the edge of the trees the sheep

175

would have plenty of contact with deer and it was well known that they were carriers of the disease. That would be the only way.

Common sense kept telling him that this was a false alarm. Only one lame ewe with a few pink blisters round her mouth meant nothing. It could be orf – a bugger of a disease from which his sheep were usually free. The symptoms were the same but often the udder became blistered and painful and the lamb infected as well, but this did not seem to be the case.

He watched Marge grazing unconcernedly. It was hard to believe she could be the cause of such potential disaster. His eye travelled over the rest of the flock, scattered again across the gentle slopes of the hill. 'My hills are white over with sheep' came into his mind. Silly to think of poetry now, but how peaceful it looked, the ewes calling to their lambs and their little voices piping back. The farm and the valley were hidden by the plump shoulder of Dancing Hill but the rest of the vale, all green and gold and chequered with dark squares of woodland, stretched out to the violet distance and the smooth silvery flanks of far away Bulbarrow and Okeford Hill.

What George most wanted to do was to call the dogs and walk slowly back down the hill, to go through the gate at the bottom of the field and trudge down the track to the farm, and most of all to be the same person that he had been when he walked up yesterday. He wanted to shed the awful fear about Josh and now the dreadful burden of his discovery, to pretend that he hadn't seen, to deny the evidence of his eyes. He wanted to cross the yard and meet Josh coming out of the house and call out to him about the weather holding and the chances of a fine day tomorrow.

Although his legs felt heavy as lead, his heart was

fluttering like a bird in his chest as he went through the process of gathering the sheep in the pens by the gate. The dogs were eager and obedient and he was grateful for that. Sly kept looking up at his face, his bright eyes trying to read his expression, sensing his growing despair and nudging his hand with his cold nose. George patted his silky head and he whined with pleasure.

Methodically, he worked through his flock, catching and examining each sheep in turn and when he let the last one free, he was shaking with exertion and wet with sweat. The effort was too much for him, he was too old for it, he knew that, and when he looked up, the sky was black and spinning and lights exploded across his vision. He fastened the gate behind him and stood for a moment looking at the ground beneath his old brown boots. He saw that the short grass was a tender green and woven with the little pink ears of restharrow and tufted purple crowns of self-heal. He loved both these little wild plants; he bent his stiff old knees, knelt on the turf and spread out his hands on the grass, then turned over and lay on his back. The words he had said most Sundays of his life came into his head, 'Lamb of God. Lamb of God, that takest away the sins of the world, receive our prayer.'

Kate lay in the cool of her bedroom, her head throbbing. She closed her eyes to sleep but the heavy torpor of the afternoon had worn off. Instead she felt strung out and wide awake. The nerve endings in the surface of her skin seemed to swarm with an increased sensitivity so that she could feel the weave of the bedspread on her back, the fine flecks in the linen of the pillow against her cheek.

Over and over she re-played the sequence of events in the car, how Patrice had slid his hand over hers, linking fingers while his thumb stroked backwards and forwards. She hadn't moved her hand away, and it was this which troubled her. Instead she had sat, mesmerised, not daring to move, frightened of Julie, whose eyes she could not seek in the driver's mirror and not wanting to interrupt the tenderness of the moment. It was the most lovely, most beautiful thing that had happened to her – for she couldn't say how long. Years and years, anyway. She felt chosen, selected, wanted, loved even. She felt like a girl again. Silly, vulnerable, desirable.

Thank goodness it had ended there. When they had bumped up the track to the farmhouse, Patrice had had to let go of her hand. He touched her thigh briefly with one finger, and then they arrived and the spell was broken. She had hurried to her room, half-blinded by the light glaring off the stone in the courtyard followed by the deep shade of the interior of the house. She had taken off her clothes and lain on the bed, under the counterpane, half expecting, she realised now, that he might come and join her, find a way of giving Julie the slip, and come to lie beside her on the white bed. When she heard steps in the passage outside, she held her breath, staring at the latch of the door, waiting for it to lift, but it was only Elspeth, she realised, going along to her room.

What had happened to her, that she had behaved so unreliably and out of character? Especially when she remembered that when Robert was describing how he and his friends had drifted between marriage partners, she had felt morally superior, an altogether better sort of person. How priggish, she thought now, how disgustingly smug and self-satisfied she must appear. Of course she believed that marriage vows were terribly important, but in that case what was she thinking of, holding hands with a man she quite frankly fancied? And at her age! She could not help a smile twitching the corners of her mouth as she thought about it. It had been lovely. Just a bit of fun. It did not mean anything. It did not change anything – though Elspeth was obviously in a huff, going off in the other car and avoiding her company.

Kate felt a little flicker of rebellious spirit. Why should she care? It wasn't as if she had done anything she was ashamed of. How could she help it if Patrice happened to find her attractive, and that was clearly what had put Elspeth's nose out of joint. She was the sort of woman who was used to being the centre of attention, Kate supposed, but really, it was hardly her fault.

She stretched out on the white bed; her limbs and back burned hot against the sheet and she moved restlessly. The heat, the wine, the company; Dolly, Patrice, Julie, her conversation with Robert seemed to have robbed her of her usual calm. She was used to being in charge, of running her busy life sensibly and efficiently but this afternoon had left her feeling strange and uncertain. It's this idleness, she thought. It doesn't suit me. I'm not used to this inactivity, this time to dwell on things.

She began to think of home, of walking on Dancing Hill, following the curves of the track as it rounded the shoulder of the hill. She thought of the dark, springy turf studded with buttercups and cranesbill and the blue pincushion heads of sheep's-bit. She thought of larks so high in the sky that they were invisible, and their song, like fast water bubbling over stones, drifting on the wind.

Gradually, her heart stopped racing and she dozed, awaking as the shadows were lengthening, the afternoon burned away. She felt different now, as if sleep had revived a sense of who she really was, and she felt dismayed by her silliness. All she had was a dull headache to show for the lunchtime shenanigans and a rather depressing feeling that she had been foolish. She also wanted to put things on a better footing with Elspeth. She was not going to be drawn into a competition over Patrice. It was too undignified and absurd.

She got out of bed and straightened the covers and went through to the bathroom to wash her face. Then she went along the passage and tapped softly on Elspeth's bedroom door.

'I hope I haven't woken you. Would you like to go for a walk? It's cooler now.'

Elspeth was lying on her bed, a book open beside her, filing her nails.

'Yes, all right,' she said, in a reasonably friendly tone. 'I need to work off that vast lunch. Give me a minute and I'll join you.'

Kate went back into her bedroom and looked out of the window while she waited. Above the green of the vegetable garden the hillside looked even more brown and burnt. There was a distant tinkling of bells and she could see two of the glossy chestnut goats jumping from rocks on the skyline.

She heard Elspeth's door open and went to join her in the passage. Elspeth had changed into her linen shirt and loose trousers and looked cool and fresh. 'Did you have a good rest?' she asked, looking at Kate curiously. 'Quite a lunch, wasn't it? I'm afraid that I drank far too much.'

'Yes, yes, so did I,' agreed Kate, glad that she was following Elspeth's neat back down the stairs and did not have to look her in the eye.

They went through the empty kitchen and out of the back door. Kate felt relieved that there was no one about.

She was sure she would feel uncomfortable when she saw Patrice or Julie again. They walked past the vegetable garden and the outbuildings and up the stony track towards the place Elspeth had chosen to sit to paint. As they walked, Kate longed to tell Elspeth what had happened between her and Patrice, to come clean and confess her silliness, but was restrained by an instinctive caution. Once these things were shared, there was no taking them back.

'What did you make of Dolly?' asked Elspeth, puffing slightly on the track. 'Quite a game old girl, wasn't she? Rather frightful, in a way, with that make-up which looked as if it hadn't been removed since she first slapped it on in the sixties.'

'Yes. That must have been when she was in her prime.'

'Women can get a sort of style rigor mortis, can't they? Clinging to what suited them when they were twenty, like pale blue frosted eyeshadow and pale pink lipstick. Think of those women one sees fossilised in the early Princess Diana era.'

'She was besotted with Patrice, did you notice?' Kate produced his name with a conscious effort to sound normal.

'She was his lover, did you know? Years ago, when he was a student and she was married to one of his professors.'

'Yes, Robert told me.' Kate did not want to be reminded. The thought of the two of them as lovers was not appetising.

'She's a wily old bird,' said Elspeth, in an amused tone. 'Did you notice how she disappeared at settling up time? She wasn't going to get lumbered with her share of the bill, was she? She came back with those mouldy peaches when she thought she was in the clear.'

'So that was it.' Kate had a sudden vision of Dolly's small

181

wrinkled, knowing eye like that of an ancient tortoise who knew a trick or two.

'Patrice is a gentleman, though,' said Elspeth, stopping to catch her breath. 'He treated her very chivalrously, I thought.'

'Yes, he did,' murmured Kate, her thoughts racing off. Had it been a chivalrous act to reach for her hand in the back of a car driven by his mistress? It was too complicated a question here in this hot place where normal rules did not seem to apply. Perhaps he had felt it was what she wanted, that a woman of her age, travelling alone, would feel disappointed if she was ignored. Perhaps it wasn't such a big deal, this whole sex thing. It certainly didn't seem to be amongst this sophisticated crowd. She thought of the disruption unwise affairs caused at home, when serviceable marriages were torn apart and children wrenched from one warring parent to another, and everyone behaved as if it was a very big deal indeed. Stupid, really, when it could all be treated as a frivolous game.

'You must be fit,' observed Elspeth. 'You could streak up this hill, couldn't you? I suppose it's one of the few advantages of yomping about after cows all day. I've always avoided exercise like the plague. I discovered very early on that lying on the sofa with a copy of *Vogue* was a much better option.'

Kate laughed, glad that Elspeth's voice was friendly. 'I couldn't be bothered to go to a gym or anything like that. I suppose I do lead an energetic sort of life although I don't chase after the cows very much.'

'There's not a great emphasis on physical activity here, is there? The only person who seems to do anything at all laborious is Monique. Patrice and Jean-Luc really have no time between cigarettes.'

'No, they don't,' agreed Kate humbly. This criticism was Elspeth putting her in her place, she realised, in case she was too pleased with herself for attracting the attention of Patrice.

'Typical Frenchmen, really,' observed Elspeth. 'Doing what they do best. Cheating, and smoking too much.'

Chapter Eight

When George got back home he went to sit at the kitchen table, his heart still thumping and his thoughts racing. He struggled to get a clear picture of all that had happened but until he could think through the implications of his discovery, he could not decide what to do next. His first impulse had been to return without seeing anyone, to shut the dogs in their run as he went through the yard, and get off down the hill. He knew that as soon as Anna had a chance she would telephone from the hospital and it was best to stay where he was and wait. He particularly didn't want to bump into Richard or Tom and have to go through it all, not now when he had this other terrible worry. He needed time to think and although he knew that the first person he should tell of his fears was Tom, he couldn't bring himself to do it. Not yet.

Just the one ewe. He thought about Marge, now penned up with her lamb, away from the others. He held a vivid picture in his mind of her mild, offended expression as he examined her mouth and the little pink abrasions around her lips. In his heart he did not think she had the disease, but on the other hand he could not be certain. In the normal run of things he would have kept an eye on her for a day or two and expected her to get better or develop further symptoms of something like orf.

Thinking of it like this made him feel calmer. It was what he would have advised anyone else to do – adopt the wait-and-see approach. If he was not such a damn particular stockman – if his sheep were turned out for summer and only a lazy eye cast over them now and then – Marge's condition would have passed unnoticed for days, even weeks. It was because of the horrors of last year, the ravages of the terrible disease, that he was suspicious of the symptoms.

Thinking this led him to the cul-de-sac he did not wish to enter. If he had even the smallest doubt he had a duty to tell Josh and Tom and to call the vet and that would automatically set off the whole nightmare chain of official reactions. His deep mistrust and loathing of Defra, of its bumbling civil servant ignorance, of its crass high-handed decisions, the unnecessary slaughter, the misdiagnosis – he could not bear to think about it. He imagined the white-suited figures stalking the farm, bringing indiscriminate death to Dancing Hill, and he knew he would rather die himself than be a witness to it.

They were his sheep. His responsibility. Yet in a way, it would be a relief to pass on the fear and share the anxiety. In the present circumstances, Tom would have to take over. He would know what to do and would get on the telephone, calling the vet, taking charge, although there would be no decisions to be made because they would all be made for them.

If he obeyed his instincts, relied on the gut feeling of an old man who had kept sheep all his life, did nothing, sat it out, he would have to carry the burden alone. He would have to pen the sheep every day and examine them until he knew for sure one way or another. It would be a long, exhausting process but it was what he would have to do if he wanted to avoid putting the fate of the farm in the hands of people he did not trust. If the very worst happened and he was sure it was foot and mouth, well, then there was no option but to report the disease and allow officialdom to take over.

The more he thought about it, the more he was convinced that he would do nothing until he was sure.

George gazed unseeing at his large old man's hands laid flat on the table. His stomach felt unsettled, his guts turned to water when he thought about Josh. They would have got him into hospital by now and maybe even seen by a doctor. As soon as there was any news he knew Anna would telephone. If he sat here in the kitchen he would be sure not to miss her call. He could pick up the telephone on the first ring. In his head he could not shape the words he might hear and could not bear to think of the future. It was too dreadful, too catastrophic, and he did not feel up to going through with it.

The kitchen was very quiet. Afternoon shadows had started to stretch across the floor and the heat had gone from the sun on the window. George sat on. He was a man who preferred to keep his own counsel, never one to go about blabbing his business, but he felt a weight of loneliness. He tried to recapture the sound of his wife moving about the kitchen, the bustle and small clatter of a meal being prepared. It would have been comforting to have her here, to worry about Josh with her, even if he chose not to reveal his fears about the sheep, but it was Kate he missed most. Kate would have shared the burden of his discovery. It was Kate he needed.

When the telephone rang, it shrilled in the silence and

gave him a start. He picked up the receiver with a trembling hand.

'Hello? Anna?' He knew it would be her. It was a bad line, he couldn't hear properly.

'Grandpa? Can you hear me? I'm in Accident and Emergency. They've just taken Dad to be X-rayed. He's conscious, Grandpa. He came to in the ambulance, swearing like a trooper.'

'Thank God!' said George, relief flooding through him. 'Thank the Lord!'

'They don't know yet how bad he is, Grandpa. They won't know until they've seen the X-rays and the results of a scan. They're looking for bleeding in the head. I'll ring again as soon as I know any more.'

'Yes, please. I'll be here, waiting.'

'I've rung Rich. I've just finished speaking to him on his mobile. He'll tell Tom. I'll have to go, Grandpa. They're moving Dad up to a ward. I promise I'll telephone as soon as there's any news.'

George put down the telephone carefully. He thought of Josh turning the air blue and hoped that there couldn't be much wrong with his head if he could still swear. Yet Anna had said he wasn't in the clear yet. They would have to wait and keep their fingers crossed for the X-rays, but it was good news all the same.

Josh was the most important thing, but relief about him was not enough to lift a terrible sense of foreboding. George sat on, not thinking of anything very much, just conscious of a weight of dread which seemed to have loaded the heavy, warm air of the kitchen. He felt it pressing on his temples until his head ached. A tortoise-shell butterfly flapped against the kitchen window. He watched it as it fluttered up and down the glass, pausing every now and then to rest with quivering wings. Poor thing, he thought, but his legs felt too weary to allow him to get up to set it free.

Anna trotted beside Josh as he was wheeled into the lift and up to the ward. She felt self-conscious now in her cut-off shorts and work boots, her shoulders bare in her vest top. They had burned red, she noticed, cut across by a line of white where the straps had been. She had not had time to change, or even grab a shirt, only to push a few things in a plastic bag for Josh as the ambulance man had suggested.

It had been terrible at first. She had really thought he was brain dead or something irreversible like that, but the paramedics went through a procedure to test the depth of his unconsciousness – looking for response to speech, then to pain, at which point he had opened his eyes, tried to sit up and begun swearing. The relief was unimaginable.

'What the fuck's going on?' he asked. 'Where am I?'

'Oh Dad!' Anna cried, her eyes brimming. 'In an ambulance. Going to hospital.'

'What the fuck?' he said again, trying to turn his head. 'What the bloody hell's going on?'

He'd continued like that for the rest of the journey. Anna apologised to the paramedics who had grinned and said that it wasn't unusual. They were used to it. 'We use what's called the Glasgow coma scale,' said one, who was rather good-looking, Anna now noticed. 'It often ends up more like Glasgow on a Saturday night!'

Once at hospital in Yeovil, Josh rode on a wave of bad temper and irritation through all the initial examinations. He refrained from swearing at the nurses, though, or Anna would have told him off, despite her huge relief that he seemed all right. His leg was badly bruised, but unbroken, and he had suspected broken ribs. It was his head that was of most concern, the rest would mend, said the gentle Iranian doctor, fixing him with large brown eyes.

'I'm perfectly all right!' he kept saying. 'There's no need for all this palaver.'

'That you must allow us to decide,' replied the doctor.

'God, Dad,' said Anna. 'You gave us a shock. You looked terrible. Honestly, I thought you were a goner. You know it was Grandpa who found you? I'm surprised it didn't give him a heart attack!'

Josh, left alone while Anna went to telephone, cursed silently. His leg throbbed and his ribs ached. When he tried to find a more comfortable position on the trolley, the pain stabbed into his side, making him gasp. The back of his head felt sore and even touching his scalp with his fingers was painful. He worked back in his mind, trying to reach into his consciousness to fill the gaps in his memory. He remembered driving the tractor into the yard and he thought he remembered going to check on the bulls, but he could not be sure that this was not because Anna had told him what had happened. George had found him in the yard, she said, with his leg pinned under the ring feeder.

Apparently there had been a fight between the bulls and Len thought the new young bull was quite badly hurt. It was all a damnable nuisance and the thing that sickened him most was that he had been warned about Frank that very morning. George would have every justification for saying, 'I told you so!'

He wondered what Kate would have to say about it. She would hear George's version, of course, that he had been warned but would not listen. She would say it was typical of him. You're pig-headed, she would say. You never will be told.

He rehearsed in his head the telephone call to France. 'There's been an accident,' they would have to tell her. That would give her a shock. She might think it was George at first. With some satisfaction, Josh realised that she would be upset, worried, would insist that she come straight home, but he wouldn't allow that sort of fuss. A few painkillers and he would be back on his feet.

When Anna came back, she found a metal chair so that she could sit beside the trolley in the corridor outside the swing doors to the ward.

'They're admitting you,' she told him. 'I've just seen the doctor. He wants to look at the X-rays and then he'll come and discuss it with you.'

'Bloody hell!' said Josh. 'What do they want to keep me in for? I'm perfectly all right. You can see I am.'

'Dad! They know what they're doing. You were knocked out for nearly an hour. You can't just ignore how serious that could be. They want to make sure that you're all right.'

Josh lapsed into angry silence.

'I've telephoned Grandpa,' said Anna. 'And Rich. He's coming to collect me in half an hour or so. I'd better get back, hadn't I? I mean, I'm not much use here, whereas I can get on with the work at home.'

Josh made an impatient noise and Anna suddenly felt a flare of anger.

'Just stop it, Dad! For heaven's sake, shut up! You've had a really bad accident. Stop being so bloody stupid!' Angry tears filled her eyes and she brushed them aside with the back of a dirty hand. Josh didn't answer. He suddenly felt ashamed. He had put them all through it:

191

George, Len and especially Anna, and it was his own stupid fault.

They remained in silence, Anna picking at a broken fingernail or drumming the heels of her boots against the linoleum floor, looking up every time the ward doors banged open. Eventually a large, black nurse bursting out of a blue uniform and armed with a clipboard came to find them and there was more form filling until she permitted Josh entry to the ward.

He was transferred to a freshly made bed in a corner and the curtains drawn round.

'Cup of tea?' the nurse asked Anna. 'Not you, love,' she told Josh. 'Not till you've seen the doctor.'

'Yes, please. I'd love one. If it's not too much trouble.'

As the nurse turned to go, the doctor himself arrived, carrying large X-ray plates. Anna held her breath. She tried to read his expression for what the results would be.

'Good news,' he said, smiling, and looking from one to the other. 'There appears to be no damage, no bleeding. You have cracked three ribs, here and here, but your neck and back are fine. See?' He shuffled between the X-rays, dropping one on the floor. He and Anna simultaneously dived to recover it and knocked heads. They both apologised and she sat back in her chair, hot, embarrassed and relieved, with what she felt was a silly grin on her face. 'So we will keep you in overnight for observation and all being well we will allow you home tomorrow. We'll warn you of danger signs – sickness, dizziness, double vision, headaches. If any of these occur, you must get in touch with your GP, or return here to A&E immediately. You, sir, are a lucky man. A toreador, your daughter tells me.' The doctor laughed, showing uneven teeth which glinted with gold.

'What about Mum?' asked Anna as soon as they were alone again. 'Do you want me to telephone her? The thing is, Dad, she'll insist on coming home if she knows that you've had an accident.'

Josh thought of Kate. He imagined being at home with her, back in the kitchen at Dancing Hill with everything back to normal. He thought of her cooking the supper, talking to him over her shoulder while he sat in the old armchair and read the newspaper, a beer at his side. He wanted her there. He wanted everything to be like it always was, like only she could make it. Without her, there was a ragged sort of emptiness at the heart of things.

When it came to it, though, he didn't want to spoil her holiday. If he brought her back, there would be a weight of responsibility on him for having done so and also an admission that he wanted and needed her. He was reminded of how he had felt about her going in the first place and how she had gone all the same. No, he did not want Anna to tell her. Let Kate find out when she got home. It would make her feel suitably contrite and give him the opportunity of being a bit of a martyr.

'Don't tell her,' he said. 'There's no need. I'll be out of here tomorrow.'

Anna nodded. 'I agree,' she said. 'Mum deserves this holiday.'

The nurse reappeared with two cups of tea on a tray. 'Here you are, love. Doctor says you can have this now.' She bustled about, drawing back the curtains. An elderly man, waxy pale, with flat yellowish hands spread like leaves on the sheet over his chest, called feebly from the bed opposite and she left to speak to him.

'I'll drink this and go,' said Anna. 'Rich will be waiting

193

for me. Is there anything you need? Pyjamas and tooth-brush and stuff are in this bag. I'll put them in the locker.' She paused. 'I'll stay at Dancing Hill, Dad. I'll ring work on Monday morning and take the week off. You can't manage now, not with everything else going on on the farm.'

Josh started to protest but she cut in, 'Oh, shut up! Just accept for once that you need help and be a bit bloody gracious about it! You're going to need to lie up and keep quiet for a day or two, and those ribs are going to be agony. I've got holiday owing me, and anyway I've made up my mind, so I'll stay, whatever you say.' She leaned forward to jab a kiss on his forehead, still cross and vehement. 'Right, I'm off.' She paused before she left the side of his bed, and again he saw tears welling in her fierce eyes. He caught hold of her hand.

'Thanks, Anna,' he said. 'I'm sorry I've made such a bloody mess of things.'

She shook her head impatiently. 'Oh, shut up!' she said again, removing her hand and clomping away in her work boots.

Josh watched the ward doors swing shut behind her and lay back and closed his eyes. His head had started to ache and although the tea had wetted his parched throat he still felt thirsty. He wished the nurse would bring him the painkillers she had promised.

On the way home another argument flared up between Anna and Richard. After she had found him waiting for her in the hospital car park, he had kissed her and shared her relief.

'It must have been terrible for you. A terrible shock. Awful to think what might have happened.'

'Yeah. I suppose I imagined wheelchairs, permanent

disability, Dad being a vegetable, all that sort of thing.'

Rich swung out into the traffic crawling through the town and told her that he and Tom had finished the silage.

'That's one hundred acres, according to Tom, with what's already been cut,' he said, pleased with the achievement.

'You've done an amazing job. Thanks so much, sweetie. You've been a star.'

'There's rolling, or whatever it's called, to get on with now. I'll start when we get back. I'll use the new tractor, shall I? It looks quite fun going up and down the slope like a ski run.'

Anna looked horrified. 'You can't,' she cried. 'It's far too dangerous. You're not experienced enough at driving the tractor.'

'Of course I can do it.' Rich stopped at a pedestrian crossing where a group of teenage boys in long baggy shorts, bare-chested and eating ice creams, dawdled across. 'Tom told me that you have to get the grass well compressed and covered up as soon as possible. It's only a question of driving up and down a slope. I've done masses of off-road driving in Africa. It's one thing I can do to help.'

'Rich, it's really, really dangerous. One of the most dangerous jobs on the farm. The tractor is very unstable on a slope. It can tip up if you don't know what you're doing. For God's sake, we've had enough accidents for one day.'

'I'll be careful. I'll take it slowly.'

'I won't let you. Dad wouldn't let you. It will have to wait until the morning. Tom will have to do it in the morning.'

'Why can Tom do it, if I can't?'

'Because he's driven a tractor all his life, Rich! He's been making silage since he was a lad.'

Richard gave a gesture of extreme impatience. They were on an empty piece of dual carriageway now which dipped and rose over green hills towards Sherborne. He put his foot down and the car roared past a milk tanker labouring on the hill. The driver had his window open, his elbow stuck out. Anna could hear a snatch of country and western music and caught sight of the man's face looking down at them in the car, knowing they were arguing.

'What is it with you, Anna?' Rich said quietly. 'There's always some fucking crisis going on and yet you won't let anyone help.'

'That's not bloody fair!' Anna shouted back, stung. 'Ah! I see. It's male ego, isn't it? You don't like being told you can't do something.'

'Oh, for God's sake! Well, if you don't want me to help, I might as well go back to London.'

'Rich, don't be like that,' said Anna miserably. 'I'm not being unreasonable or making an unnecessary fuss, I promise. Ask Tom. He'll tell you.'

They drove in edgy silence until Richard stopped at traffic lights on the edge of Sherborne and looked across at her.

'And you can't go back now,' she said. 'The traffic will be diabolical. Everyone trails back to London early evening. Leave it until much later.'

'Jesus! Is there anything else I don't know that you need to tell me?' he asked sarcastically, shaking his head at her, but with his kind face softening into a smile.

'Yes. I'd like to thank you properly. For your help.' Anna raised a hand and wiped his long hair out of his eyes and pulled his head down to kiss his mouth. He tasted salty and she could smell his sweat. The traffic lights changed and the car behind sounded its horn.

'Come inside when we get back,' he said urgently. 'Come inside and shag the daylights out of me and I might forgive you.'

'Can't. I must go and see if I can give Len a hand. There's a hell of a lot to do.'

They drove back in silence after that, Anna watching the fields slip past, thinking of her father. It had felt so strange to leave him lying there in a hospital bed. He had looked vulnerable and even frightened and she had never seen him like that before. She felt sorry now that he had made her angry. She supposed it was the shock and then the relief to find he was all right that had made her flare up. She still felt maddened by his attitude. He was so stubborn and difficult to get close to. She wondered for an uncomfortable minute if that was how Rich saw her. Thinking this, and to make amends, she put a hand on his thigh and he smiled and put his own hand on top and then slid hers towards his crotch.

They were nearly back now. As they turned onto the farm drive past George's bungalow, there was no sign of life.

'I telephoned Grandpa from the hospital,' said Anna. 'To give him the good news. He was so relieved, poor old thing. His voice sounded really odd. Strained, somehow.'

'I'm not surprised,' said Rich as they pulled up in the yard. 'It must have been a terrible shock for him, finding your father like that. Well, if you're going off with Len, I'm going in to get a beer. I'm bloody parched, I can tell you.'

'Save one for me,' said Anna, disappearing across the yard at a trot.

Rich found Tom in the kitchen, writing a note at the table.

'Ah, you're back,' he said, looking up. 'This won't be necessary then.' He scrumpled the paper. 'I was just leaving a message for Anna. George telephoned to tell us the news. Thank God, eh?'

'Yeah.' Rich went to get a beer from the fridge. He held the can aloft. 'Want one?'

Tom looked at his watch. 'No, I'd better be getting on back. What's the final score, then? With Josh?'

'Cracked ribs and concussion. They'll keep him in overnight and let him out tomorrow. I don't know that he'll be up to much for a day or two.'

'Good thing we finished cutting. I've just brought in the last load.'

'I wanted to do the rolling but Anna got in a strop about it.'

'Quite right. It's a dangerous job. Josh and I always do it ourselves.'

'Ah. That's what she said.' Rich peeled back the ring pull and sat at the table. 'You'll manage OK, will you?' he asked. 'Anna said she's going to stay a few days, to help out.'

'That's good of her. Josh will hate her doing it, but he will definitely need a hand this end. Actually, she's bloody useful on the farm. Much more use than the boys ever were.'

Richard felt instant sympathy with Anna's brothers, thus written off. No wonder they both embraced London life with such enthusiasm.

'Having it in the blood isn't always enough then?' he asked idly, draining the can and wiping his mouth.

Tom considered. 'It's aptitude as well, like most jobs, but background helps more than anything. Understanding the life.'

'Ah.'

'Actually, it can work either way. Farmers' children seem to love it or loathe it. The first lot feel miserable doing anything else and the others put as much distance as possible between themselves and a muddy field.'

'Like the offspring of vicars,' said Rich. 'I was at school with sons of a bishop. One went on to be an army chaplain and the other's a drag artist.'

'It's different for girls, of course,' said Tom. 'Although my father maintains that farmers' daughters make farmers the best sort of wives.'

God, thought Richard, dropping his can in the bin, you couldn't get away with that sort of remark anywhere but deepest Dorset or possibly some backward areas of Afghanistan.

'That's what I came up against when I married Susie,' said Tom, getting up to go. 'She's had to battle against that prejudice for years. She calls it a bloody closed shop.'

She's not far wrong, thought Rich later, helping himself to another beer. He thought about the afternoon, how he had enjoyed working with machinery, liked the juddering power of the tractor and the sophisticated hydraulics, liked the speed and efficiency of the modern equipment, but Anna really got up his nose at times. He loved her and fancied her something rotten, but when she was down here on the farm she could be bloody irritating. That business about the silage clamp was only part of it. He knew that he was perfectly capable of doing the job but, oh no, he hadn't been born with a straw in his mouth.

There was something about these farmers. It was evident in Josh and old George and was coming out in Anna as well – a sort of built-in sense of superiority, like belonging to some exclusive club. They knew everything about everything in the country and didn't believe anyone else could be trusted. They liked to think that they were the misunderstood guardians of the countryside and everyone else was against them, from ramblers to dog-walkers, picnickers, the government, the weather, everything. They were the biggest load of whingers he'd ever come across while at the same time holding out their hands for subsidies. As far as he could see, and with, he admitted, only a vague understanding, they brought most misfortunes, including BSE and foot and mouth, on themselves and then howled for compensation. They polluted and desecrated the countryside with their hideous buildings and their plastic sacks and their chemicals and poisons and huge machinery and then wanted grants to put in hedges and wildflower verges and whimsical hedgehog colonies. As far as Richard was concerned, the sooner British farming bit the dust and all food was imported, the better.

Anna was a lovely girl, beautiful, sexy and bright, but he liked her better in London where she dropped this country girl posturing and seemed like any other female in her twenties, hard-working, hard-playing and good fun. When they married, and Richard thought in terms of when rather than if, he would make sure that they always remained with their feet firmly on concrete. Put her in a pair of green wellies and it meant trouble.

'So I'm going to stay and lend a hand for a day or two,' finished Anna. Len stood in the doorway of the calf shed, rubbing his chin. He didn't know what to think. Anna was a useful sort of girl but there were a lot of jobs she couldn't do. They would still be hard pushed to keep things going.

'Well, don't look so pleased!' said Anna. 'I'm obviously

not the partner of your choice, Len, but I'm the best you'll get. I'll give you a hand with the bull after I've checked those heifers due to calf.'

Len shook his head, but there was nothing for it but to get on with the job. He didn't like these upsets to his routine. Dealing with Josh had shaken him right and proper, especially making that emergency telephone call, having to tell the duty doctor how to find the farm when he didn't appear to know the district and didn't understand half of what Len said, the milking delayed, his cows upset, the milk yield down. It had been an afternoon he wouldn't forget in a hurry. He'd have liked to have clocked off early, got back to his cottage and related it all to Rita over a cup of tea. As it was, he didn't know when he'd finish, and now Anna putting her spoke in. He didn't like it, not one bit. Gloomily, he plodded off to feed the calves.

Anna went to check on the cows who were in the field behind the dairy, known as the maternity ward. Two of them looked about to calve but the rest showed no signs of imminent labour. With any luck they would just get on with it without the need for intervention, but the heifer in the barn had gone into labour. She was flat on her side and straining and Anna could see one tiny neat hoof emerging from her rear end. She would have to get Len to come and look. She wasn't experienced enough to know whether it would be a straightforward birth.

First Charlie had to be dealt with. Slowly, because he was still jittery and nervous, she and Len guided him into the cattle crush and closed the gate behind him so that he was held between the high metal bars, unable to turn round. He could still rear up and toss his great head about but he chose to stand still and quiet while they bathed his bleeding eye. He and Frank had bashed mercilessly at each other's heads, and Anna could see that beneath Charlie's choirboy curls, the skin was bruised and swollen. She hung over the crush and stroked his enormous mound of cream shoulder.

'Watch yourself!' snapped Len. 'He could break your arm without knowing he'd done it.' Carefully he swabbed at the eye while Anna kept the bull's head steady with a rope halter. They gave him a shot of antibiotic and then let him loose. He went to stand dejectedly in the corner.

'He's so depressed. I can see where the term "bullied" comes from,' said Anna. 'Can't we put him out with the cows? That would cheer him up.'

'He'll need another shot tomorrow. He can go out after. Now let's look at that cow.'

Together they went round to the barn, passing on the way the hammer and wire cutters and coil of wire left by the fence that George had mended.

'That's not like him, leaving things lying around,' said Len, collecting them off the grass. 'He's made a good job, though. There's no one as handy as your granddad.'

'He'll have forgotten he left them there,' said Anna. 'He must have thought he'd pick them up on his way back from the sheep and then walked right past them. He's getting forgetful, I've noticed that.'

'Who exactly is Archie?' asked Kate, once Elspeth had caught her breath and they started walking again. 'You've never really told me.'

'Haven't I? Well, it's no secret. Sir Archie Findlay. He was Minister of Health in the last but one Tory government. The love of my life. I am utterly, utterly devoted to him, but when we met he had been married for twenty years and so that was that. I knew the situation from the start.'

'He never considered divorce?' asked Kate.

'Never,' said Elspeth emphatically, 'and I never asked him to. I didn't think, and still don't, that to ask a lover to destroy the happiness of his wife and his children is a loving thing to do. It's more like an act of terrorism in my view. He was perfectly well married, you see. His wife was a pleasant woman, a good wife, and he loved her.'

'How could he have done? To have an affair, I mean?'

They were both walking, watching their dusty feet on the stony rutted track. Now Elspeth stopped and turned to look at Kate.

'Of course he did!' she exclaimed. 'But in a totally different way. With me he had passion, fun, excitement, relief from the tedium of life with a rather dull but nice woman. It was a very good arrangement. I like to think that I had the best of him, but on the other hand, I do believe he was a kinder, nicer man at home because of me. We observed very strict rules. I never went to his house and never once telephoned him. Mostly we avoided meeting socially, but if we did, I strictly observed the role of PA and nothing more. I don't believe I ever humiliated or embarrassed his wife. In the end we became quite good friends. I think she must have known the truth but she chose to be tolerant when she realised I was not going to upset the apple cart.'

'I see,' said Kate, glimpsing a life so far from her own, a relationship so different from anything she had experienced, that she found it hard to imagine.

'His wife died five years ago, so I have him to myself now,' said Elspeth. 'Dear old Archie. He'll be eighty-eight next year.'

'So do you live with him now?' asked Kate.

'Oh no! Not likely. He has a full-time housekeeper. He's very comfortable and well looked after. It would have been a great mistake to change the nature of our relationship. I'm still his occasional treat, you see. Something to look forward to. He knows I'd be useless at breakfast trays and bed baths and that sort of thing, and there are his children to consider. They wouldn't want me ensconced with their father after all these years.'

'So how often do you see him?' asked Kate, intrigued. Archie was older than George, she realised.

'Once a week at least. We speak every day, sometimes several times, and I often go round for a drink in the evening and occasionally we lunch together or go out for an early dinner. We totter round the corner to an Italian restaurant where Archie has been going for forty years.'

They walked on in silence. Kate tried to imagine the mechanics of this relationship. It seemed so exclusive, so well regulated, so glamorous. She imagined Elspeth getting dressed to meet her elderly lover, sitting at a dressing table to do her face and spray on scent. She thought of the muddle of her own life, her love and concern for her children, for Tom, for her father, the demands of the farm, her business, and somewhere, pushed to one side from his original place in the centre of it all, was Josh. Predictable, reliable, steady as a rock but rarely the person she considered first. She couldn't remember the last time she had thought about him in romantic terms. They had grown careless of each other, that was it. What had grown up round their youthful love, like suckers from a tree, had eventually taken over completely. Perhaps this was always the case in a healthy, strong marriage, that it became an enduring framework for all the other stuff of life. Surely the relationship described by Elspeth was far from normal, just two people doting on each other, gazing into each other's eyes to see a reflection of themselves. It was easy to write it off as a selfish indulgence, but why, then, did hearing about it make her feel envious and as if it was she who was missing out in some way?

They reached the brow of the first hill, past the big pine under which Elspeth had planted her easel, and the track now wound through a rocky waste and on up towards another set of buildings, the roofs of which were just visible above the pines. The cicadas had started up their insistent thrumming and the shadows were darkening between the trees.

'Is this another farm, do you think?' asked Elspeth. 'What a ramshackle collection of buildings.' A dog began to bark and then ran down the track towards them – an ugly yellow and white mongrel with the thick shoulders of a fighter and a curly tail. Kate spoke to him and he stopped, hackles raised. Under the trees in front of a low, single-storey wooden house, a clutch of assorted chickens sunbathed and scratched and to one side, within a railed patch of scuffed garden, a small naked girl stepped out of a plastic swimming pool and ran indoors.

A young woman came to the door of the house and shaded her eyes to look in their direction, then called to the dog and stepped out to meet them. With a shock, Kate realised that she was also naked. Although young and slim, her breasts hung like empty hot water bottles, half-way down her chest, and there was a deep triangle of dark hair between her legs.

'Yes?' she called out. How does she know that we are English? thought Elspeth, at the same time as she and Kate felt compelled to move forward, polite and smiling, as if this was a perfectly conventional meeting. The woman reached the railings and stopped. She had cropped dark hair and was very tanned. She was completely unembarrassed and made no attempt to explain her nakedness or apologise. The child reappeared at her side dressed in a long, dirty cotton frock, her feet bare.

'You come for cheese?' the woman asked. 'Honey?'

'Oh yes, that would be lovely!' said Elspeth, glad that she had money in her trouser pocket.

'Come.' The young woman opened the gate and led the way towards one of the outbuildings. As they got closer, Elspeth noticed that she had a diagonal scar right across her chest, a silver line almost from shoulder to waist.

She opened the door of the shed and let them in. 'Here,' she said, indicating a small table loaded with pots of jams and honey, and a large fridge. She turned to open the door and show that it was stacked with little golden discs of cheese. It was hard to admire and take an interest in the cheese, thought Elspeth, with the woman's bare arse in the way.

'A moment,' she said and disappeared out into the dusty yard towards the house. The child lingered on, leaning against the table, watching them with interest. She began to pick her nose with a dirty finger.

'Well,' said Elspeth, looking round. 'What an extraordinary set-up.' Kate made a face back at her and shook her head in amazement. She picked up a leaflet from the table.

'Do you think this is part of the co-operative they were talking about at lunch? Apparently Patrice went into a cheese-making business with some neighbours.' She read the leaflet which was printed in French. 'It's all bio whatsit and multi-orgasmic,' she said. 'Rather as you would expect. "*Nous sommes très attentifs au respect des fragiles équilibres naturels . . .*"'

'Very *naturel*, I'd say,' said Elspeth, looking out through the door towards the house. 'Watch out, she's coming back. Half-dressed this time and with a dwarf man in tow. No, it's not. It's a woman who looks like the smaller of the two Ronnies!'

The child continued to stare solemnly and Kate smiled back at her, with no response.

The two women joined them in the little makeshift shop. The first had put on a pair of patchwork shorts but was still bare-breasted, the other, who also had cropped hair and a nose ring, wore stained dungarees and a T-shirt. Elspeth had chosen two pots of lavender honey and Kate added a third and a bar of handmade soap.

'Goat soap, do you think?' she whispered to Elspeth.

'No, not goat soap,' said the dungareed woman drily. She had a square chin and a pug nose in a face which looked as if it were pressed against a window. 'This soap is made from pure beeswax.'

'Oh,' Kate said, embarrassed. 'It smells wonderful.'

There was a lot of sighing and discussion over the complexities of change for Elspeth's note and the child was sent into the house for a tin box of coins while the smaller woman cross-examined Kate and Elspeth.

'Ah, you stay with Patrice,' she announced when she found where they had come from. 'He is our business partner.'

'I thought so,' said Kate. 'He said something about a cheese co-op.'

'Only a sleeping partner,' said the woman significantly, giving Elspeth an arch look.

'Good Lord,' said Elspeth in an aside to Kate. 'I think we should get out of here.'

'You come to drink tea with us now, like English ladies,' announced the dungarees. 'Beneath our tree. Camomile tea,' and she caressed the bare neck of her friend.

'No, no, we must be getting back,' said Elspeth firmly. 'It's very kind of you, but another day,' and picking up her change and the honey from the table, she swept out, Kate in her wake.

They stumbled down the hill, snorting with suppressed laughter.

'What was all that about?' said Kate. 'Were they really lesbians, like it looked?'

'I'm sure they were. That ugly little mannish one thought we were, too. That poor child. What a way to bring up a daughter.'

'Unconventional,' said Kate, 'but healthy and secure, I should think. What an extraordinary day this has been. I haven't met so many bizarre characters in the whole of my life, although I suppose you'd hardly expect to in Dorset.'

'Look,' said Elspeth as they dropped down towards the farmhouse. 'Here comes Patrice. He seems to be herding the goats.'

Kate felt her heart rev as she looked down the hill. Patrice was winding his way towards them, wearing his straw hat, smoking the inevitable cigarette and driving four or five of the goats in front of him.

'Patrice! Hi! We're up here!' called Elspeth. He stopped and looked up at them.

'Ah,' he cried. 'I did not know you ladies were up on the hill. You have had a good rest? These goats belong to our neighbours. I am encouraging them home. One minute and I will be with you.'

They watched him march on up the path, the goats skipping before him, raising little clouds of dust from their scrabbling hooves, their bells tinkling merrily.

He arrived beside them and Kate moved over to make room for him on the narrow path, glad of the diversion provided by the goats. He seemed quite natural and easy and from his manner she guessed that he had not spent the afternoon agonising over the etiquette of holding her hand.

'These animals come from the next farm,' he explained. 'They visit us to eat our vegetables. Go home! Shoo!' He waved his arms at the skittering creatures who trotted off indignantly, their tails in the air. 'From here they will find their own way. Now,' he said, taking off his hat and wiping his brow with his arm, 'may I accompany you?'

'We were on our way back,' said Elspeth. 'We've just been to the farm. Look. We've bought honey.'

'Ah,' said Patrice. 'So you have met our neighbours? Clara and Lisl. They are Swiss ladies. A little strange but very pleasant. Lisl, she was a policewoman, and Clara a sociologist. Now they lead the natural life here.'

'Yes. Very natural. We saw.'

Patrice laughed. 'You were not shocked, I hope? Here in the south it is possible for people to live as they wish.' He cupped his hand beneath one of Elspeth's elbows and started her off down the track as if she were in need of support. Kate trailed behind, conscious of being awkward and silent. The sun was going down and in a moment it would be getting dark.

Anna banged into the kitchen, her face radiant. 'We've had a lovely calf, Rich. A big bull calf. A beauty.'

Rich, sitting in the armchair watching television, took in

her hot, shining face and filthy clothes. 'Great,' he said. 'All your own work, was it?'

'Well, it was a first calf, and a big one. It took a bit of manoeuvring. Poor Judy – that's the cow. She had quite a struggle.' She went to the sink to run herself a glass of water. She gulped it down and wiped her mouth.

'You look as if you need a bath,' he said.

'Yeah. I'll put all these clothes in the washing machine.' She went through to the washroom and began to strip off. She reappeared wrapped in a bathtowel and came to stand in front of him and put her arms round his neck. They were, he noticed, far from clean, smeared with something unspeakable. A strange smell clung to her. He pulled back, making a face.

'It's Lubigel,' she said, undeterred. 'I've had my arm up a cow, remember?' Rich pushed her away.

'How revolting!' he said.

'No, it wasn't. It was utterly wonderful. It's marvellous to see a healthy calf born like that. It cheered Len up. Despite himself, he was quite nice to me for the first time this afternoon. Admitted I'd done a good job.'

She sat on his knee but he leaned back, refusing to touch her.

'Go and have a bath first,' he said.

'I will.' Teasing, she seized one of his hands and slid it between the edges of the towel to find her bare skin, so that when she got up he caught her hand and pulled her back to straddle his knees. The towel fell to the floor and her naked breasts brushed his face.

'Have the bath later,' he whispered. 'That Lubigel's driving me wild, you witch!'

Anna laughed and tried to climb off but now he wouldn't let her go.

'Anyway, I took all the hot water,' he confessed, turning her over onto the floor.

In the bungalow at the foot of the drive, George sat in his armchair in the dusk. He had poured a glass of whisky but it remained untouched beside him. The French windows were open onto the garden and he could smell the scented stocks which Kate had planted round the door. Across the valley the falling dark spread blue shadows so that the trees along the stream had become a deep forest which marched along the bottom and up the black hill beyond. The light was nearly gone from the sky except for curds of yellow and gold on the horizon as the last rays of the sun disappeared. He could hear a cow calling to her calf, persistent and melancholy, but otherwise all was peaceful.

He sat quietly, his spotted old hands resting on the arms of his chair but his heart still full of dread. Behind the farm, up on Dancing Hill, he could imagine his sheep, ghostly white on the flanks of the field, grazing peacefully or lying, ewe with lamb, in the shelter of the trees. Mild, gentle creatures in a well-tended flock. He could not guess what fate awaited them. Awaited them all.

Chapter Nine

It was easy, as the evening dwindled, to delay Rich's return to London. Finally, he decided he would drive back in the morning, leaving at about five thirty when it was light. Anna took a shepherd's pie out of the freezer and then overcooked it while she had a long bath. They had to chip the cindered edges from the dish, but it still tasted good. They finished their makeshift meal with thick slices of Kate's plum bread. They had forgotten to start the dishwasher in the morning and so they switched it on and left the plates of the evening to join the growing pile of dirty crockery on the counters. Anna put the dish on the floor for the dogs to finish off and then she and Rich collapsed on the sofa in front of the television and were both asleep in ten minutes.

Anna woke him after midnight. She'd been out to check on the cow and calf and her body felt cold and clammy as his warm hands reached for her.

'Come to bed,' she said. 'For a few hours at least.' Together they mounted the stairs and climbed into Anna's unmade bed to make love again.

When the alarm clock rang at five o'clock, it was light but the house was quiet and Rich found he was alone once more. Forcing himself into action, he gathered his things, picked up his bag and went downstairs. The back door stood wide open and he went out into the yard to see where Anna was. The dogs had already been let out and Patch came to greet him, weaving backwards and forwards, his plumy tail wagging cheerfully. Rich pushed him away; he didn't want to get covered in dog hair and slobber. There was no sign of Anna.

Going back inside, he put the kettle on for a quick cup of coffee and spooned instant granules into a clean mug from the dishwasher. Glancing out of the window, he saw the whole valley was filled with a white lake of mist, floating halfway up the trees and transforming the green hillsides into a shimmering watery landscape lit by a pearly dawn light.

He stood gulping at the scalding liquid and then felt impatient to be off. He didn't have time to wait for it to cool, so tipped it away down the sink. Wondering where Anna was, he went out to his car and slung his bag in the back and looked round the yard. Len must already be milking because he could see a line of cows making their slow way out of the parlour, and then Sly and Bonnie appeared from one of the barns and came forward to greet him. That's where Anna would be. What the hell was she up to at this time of the morning?

He walked over to look for her and stood with his hands on the top bar of the gate looking into the barn. In the far corner stood a black and white cow and, beside her, swaying on spindly knock-kneed legs, was a new calf. The cow turned and gently nudged the little creature who pressed underneath her to drink from her udder. Anna, in her pyjamas, was sitting on a straw bale, watching. She looked up when he called her name, and then came over to him, pulling her loose hair back with both hands.

'The calf is fine,' she said, her face tired but transfused with happiness. 'He's really strong this morning. He's a greedy little so-and-so, butting his mother to get at the milk.'

'Oh, great,' said Richard, wondering why it was such a big deal. Weren't all these animals on a conveyor belt to the abattoir anyway? 'Is this the one that was born yesterday evening?'

'Yes. The one I helped with.' She picked up one of his hands and kissed it. 'Are you off?' she asked.

'Yeah. I've got to call in at the flat and have a shave and change of clothes first, so I'd better get on my way.'

Anna climbed onto the second bar of the gate so that she could lean over and kiss him. She looked lovely, he thought, and he undid one of her buttons and put his hand inside her pyjama jacket. God, if he didn't drag himself away he'd have to have her, here in the barn.

'Thanks for coming, sweetie,' she said, balancing on the rung in her wellington boots, holding his face between her hands. 'Thanks for all the help. It's made such a difference having you here, what with Dad's accident and everything. Drive carefully. Give me a ring when you get there.'

'I'll do that. Hope your dad goes on OK.' He started to walk backwards, throwing her a kiss.

'I've been thinking,' she said, not wanting to let him go.

'What?'

'You've enjoyed it, haven't you? The farming, I mean.'

'Yeah. You know I like tractor driving. Was that all you've been thinking?'

'No. I can't tell you it all now. I'll tell you when I get back to London.'

'Good or bad?' He stopped in his tracks, his attention caught. He had to hear now.

'Oh, good. Definitely good.'

'You've got to tell me. It's not fair not to. Is it about us?'

'Um, sort of. Indirectly. More about the farm than us.'

Rich pulled a face and sighed elaborately. 'In that case I think I can bear to wait.'

George was up early as usual. He hadn't slept well and had risen before it was light to make a cup of tea. He had taken it back to bed and then must have dozed off because when he woke again at five o'clock he was sitting upright with the light on. He had tried to read a few pages of a book Kate had got him from the library, a history of the desert campaign in the last war, and although it interested him, the words slid through his mind without making any impression.

He was glad to be up and about, with the routine of the morning to carry him along. He was in the kitchen rinsing out his tea mug when he saw Richard's car turn onto the lane. He glanced at the kitchen clock. Five thirty. He'd be driving back to London, no doubt. George knew how hard these young people worked in the City. They might earn more money than he considered defensible, but they put in the hours, you had to grant them that. And the commuting! Journeys to work of a few miles that took over an hour, stuck in traffic or squashed in the Tube. He knew he couldn't have stood it. When he was younger he'd been up to Smithfield most years, and as far as he could see office workers were herded up worse than cattle. In fact there was legislation to prevent cattle being transported in such conditions. The RSPCA should take a bit of interest in the human animal, in his opinion.

He listened to the radio while he shaved, to the fat stock prices and *Farming Today*, as he had done most mornings of his life, but he couldn't keep his mind on the programme. A few sentences floated across his brain: 'The launch of a new voice for farmers, fighting for a viable future for family-run farms'; 'Steady decline in independent farms'; 'Eleven farmers gone out of business every day for the last fifty years'. He turned the radio off. He didn't have the heart to listen, not when the immediate future occupied all his thoughts.

Slowly, he went through his morning chores, made his bed neatly, straightening the counterpane Pat had chosen the year she died, swept the kitchen floor, started a small load of laundry in the washing machine and then put together his simple breakfast, making two slices of toast and another cup of tea. He sat at the table and forced himself to eat. It was no good going to pieces and not looking after himself properly. He'd need his strength to get through the next few days.

As soon as he had washed the dishes he would get on up Dancing Hill. He would have to call in at the farmhouse to hear news of Josh, see how they were going to manage with him out of action. Tom had telephoned last night to say that he would be out of hospital today and that Anna was staying at home for a day or two, but the silage would need to be finished and it was heavy work, hauling all the old tyres on top of the heap to keep the plastic in place. George didn't see that Anna could do it on her own. It wasn't girls' work. It occurred to him that they wouldn't be needing the silage if his worst fears were realised. They wouldn't need it because there would be no livestock to feed.

Taking the crusts from his toast out to the garden for the birds he saw that the valley was filled with a floating white mist, draped like a flimsy scarf along the trees down by the stream. The grass was silver with dew and Tom's cattle left dark snail trails behind them as they moved down to drink. The sky was very pale but the tops of the trees were already gilded with a dreamy, golden light. It would be a while yet before it was hot enough to burn off the mist and then it looked as if it was set for another beautiful day. There was Kate going off to France for sunshine! She could have stayed put and had all she wanted right here on her doorstep without having to hobnob with the bloody French.

Collecting his cap and stick he closed the back door behind him and set off up the drive towards the farmhouse.

Kate and Elspeth enjoyed a leisurely breakfast in the sun. Someone had been into the town and there were large, warm croissants and pain au chocolat on the table, with bowls of milky coffee, a pot of cherry jam and a plate of ripe peaches.

'Isn't this just perfect?' said Elspeth appreciatively, breaking open a croissant. Its crisp golden flakes scattered over the table as she pulled apart the delicate creamy layers within and spooned on glistening blobs of black jam.

'It's not just the yummy food, it's having time to sit and enjoy it. No telephone, nobody needing something. No Josh asking what the time is, or wanting a telephone number. For some reason he's never worn a watch and so over the years I've become a sort of speaking clock.'

'It's deliberate helplessness, isn't it?' said Elspeth. 'In all my working life I've never met a man who made himself responsible for knowing telephone numbers. They always say, "Have we got so-and-so's number?" to save the bother of having to look it up for themselves. Archie's exactly the same. If I'm not around, he'd rather ring

Directory Enquiries than bother with the telephone book.'

'The next generation will be different. They have everything stored in the memories of their mobile telephones and computers, don't they?'

'Yes, I suppose so, until they wipe them all out, by mistake!'

Kate helped herself to a peach. Its deep pink skin was soft and furry and warm in her hand. She sat for a moment stroking its surface and enjoying the sun on her face. She heard someone come out of the kitchen and then Patrice spoke from behind her.

'More coffee, ladies?' He laid a hand on her shoulder and pressed down, quite hard with his thumb. She turned to look up at him and as he took his hand away he traced his fingers very gently along her neck. The gesture was so small, so slight, but Kate felt herself blushing. Patrice was unabashed.

'Your cheek is like the peach in your hand,' he said. 'See. The same tone, the same pigment.'

In his other hand he carried an earthenware coffee pot and he leaned over her shoulder to fill Elspeth's cup.

'Lovely breakfast, Patrice. Everything is delicious.'

'I am glad. May I join you?' He indicated another chair at the table.

'Of course. Please do.' Elspeth moved her scarf off the chair and Patrice sat down, crossing his long legs and taking a cigarette packet out of his shirt pocket. Kate said nothing, but moved her chair a little further away so that their knees were not touching. She put the peach on the table beside her plate.

Patrice lit his cigarette and drew on it deeply. 'Now we will talk about the painting,' he said, and began to explain

219

how he wanted each of them to work at their landscapes. As he talked he took a small penknife out of his pocket and with the cigarette stuck to his lip and his lazy, seductive eyes half closed, he took up the peach and began to peel back its skin and cut into its golden interior. Juice ran over his fingers until finally he had carved four perfect quarters and the dark red stone lay neatly separated from the flesh. Spearing a quarter on the tip of his knife and without pausing in his discourse to Elspeth on how she needed to concentrate on light and shade, he offered the fruit to Kate who realised at once that she was caught in some sort of ritual. Hesitating, she took the peach from the knife and put it into her mouth. Patrice glanced at her and smiled. Her mouth full of juice and sweetness, she smiled back.

Elspeth watched, transfixed. It was one of the most seductive scenes she could think of. No wonder Kate had hesitated. The implication had clearly not escaped her, ingenuous though she was. Then Patrice, still talking, offered her, in turn, a similar piece of fruit, but the action was so different, so stripped of erotic intention that she shook her head. She would never accept the role of a pretty girl's fat friend. She gave Patrice a knowing look. 'No thanks, Patrice,' she said briskly. 'I'm keen to get started. I'm going to collect my things.' She stood up and as she did so noticed Kate reach forward and help herself to the remaining fruit from the plate.

'First, come into the studio, please, and we will talk about your work,' said Patrice, also getting up. The moment of sexual tension was gone, the atmosphere now workaday. He led the way further down the terrace to where the outside door of the studio was framed by terracotta pots filled with geraniums.

Kate let them go, finishing her peach, and when she

eventually rose and followed slowly, as she passed the open kitchen door she noticed Julie standing just inside, an onion in one hand, a knife in the other. On her face was a *'j'accuse'* sort of expression. Goodness, thought Kate. Don't look at me like that! It isn't as if I've done anything! But as she trailed after the other two she could not deny the intoxicating pleasure of being found desirable.

Well! thought Elspeth, twenty minutes later as she made her way up the hill to her painting position. Just as she had expected, and irritating though it was, Patrice was evidently working hard to seduce Kate. Whether he would be successful or not, she couldn't guess. Kate seemed to her to be a sensible sort of woman, an Englishwoman of the type he might not have met before. However, his strongest card was that no doubt she was terminally neglected by her husband. Elspeth could almost guarantee that fact, and there was no one more vulnerable than an unappreciated, long-married woman.

If Kate had any sense, and if she felt so inclined, she should accept his advances and have a damn good time, then go home, be nice to the husband and forget all about Patrice. But it rarely worked like that. Ridiculous notions of falling in love would take over and then the trouble would begin, the heartache and destruction which, in the long run, benefited nobody. It was not a scenario that Elspeth wished to have any part in.

Women, on the whole, especially ingénues like Kate, misunderstood the nature of these sort of relationships, lacked the steeliness and self-control to realise that there could be a heavy price to pay for the thrills of sexual dalliance. It was like investing in a speculative way in a foreign currency, she thought, believing that the coin could never be debased, and then being scuppered by devaluation. Oh, the weeping and wailing and gnashing of teeth when the investment was found to be worthless. She had no patience with such foolhardiness.

She stopped to get her breath and turned back to look over the farmhouse. How pretty it was, with its tiled roofs and all its pots of cascading geraniums and petunias, nasturtiums and fuchsias. Kate should try to see Patrice as a sort of bedding plant, she thought, just a lovely splash of temporary colour to brighten things up. She could think of her good, dull husband as a well-established but less exciting perennial and keep him beautifully mulched and lovingly looked after in a permanent place in the flower-bed. Then all would be well. Pleased with her analogy, she set up her easel and started to paint.

Down below the farmhouse Kate was also about to begin work. She was thinking of Josh, thinking quite fondly of him and realising that she missed him. If he had been a different sort of man, she thought, and if they had a different sort of relationship, she would have telephoned him this morning. She would have rung up after breakfast, when Patrice's attentions had filled her with such light-headed, silly happiness, just to tell him she loved him and to hear him say, 'Darling, what a lovely surprise! I love you too. I love you and miss you!'

Instead, the real Josh would say, 'What's the matter? Is something wrong? Isn't it rather extravagant to be ringing at this time?' He would think she had gone off her head and his voice would be full of disapproval. But for all that, he's a good husband, thought Kate, as she squeezed a delicious tomato red onto her palette. Stead-fast and true, unlike Patrice, who must be totally unreliable and a nightmare to live with.

However, as she painted happily in the sunshine, it was to Patrice that her thoughts kept returning. He's made me feel attractive again, she thought. He's made me feel desirable and as if life is full of possibilities. Dangerous possibilities, maybe, but at least something a lot more exciting than the same old plod of home.

George got Marge into the corner of the pen and with the handle of his stick hooked round her neck, held her there while he got close enough to catch her. Her lamb scudded away, bleating, but Marge stood quietly while he examined her mouth. His eyes were blurred this morning and he had to blink to clear his vision, to make sure that what he saw was right. The small lesions were still there, but they were no worse and, he thought, less defined than yesterday. They looked as if they were healing.

Heaving her over onto her back he examined her feet, which were still clean and cold. Her udder was clear of infection and when he pulled her to her feet she trotted off only slightly lame. If he let her back into the flock now he would defy anyone, a vet even, to notice anything out of the ordinary about her.

A flood of relief overwhelmed him. Just as he had thought, it was nothing serious. Whatever it was that produced the freak symptoms had passed, and he was almost certain there was nothing to worry about. He straightened up and, taking off his cap, wiped his brow with his sleeve. It was hot already, early as it was. There had been nobody around when he went to collect the dogs from the yard. Len was finishing the milking, but there was no sign of Anna. Now, with his mind at rest, he would call in on his way back. He looked forward to a cup of tea at the kitchen table and a bit of a chat with his granddaughter.

First, he would pen the rest of the flock and check them over. Even though he was reassured, you couldn't be too careful, he thought, not after a scare like that. Whistling to the dogs, he sent them to gather the sheep from the hill and bring them down to the pens at the bottom. Sly and Patch shot off, moving like arrows up the flanks of the slope, before dropping onto their bellies at his command. Old Bonnie waited by his side, her ears pricked, her bright intelligent eyes watching every move. When the moment came he would send her forward to nudge the sheep into the pen.

The sheep looked up from grazing and began to gather into a bunch as the dogs worked forward. The first of the old ewes started to trot down the hill and the others followed, the lambs bumping nervously into their mothers. Bonnie glanced up at George and he put a hand on her head. 'Wait, girlie,' he said. 'Wait a minute now.'

Sly and Patch were circling behind, turning the stragglers who tried to shoot away to the sides, until the lead ewe stopped nervously beside the mouth of the pen. 'On you go,' said George and Bonnie streaked off, dropped, and then nudged forward, dropped again. The ewe swung away but Sly was there, outflanking her. She stopped, considered, and then with an independent air, as if it had been her intention all along, strolled into the pen. The others followed and Bonnie guarded the entrance as the last one sidled in.

George stumped over to lift the hurdle across the opening and rewarded the dogs with praise. Then moving amongst the bobbing backs of his sheep, he worked methodically through the flock, inspecting each one in turn. The first four ewes were clear, but the fifth made his heart falter. Quite clearly, around her neat little white mouth there were signs of abrasions. The sixth was the same and then the tenth. By the time he had finished, eight of his twenty-five ewes were affected.

Separating them from the rest of the flock took time, then checking the water trough and emptying bags of nuts into the feeder. It was easier to work than it was to stop and think, but when he paused, a sense of defiance came over the old man. It seemed to him that he alone stood between Dancing Hill and the terrible consequences of reporting a suspected case of foot and mouth. Only two of the sheep were slightly lame, none seemed distressed and he still could not be sure what they were suffering from. He was determined now that with Kate away and Josh laid up, he would tell no one. Like Marge, these sheep would get better and no one need ever know.

It was early in the afternoon before Anna helped her father out of the Land Rover and into the house. The dogs barked joyfully and Len appeared from the dairy to see if he could help, but Josh shook him off.

'I can manage,' he said. 'If Anna will just give me that stick to lean on. These ribs hurt like buggery, I can tell you. The leg's bloody painful too.'

'We thought you'd had it, we did,' said Len, pursing his lips and shaking his head. 'We thought you'd turned up your toes. Terrible fright you gave us.'

'Yes, well, I'm all right,' said Josh irritably. He moved stiffly, like an old man, Anna hovering on one side and Len behind, relishing the drama.

'How are the bulls, Len?' he asked, as they reached the back door. 'There was a fight, so Anna says. No doubt

George will be round any moment to say "I told you so!" '

'I'll say,' said Len. 'Went at it hammer and tongs from the look of the new one. He'll be all right, though, in a day or two. We patched him up, didn't we, Anna?'

'Yeah.' Anna smiled back, glad of the acknowledgement.

Reaching the kitchen, Josh eased himself into the armchair, his face creasing with pain as his ribs protested. Bonnie pressed her nose into his lap and he put a hand on her head, thinking, God, it's nice to be home. 'Put the kettle on, Anna, there's a good girl. Hospital tea is like gnat's piss.'

Anna dropped several bottles of painkillers into his lap. 'You'd better take these, too. Every four hours, the doctor said.' She went to fill the kettle. 'Do you want a cup, Len?'

'Wouldn't say no. It's dry work out there in the sun.'

'Afterwards, will you come and look at that other cow I told you about? I think she's gone into labour.'

Josh leaned back, trying to ease the pain in his ribs. His leg throbbed continually and he longed to be back in bed. After he had had a cup of tea he would go and lie down upstairs. Anna and Len's talk about the farm should have interested him, but his head felt full of something like lint, which fuzzed the edges of everything they said, and he found it hard to concentrate. Stuffed into the plastic bag containing his things from hospital was a sheet of printed instructions for victims of concussion. The doctor had been through all the danger signs with him, complications which he should not ignore, and had warned him that he should take it easy for a day or two and expect to feel tired. He had had a restless night, only sleeping in snatches between all the comings and goings on the ward, and his eyes now felt heavy with sleep.

He listened to Anna and Len talking and when he had

finished his cup of tea asked for a hand to help him out of the chair. 'I'm going to lie down for a bit,' he told them. 'You can't get a wink of sleep in hospital.'

Anna went with him, a step behind him on the stairs as he mounted slowly and painfully, and when they got to the landing he saw through the open bedroom door that his bed was still unmade and the curtains drawn.

'Sorry, Dad. I haven't had time to do anything in the house. Shall I straighten it for you?'

'Don't bother,' he said, sitting on the edge. 'I'll only mess it up again.'

The news of Josh's accident spread fast through the farming community. By lunchtime, Tom had had several calls from immediate neighbours. Most were as busy as they were at Dancing Hill but nonetheless were offering help when they had their own silage or hay cut.

'We've been flat out over the weekend,' he said to Paul Hobbs, whose land marched with theirs. 'We finished the silage yesterday, so we should be OK if we can get it rolled and covered today.'

'You're better off than we are, then,' said Paul. 'I'm still waiting for the contractors to come and finish. I can send Joe over this morning to help if you could do with an extra pair of hands. I know you're a lazy bugger. You'll never manage on your own.'

'Thanks, Paul,' laughed Tom, good-naturedly. 'We just need to see if Josh can drive the tractor in a day or two. If he can, we'll be OK. It's only concussion and cracked ribs he's got. Nothing serious. Thanks for your offer. Can I get back to you?'

He put down the telephone and turned to Susie who was in the utility room, feeding sheets into the washing machine. 'Why do you always say no to help?' she asked in a small, pained voice. 'You said that Josh being out of action couldn't have come at a worse time. When was it you finished last night? Eleven o'clock? I hardly saw you all day.'

'Sorry, darling,' he said, going through to collect his overalls and pausing to kiss her head. 'You know how it is. But I can't take Joe from Paul today when we are further on with the hay than he is.'

'Well, you've got to think of our guests. They don't want to be disturbed by tractors coming and going at all hours.'

'We didn't have any guests last night.'

'No, but we might have done. You've got to think of that. Especially when we make more money from B&B than we do from farming.'

Tom sighed as he put on his overalls. 'That doesn't mean we stop work, does it? Everything still has to be done as usual.' His voice was patient but he wondered how Susie could return to this theme time after time. It was the same with all farmers – no one was making any money. Breaking even was the best they could hope for. She knew it, but her solution was to get out, as if it was as simple as that.

'Have you been in touch with Kate?' she asked, changing tack, but staying with a subject which annoyed her. Tom realised that she was looking to be irritated, in the sort of mood that seeks to niggle and fault-find.

'I don't know if Josh has,' he said evasively. 'Or Anna. I told you she's staying on to help?'

'Isn't she supposed to have a high-powered job? How can she just take time off?' Susie's tone was indignant.

'*I* don't know, Suse. Presumably she's squared it with them. It's hardly my business, is it?'

'If I was Kate, I'd want to know about Josh. It's amazing if no one tells her in case it spoils her holiday, while all the extra work falls on you.'

'It isn't strictly like that. You know it's not. The silage is nearly finished. There wouldn't be much Kate could do that Anna can't, and Josh hates a fuss. He wouldn't want her to come home for him. After all, she's only got a week and it's the first time in living memory that she's ever been away.'

'So do you call me going up to see my mother "going away"?' asked Susie defensively. 'Because although we go to a health farm, I can tell you it's not much of a holiday with Mummy, and I'd like to point out it's her who pays for it. Not one penny comes out of the farm.'

'I know, darling, I know! Don't get so worked up! I'm not saying anything about you. We were talking about Kate, remember?'

Susie's pale blue eyes started to fill and she went to stand at the kitchen window with her back to Tom. He knew what was coming, what had been initiated. It was all old territory. Surreptitiously, he looked at his watch and wondered how long it would take to calm her down. He went and put his arm round her shoulders.

'It's because we had no children.' She spoke in a trembling voice. 'Because we had no children, no one thinks I have any need of a holiday or a break. They think I just do what I like all day, that I'm selfish or something, as if it was my fault.'

'Of course they don't. Come on, darling. Don't be silly. Nobody thinks that.'

'Yes, they do. Your father. Kate, Josh. They all do. I once heard Kate saying something about how I'd done this house so nicely. She said, "Of course Susie's had the time.

Not having kids about makes all the difference." '

Tom couldn't believe his sister could be so tactless. His father perhaps, but not Kate. It was probably one of the things Susie misinterpreted.

'If she said it, she didn't mean it,' he protested. 'I know she didn't.'

'You would stick up for her and not believe me.'

'That's not what I said. Now calm down, Suse, there's a good girl. Josh gets out of hospital today so why don't you come up to Dancing Hill with me? You can judge for yourself. If you think Josh looks as if he could do with Kate at home you could suggest you telephone her. Tell him how you would feel in the circumstances. He's such a selfish so-and-so he'd never work it out for himself.'

'It couldn't *be* me, though,' said Susie, sniffing but triumphant, 'in these circumstances, could it? Because I would never have gone off and left you in the first place.'

Out in the barn Anna had her arm in the cow, trying to work out the position of the calf's other hind leg. It seemed to be doubled back at the hock, and she had to push the protruding foot back inside the uterus and then search for its partner. With a bit of manoeuvring, she managed to locate and release the folded leg and draw both feet out together.

'Well done, girl,' said Len. 'It's having smaller hands as what helps. We can get the ropes on now.' He began to tie the little legs above the fetlock joints and loop the ropes round the winch.

'Hang on a minute, Len,' said Anna. 'I'm going to have to have a rest. God, this isn't something an impressionable girl should have to do. It puts me off childbirth, I can tell you. Elective caesarean for me, every time. I want to be fit to sit up in bed for the champagne.'

Len wasn't listening. 'If we don't get 'er shifted soon, we'd best get the vet or we'll lose the cow. Must be a bloomin' big calf. I don't know as it's still alive.'

'Poor thing,' said Anna, touching the perfect little protruding black hooves which looked as if they had been polished with a shoe brush.

'Come on then. Let's have another go. We might do it yet.'

Len moved the winch on a couple of ratchets with each contraction, while the cow rolled her eyes and frothed at the mouth. Anna rubbed her neck. 'Good girl,' she said. 'Come on, girlie, you'll soon have a lovely baby.'

'We're nearly there,' said Len and, grabbing the legs in both hands, he twisted and pulled with each massive contraction until the calf's rear end slid out in a slimy bloody sack. 'We've got to get the head out or the bugger'll drown.'

'We can't lose it now!' cried Anna. 'Come on, Len, try again.' They both took up the ropes and when the next contraction came they pulled until Anna's hands burned. This would surely kill the poor cow, she thought, who was flat out on her side and looked exhausted. Then there was a sudden slurping sound and the head was released in a rush and Anna and Len staggered backwards.

'Is it alive?' she asked as Len bent over the calf. He pulled the birth sack from the head of the limp little body on the straw.

''Er's not breathing,' he said.

Anna laid her hand along the calf's left side, searching for a heartbeat.

'I've found a pulse!' she said, looking up, excited. 'The heart's beating! We can save her. Come on, Len, help me.'

Together they hauled the calf up by its hind legs, struggling to suspend it upside down to free the airways of fluid.

'It's too heavy!' wailed Anna. 'I can't hold it up!'

'Hang 'er over the gate,' said Len, dragging the inert body across the barn. Together they hauled it up and suspended it, dangling down over the top bar of the gate while the cow, sitting up now on the straw, watched anxiously.

'That'll do,' said Len, allowing the calf's body to flop back onto the straw.

'Mouth to mouth,' said Anna. 'I've seen Dad do it.' She knelt beside the little bloody body and lifted the large head on the limp neck. The eyes, with their fringes of thick white eyelashes, were peacefully closed. Pinching the perfectly formed little nostrils, Anna put her own mouth over the rubbery pink lips and breathed into the calf. Then she pressed on the lungs to try and start them working and repeated the process over and over again while Len stood shaking his head.

'You're wasting your time. We've lost this one,' he declared gloomily. 'Lovely big heifer calf, too.'

Anna, taking no notice, kept up her efforts until, scarlet-faced, she looked up and cried triumphantly, 'She's breathing, Len! She's breathing! Look!' Almost imperceptibly the frail little sides were rising and falling. The cow, on her feet now, with the afterbirth straggling from her rear end, watched from the corner.

'Blow me,' said Len, squatting down beside Anna. 'I thought 'er had snuffed it. You've done well there, girl. Best get 'er moved. Move 'er to the mother.'

Together they heaved up the limp body and carried it to lie in the straw beside the cow who sniffed at it curiously and then began to lick, her thick pink tongue working

232

over the damp whorls of black and white hair, drying off the wet and blood, stimulating the circulation, reviving the flickering spark of life.

'That's nature, that is,' said Len. 'Mum doesn't want to lose 'er now.'

They watched in silence. From where they stood there was not much sign of recovery but they had to hope that the little heart was beating and the lungs struggling to fill. Anna realised that she was still shaking from her exertions and that her cheeks were wet. She wiped at them with the back of her filthy hand and sniffed. She felt moved by a great wave of love for the little black and white scrap collapsed on the straw whose life she believed she had saved.

Later, well after midnight, from across the landing Josh heard Anna getting up and going downstairs. She would be going to check on the calf, he reasoned, and he lay, listening, straining his ears to hear her crossing the yard under his window. The dogs barked briefly and he heard her speak to them in a low voice. Then all was quiet again. Josh had been too uncomfortable to sleep and now he felt the need to have a pee. Getting out of bed was bloody agony but he managed it and set off across the landing to the bathroom. That done, he stood at the top of the stairs listening for Anna. What would she find in the barn? The calf's chances were marginally under fifty fifty, he reckoned, and he knew she would be upset if it died. It was always hard to lose what should have been a healthy animal, but she should be glad that she had saved the cow.

He stood and waited and when he did not hear her come back he lowered himself painfully down the stairs, hanging on to the banisters and pausing after each step.

Getting out to the barn was a bit easier. The electric light shone from the open door, and when he went in he saw the cow standing in the corner, the calf folded at her feet. Its markings were very bright under the striplight. Anna, squatting beside it, looked over when she heard him come in. She had pulled a sweater over her pyjamas, rubber boots on her feet. Her hair was loose and tousled and her face had the slightly swollen look of someone awoken from a deep sleep. She looked very young, thought Josh tenderly, like a child. He went to stand beside her and put his arm round her shoulders.

'How is she?' he asked.

'So so.'

'Has she been up, do you think?'

'I don't think so. All her effort is going into breathing.'

'It was the long labour and oxygen deprivation and probably fluid in the lungs, but she might still pull through. They do sometimes. Gather strength just when you think they've had it.'

Anna put a hand to her mouth and, glancing at her, Josh saw her eyes had filled with tears.

'Come on,' he said gently. 'You're a farmer's daughter. Life and death. It happens every day.'

'I know, I know. But I do want her to live, I really do. She's so perfect and she had such a battle to be born at all.' With a finger she stroked the whorls of hair on the crown of her head. One of her ears twitched slightly but the eyes remained closed.

'Shall we help her to her feet, Dad? We could support her between us. Try and get her to feed.' She had forgotten that Josh's cracked ribs would make it impossible.

'Not yet. Give her a bit more time. The best thing is to leave her with her mother to work over with her tongue.

234

All that rhythmic licking has a purpose. It's more effective than anything we can do.'

They watched mother and calf for a moment and Josh said gently, 'Come in now and get some sleep. Come and look at her again in an hour or two.'

Anna sighed and got to her feet and together they slowly left the barn. She paused to turn off the light and they went out of the gate into the dark yard. She took Josh's arm and he winced.

'Sorry, Dad. You poor old thing. I'd forgotten you're injured.' Halfway across the yard she suddenly said, 'I've been thinking about the future, Dad. Thinking about Rich. Should I marry him, do you think?'

Josh hesitated. He hadn't anticipated such a question. He could not tell from her voice whether she wanted a serious answer and he stopped, seeking her face in the dark.

'Don't ask me that,' was all he could think of to say. 'That's for you to decide. You'll know if it's right or not. But Mum and I like him.'

'How do you mean, I'll know if it's right or not? I wouldn't ask you if I was sure.'

'If you're not sure, then don't.'

'But how were you and Mum so certain of each other? You were so young. Mum had hardly met anyone else. She'd hardly been off the farm.'

Josh considered. He didn't really know what Anna was after. Did she want him to claim that their marriage had been one long love story, a perpetual honeymoon? She knew that wasn't true. She couldn't have grown up in the family without realising the tensions and irritations that existed between him and Kate. Or was she looking for him to say that although they were certain then, such certainties can't last and that with hindsight they had been wrong to marry so early, before they knew anything about the real complexities of life.

Neither was true, anyway. He wasn't a believer in romantic love, all that women's magazine tosh, and he and Kate were certainly not soppy about each other, God forbid, but they muddled along OK. That was about the sum of it. They got on OK. They liked each other, were good partners, knew one another, made allowances. He couldn't see that you could hope for, or expect, more than that. He didn't hold with all this introspection anyway, all this analysing relationships and delving into feelings or lack of them. It was a dangerous activity, especially when women got going on it.

Last Saturday he'd met a young farmer friend of his at Taunton market and thought he had looked a bit down in the mouth. It turned out his wife of ten years had just taken the children and left him, said he wouldn't communicate, wasn't aware of her needs or some such rubbish. They had a lovely farm, a fine herd of cattle, healthy children and he was an honest, hardworking young man, so what more could she have wanted? Now she was living in a flat somewhere in the town and unless he could talk her into reconsidering, everything would have to be sold.

It was a mystery to Josh. What had this young woman hoped for in marriage? What extraordinary expectations had she had? Her husband reckoned the trouble had started at her yoga class. She'd met up with a coven of women there who led her to believe that her husband wasn't committed enough to her because he went to sleep in front of the television every evening. The fact that he'd been up at four to do the milking seemed to have escaped them.

'I'm not the person to ask,' he said finally. 'We just did what seemed right at the time. I've not regretted it. I can't speak for your mother, though.'

Anna squeezed his arm. 'I wouldn't put up with you,' she said fondly. 'Mum must love you or she wouldn't either.'

Josh smiled in the dark. 'That's about it,' he said. 'Putting up with each other is about the best you can hope for. You can't go far wrong if you keep that in mind.'

When they got back into the light of the kitchen, the closeness they had felt outside was lost, the intimacy over.

'Is there anything you want, Dad? I could do with a cup of tea. Would you like one?'

'That would be lovely. Thank you, Beano.' He slipped easily into using her old nickname. She filled the kettle and put it on the Aga, the soles of her bare feet picking up the grit of sugar spilled on the floor. Waiting for it to boil, she stood on one leg and then the other, wiping each foot in turn on her old Snoopy pyjama legs.

Josh eased himself back into the armchair. He couldn't face the effort of getting back up the stairs just yet. Anna made the tea and handed him a mug and said she was going to bed and to call if he needed her, but he told her he was more comfortable sitting where he was. It was good to be home even if the kitchen looked as if a bomb had hit it. As well as all the dirty dishes, someone had left the Sunday newspaper crumpled on the floor and the table was littered with everything that had not been put away. A packet of sugar, got out of the cupboard when the bowl was empty, had been knocked over and gritty grains crunched underfoot. The cake tin, a cornflake box, a bottle of ketchup, a packet of biscuits, two days of junk mail, suncream and a cotton scarf lay amongst a collection of what Josh thought of as 'stuff'.

Discarded clothes had piled up on chairs. Sweatshirts, T-shirts, caps, trainers. Where had all the mess come from and how had it appeared so quickly? It seemed to have engulfed them like a tide, building up imperceptibly until they were awash. Of course, it was Kate who normally manned the defences to keep this detritus under control. She was constantly sifting and storing, stacking in cupboards, folding, dividing, putting little piles on the stairs to go up with the next ascending person, although of course it was only ever she who bothered to stop and pick it up.

Anna didn't seem to notice. It was as if she had had a female role bypass, thought Josh. She was perfectly happy to shove things aside in order to put down her plate on the crowded table or to drop her clothes on a chair and leave them there until she next needed them. She wasn't always reaching for the dishcloth, which Kate practically wore as a permanent accessory when she was in the kitchen. In fact, Josh couldn't think of Anna using a dishcloth at all. No, she certainly wasn't good wife material in that way and Josh wondered if Richard noticed or minded. He supposed that once a relationship had moved into the bonking phase, which clearly theirs had, whether or not Anna had any aptitude for housewifery would not be uppermost in her lover's mind. He had to admit he would have been the same.

It seemed incredible in the current sexual climate that when he and Kate got married she was still a virgin. Technically, anyway. When he met her she had only just started at art school and had no real experience of life away from home. He had come to Dancing Hill as a residential farm student and their romance had to be conducted under the keen eyes of George and Pat.

Although the sexual revolution was supposed to have happened, it certainly hadn't reached Dorset, and rumours of a changed moral climate only made Kate's parents more vigilant.

They lay naked together in her narrow bed in the seaside town where she was a student, but she was too terrified to go the whole way and he too chivalrous to make her. He used to drive back at the end of one of these weekends fuelled with love and desperate with frustration. It was ridiculous, he thought now, this hesitating on the brink, but ultimately it was what made them marry so young. It was the only way to get regular sex.

When Josh eventually made it back to bed he found lying down was too painful and so he took the pillows from Kate's side and propped himself up in a sitting position. He reached to turn out the bedside light and as he did so an unmistakable scent came to him from the pillowslip. It was Kate's. He couldn't remember the name of the stuff she used, wasn't sure he had ever known, but it was what she always smelled of. He buried his face in the pillow and moved a leg and arm across into the cold of her side of the bed. He really missed her. Perhaps he should have tried to tell Anna how he felt about her mother. Perhaps that was what she wanted, but truthfully, he couldn't have done it. He didn't have the vocabulary. It was the sort of thing that went without saying.

Across the landing, Anna heard her father go to the bathroom and then the light went out on the landing and the house was dark. Through her open window the night breathed with the noises of the countryside, a distant cow mooed to a calf, a fox barked and a cock pheasant gave its football rattle call from Hanging Wood. She felt wide awake now, not just as if sleep had deserted her but as though her mind was particularly clear and sharp. Any questions she asked herself would be answered with a clarity which often eluded her during the day.

She stared into the darkness, thinking about the week-end and knowing that she had arrived at a decision which had bothered her for some time. She was so certain now that all the subsidiary questions and answers fell neatly into place and suddenly she could see the pattern her life would take. When she got back to London she would hand in her notice and warn Jeremy and Tim that they must look for a new flatmate. Then she would tell Rich that she wanted to marry him in the near future, if he would have her, because what had come to her as she lay in the dark was the conviction that she wanted to farm on Dancing Hill.

Chapter Ten

One look at the state of the kitchen convinced Susie that, very far from managing, Anna and Josh were fast sinking into a state of chaos. She and Tom found the pair of them sitting at the kitchen table on which it would have been hard to find the space to put down an eggcup. Under the table, Patch was standing with his two front paws in a dish containing the burnt remains of a meal, noisily scraping away at the edges with his teeth. There was a bundle of unironed laundry on the armchair and every counter and surface was a muddle of things not put away or dirty mugs and dishes. The dishwasher stood open but had not been unpacked and the sink was full of saucepans. Susie looked round, horrified.

Anna, seeing her expression, got up from the table, and Susie saw that although it was after nine o'clock in the morning, she was still wearing pyjamas but also had on a pair of dirty rubber boots. Her long dark hair was a tangled mess down her back and she looked very tired, with dark smudges under her eyes. Josh, on the other hand, looked better than Susie had expected. He, at least, was dressed and shaved. He turned stiffly in his seat and said, 'Can't get up, Susie. Too bloody painful.'

Anna came across and kissed her aunt. 'Morning, Susie.

Morning, Tom. Excuse my outfit. I haven't had time to get dressed yet. I was up with a calving in the night. Dad and I were having a cup of coffee. Do you want one?' and she went to put the kettle on the Aga.

'Here, sit down,' said Josh, pushing back a chair and tipping a pile of magazines and newspapers onto the floor.

'So how are you?' asked Tom. 'Thank you, Anna, I will have a cup if you're making one.'

'Not for me,' said Susie grimly. 'I had one at home. We've come to see what the situation is. How you are coping.' She gave the kitchen a sweeping glance, as if what she saw said it all.

'Fine,' said Anna. 'Really, really well. As soon as I'm dressed I'm going to help Len with the bulls. We've got to yard up Frank and see if he's all right after the recent shenanigans. Hey, Uncle Tom, I delivered a beautiful heifer calf last night. A real stunner. We thought we'd lost her, didn't we, Dad? She was back to front and every which way, but she's OK this morning. Up and feeding, and really strong.' She beamed at them happily as she spooned coffee into mugs.

'When does Joyce come next?' asked Susie, knowing well that it was Tuesdays and Thursdays that the young woman who cleaned for Kate turned up to bang the Hoover round and mop the kitchen floor. 'You'll have to clear up for her or she'll walk out, you know. She won't put up with all this.'

'Oh, yeah,' said Anna cheerfully, looking about the kitchen. 'It won't take me long. We got in a bit of a muddle over the weekend with one thing and another. Dad and I don't notice, do we, Dad? Happy as pigs in shit, we are.' She passed Tom his coffee and stuck a teaspoon in the packet of sugar.

'So what's the score, Josh?' asked Tom. 'Phil telephoned this morning to offer us a bit of help with the silage, but I said I'd see what shape you were in. Do you think you can drive the tractor?'

'I'm sure I can,' said Josh. 'I'll be fine when I'm up in the cab. It's just moving about that hurts. I'll do the rolling, if you and Anna can get the sheets and the tyres on. I don't want to take Len off the cows because what with milking and the calves and calving, he's up to his eyes. If he can't manage, we'll have to get a relief milker in.'

'What about the rest of the hay? The forecast looks good for the next few days. We need to get it turned today and tomorrow and baled on Wednesday.'

'I should finish the silage by lunchtime and I'll go on down and start turning this afternoon.' He gestured towards Anna. 'Having this girl at home to lend a hand is what has saved the day.' Anna grinned back at him and took a mock bow.

'What about your job?' Susie asked her. 'Can you just take time off like this?'

'I telephoned my line manager this morning. Explained it was a family crisis. She was very understanding. I can take until the end of the week if I need to. It will have to count as holiday, but there you are. The weather's so lovely and I'd far rather be down here, out in the sunshine, than at work.'

'I don't think your mother would be at all happy with any of this,' said Susie. 'She wouldn't want you to give up your holiday, Anna, and I really don't think you should be driving the tractor after being concussed, Josh.'

'So we don't tell her,' said Anna blithely. 'Dad and I decided that yesterday. We don't want her worrying.'

'Don't you think she ought to know?' persisted Susie.

'I'd certainly want to be told if Tom had what could have been a very nasty accident.'

'But it wasn't,' said Josh, rather irritably. 'That's exactly the point. It wasn't a nasty accident. I am perfectly all right apart from a few bruises. I've been knocked out so often that I can't get excited about minor concussion. I fell off ponies onto my head on a regular basis as a child and knocked out any brains I had left playing rugby. Really, Susie, there's no need to worry about me. Kind though it is of you,' he added.

Susie drew in her breath and made a disapproving mouth. 'Well, I think you are being very stubborn and silly,' she said. 'I think you should let Kate know and then she can make up her own mind.'

'But we know what she'd do,' exclaimed Anna. 'If we told her, she'd be on the next train home and we don't want that, do we, Dad?'

Here we go, thought Susie. Ganging up and treating me like a fool and an outsider. She glared at Tom for support but he was poking about in the biscuit tin and refused to catch her eye.

'Tom,' she said sharply. 'What are you doing in that tin? You've only just had breakfast!' He looked up and smiled at her disarmingly.

'Have I? It seems a very long time ago to me,' and put a chocolate digestive in his mouth.

'I'm off to get dressed,' said Anna. 'Len will be waiting for me. I don't think he'd appreciate my pyjamas.'

'Give him a heart attack more like. He'd never get over it,' said Tom.

Anna paused at the door and said to Susie, 'Don't worry, Susie, I'll clear up in here this evening. I promise I won't let the mess force Joyce to take industrial action,' and she whisked out with a cheery wave.

Susie was left feeling dissatisfied.

'So what can I do to help?' she asked finally. 'Are you all right for food? I know it's no use asking you for meals because you won't come, but I can leave something here for you to heat up.'

'That's kind of you, but I think Kate left the freezer bursting with rations for me. I'll get into trouble if I don't use them,' said Josh. 'She'll take it as a personal insult if she gets back and finds I've spurned her frozen shepherd's pie.'

'Well, what about shopping? Do you need anything?' asked Susie. 'I'm going into town later on.'

'Oh, wait a minute. She said something about fruit. She said we'd need some fruit during the week. Could you get some apples and bananas, maybe?'

'Of course,' said Susie. 'What about veg?'

'We've got plenty in the garden. Thanks anyway, Susie.' Josh made an effort to be nicer. 'By the way, George enjoyed his lunch. It was kind of you to have him and the colonel. I expect you heard the same old stories for the hundredth time. They're both as deaf as posts so they don't bore each other.'

'It was nice to have the company,' said Susie pointedly. 'We'd have been living off that casserole for a week otherwise.'

'Have you seen George this morning?' asked Tom. 'I thought he sounded a bit odd on the telephone last night. A bit distant. Must have been a shock for him, finding you like that.'

'He telephoned not long after we got back from hospital but managed to refrain from saying "I told you so". I'm surprised he hasn't been in this morning, come to think of it. He doesn't like Kate being away, that's the thing. She spoils him, as you know, so it's put his nose thoroughly out of joint.'

Both men chuckled, and then Tom said, 'Is he doing anything to help? I think he's better with a job to do. It gives him something to think about.'

'He's feeding the dogs in the evening and doing Kate's chickens last thing. There's not much else he can do. He certainly can't drive and I don't like him in amongst the stock. He's not steady enough on his feet. Give me a hand up, will you, Tom? I'm ready to start, if you are. You may have to get behind me with the pitchfork to get me into the cab but I'll be fine when I'm up there.' Painfully, he got to his feet.

Tom turned to Susie. 'OK, darling? I'll be back at lunchtime.'

Susie nodded. She managed a smile and as Josh moved slowly across the kitchen he said, 'Thanks, Susie. Thanks for your concern.'

Left alone, Susie stood looking at the mess again. She really would not know where to start. She wondered how a girl like Anna could be such a slob in the house. You couldn't expect men to tidy up, but she would have thought a girl would have made some effort to keep the place under control.

Perhaps she should just unpack the dishwasher while she was here. She had guests turning up for two nights but they would not be arriving until late afternoon. She was putting the first lot of clean mugs in the cupboard when Anna came thumping downstairs wearing shorts and a T-shirt and working boots. She had tied her hair back under a red scarf, worn in a triangle, like a peasant. She saw what Susie was doing and came over and put an arm round her and gave her a hug.

'Thanks a lot, Aunt Susan,' she said. 'You're a star. Don't do anything else. Please, promise me.' She picked the suncream off the table. 'Now I'm off to the bulls. Honestly, the size of their bollocks makes a poor girl feel quite faint! Hey, will you come and see my calf before you go home? She's so beautiful,' and she clumped out of the kitchen, whistling cheerfully.

Susie carried on with what she was doing. Her heart felt lightened from the tight band of unhappiness that had been constricting it all morning. It was better to be useful, to help people, she thought, than dwell on what could not be changed. Anna had made her smile. It was nice that she joked with her, treated her almost like a friend.

She finished unpacking the dishwasher and started to load it with the dirty crockery piled up on the counters. She retrieved the dish licked clean by Patch and wedged it in the machine.

It would not take her long to get the place a bit straight and then she would fold the pile of ironing and give the floor a quick sweep. There was something rewarding about doing Kate's job. She knew this was partly the smug satisfaction of being virtuous. She imagined how it would make Kate feel when she heard that while she was swanning about on holiday, Susie had been doing her housework. Susie couldn't help but be a bit pleased at the prospect, but she was also glad to be able to help, to be involved in the crisis, to be part of the team. Thinking about this made her realise that she felt touched that Anna wanted her to see the calf. She didn't think anyone had ever suggested that she might be interested in anything like that before.

She was pegging out a line of washing she had found

247

wet in the machine when she saw George cross the yard. His head was down and his shoulders stooped and he seemed to be hurrying. He did not see her but there was something about him that alarmed her. She realised that he looked preoccupied, sunk in thought, not his usual self which would have meant taking his time in the hope of bumping into someone in the yard. There was nothing he liked more than the excuse to stop and have a little chat about what was going on on the farm.

Susie watched him disappear round the corner. It was strange that he hadn't called in to inquire about Josh. She would have expected him to want to be in the thick of it all. Thoughtfully, she continued pegging out the clothes. When she finished she would go and see Anna's calf and then get on into town, but this afternoon, when she was organised at home, she would call in on George and see if she could find out what was the matter.

Elspeth held out her arms in the sunshine, admiring their slimness and pleased to see that they were turning very slightly brown. A pretty colour, she thought, like a milky cappuccino. She valued her fine, smooth skin and had no intention of overdoing the tanning. In her view, the weathered look was not flattering on an older woman and the saddlebag complexion seen so often in the south of France was positively terrifying. Nevertheless, she would like to go home looking healthy and be rid of her London pallor.

Indeed, she did feel well and rested. There was no doubt that this was a relaxing holiday. She was enjoying the long slow days, the leisurely meals and the peace and quiet of the wooded hills. She was sleeping well, which was un-usual for her, and the nights were dark and utterly silent.

There were wonderful stars, of course, all the more start-ling because of the velvety blackness. She thought with distaste of the yellow glow that hung all night over London and the ugly green half-light that seeped into her flat and made it feel like a gloomy aquarium.

She did not want to think about her situation, not while she was on holiday, but now she had started on that train of thought it was hard to stop. She was immediately aware of a downward drag on her spirits and knew that the familiar scenario would play through her mind until she gained control and shut it off. She should be grateful that Archie had helped her to buy her flat outright and that it was in a pleasant part of central London but recently she had felt almost like a stranger in an area in which she had lived for thirty years.

She had the horrid realisation that it was not only that London had changed, become an uglier, dirtier, more violent place, but that as she got older she was losing her place at the heart of things. When she was younger it had seemed that all the delights of the city were at her disposal. She went out at night, ate at fashionable and expensive restaurants, bought clothes from exclusive shops. There was always a wealthy and admiring man to spoil her. These days, with dear Archie almost housebound and most of her friends from her days at the House of Commons retired and moved away, she felt increasingly alone.

It was loud-mouthed young people in their hideous trashy clothes who ruled the roost these days. Media people, City people, property developers, who talked a language she hardly understood, they were the new aris-tocracy. She didn't like their bars, their trendy faddish restaurants or their absurd designer shops but she had to recognise that things had moved on and that she had been left behind. This was no surprise. In fact it was what one expected as one got older, but she regretted the changes and the sense of the city becoming an alien place and her own part in it shrinking and dwindling.

As a guide, she could still talk confidently of the wonderful landmarks, the historic sites, the palaces and parks, the churches, the galleries, the exhibitions – these were unchanging, it was everything else that seemed to have shifted and altered. She had begun to wonder if when she retired she really wanted to stay in the flat. She had always considered herself a true Londoner but now she began to question what it would be like to grow old and possibly infirm and at the mercy of the creaking National Health Service. It did not take a genius to see that the over-crowded doctors' surgeries and beleaguered London hospitals were stretched to capacity. She would be hard up, she knew that, and what would it be like to eke out her savings, penny-pinching, scraping along and for God knows how long? Old people lived for ever these days. And if not London, then where? She had no family, an only child, parents long dead, no ties anywhere, only Harry in America and she had no intention of landing on his doorstep.

These were gloomy thoughts and she tried to resist them but she knew that sooner or later they would have to be confronted and addressed. She had no idea what the solution would be, had to trust that something would become clearer as time went by, and of course it was Archie who kept her in this state of suspended decision-making. While Archie was still alive she would stay where she was. Archie was at the centre of it all.

She was well aware that his two daughters were jealous and suspicious of her, but she had long known the contents of his will and they had nothing to fear. Indeed, they should be bloody grateful that she had behaved as honourably as she had. He was providing her with a small allowance and a painting from his considerable collection. She had chosen a small bright landscape by a relatively unknown Spanish artist and Archie had nodded his approval.

'Wise choice, my dear,' he had said. 'He's not so fashionable at the moment, but he will be. Think of this little picture as your nest egg.'

'You silly old thing,' she had said. 'That's not why I want it. I chose it because it looks exactly like the heavenly view from the window of that parador we stayed at outside Salamanca. That was one of the happiest times and whenever I look at it, it will cheer me up and remind me of you.'

'A wise choice all the same,' persisted Archie, a canny old Scot. 'You can't live on sentiments and you never know, you might need to sell it one day.'

Elspeth thought of that landscape now as she looked at her own painting set on the easel in front of her. She knew what she wanted to achieve, a sense of heat, of light and shade, of the dry earth and the hard sky, but she also wanted somehow to capture the vigour of the place. True, the heat made one feel lazy, torpid almost, but there was also a heightened awareness of being alive, as if one's pores were opened by the sun to receive every sort of reviving, revitalising sensation. It was a bit like being a car and running low on petrol, she thought, and then having one's tank refuelled. She wasn't altogether pleased with this analogy, because as a pedestrian who had never owned a car, she rather disliked them. Maybe it was more like being a lizard, mopping up the sunshine, but this made her think of wrinkled reptile skin and the wide-eyed, wind tunnel stare of the serial face-lifted. In simple terms, this time to relax, to observe, to paint, to eat simple, delicious food and drink lots of wine, had replenished her spirits and revived her senses.

She was not going to spoil this pleasure with gloomy thoughts about the future and, looking hard at her painting, she tried to work out what it was she should do to suggest this source of vitality that ran like a mineral vein through the place. Perhaps her colours were too wishy-washy, too tentative. Perhaps she should be bolder. After all, it was the glowing colours and the strong brushstrokes of the little Spanish painting she loved which made it come alive, that gave it its optimism and its power to reflect intense personal memory.

Taking up her brush she was about to begin again when the sound of a noisy vehicle on the road below the farmhouse caught her attention. Peering downwards through the trees, she saw a truck pull into the courtyard and a man get out and slam the door. A brown and white spotted dog, some sort of retriever, jumped out of the back and ran to lift its leg against the pots of geraniums, as Jean-Luc appeared from the barn and greeted the visitor. Then Elspeth realised who he was: Bernard, their neighbour, the rather jolly builder she had sat next to on Saturday night. After some discussion, she saw Jean-Luc gesture up the hillside and then the two men went together into the house.

Thoughtfully, she turned back to her canvas.

Below the farmhouse, Kate also saw the truck arrive, winding up the road beneath her in a cloud of dust and then turning through the gates of the farmhouse. Shortly afterwards Patrice appeared on the path from the house, carrying a stool and a large sketchpad. She was not surprised to see him. She had thought he would come.

'This is a good place you have chosen,' he said, positioning his stool on a flat piece of ground, the habitual cigarette stuck to his lip. 'It is the arrangement of roofs, trees and the hills beyond that is interesting.' He gestured with his arm towards the landscape.

Kate made a noise suggesting agreement. What he had said seemed like a compliment but she was not altogether sure that she welcomed his company. It made her feel on edge and one of the things she enjoyed was the chance to be alone, to paint in silence.

After a promising start, she was dissatisfied with what she had achieved. Her picture was frankly boring, like a painting copied from a postcard, and she did not know how to make it more expressive. The colours and forms were technically quite accurate but they didn't convey what she felt about what she saw or what she wanted other people to see, and now she felt uneasy with Patrice sitting beside her. He would surely notice that she was stuck, just twiddling and tweaking, not getting on with it, and then there would have to be a discussion which might be embarrassingly personal.

She watched him from under her lashes. He was sketching fast, one brown arm resting on the page, the other moving the pencil across it. Two of his fingernails, she noticed, were rimmed with paint, the others clean and healthily pink. The rolled-up sleeve of his linen shirt was splattered with white paint. He was concentrating, breathing quite heavily through his parted lips, his eyes darting from the view to the page. He seemed to be totally immersed in what he was doing and it was as if those long fingers had never touched her neck or that hand reached out to hold hers.

What exactly is going on? thought Kate. How can he suddenly retreat from me? A short while ago she thought that she occupied his thoughts in some way, that he had some sort of intentions towards her. Now he sat a few feet away, apparently unconscious of her presence. Here they were, alone, hidden from view, and she might have expected him to make some sort of move. She found that she was disappointed and that she wanted to reach out and touch his long denim thigh, to draw his attention back to her.

Whatever is the matter with me? she thought. This is just lust that I'm feeling. I suppose I ought to try and suppress it, behave properly, but I don't want to. What harm can it do? Instead, she shifted her seat and tried to concentrate on her painting, but could not stop thinking about Patrice. Really, he was the exact opposite of Josh. Expressive, creative, sensuous, sociable, and probably unreliable, fickle, tempestuous, too. She imagined he would be good in bed, good at sex. She had a sudden clear picture of lying naked in his arms, feeling slaked and satisfied while he smoked a post-coital cigarette.

It had been ages, years, probably, since she had thought about exciting sex. She and Josh had grown lazy and undemanding. He was usually too tired and she was too bored. She would rather put on her night cream and read her book. They didn't think of each other like that any more, there were too many other things to deal with. Money worries, the children, the farm, her father, they all took up too much time and energy. What had started out as being such a powerful force had dwindled away until they were bound together by all the other things that had grown up between them over the years and sex was not important any more.

This was normal, she thought, in a long marriage. Despite the barrage of sexually explicit stuff that was churned out relentlessly by the media, surely sensible, grown-up people didn't believe it to be the be all and end all? Lack of it didn't mean that they didn't love one another and she certainly didn't blame Josh for fancying her less. She had lost confidence in her body as she had got older and was conscious of sagging and puckering flesh and all the other signs of ageing. She didn't feel she was sexy any more, which made Patrice's interest in her the more intriguing and the more delightful.

What I want, she thought, as she rummaged about among her tubes of paint, is for him to make love to me. I am very surprised to find that I want it very badly. It's got nothing to do with real love or even affection. I like him because he's charming and attractive but I don't want a relationship with him. God, think of poor Julie. Who would want that?

Patrice was sketching fast, moving between pencil, charcoal and chalk, flipping over the pages of his sketchbook. He drew beautifully, thought Kate enviously. With a few deft lines he captured the shape of a tree, the winding path, the angle of a building. She watched for a while, transfixed, until he suddenly put down his pencil and said, 'Now,' as if he had just become conscious of her. 'What is the matter, Kate? Your painting is not progressing?'

'No, it isn't. Not how I want it to, anyway,' she confessed.

He got up from his stool, propping his sketchbook carefully against a tree, and came to stand behind her. He said nothing and Kate, embarrassed, blurted out, 'It's so flat and dull. It has no expression . . .' she tailed off.

'No,' he said after a long wait. 'I think you are wrong. It is quiet, not dull. It is gentle and shows an affection for these things you paint, the old cart, the broken chair by the barn door, the chickens. These are the things which interest you. I can help with some of the problems – we can increase the quality of the shadow here and here, and the roof is perhaps too much drawing the eye here. We can work on this. No, you should not be disheartened. Your painting speaks of you.' He dropped both hands on her shoulders.

This was what Kate dreaded. She would now have to try and explain how it fell short of what she wanted to achieve.

'It's too restrained. I want it to be more emphatic, to speak more strongly of the lives led here, the hard work, the heat, all the human stuff that has gone on in this old house. Sadness, happiness, birth, death, love, hate – all of life, I suppose,' she finished lamely.

Patrice said nothing. He moved his hands from her shoulders and indicated that she should get up. She did so, thinking that he wanted to take her place in front of her easel, but he caught her arm and turned her towards him.

'Ah, Kate,' he said, taking off her hat and dropping it on the ground and moving her hair from her hot forehead. Gently he drew her to him and put his arms round her. She felt foolish, standing there with her own arms by her sides so she encircled his waist, loosely, not wanting to press against him.

'Kate, Kate,' he said again, softly. 'My lovely Kate,' and he lifted her chin with a finger and looked into her eyes. 'You have, I think, a more passionate nature than I had supposed.'

She blushed. Just get on with it, she thought, imagining

he was going to kiss her, but the next moment he sighed and released her. Embarrassed and confused she moved away and then bent to pick up her hat which she found he had been standing on.

When Elspeth came down off the hill, very hot and feeling dusty and thirsty, despite Patrice having appeared halfway through the morning with lemonade, she was pleased to discover lunch already set under the vines. Nobody was about although there was a clattering from the kitchen and she went up to her room to wash and re-apply her make-up. The heat was making her hair behave oddly, lying flat and limp in what she thought was an unflattering way, so she tied a kerchief round her head which perked things up satisfactorily, and sprayed herself with scent. She turned this way and that in front of the glass and was pleased with what she saw.

When she went downstairs she was glad she had made an effort because the men had by now gathered at the table, including Bernard, who got to his feet and kissed her hand gallantly and indicated that she should sit beside him. He filled a glass from the carafe of white wine on the table and handed it to her. Taking up his own, he clinked his glass to hers as if they were sharing a toast. His stout body, his chest like a drum, looked comfortingly solid in his blue workman's shirt. He would be a nice man to lean against, thought Elspeth, and she liked his sunburnt face with its generous features and lively brown eyes and the swept-back thick curly hair going a distinguished silver-grey. It was a big, good-humoured face without being peasant-like or coarse. If she were a casting director, she could easily imagine him as a twinkly peer of the realm in ermine robes, or a benevolent captain of industry or a rather jolly bishop.

She smiled back happily and looked round the table. Patrice, barefoot as usual, as tall and lean as Bernard was barrel-like, was cutting a loaf of country bread into thick slices, and Jean-Luc was gathering up some papers which had been spread about the table and putting them back in a document holder. Monique came in and out from the kitchen with plates and a bowl of salad. From her sleeveless blouse her underarm hair sprouted thick and dark as she reached across the table. Slightly off-putting, thought Elspeth, but what one expected from the French. There was no sign of Kate.

Julie emerged from the kitchen looking hot and shiny-faced, carrying a dish full of golden, freshly fried squid. She stood holding it, wearing a martyred expression, until Patrice, without a word or a look, took it from her hands and put it on the table, at which, as if dismissed, she turned and silently went back to the kitchen.

A moment later, Kate appeared looking rosy-cheeked and pretty. Her shiny curling hair, the whiteness of her teeth and the faded pink cotton shirt gave the impression of natural good health. This holiday is doing her good, thought Elspeth, watching Patrice pour her a glass of wine. She looks really well and happy.

'George!' called Susie, knocking on the open door. 'Are you there? Dad?'

There was no reply so she went in. The kitchen was tidy and empty, the table cleared, the floor swept. The newspaper lay on the counter, still folded and unread.

'Dad?' Susie looked into the sitting room and saw George sitting in his armchair by the open French windows. He's having a little afternoon doze, she thought, but then realised that his eyes were open and he was staring through the windows, but in an unseeing way, as if his mind were far off. The expression on his face was one of deep sadness and for a moment Susie was frightened. Such grief was private, surely. He would not want to show that terrible, revealing face to anyone, least of all to her. He would want a moment to recover himself after he realised that she was there.

She backed out of the doorway, her heart thumping, and stood inside the kitchen, feeling awkward and wondering what to do. She was tempted to creep away, unnoticed, pretend she hadn't seen, maybe send Tom down later on to find out what the trouble was. But Tom was so busy and he might make an excuse, say she was imagining things. No, she had better go through with it now she was here.

She tapped lightly on the sitting room door and called again, louder this time. 'George? Are you there? It's me, Susie.' She heard a shuffle from the chair and then the sound of the old man getting to his feet. It was safe now for her to appear and when she looked round the door she was relieved to see that George looked much the same as usual and the terrible expression had left his face.

'Oh, it's you,' he said. 'I didn't hear you come in.'

'The door was open. I knocked but I don't think you heard. Look, I've brought you a bit of quiche for supper. I've left it on this plate, here. I'll put a teacloth over it to keep off the flies.'

'That's very kind of you,' said George stiffly. 'You shouldn't have bothered. I've got a bit of ham in the fridge.'

'Would you like a cup of tea? I could do with one. It's still so hot. It's funny, isn't it, that tea is so refreshing?'

Susie prattled on, not knowing how to introduce the questions she wanted to ask.

'Well, I usually have one about now,' he said. 'Then I'll be back up to the farm. I told Josh I'd feed the dogs.'

'I'll put the kettle on then,' said Susie, grateful for something to do. 'Have you seen Josh today? You've called in, I expect.'

George looked shifty. 'I didn't. Not this morning. I had work to do with the sheep.' Damn, he thought, next thing she'll be telling Tom. What does she want, poking her nose in, asking questions?

'What are you doing? They've all been sheared, haven't they? It's hot for you to be working out in the field.'

George turned away, mumbling something about fly strike. The woman was so ignorant he could tell her anything to get her off his back.

Susie finished making the tea and put the mugs on the table.

'Biscuit?' she asked.

'There's a cake in the tin. Kate left me a sponge cake.' He pointed to the cupboard and she reached up and got out the old green tin. She cut two slices and put them on tea plates, and while George tried to eat, although the cake felt like ashes in his mouth, she went on talking about the accident, about Anna staying to help, about the silage and about the haymaking. He tried to respond as she would expect him to but she was making his head swim with all the talk and all the questions. Finally he heard her saying, 'So I wondered if there is anything wrong. I thought I must come and ask and see that you're all right. You haven't had any bad news, have you?'

'Bad news?' he said. 'What bad news?' She had confused and alarmed him now.

'I just hoped you weren't worried about anything. That you would tell me, if you were. With Kate away.' Susie started to flounder. George was staring at her across the table.

He realised that she was on to him, that she had noticed his altered behaviour, but instead of interpreting her questions as concern for him, he saw them as provoking and inquisitive.

He pushed away his mug and stood up. 'I don't know what you mean, Susie,' he said. 'I don't know what you're carrying on about. If I need help, I'll ask for it. Or advice, come to that. Now, if you've finished that tea, I'm going on up to feed the dogs.'

Susie, her cheeks blazing, knew she was dismissed and collected the mugs to rinse them under the tap. You horrible, rude old man, she thought. That's the last time I trouble myself over you. Rise above it, she told herself. Don't get upset.

'Well, I'm glad I was wrong. Obviously,' she said in a deliberately bright tone. 'And don't forget the quiche for your supper.'

George followed her out of the kitchen door. 'I can't eat pastry at night,' he said as she got into her car.

Bugger off, then, she said to herself as she drove away.

Much later Anna and Josh sat at the kitchen table on Dancing Hill, eating beans on toast in companionable silence. They both felt extremely tired and Josh knew that he had overdone it. His head ached and every time he moved his ribs screamed, but the silage was finished and that was the important thing. They had spent the afternoon haymaking which, if the weather held, they would finish tomorrow. The forecast was good and the evening

261

sun had dwindled in a sky turned fiery gold.

Anna had lost count of the number of old tyres she had hauled into place, most of which had been half full of winter rain which had tipped out and run down her arms. Her shoulders and back ached and as soon as she could summon the energy she would go and lie in a hot bath. Her last job had been to check on the new calf, who was now firmly on her feet and butting greedily at her mother's udder. Tomorrow they could be turned out in the nursery field behind the barns. Anna had traced the white heart-shaped mark on her forehead and the little buds where her horns would grow. Her silky coat was smooth and soft and her large, liquid black eyes were bright. She was so brimming with life that it was hard to believe that such a short time ago she had only hung on by a thread.

'Another beer, Dad?' she asked, getting up.

'Please,' he replied, wincing as he turned in his seat.

'Susie sorted us out this morning,' said Anna, her head in the fridge. 'Wasn't it kind of her? We'd let things get in a bit of a mess, you and me.'

'She was longing to put her oar in though, wasn't she? Longing to interfere.'

'Dad, that's so unkind,' protested Anna, coming back with the cans. 'She was just concerned, that's all. What's more, she just got on with it. Did something practical to help. She was really sweet about the calf. She spent ages admiring her.'

'I know. You're right. I'm grateful, really. We've got Joyce coming tomorrow, haven't we? She'll get us straight.'

'Actually, we haven't. There's a message on the answering machine. Her little girl's ill. She'll try to come in later in the week.'

Josh groaned. 'Bloody hell! What next? Is there anything else that can go wrong?'

'Honestly, Dad, don't be so gloomy about everything. Poor Joyce, you should say. Or poor Joyce's little girl. We can manage if I make a bit more effort to clear up as we go.'

'I suppose so.'

They sat in silence again, drinking their beers from the can.

Anna wondered if this was the right moment, and then encouraged by the companionable atmosphere between them, she said, 'Actually, Dad, there's something I've got to talk to you about. Something important.'

It was later still, after they had sat and talked at the table for an hour or two, after she had argued and explained, implored and even at one stage burst into tears, that Anna eventually got out of bed and stood by the open window. Outside, the dogs were barking frantically in the yard, the high-pitched almost hysterical bark that always indicated trouble.

Pulling on her old towelling dressing gown, she went out to the landing. Her father's door was a little open and she could see that he was sitting up in bed, sound asleep, doped by alcohol and painkillers.

Barefoot, she ran downstairs and unlocked the back door. The moon was bright and the yard was filled with silver light. The collies were leaping at their netting, twisting in the air and falling back. Anna stopped to pull on her work boots and then, with the laces untied, she ran outside. She couldn't see what had upset the dogs, could not see anything out of the ordinary, but as she struggled with the rusty bolt to open the door of the run, she heard what had disturbed them. Suddenly as frantic as they were, she threw back the door and they burst out and flew screaming across the yard. She ran after them, shouting, knowing where to go, dreading what she would find. A few paces short of the gate into the back field, she trod on one of the flying laces, tripped, and unable to save herself went headlong, face first onto the concrete.

Chapter Eleven

When Anna limped back into the kitchen she was an alarming sight. She had ripped the knees out of her pyjamas and shreds of cotton now stuck to the bloody mess. The palms of her hands burned and smarted and she had skinned an elbow. A split lip had swollen and stiffened and blood and gunge from her nose smeared her face. She sniffed, trying not to cry, but what she most wanted to do was throw herself in the kitchen chair and howl.

Her hands and wrists and the sleeves and front of her pyjamas were splattered with drying blood and she thought that she might need to be sick. Bile rose in her throat and she went to the sink and drew a glass of water and then ran the tap over her hands. She watched the water gush from clear to deep red and finally to clear once more.

She sat down shakily but the smell of blood made her feel sick again and she hurried back to retch into the sink, then yanked off her filthy pyjamas and, standing naked, stuffed the bloodied garments into the kitchen bin and closed the lid. She couldn't remember where, in her haste, she had thrown off her dressing gown. She picked one of Josh's work shirts off the laundry pile, neatly folded by Susie, and pulled it over her head.

She sat down again and examined her knees. She had forgotten how much skidding across the yard could hurt. Her injuries were reminiscent of childhood and all the spills she had had over the years from bicycles, roller skates and skateboards, resulting in agonising scrapes from which the bits of dirt and grit had to be painstakingly removed. Now, one knee was cut, lacerated by the concrete and turning black and bruised where it wasn't still bleeding. The other wasn't so bad, just red and sore with pink open grazes across its surface. She picked off some of the threads of cotton which had dried in the crusts of blood. In a minute she would have to find some antiseptic and cotton wool and set about bathing her wounds.

She shut her eyes in misery but even then the horrible scene floated across her mind. After she had scrambled to her feet and, ignoring her injuries, climbed over the gate and run into the field, the dogs were already howling away, right across to the dark hedge at the bottom where they checked and worked up and down, noses to the ground, whining and barking hysterically.

The henhouse door was wide open, as she feared it would be, and all across the moonlit grass were strewn the bodies of Kate's chickens, some fluttering pathetically, some lying still in awkward bundles of skewed feathers.

'Oh fuck, fuck, fuck!' Anna cried in anguish, and began to run between the birds, trying to work out which were still alive and which mortally wounded. A quick check in the house revealed seven or eight traumatised chickens crowded together on the perches, cocking their heads and gaping in terror. Kate closed and bolted the door and went back to the others. Although she hated to touch them, she gathered up the twitching, injured birds and laid them side by side on the grass. She would have to finish them off, bring their suffering to an end. Several had wings and legs torn off or their throats half ripped out and she could not see one which had any chance of recovery.

She searched round for something to use as a cudgel. Her mother would wring the birds' necks with a swift pull of her wrist, but Anna did not know how. She dreaded what she had to do but she had to go through with it, especially after her conversation with her father, to show that she could. Whimpering, she pulled part of an old fence post out of the hedge and went back to the injured birds. A swift bang on the head would be sufficient, but although she raised the weapon in her hand, she couldn't do it, couldn't smack it down on a living creature's head. She looked round desperately. What else could she do? The longer she dithered, the more they suffered. She thought wildly of driving the tractor over the bodies, but that seemed just as horrible. She laid out the first hen, its eye wide and blinking, despite its open throat and torn-away breast. Raising the post she banged it down on the bird's head, and again. Thank God the eye closed and the body went limp. Feeling sick, she saw that her hands were splattered with a spray of blood. The next one was worse because although one wing had almost been torn off and a leg broken, the bird still fluttered on the ground and she had to hold it down with a boot while it flapped and struggled. She began to weep silently, salty tears running down her cheeks and into her mouth, mixing with the blood from her lip.

The dogs gathered round her, back from hunting, excited by the smell of blood and causing more agitation and distress among the injured birds.

'Go away!' she shouted, kicking out at them, swinging the post to drive them off, and they shied away to sniff at the heap of dead bodies she had put to one side.

She moved down the line of birds, glad that two had died by the time she got to them, bludgeoning those that still lived until the last one was despatched and she stood up, her hands sticky, her pyjamas splattered. It was the most horrible thing she had ever had to do. Still weeping, she cast angrily in her mind for who was to blame. Whose job was it to shut up the hens? Grandpa. It was Grandpa who had said he would do it. He must have forgotten and the bastard fox had got in.

Sixteen in all, as far as she could see. He had slaughtered sixteen. Probably he had carried one away with him when the dogs chased him off. She hadn't seen the cockerel. Perhaps he had been dragged off across the fields to the earth, to the waiting vixen and cubs.

Back in the chair in the kitchen, Anna examined her injuries and blubbed like a child. She wept because her hands and knees hurt, and because of the horror of what she had just had to do. She wept because she was so tired and because her father had been dismissive about her plans for the future. She wept because someone would have to tell Grandpa it was his fault that her mother's chickens had been killed and she knew how upset he would be. She wept because she wanted her mother. She wanted Kate to be there to bathe her cuts and put her to bed, to take charge of things and restore some order, to make her father see sense. It was pathetic, she knew, to want her mother. She was nearly twenty-six, for God's sake, but she couldn't help it. When she felt as bad as this, no one else would do.

Early next morning, as George trudged up the hill to the sheep, he saw the dead hens where Anna had laid them by the gate and it took him only a moment to realise what had happened. The work of a fox was easily recognised. What took longer to comprehend was his own role in the affair and he stood, horrified, while his promise to Josh came back to him and he realised it had been left to him to shut the hens in at night and he had clean forgotten.

There were no two ways about it. It was his fault. He counted the corpses. Sixteen out of the two dozen or so fowl Kate had in her flock. Poor things slaughtered out of blood lust, the fox's love of killing, not even to feed the cubs. Of course, he could replace them, get on to Mike Gledhill who always had some point-of-lay pullets for sale over at Bishops Barton, and replace them before Kate got back on Saturday, but that wasn't the point. What mattered was that it was through his carelessness that they had met their grisly end. He had clean forgotten them and the one thing you couldn't do when you were responsible for livestock was to be careless.

He stood looking at the pathetic, mutilated bodies and realised that apart from the suffering and loss of life, what he also minded was how badly it reflected on him in the eyes of the rest of the family. Josh would never forget, never allow him to forget. He'd never trust him with doing a job again, and quite rightly, if he couldn't be relied upon. It was old age, he supposed, that had wiped it out of his mind. That, and the worry over the sheep. He turned one of the dead chickens with his stick. The fox had stripped out its throat and the ground on which it was lying was black with blood. Soon the flies would arrive. He had best get the bodies moved. He glanced up at the house but there seemed to be no one about and he wanted to clear the evidence away so that there was no reminder of his failure still lying there this morning for all to see. He wondered who had found them, who had laid the bodies out like this along the drive. Glancing at the henhouse he could see that the door was still closed so someone had been out here during the night and shut the run. Josh, probably, despite his broken ribs.

It was early still, not long after six, but George had been awake since four and was impatient to get to his sheep. Now, he would have to see to this unpleasant job first. Hurrying, he went to the cart shed and found three plastic feed sacks. He chucked the mutilated bodies into the bags and tied the tops with baler twine. Later, when he'd been up to the sheep, he would come back and bury them. He felt furtive and ashamed as he worked, glancing over his shoulder, hoping no one was observing him and glad that Len was busy in the milking parlour.

As he went back through the yard he let out the dogs who were squirming with joy at the wire of their run and they bumped against his knees, eager for a word of welcome and encouragement. He bent down to stroke old Bonnie's silky head and she licked his hand, her ears flattened in greeting, her intelligent eyes searching his face. It seemed to George that she sensed his despair and she was trying to comfort him. If only it could be so simple. If only it could.

'Good old girl,' he murmured. 'Good girl,' and then with the three dogs at his heels he began to walk up the hill. The sun was golden through the mist now, bathing everything in a warm glowing light, although the distant trees of Hanging Wood were still standing in a sea of white and he could not make out his sheep on the misty slope of the hill.

As he got nearer to the pens he could hear the ewes calling, impatient to be free to get back to the summer grass, their lambs echoing their cries. Anxiously, George looked over their bobbing heads, searching for signs of illness or distress and then let himself in amongst them, his heart filled with dread at what he might find. He began to work methodically through the sheep, catching each one in turn and examining it carefully. The ewes were large and heavy to handle and his back ached from the effort but as his work progressed, his spirits began to lift. None appeared to be any worse than the day before; if anything, most seemed a little better, the abrasions round their muzzles less pronounced and none, except old Marge, were lame. He stood up and let her struggle upright and trot unevenly away. How many days had it been? He was losing track, but he could still do the simple arithmetic involved. The numbers of sheep affected had gone up steeply since the first day, he knew that, but whatever it was that they were suffering from did not seem to have acute symptoms, at least not yet. This was not to say that they wouldn't develop later.

The lambs he could not get hold of. They moved too fast, shot between his legs, dodged away from his open arms, his outstretched hands. It would take a younger shepherd to catch them. I'm too old for this, he thought gloomily. I am an old man who can't do the job any more. He remembered Kate's chickens and felt worse. He was unreliable as well. Not to be trusted.

He felt dizzy from his exertions, from all the work bent over, and he straightened up and held onto the gate to keep his balance. The dogs lay on the ground outside the pens, watching his face and whining in anticipation of being given a job to do. Shading his eyes, George looked up the hill. The remainder of his flock were spread across the lower slopes, the presence of the penned sheep keeping them from straying up to the higher ground. From where he stood they all looked well enough but he would have to look them over properly. He spoke to the dogs and indicated that they should get to work and they sprang forward and fanned out to move the sheep down to the holding pens.

George stayed where he was and watched carefully. The lead ewe trotted down the hill, head high, and the rest followed and as they bunched to get through the gate into the pen he was able to run his eye over each one. They looked all right. He hardly dared to believe it, but they looked all right.

In the farm kitchen, Josh moved about stiffly, putting the kettle on the Aga for a cup of tea, getting the bread out of the bin, shuffling between the cupboards looking for the marmalade which he imagined Susie must have found a new home for. If anything, his ribs and bruises were more painful than ever. He knew that he hadn't done himself a favour by working all through the previous day, but on the other hand he believed it was better to keep moving. If he stopped and lay about like an invalid he would stiffen up worse than ever.

There was no sign of Anna and he mused ruefully that despite her protestations of the night before, the farmer's habit of early rising was a hard one to establish. He felt confused and disturbed by the discussion that had taken place between them. Of course, he had been aware that his daughter had flirted with the idea of wanting to farm but never for a moment had he suspected that she was serious. Three years of business studies at university and then a job with a finance house in London had led him to assume that she wanted a very different sort of life.

Farming was in such a state of decline that it had been a

relief that none of his children had considered carrying on at Dancing Hill and it was a comfort to him and Kate that all three were set on successful careers away from agriculture. That did not mean that he would not have been glad if either of the boys had been keen to take over. In theory, it would have been a joy to have a young partner, to feel that the farm was going to stay in the family, but a daughter was different.

It was true that she was capable and competent and that she had always loved the outdoor life as a child, but it was more complicated than that. Physical strength counted, for one thing. A stock farm involved hard physical labour, lifting bales and feed sacks, and working amongst beasts whose bulk could reach several hundredweight of potential danger. Look at the accident that had just happened to him. That was a case in point.

There were other implications. The unsocial hours, the isolation of living and working on Dancing Hill where it was not unusual for him to talk to no one outside the family but Len and the tanker driver for days on end. The exhaustion that set in during the winter when the incessant wet of the last few years made stock-keeping a misery of mud and disease.

It was all very well for her to think of playing at farming when the weather was good and she had successfully delivered a healthy calf, but that was nothing like the whole picture. She should know that. She had, after all, been brought up a farmer's daughter, so why was it that she had this romantic notion that she would like to take it on full time? He couldn't understand it. He had pointed out the financial implications, the loss of salary, the lack of a career structure and little hope of making a decent living in the foreseeable future. What about clothes, he had asked her, holidays, the chance to buy her own flat, her rich and varied social life? What about Richard?

She had brushed all these objections aside. Said she knew what she wanted and that she did not need to be told the downside, that she wasn't that stupid. She said that Richard would support her, that he understood how she felt, but Josh wasn't so sure. It was different when the farming was the man's job and he had the backing of a wife like Kate. True, she contributed to the farm income with her little business, but more important were the unpaid hours she put in and the fact that Dancing Hill was something that they shared.

It would not be like that with Richard. He was a city boy, a townie. He had lent a useful hand this weekend, that was true, but he wouldn't want to do that on a regular basis and Josh knew enough about men to guess that it would not be long before he started to resent Anna's commitment to a way of life he could not share and was not really interested in.

Had it been either of the boys who wanted to farm, there were enough local girls, farmers' daughters, or at least country girls born and bred, who would know what was expected of them as a farmer's wife. As far as Josh could see, that would be a different thing altogether. It was no use pretending that there was some new way of arranging this gender role thing. The reality was that farming was an occupation better suited to a man with a good wife. It didn't matter what Cherie Blair or her ilk might have to say about it. Hobby farming was something else. He knew a number of women who kept a few rare breed cattle or a small flock of fancy sheep, but if you had to make a living out of it, it was unsuitable for a woman.

He'd said all this to Anna and she had reacted by getting

angry and exasperated, telling him that he was unbeliev-able, that she hadn't heard such insulting, sexist argu-ments in all her life, that modern farming was a profession like any other and that questions about her personal or social life were nobody's business but her own.

He had shouted back not to be so stupid, that farming was not like other jobs, she knew it wasn't, it was a way of life and that being a woman made a tremendous differ-ence. 'Look at Mum,' he had said. 'She would never have wanted to take on the farm on her own.'

'How do you know that?' Anna had flared at him. 'Have you ever asked her? Of course you haven't, because it has suited you to have her as an appendage all her life. It's a male conspiracy, Dad. That's what it is! She'd be as capable as you are of running this place and you know it. No, it suits you to have her as an unpaid farmhand and house-keeper. What man,' she had spluttered, 'what man would put up with that?'

He hadn't had an answer and sat looking at her. Was that really how she saw it? He wondered what Kate would have said had she been there. Surely she wouldn't have agreed. Anna made him sound like an oppressor, some sort of tyrant, while he knew that was not the case. The arrangement between him and Kate was normal. It was how things were between a husband and wife who farmed.

They had carried on like this until, worn out, Josh had said, 'OK, Anna. Let's draw a line under this for now. We'll both have to think about it. About the implications.'

She had had to accept that. She said, 'Just as long as you know that I'll not let it drop, Dad. That I'm determined. I've started on a business plan. I've been playing around with it at work for ages, looking at the options, trying to work out a future. It could involve us all. You and Mum, Tom and Susie. The boys, too, if they're interested.'

He had to take her a bit more seriously then, but all he did was make a dismissive noise in his throat and turn to go to bed. It was too much, to hit him with a scheme like that, out of the blue. Now, as he spread marmalade on his toast, he wondered why he found Anna's idea so unsettling. It wasn't only the objection to her on the grounds of being a girl, there was also, he realised, a reluctance to relinquish his position in any way. He was too young to think in terms of moving over to make room for anyone else. For goodness sake, it felt as if he had only just sidelined George, had only just begun to farm in his own way. Having Anna on the scene, full of new ideas, would be a pain in the neck. He wasn't ready for it.

The kitchen was warm, the morning sun flooding in the window. As he took his breakfast plate to the sink he glanced out and across the valley. Down along the stream the shadows were deep and blue but the mist had started to burn off. Another perfect day but he could take no pleasure from it. Instead, he felt thoroughly discomfited. Kate should be here, that was the thing. He shouldn't be having to deal with Anna on his own, trying to make her see sense. If Kate had been here they would have talked the whole thing through and this morning as she got him his breakfast they could have discussed it again, agreed what line they would take.

Feeling irritable, Josh made himself a cup of instant coffee, moving the first aid box out of the way as he looked for the jar. Of course, he thought, that wasn't strictly true. If he was honest, he would be more likely to have lapsed into an uncommunicative mood and Kate would be trying to humour him, to draw him out, to make things easier between him and Anna. That's what she always did. The point was, however, that she should be here, just doing whatever it was she did, so that this morning he could have gone off to turn hay, knowing that when he came in at lunchtime, still morose and silent, she would have taken the burden off his shoulders, talked to Anna, smoothed things over, and little by little he would have allowed his bad mood to lift. As it was, he did not know how to deal with it.

Lifting the lid of the bin to chuck away the empty coffee jar, he saw, right on the top, a bundle of bloodstained clothing. Horrorstruck, he lifted out Anna's pyjama jacket.

'Today, ladies,' announced Patrice at breakfast, 'I have a suggestion to make. After a morning of painting, would you, later this afternoon, like to visit the gallery of Dolly in Seillans? She has an interesting exhibition opening tomorrow and we are invited for a preview.'

Elspeth and Kate exchanged glances.

'What sort of exhibition?' asked Elspeth.

'A selection of innovative conceptual work by young artists. It is called "Mutations". I think you will enjoy it. Contemporary work is always stimulating.'

'Well, I'd love to see it,' said Elspeth decisively. She always enjoyed a jaunt and was curious to see more of Dolly and where she lived.

Kate hesitated. With Elspeth committed, it looked as if she now had no option, but really she would have preferred to paint peacefully at Arc en Ciel.

'Kate?' asked Patrice, looking at her expectantly.

'Yes, that would be lovely. Thank you.' To have said that she would rather stay on her own would have caused the sort of attention that she disliked.

'That is decided then,' said Patrice, smiling. 'After lunch and a little siesta, we will set off.'

'Will we come back here to dinner?' asked Kate, dreading another meal like the last, with Dolly all but devouring Patrice and Julie suffering silently.

'Yes, we will come back. Julie is preparing paella for tonight.'

'Wonderful. I adore paella. Is it really Tuesday today?' said Elspeth. 'I don't like to be reminded that we only have three more days. It has gone so quickly. I dread to think of being back in London on Saturday.'

'But you must return to us,' exclaimed Patrice. 'Always, our visitors come back. Next time, you come as friends and you stay longer.' He looked at Kate and smiled.

She said hastily, 'I daren't hope for that. I'll just have to make the most of the three remaining days.' As soon as she said it, this remark seemed to her to be loaded with an inappropriate longing, and she blushed.

'Ah, Kate,' joked Patrice, putting an arm round her. 'It is to be goodbye for ever? I don't think so.' He withdrew his arm and stood up. '*Eh bien*, my friends, are you ready to begin work?'

'I must get my hat,' said Kate. 'I left it upstairs,' and leaving the terrace she went back into the house. The kitchen door was open and she heard Julie on the telephone having an excitable conversation in French. There always seemed to be some sort of drama going on here, she thought, unlike at home where day followed day in a predictable routine.

Tuesday was market day and Josh and Tom would be taking some steers for sale. She had sorted out the paperwork before she left. Afterwards, the two of them routinely went for a pie in the pub and a gossip with other farmers; always gloomy talk, and a chance to grumble amongst themselves. It was also the day when she would normally deliver the cakes and pies which she had made on Monday. She thought of her route round the villages, dropping off at the butcher in Sharston, the post office and general store in Alston which was making a name for itself by specialising in locally produced food, the little supermarket in Stur, the pub in Bishops Barton. She would do the same round on Friday, stocking everyone up for the weekend.

It was hard not to think about Dancing Hill in the rain as she had left it, and Josh gloomy about the hay and silage. George would be dismal too. She could almost imagine the conversation, word for word, about climate change, how unnatural it was that year followed year of wet summers and mild winters. He would reminisce about the long, hot summers of his youth and she would think, it can't always have been like that, not always perfect farming weather.

Picking her hat off the chair by the window she was drawn to the view of the green and scarlet and white of the kitchen garden where the peppers and tomatoes, courgettes and lettuces grew in such profusion out of the meagre-looking soil. Patrice and Monique were making their way between the rows, Monique carrying a blue bowl into which she was tossing black pods of beans. They were laughing about something. Patrice had donned his battered straw hat and Anna admired his broad denim shoulders and his long legs in his paint-splattered jeans. Ordinary work clothes but worn with such style and insouciance. Kate thought of Josh, in his country checked shirts and battered moleskin trousers. What was the difference? It was something to do with being easeful, she thought. That was just the word for Patrice, comfortable and easy and enjoying life. Kate could not say the same for Josh who had a permanent edge of combativeness.

Watching Patrice, she realised that Josh never strolled but always hurried and it was rare to hear him laughing these days. He was always tossing down the newspaper in disgust, slamming about because of the weather or the price of milk, struggling to repair a piece of machinery while the fools at the agricultural engineers had ordered the wrong replacement part. It was all such a struggle. There was never any time to step back and just enjoy what they had, they were always bracing themselves for the next downturn of fortune. Had he always been a prophet of doom? Kate didn't think so. Poor old Josh. Farming was full of despairing voices.

The sound of Patrice's laugh floated up to her. He was a man who seemed at ease with himself despite his irregular relationships, his ramshackle lifestyle, his tumbledown farm, his less than professional painting school. Kate could not begin to guess whether he had financial concerns or any other stressful issues to deal with. The impression he gave was that all was well and that there was plenty of room for laughter and enjoyment and that was what life was for. Perhaps it was the sunshine, she thought. Perhaps it was the sunshine which made everything seem so possible.

As Elspeth trudged up the hill she was thinking of Archie. In three weeks it would be his birthday. The invitations had gone out several weeks earlier. They had done them together, like in the old days when she had been his secretary. He had wanted to invite everyone he knew and she had to suggest gently that at his age it would be better to reduce the list, cut out the professional contacts, keep it to those who were true friends. Then she had pencilled through all those who had kicked the bucket since the last time Archie had hosted a party, and that crossed off nearly a fifth of the list.

He had watched her write the invitations and put them into the envelopes which she had printed on her word processor and then, later, he had telephoned to check that she had posted them on her way home. From then on he was in what she called 'a state', telephoning every five minutes to check that they had invited everybody.

'Archie!' she had to say. 'You've forgotten, darling. Chummy died last year. You went to his funeral. Remember?'

'Well, I'm damned! Chummy? Dead? Are you sure?'

'Yes, I am, darling. It was at All Souls'. Remember?'

'No, no, dearest. That was Budge. That was Budge's funeral.'

'No, darling. Budge died too, but he was cremated. Basingstoke. Then back to his daughter's house. We went together on the train. It was terribly cold and the vicar was a woman.'

'So she was. With enormous breasts. Was that Budge's send-off? He would have enjoyed that, wouldn't he?'

Then he started to agitate about replies, beginning from practically the day after she had posted the invitations.

'Bloody rude, I call it!' he had shouted down the telephone. 'Bloody rude not to bother to reply! I shan't invite the buggers next year!'

'Darling, they will have only just got the invitations. I only posted them on Monday.'

Elspeth smiled to herself as she set up her easel. Dear Archie. The signs of ageing were endearing in him, along with his remaining wit and the pure strain of his love for her. When she got home she would telephone the caterers and check the arrangements. Archie wanted the same format every time: a choice of spirits to drink, proper drinks he called them – champagne was only for women and interior decorators, his term for homosexuals – served with smoked salmon and caviar blinis. It was always a good old 'do', and thank God the dreary, disapproving daughters never came, although Elspeth insisted that Archie invite them. They disapproved, she knew, of what they thought of as his extravagance. Last year, one of them, Alison, married to a dentist in Great Missenden, had complained to her father of his expensive lifestyle. 'Do you know how much it costs us to send Jemima to Wycombe Abbey?' she had asked, 'and Marcus to Caldicot? Yet you don't think twice about shelling out a term's fees on a party!'

Surveying her painting, Elspeth wondered whether, when it came to it, it would be worth framing and giving to Archie on his birthday. Home-produced presents had plenty of scope to be embarrassingly awful, but she would like to give him something that she had put more of herself into, something that represented more than a quick dash through Fortnum's. From now on, she decided, she would paint with Archie in mind.

Dolly's exhibition was the most extraordinary thing Kate had ever seen. As Patrice had suggested they set off as the afternoon shadows started to lengthen, just the three of them in the battered old Citroen. Patrice had spruced up for the occasion, putting on a clean pair of jeans and a dark red shirt, sleeves rolled up as usual, and with a blue and white kerchief tied round his neck, along with his reading glasses tied on a piece of string, and it was this touch which Kate liked. The carelessness of the string prevented the scarf trick from looking poncy or precious, she thought. He drove with an arm out of the window and again pointed things out as they went, stopping once to herd some sheep off the road and a second time to take a photograph of an old house where three men were repairing the red-tiled roof.

'I like to keep a record,' he explained. 'To catalogue changes. In the winter I am going to make a painting of the area. A big work.'

Kate sat in the back, behind Elspeth, enjoying the hot wind blowing through the open window, closing her eyes as the sun flashed on and off her face as they passed between the trees. Then she must have dozed because it seemed no time at all before they were arriving, twisting through steep streets and then turning into a courtyard behind a tall, elegant stone house. Several young people busied in and out, carrying pieces of furniture to a barn, and then Dolly appeared, glass in hand, looking more bizarre than ever in a multi-coloured Spanish skirt with a looped hem and a black, bat-wing shirt and turban and enormous hoop earrings. She swooped on Patrice who embraced her fondly and then turned to Elspeth and Kate. Kate was surprised by the warmth of her welcome. The wonkily drawn scarlet mouth hovered by both her cheeks in turn as Dolly clasped her to her bosom. She smelled of scent and, faintly, of frying.

'Come in! Come in, darlings!' she cried, before reverting to gabbled French. Patrice listened carefully to her monologue, his head inclined towards her, laughing, smiling, responding really so warmly, with such interest and involvement, that Kate was struck again by what a nice man he was. Today, she noted Dolly's manner was quite different. She was no longer rapacious or flirtatious and when she put a hand on his arm it was to emphasise a point rather than make a suggestive gesture.

They made their way through the back door of the exhibition, into a tall-ceilinged room painted a pale, dove grey. It was empty apart from a beautiful, glowing Persian carpet set in the middle of the bleached floorboards and in the corner something which Kate thought a workman had left behind – a pile of rubbish covered by a rubber sheet.

It took her a moment or two to realise that this was, in fact, the exhibit, the work of art, and as she and Elspeth stood, in awe, Dolly explained its significance in a torrent of French.

The next room was neatly divided into quarters by a series of plastic-wrapped bottle shapes and in the third a rubber life raft leaned against an elegant Louis XIV chair. Kate felt a strong urge to bustle through the rooms and tidy up, but that was obviously the whole point: unexpected things in unexpected shapes in the wrong place. She struggled to take it all seriously, as Patrice and Dolly obviously did. Elspeth had wandered off to get a glass of wine and through an open door Kate could see she had found a very handsome young man who was explaining the concept behind the collapsed tent in the fourth room.

Kate turned her attention to the rest of the gallery and realised that, despite Dolly's air of dereliction, this was a well-run place. The entrance hall was stylishly arranged with some lovely small pieces of modern sculpture and the printed flyers for the gallery and the exhibition were professionally produced. I misjudged her, thought Kate, looking around. She's not just an old soak. It takes direction and drive to run a place like this.

Dolly appeared in the doorway and held out her hand.

'Come!' she commanded imperiously, and Kate followed obediently, back through the room where Patrice was helping to hang a banner proclaiming 'Mutations' in strange red letters, and up an elegant, curved staircase. Dolly's stout little legs were encased in the same laced-up boots as before and Kate was conscious of the padding of fat over her haunches as the Spanish skirt mounted the stairs in front of her.

From the first landing they entered a light and spacious apartment where a pair of long windows opened on to a roof terrace. Dolly bustled into a galley kitchen and emerged with a bottle and two glasses which she gave to Kate and went back for two more and a dish of olives.

'Before the others come, I have something to show you,' she said, leading the way into a drawing room furnished with antiques. She put what she was carrying down on a table and reached for a framed photograph.

Kate looked. An old photograph, she could tell. Two men and a pretty, dark woman, laughing at a restaurant table.

'You see,' said Dolly watching her face. '*C'est moi.* And also my 'usband, 'ere,' she indicated with a scarlet finger, 'and Patrice.'

He had been beautiful. Kate was not surprised. She looked again, smiled, shrugged and nodded. What was she supposed to say? It was an odd moment which felt almost conspiratorial, as if she was being let into a secret.

'You all look, um, young and happy. And beautiful.'

'Of course. We were.'

Kate put the photograph down and looked at Dolly, wondering what was coming next.

'I loved 'im, you know,' Dolly said. Kate wasn't sure to which man she was referring. She made an interested sort of face to tide over the moment.

'I loved Patrice and I loved Charles. Two men. It is possible, you know. Oh, you English! You know nothing of these possibilities. For you, all is front page of newspapers. Scandals and shame. 'Omosexuals! Bishops! Spanking!' She shrugged disdainfully. 'It 'as no class. The stuff of the gutter.'

'Didn't Charles mind?' asked Kate stiffly. She did not welcome this sudden intimacy between herself and Dolly, a woman whom she hardly knew and was not sure she liked.

'Why not? I did not 'urt or desert 'im. And no 'umiliation. Never. Just a little clever management. That was all.'

'Really?'

'So I tell you. If you want 'im, do it! Fall in love!'

Kate looked at Dolly in astonishment. Behind Dolly's head, a large, dirty-looking pigeon landed on the sill of the open window and looked in with a beady eye. It seemed to Kate that both were waiting for her reply.

'But I'm happily married,' she said.

Anna woke to her father shaking her. She opened her eyes and saw him standing beside the bed, saying, 'What the hell's happened? Are you all right?'

'Yeah, yeah,' she said in a voice husky with sleep. 'Yeah, I'm fine.'

'Your face! What happened?'

'I fell over, tripped on the concrete last night.' She sat up, feeling her swollen lip with a finger and then showing her father the grazes on the palms of her hands. 'My knee is worse. Ouch!' She patted at the bruised and broken skin.

'For God's sake!' said Josh, unreasonable irritation sweeping over him, replacing the awful lurching anxiety that had driven him painfully up the stairs after his discovery in the kitchen.

'It was an accident, Dad! I tripped on a bootlace. It was Mum's hens. The fox got in.'

'The fox? How? George said he would shut them up!' He stared at his daughter's face. 'You don't mean . . .'

Anna nodded. 'I'm afraid so.'

'How many?'

'I don't know, Dad. It was dark.' Anna shied away from the truth. 'A lot.'

'Bloody hell! Bloody hell! The silly old fool! God! He can't be trusted any more. He must have forgotten!'

'Dad! Anyone can forget things. I do all the time. It was something out of his routine, that's why he forgot.'

But Josh was fuming about the room, picking up Anna's hairbrush and putting it down again, going backwards and forwards to the window, his face puckered with anger.

Movement in the yard below caught his eye and he saw George and the dogs coming round the corner. He watched for a moment as the old man went slowly to the outhouse where the dog food was kept, with the collies weaving around him in expectation of breakfast.

In the light of what Anna had just told him, the unhurried figure, the lack of agitation in the slow movements made Josh angry. The old fool, pottering about like that, he thought bitterly. He's just another burden. One more thing I have to contend with.

Chapter Twelve

Although Susie felt she had every excuse to wash her hands of George, she had not forgotten that he had a doctor's appointment on Wednesday morning and that she had promised Kate that she would take him. She had quite a rush to get the breakfast for her two sets of guests out of the way, but fortunately both couples had come armed with Ordnance Survey maps, red socks and walking boots and were clearly eager to make an early start.

'The south-west coastal path,' announced one of the men as he tucked into local pork sausages and grilled tomatoes. 'That's what we are tackling today.' Susie thought his wife looked as if she would have liked to lie in a deck chair in the garden, but her husband was running a little wheel over the map, working out the mileage, and it was obvious that there was no opt-out clause.

'You've a lovely day for it,' she said to her, encouragingly, 'and there are some good pubs near where you're going.'

'Oh no,' said the man, looking up. 'We've got over twenty miles to do today. We'll not be stopping at a pub.'

'Oh, I see. Well, remember you're on holiday!' said Susie, noticing his close-set eyes and mean little mouth and thinking of the perilous clifftop paths which, had she been his wife, would have provided tempting opportunities.

The other couple were older and more relaxed. Comfortable, round people, whose walking route would lead them in and out of coffee shops and tea rooms and allow a bag of chips and a Devon ice cream on the seafront at West Bay.

Susie waved them off and set about her chores with an eye on the clock and at half past nine hurried out to her little car to go and collect George. All along the lane the gates were open and the hedges festooned with loose swathes of hay, snagged off the loads brought up to the barns. She could see two tractors moving along the big field at the bottom, leaving a chequerboard pattern of giant bales behind them.

Tom had told her that Josh had worked the last two days as usual and it made her cross to hear it. Really, he was impossible. It was all part of a martyrdom complex, in her view, and the chance to feel superior so that when, for instance, she insisted Tom stayed in bed when he had flu, she knew that Josh and George got together to have a grumble, reminding each other of how they never took time off, in George's case not since the winter of 1964 when he had pneumonia.

She had to remember it was historical, Tom told her, part of the tradition of small stock farmers who never had a holiday or even a day off, but she couldn't see what that had to do with anything. You could just as easily say that a horse and cart was a traditional way of getting about, or that they should cut the hay by hand. To Susie, it was more to do with the cussed nature of the men involved, the stupid determination not to give in, not to weaken, even when a couple of days in bed might mean a quicker recovery in the long run.

Reaching the bungalow, she drew up outside the back door and sounded her horn and when George did not appear she got out to shout for him. He must be about somewhere. Tom had reminded him yesterday that she would collect him at a quarter to ten.

The kitchen was empty, his breakfast plate and cup set on the draining board, the dishcloth draped over the tap to dry. The sitting room door was open and when she called into the bedroom she heard no sound of anyone about. She checked the bathroom. Empty. Going back to the kitchen she saw that George's cap and stick were missing. He must have gone out, gone up to the sheep, more than likely, and forgotten she was coming for him.

Annoyed, Susie checked her watch. If she drove on up to Dancing Hill she could see if he was in the yard and, if not, take the car right up the hill to the sheep pens. When it was dry the track was passable and if she found him within the next ten minutes they could still make his appointment. With a determined expression she set off.

The yard was quiet, with no sign of Len, Anna, or the dogs. Susie noticed that the same washing was still hanging on the line where she had pegged it on Monday and the back door of the farmhouse stood open. She shouted from the washroom but there was no answer and she hurried back to her car and drove round the buildings and up the track. It was not far to go, just round one curve of the hill, and there were the pens and there, as she thought he might be, was George, at work amongst the sheep. Really, it was too bad, she thought self-righteously. It wasn't only her own time that was wasted, it was the doctor's as well.

She got out and slammed the door.

'George!' she yelled. 'What are you doing? You're

291

supposed to be at the doctor's!' He didn't hear but continued bending over one of his ewes, holding her head between his hands and turning it this way and that, examining her muzzle closely.

'George!' she shouted again. Sly and Patch got up from where they were lying and came over to greet her. Bonnie remained where she was and watched, nose on paws, her tail thumping the ground.

George noticed the dogs trot off and looked up to see what had attracted them. Even when he saw Susie standing, hands on hips, he didn't seem to realise the significance of her appearance.

'George!' she shouted for the third time, tapping her watch. 'You're supposed to be at the doctor's! What are you thinking of?'

He stood up and then let the ewe go and took off his cap and wiped his brow with his sleeve. He didn't know what to say. He had forgotten. Clean forgotten. Susie came to the side of the pen, her face etched with exasperation and annoyance, but the old man's expression softened her mood. He looked stricken. That was the only word to describe it and her apprehension concerning him came back. She felt sure there was something more wrong than a missed appointment.

'Did you forget?' she asked in a gentler tone. 'I thought Tom reminded you yesterday. He told me he had.'

'Yes, he reminded me,' said George in a strange, resigned voice. 'He reminded me all right.'

'Well, it's too late now,' said Susie, looking at her watch. 'I'll have to ring the surgery. I've got my mobile in the car.'

As she went back to make the call, George stayed where he was. The ewes bunched in the corner of the pen watched him warily, those he had not yet checked stamping their feet nervously. Doctor or not, he had got to get on with the job. He had to stick to what must be done. It was more important than anything else.

Susie came back. 'That's that,' she said. 'I've made you another appointment. Same time next week.' She stood watching him. Risking an impatient answer she asked, 'What are you doing, anyway? What are you looking for?'

'Fly strike,' he mumbled, turning away so that she did not see that he was lying.

Susie was not going to give up. There was something going on and she was determined to find out.

'Tell you what,' she said. 'It's such a lovely morning, I'll walk up to the top of the field and then when you're done, I'll give you a lift back. We'll have a cup of coffee, shall we, at Dancing Hill?'

She didn't catch George's answer and, frankly, didn't care what he said, but set off up the hill. As she walked, she noticed how the toes of her trainers kicked up little spurts of dust and was surprised how quickly the ground dried out. Last week it had been waterlogged like a sponge but now it was hard and rutted. The side of the hill was ridged with the paths made by the sheep and, between, the grass was short and springy. It was old turf, she knew that, and studded with clumps of small flowers, speedwell and restharrow, daisies and buttercups.

It was steep towards the top and she felt her breath become shallow and fast and sweat trickled between her shoulder blades. She would walk to where the old iron fence skirted the dark edge of Hanging Wood. There was a good view from there and she could keep an eye on what the old man was up to.

It was twenty minutes before she puffed down again. She had watched George penning the remainder of the flock and not until she saw him turn them loose again did she start down.

'Finished?' she asked as he filled the feed troughs for the sheep left in the pens. 'Ready for that coffee? It was lovely up there. A beautiful view. There's going to be a wonderful crop of blackberries. They're growing all through the fence at the top. I must remember and come back in the autumn. I love blackberry jelly, don't you?'

George stopped what he was doing and turned to her.

'What did you say?' he asked in a strange, urgent tone. 'What did you just say?'

She stared at him. 'Nothing. I didn't say anything.'

'Yes, you did. The blackberries. You said something about blackberries.' Looking at him, Susie felt a sudden panic. What had she said? Something stupid? Something that showed her up?

'I just said that there's a good crop of blackberries this year. They're all green now, of course, but there are lots of them. The brambles have grown through the fence.'

As she spoke, she saw George's face collapse. She saw his mouth drop open, his chin sag. She saw his shoulders droop as if they had suddenly been relieved of a burden.

'That's it!' he said slowly. 'That's the answer. You've found the answer.' He closed his eyes and sank his chin on his chest and let his hands dangle by his sides in an attitude of surrender.

'What? What is it, George?' Susie asked, alarmed.

'You've given me the answer!' he said again. 'All this time, I've been trying to work it out!'

Suddenly, he was busily active again. He opened the gate to the pen and began herding the sheep out. Marge did not need telling twice. In a determined trot she was through the opening and back up the hill, her lamb bleating by her side, back to grass and freedom. The others scuttled after her, a bobbing surge of agitated woolly bottoms.

George watched them go and then turned to Susie and caught hold of her hand. His face was transformed by happiness and relief. 'Thank you! Thank you!' he said.

'For what?' she asked, laughing nervously.

'For telling me! For telling me what was wrong!'

'What? What did I tell you?'

'The sheep. What's been wrong with the sheep. The buggers have been eating the brambles!'

Half an hour later they sat at Kate's kitchen table over mugs of coffee. Relief had made George garrulous and he went over and over what had happened and Susie, listening to him, had no doubt of the strain he had been under.

'I still don't know why you didn't tell anyone,' she said. 'Surely it would have been better to let Tom or Josh know what you suspected.'

'Oh, aye, it would have taken the pressure off me, but I knew that they wouldn't bide their time and wait and see. Josh, now, he's hot-headed – he'd have been straight on to the vet and the ministry and all hell would have been let loose. Look at last time! Look at all the unnecessary slaughter, all the mistakes that were made. I couldn't let that happen, not when I was pretty sure it wasn't foot and mouth they'd got. I didn't know what it was, but I didn't think it was that.

'Trouble is, you see, in the old days I'd have walked that field, been to the top, checked the fences, kept an eye on things. That's what a farmer should do, that's the way he knows his land. These days that hill's too much for me. I haven't been up there since Josh and I went up in the

Land Rover last spring to move that fallen tree. I'd forgotten about the brambles, see. Forgotten that they would have grown through the railings since last year.'

He paused and Susie said, 'Well, thank goodness I decided to go up there this morning and then mentioned it to you. I was sure there was something wrong. I thought there was the other day. When you bit my head off.'

George looked uncomfortable. 'I'm sorry,' he said humbly. 'I was rude and ungrateful. I know that. I'm sorry.'

Susie leaned over and touched his hand. 'That's all right,' she said. 'I'll forgive you this time.'

'It's been a bad few days,' he admitted. 'What with this and then Kate's hens. You heard what happened to them? That was my fault. I was supposed to shut them up.'

'The fox got in, didn't he?' There was always a drama going on with the livestock as far as Susie was concerned. One thing after another. 'Why was it you who was supposed to shut them up?'

'I told Josh I would. I was trying to help. Oh, I know what he thinks. He hasn't said anything because I've kept out of his way. Been lying low.'

'But you're an old man!' said Susie indignantly. 'Did he really expect you to come up the hill in the dark every night to shut the henhouse door? Why couldn't he have done it? He's well enough to drive a tractor all day, apparently. Or Anna? You were the last person who should have been given that job to do. Really! Sometimes men are so *thick*!'

'Well, I told him I would,' said George simply, 'and I let him down.' He was touched by Susie's outrage on his behalf, but it did not assuage his guilt. 'Kate will be upset when she gets back. I know that for sure.'

'We can replace them, can't we? Get some more before she gets back?'

'I've already ordered some pullets from Mike Gledhill. He's bringing them over on Friday, but they won't be laying for a week or two. She'll be short of eggs until then.'

Susie looked thoughtful. 'George,' she said. 'Do you think he has any of those birds that lay the very brown eggs?'

'Marans, you mean. Or Welsummers. He might do. Why?'

'Would Kate mind if I bought a few extra to put in with her flock? I've often thought it's silly that I buy eggs when I could have them from the farm, and my visitors would love the ones with the dark shells. They would look so pretty in blue pottery egg cups on the breakfast table.'

'When I get back, I'll give him a ring and ask. Get him to put in half a dozen for you.'

'Thanks, George.' She sat back, smiling.

They looked at one another with real affection. He's not such a bad old stick, thought Susie. I feel as if I'm on his side for once.

She's a good girl, thought George. No doubt of that. A good girl.

'Now then,' said Susie, getting up. 'They've let this place get into a state again. I'm going to load the dishwasher and clear up in here, and I'd like you to go and get the washing off the line. Look, here's the peg bag.' She put it into his hands. 'And then would you mind picking me some beans from the garden? Josh won't miss them and they'll be just the thing for my visitors' dinner tonight.'

Bossy, though, thought George, ambling off with the gingham bag with 'pegs' embroidered on the side. Not that he minded. Somehow, it was a comforting feeling to be told what to do.

★ ★ ★

In the days since their dreadful battle, Charlie had fallen in love with Frank. As George had confidently predicted, now that supremacy had been established, the two bulls grazed peacefully side by side, and Frank was full of fatherly interest in the young pretender, butting at him playfully and nibbling at his shoulder, while Charlie would look up, his great brow furrowed in concern, if Frank strayed a few yards away.

Their injuries had started to heal and as Charlie's bruises subsided and his eye re-opened, it was Frank who dominated his vision, the dry cows with whom they were turned out of no interest at all. Anna stood watching the big blond bull devotedly dogging the footsteps of the smaller black Angus as he lumbered down to the water trough to drink.

'Do you think he's gay, Len?' she asked. 'A ladyboy?' They had just finished giving Charlie his last shot of antibiotic and released him from the crush, where his only concern was being separated from Frank. In the end they had brought Frank into the yard and then Charlie was docile as an old sheep, rolling his eyes to look over his shoulder and check that lover boy was still there beside him.

Len snorted. 'We'll be sending him back if he is! A nancy's no use to us. It's hero worship, that's what. After he's served his first cow, he'll get the taste for the other all right.'

Anna grinned. It was ludicrous to think of Len as a sex therapist.

'My calf looks well, doesn't she?' she said, stooping to gather up the used syringe and the plastic wrappers from the ground. 'She's grown, I'm sure. You'll be separating

298

her from the cow soon, won't you? Putting her in with the other calves?'

'One more day. I give them an extra day when they've had a difficult birth.'

Anna nodded. It was the aspect of dairy farming that she hated, when the calves were taken away. She had vivid childhood memories of the bellowing of the frantic mothers. Day and night they called for their babies, before they forgot them and meekly joined the rest of the milkers. A week or two later and they did not even recognise their own calf. Still, it was distressing and something that most people who picked up a carton of milk in a supermarket had no idea about.

'I'm off this evening, Len. Back to the big smoke. I reckon Dad can manage now, and Mum'll be back on Saturday.'

'Ah.' Len was not given to wasting words. Anna had vaguely hoped that he might say something complimentary about her farming.

'I've loved it. I've loved helping out,' she prompted.

'Ah,' Len repeated, nodded sagely. 'Your mum'll be back then. Saturday.' This was said as a statement, a confirmation.

'Yes.'

Len made a satisfied face. 'Let's hope she'll have done with gadding about. What with your dad and losing her chickens.' Anna realised that he was managing to blame Kate for both these mishaps. They were proof he'd been right. That no good would come of her going off on holiday. She imagined him sucking his teeth as he told Rita how he'd known all along.

'Reckon it's been too much for your granddad and all,' he announced in a doomladen voice.

'Why? Grandpa's all right.'

299

'Didn't look too bright when I saw him this morning. Aged ten years since your ma's been gone, I reckon.'

Anna felt alarmed. She'd been too busy to bother much with her grandfather and now she felt guilty. Len was an old stirrer but it would be awful if what he had said was true.

Leaving him to stomp round to check on his bovine maternity ward she went back through the yard to collect the tractor. She had planned to get on down to where they were haymaking and make a start on moving the bales but perhaps she would stop at the bottom of the drive and call in on her grandfather first.

As she climbed up into the cab she noticed Susie's car parked outside the back door and a moment later George himself came out, clutching a small, pink gingham bag in his hand, and started to take the washing off the line. Anna paused, amazed. Len was right. Something very worrying was going on.

'I couldn't believe my eyes, Dad,' she said later, as Josh drove her to the station to catch the London train. 'Grandpa! Doing household chores! Aunt Susie had rounded him up to help. I don't know what had gone on between those two but when I caught him bringing the washing in and went to find out if he was suffering from some major personality altering illness, the two of them were as thick as thieves.'

'Susie's had a lot of practice at organising the work force, remember. She's always getting after poor Tom. He doesn't get a moment's peace.'

'I know, but Tom's incredibly good-natured. Unlike Grandpa, who appeared to be trotting about doing her bidding. Then she asked me if I'd show her how my calf was getting on and she went out to the barn with me and was really interested. All in her sparkly white trainers. Are they on something, Dad? Smoking weed together?'

'Must be,' said Josh, halting at the junction of the main road to the station. After a few moments of waiting for a break in the steady stream of cars, he hit the palm of his hand on the steering wheel and exclaimed, 'Look at all this traffic! It's like the bloody M25!'

'It's been a lovely day. Everyone's been at the sea. Anyway, what do you know about the M25? Four cars together in a row is a traffic jam to you!'

'Why haven't these people been at work? Who can just take the day off at the drop of a hat?'

'Dad, stop being so grumpy. Just because you're in a bad mood.'

'I'm not in a bad mood.'

'If you're not, is this how you are all the time these days? Poor Mum!'

They drove in silence for a bit and then Anna said quietly, 'When I get back to London, Dad, I'm going to talk it all through with Rich and then I'll come down next week with a properly worked out projection for the farm for the next five years. A properly drawn up business plan. I'll prove to you that having me on board makes sense. All I ask of you is that you keep an open mind until then.'

Josh said nothing. Half his attention was on looking over the hedges to see how other farmers were getting on with hay and silage making, the other half was struggling to find the right way of saying goodbye to Anna and thanking her for the time and hard work she had put in, without offering her any long-term encouragement. In the end, as they drew up outside the station, there was a confusion of cars and taxis and he couldn't find anywhere to stop and all he could do was lean across and kiss her and say, 'Thanks, Anna. You were great. Saved the day.'

She accepted his kiss and then climbed out and yanked her bag off the back seat. She slammed the door shut and then stuck her head in the open window. Her bruised lip gave her mouth a sexy swollen look and, patched up with lipgloss, no longer looked the result of an accident. Her face and arms were glowing brown after five days in the sun and her hair, still wet from a shower, swung in a thick pony tail on her bare shoulders.

'Bye, Dad. Thanks for the lift.' She narrowed her eyes at him. 'I won't give up, you know,' and she was off.

Thoughtfully, Josh drove home. Anna treated him as if he were a grumpy old man, a comic television soap father. This was a surprise, in a way, because he considered that his was the generation that had kept abreast of things. Computer literate, with an ability to accept change and to understand the impact of global markets, he felt that there was not much he needed to learn from Anna's lot. What did she think she could bring to the farm, for goodness sake? That she could teach him anything at all was an arrogant assumption on her part.

Still, she had been a terrific help. Without her they would never have kept up with the round of stock work as well as everything else. She had freed him to stick to the tractor-driving which was all he could manage with his ribs buggered. It had also been nice to have her company.

Josh's head started to ache as he drove back into the evening sun. There was something about the sky which suggested a change in the weather. Mountains of violet cloud had settled on the pinkish horizon, here and there shot through by a clear yellow light. He doubted that the good weather would hold.

That'll keep this lot at home, he thought, as he waited for a break in the traffic to cross the main road onto the lane. From then on it was unusual to meet a vehicle coming the other way and if you did, you expected to recognise the driver and would probably nip into a passing place and wind down the window to have a chat as you drew level. After the next bend came the grassy triangle where the no through lane from Holbrook Mill came in on the left and the little scarlet postbox was attached to the oak tree. Whoever came to post a letter here these days? wondered Josh as he went by. There had been farm cottages along the lane, five or six families, in George's day, but they'd been knocked into two and both were now empty most of the year. Owned by London people, who came for the odd weekend. Once, Josh had been surprised to see Len cutting the grass there, but then it was in his own time and why shouldn't he? He just hoped they paid him well.

He was driving through their own land now. On either side of the lane lay the fields of Dancing Hill Farm, and characteristically Josh saw less the beauty of the landscape, more the jobs that needed doing. The ditch along the lane ought to be cleared. That could be left for the winter, and while they were at it, the field drains needed attention. Today's heavy machinery shattered the old underground clay pipes and then there was trouble with flooding. He thought of George's day when the farm employed a man just to do fencing and ditching, and kept him busy all year round.

When Josh first came to the farm, the ditcher was an old chap called Ned Parsons who lived in one of the cottages he'd just passed. Josh could see him now on his old sit-up-and-beg bicycle, a sack of implements tied on the rack at the front, his shovel over his shoulder and his terrier, Tinker, trotting alongside. Ned would take a week or two to cut and lay a hedge and it was a work of art when he had done. These days it took an hour or two to go along the lane with a mechanical slasher which mutilated the top of the hedge, and that had to suffice, along with a strand of barbed wire. The hunt made an effort to encourage proper hedging, even ran a hedge-laying competition, but not many people had the time for it any more.

Passing George's bungalow at the end of the drive, Josh noticed that the colonel's car was outside, less parked than docked, its rear end sticking out into the lane. He wondered what the two old codgers were up to, what they would be talking about as they sat side by side in the sitting room by the open French windows, whisky glasses in hand. Banging on about the past, he supposed. Reminiscing about how things had been, maybe exchanging a bit of gossip. Tony was always up-to-date on hunt news, things like how the new kennelman was getting on, and who had said what to whom at the hunt supporters' club cheese and wine party.

He thought of what Anna had said about Susie's influence, and could not help smiling at the idea of George being chivvied to help in the house. It wouldn't do him any harm at all and might encourage Kate to fuss over him less. The loss of the chickens still made Josh angry, but in a way it evened things up. He'd made a mistake with the bulls and then George had blotted his copybook big time. The pair of them had avoided each other's company since – both shamefaced, he suspected. It was silly, this sort of one-upmanship, but he supposed it was only natural when families worked together. Which brought him back to

Anna and her crackbrain schemes. As he turned into the yard and the collies ran joyfully across the yard to greet him, he looked at the barns where the giant bales were neatly stacked and the silage clamps were full, the old tyres Anna had heaved into place pockmarking the shiny black plastic, and felt satisfied.

All told, a job well done. Getting stiffly out of the Land Rover, he thought he would enjoy a quiet beer in the kitchen before having another look at the cow that was due to calve. Now things were calmer, more back to normal, he missed Kate more than ever. Susie had done a good job tidying things up, but he missed the routine Kate imposed. Supper would be on the go by now, the evening news on the radio. He would sit in the armchair with his beer and the newspaper, while she chatted about the day. She always complained that he was uncommunicative but you didn't need to be yapping on all the time to be communicating. He'd listen in silence and then throw down the paper and ask what time supper would be before he went out again.

Only three more empty evenings and then she would be home and things would be back to normal.

'Tony, I need your advice,' said George as they sat in the evening sunshine, much as Josh had imagined, glasses in hand. 'You know about this sort of thing.'

'What sort of thing?' asked Tony. 'I don't know that I know much about anything these days.'

'I want to send someone a bunch of flowers,' said George. 'You know, one of those big things with ribbons and all that carry-on.'

'Good Lord!' said Tony, looking at his old friend. 'Not smitten by someone, are you, George? Flowers for a lady?'

'Don't be a bloody fool,' said George. 'Anyway, we needn't go into who they're for. I just need to know how you go about it. Can you do it over the telephone?'

'Of course you can. Just ring the buggers up and tell them where to send them and they do all the rest. Like for a funeral.'

'But what about the card, eh? How do you get the card done?'

'You tell them what to put and they write it on the card for you.'

'So who would you go to? I'm out of touch with shops, these days. Where's a good flower shop?'

'Sure to be one in Stur. Look in the Yellow Pages. Have you got it there? Here, give it to me.' Tony adjusted his glasses and scrabbled through the pages of the directory. 'Look, there are a lot of them. Take your pick. The Flower Barrow, Blooms, the Flower People. Any of that lot would do.'

'I can put it on my plastic card thingummy, can I?'

'Of course you can, George. That's what they're for.'

'That's what I'll do then.' George sat back, satisfied. He'd get on with it in the morning. Insist on something special. Make sure the flowers were fresh.

'You're being very mysterious,' observed Tony. 'Aren't you going to tell me what this is all about?'

'They're a thank you,' said George, 'to someone who's helped me out. That's all I'm telling you, you nosy old bugger. Here, give me your glass. You look ready for a top-up.'

Tony took off his spectacles and wiped his rheumy old eyes. 'Thanks, George. Always ready for a top-up. This weather gives one a terrible thirst.'

306

Richard was at Waterloo to meet Anna off the train. He stood waiting amongst the thronging mass gathered round the departures board. Anxiety and tension rippled through the crowd as they watched the rotating electronic messages, heads tilted, necks straining, poised to make a dash for their platform when it was indicated, knowing that if they were not quick off the mark they would not get a seat. There was nowhere to sit and nowhere to throw away the empty paper coffee cup he held in his hand. One train cancelled, another delayed, a points failure outside Clapham Junction – all part of a commuter's life, and he knew that he couldn't tolerate it. If you worked in London it was better to live over the shop, he thought. Walk to work if possible and cut out this whole ghastly experience.

Anna's train was only ten minutes late and he watched for her amongst the alighting passengers. There she was. Christ, she looked well. Really brown and healthy and casual clothes suited her – jeans and flip-flops and a cotton vest and her hair just yanked up like that in a pony tail. She saw him and waved and, hitching at the strap of her backpack, dodged through the people towards him.

'You look lovely!' he said, kissing her on the mouth.

'Ouch! I've got a bust lip! Look!' She pulled at her bottom lip to reveal a crack.

'Poor darling! How did you do that?'

'Long story. Are we going to have dinner somewhere? Let's walk along the river. I've got a lot to tell you.'

Later, after they had shared two bottles of wine at a table outside a pub overlooking the sliding grey waters of the Thames, with the outline of the city as a backdrop, Richard felt as if he had been caught in a Before and After trick. Before Anna had told him about her decision, he had felt secure, full of love and unspoken plans for the future. After, he felt cast aside, adrift, uncertain, and as if all the things he had been sure about had been hacked away.

'What I can't believe is that you've made this decision without any reference to me at all,' he complained. 'I can't believe you could do that, Anna, when I thought we had agreed that we had a future together.'

'Of course we have! What I've decided has nothing to do with that. Why can't you compromise? Why can't we have a commitment to each other, as well as me take up farming? Why do the two things have to be mutually exclusive?'

'You know why. Because farming isn't like, say, giving up your job to be an artist, or a plumber, or something. As you know, it's a lifestyle choice, and it's not one I want to make.'

'Why not? It's me who'll be doing the farm work. I'm not asking you to take it up.'

'I don't want to live in the country and I don't want to commute. OK? And I'd like to see you on occasions, as well.'

'So it's all what you want or don't want, is it? What about what I want?'

'Of course I want you to be happy. I thought you were. Living in London. I thought this was where our future lay. Not shovelling shit in the sticks, anyway.'

'Well, you were wrong. I know more strongly than I know anything that I don't want to go on in my job. I don't want to stay in the city. I know I want to farm.'

'What about marrying me? What do you know about that?'

Anna hesitated. Up until now they had carefully dodged using the M word. Now it was out in the open. She looked down and twirled the stained beer mat on the table, then shrugged.

'The way you've reacted to all this . . . I don't know . . . it casts doubts, doesn't it?'

'I don't have any doubts,' said Richard quietly. 'I love you and I'd like to marry you.'

'Yeah. With provisos. That I stay on here and don't take up farming.'

'Well, yes. But not because that changes how I feel for you, but because of the obvious practical difficulties.'

'So you don't love me enough to support me in what I most want to do?' She looked up, eyes blazing.

'No.' Richard sat back. 'I love you enough, but I know that it wouldn't work out. It wouldn't be fair to either of us. Playing about on the tractor in the sun for a couple of days isn't really farming, so don't pretend to me that I'd like it if I gave it a try. I'm as sure about that as you seem to be about everything else.'

They sat in miserable silence. Anna looked across the river and wondered if what was happening here at this pub table would be something she would regret for the rest of her life. Eventually she sighed and, picking up her bag from under her chair, stood up.

'I suppose that's it then,' she said.

Richard remained sitting. 'The choice is yours,' he said, shrugging, an expression of infinite sadness on his face.

'Thanks,' said Anna quietly and leaning across the table kissed the top of his head.

In Elspeth's experience there was always a time during a holiday, perhaps only the odd half-hour, or an evening, or sometimes even a whole day, when she wished she was at home. This reflective mood hit her on Wednesday evening.

She had been painting while the afternoon light faded and had experienced a rush of energy, almost a sense of recklessness as the sun set. She was suddenly sick of being careful and of the painstaking work she had put in, fiddling about, trying to get an accurate representation of what she saw, and seized with boldness had started to apply fresh paint thickly and dramatically.

As she painted, she thought of dear Archie as the much younger man for whom she had first worked. She thought of the tenderness that had grown between them, the excitement of discovering he loved her, of the passion that they had shared and of the enduring, loving friendship that sustained them. He has been the centre of my life, she thought as she used her palette knife to spread colour, and this is for him. He has lit every corner of my life, and this is for him. As she worked, her painting started to glow with colour. It no longer resembled the tranquil scene in front of her, the rocky hillside, the line of trees, the darkening sky. It had begun to represent something else and as she painted Elspeth felt tears well in her eyes and start to slide down her cheeks.

Eventually she put down her brush and sniffed loudly, twisting her mouth and wiping at her eyes. Ridiculous, she thought. Such sentimentality. She couldn't bear weepy, whiny people. Still, she would give anything to be at home now. Or at least back in London with Archie. She would have liked to have told him that she loved him. One more time. The longing became so acute that she felt she couldn't breathe and she stood up and stretched her arms above her head to try and release the congestion she felt in her chest. Her painting was finished. She didn't want to do any more. It was crude, embarrassingly bad, but it was what she had felt like painting. She didn't care what anyone else thought of it. She could never look at it without remembering this moment when she knew with a piercing insight that Archie was the love of her life and there would be no other. That was that. Finished.

She sniffed again and began to pack away her paints, screwing on the tops of the tubes, wiping her brushes with a rag. She could hear the sound of goat bells tinkling in the distance, trotting home to the lesbians, she supposed. Down at the farmhouse poor old Julie would be chopping up something or other in the kitchen, suffering because of Patrice, and Kate would be busy resisting his charms. What fools love made of them all.

Chapter Thirteen

Anna passed a miserable evening, glad that her flatmates were out and she did not have to face anyone – though one of the good things about sharing with men was that they didn't probe one another's moods or take a huff if one of them preferred not to talk. She wouldn't have to explain too much what had happened between her and Rich, either. Relationships were simple to Jeremy and Ned. Things were either going well and they were bonking their current girlfriend, or they weren't, and they weren't, with not much in between.

The telephone rang a couple of times and each time she thought it would be Rich, but it wasn't. She roamed sadly around the flat, unable to settle. What do I want? she thought. Do I want him to ring me and say he's made a big mistake and that he has reconsidered and wants to make a go of things? She realised that she did, very much, but later, lying in her bath, she thought not. This had to happen, she decided, and better now than later. There were too many differences between them and she admired Rich for his honesty and courage in precipitating the crisis, because she knew, she really knew, that he loved her.

On the other hand, she thought as she stood with a Diet Coke at the kitchen window, looking out at the chimney pots and back gardens, if he really loves me, why can't he understand that this is what I need to do? What sort of love is it that is conditional on my conforming to his idea of me? And why should it be me who has to give up the farm, while he doesn't have to sacrifice anything at all? A feeling of indignation towards him started to mount.

She went to lie on the sofa and stared at the ceiling. She felt dissatisfied with how things had been left. They had known one another for so many years, been so close, how could they have arrived at this awful impasse, so that although she had a strong urge to telephone him, she felt that she should not? It would compromise her position, suggest that she was weakening. Which she wasn't, but God, did Rich know how much this cost her, how much she was going to miss him? He was a mate, her best friend, as much as anything else.

Of course, she could ring him now and say she had made a terrible mistake and he would come round and they would make love and the whole bloody thing would be forgotten. But she couldn't do that because she would not give up the farm and she realised that for once he would not give way however much she wheedled. There had been a new steeliness in him, a quality which she realised that she had always felt he lacked. Typical that he should show this strength on the very occasion of their breaking up.

She swung her legs off the sofa and started to prowl about again. He was right in saying that she must want to farm more than she wanted him, ergo she didn't love him enough. Certainly not to marry him. But what she didn't want was being made to choose. It seemed so unfair of him not to even consider some sort of compromise. That's what it was, unfair and unreasonable.

But still she wanted him to telephone. Why? She realised that she wanted him to tell her how devastated he was. She wanted to know how much he was suffering because he bloody well ought to be. That can't be true, she stopped herself, horrified. I can't really want him to be distraught. I'm not that selfish and horrible.

Sadly, she found she was. The only comfort she could derive from the situation would be knowing that Rich was very, very unhappy. In the end, she gave way and telephoned his mobile. It was switched off.

She sat picking at the scabs on her knees and with a conscious effort to stop brooding over Richard, thought instead about Dancing Hill. The next couple of days she would work really hard at the business proposition she had promised her father and then she would go down next weekend, maybe on Sunday, after her mother was back and had caught up with things, and present it to them.

It was exciting. Really, really exciting and she knew it could work. She imagined getting up every morning to do a job which she loved, rather than just plodding off to work because she had to. She would have to think about where she was going to live. She couldn't go back to her childhood room at Dancing Hill. Not as an adult. She had vaguely thought about renting a cottage. There were always one or two available on the nearby estate. She must put that down on her list of things to look into. She wanted to have a watertight case when she presented it to her parents. Any holes in her argument or sloppy thinking and her father would be on to it, trying to prove that she was just a blue-sky dreamer.

Shit! she thought. He can't think that. Not when he knows I've sacrificed Rich.

She stood up to go to the bathroom and, catching sight

of herself in the glass, said out loud to her reflection, 'This is the face of a girl who has just given up the man she thought she loved.' However tragic she made it sound, she looked no different. Just brown and well, even when she made mournful faces at herself. Funny that she hadn't cried, when she had been blubbing most of the last few days – about the calf, about the chickens, when she fell over and grazed her knees.

The thing is, she thought, going into her bedroom and pulling out a box from under her bed, this isn't a tragedy, it is a decision we've both made, a grown-up choice, and although I'd like to lie on the floor and cry and drum my heels, I am not a child any more. There is a price to be paid for everything and whether later on I will think I have made a terrible mistake, I don't know. I've got to have the guts to do this thing because I think it's worth it, and weeping and gutsiness don't go together. What it is, though, is really sad. A really sad decision we've had to make and I feel bereft and miserable because of it.

She opened the lid of the box, which was full of sentimental bits and pieces that chronicled her long love affair and poked about amongst them. They looked a pathetic little whimsical collection of theatre tickets and postcards, champagne corks and pebbles from beaches where they had made love. This lot will have to go, she thought. I'm not going to take all this with me into my new life.

Before she emptied the contents into a supermarket carrier bag to go out with the rubbish, she kept two items to one side. One was the invitation to a girlfriend's twenty-first birthday party where she had first met Rich, and the other was a paper napkin from an Indian restaurant on which he had written, 'I love you. Is that OK?' dating from the first time they had spent a night together.

Proof. That's what these two are, she thought, as she found an envelope in which to keep them safe. Proof that we meant a lot to each other, that it wasn't wasted time we spent together, and of course she didn't really want Rich to be unhappy. Not for too long, anyway. Standing, holding the bag in one hand and the envelope in the other, she felt full of regrets and had a terrible urge to return the whole lot to the box, to reel back the events of the evening to when things had been so good between them. Instead, she marched through to the kitchen and shoved the bag in the top of the bin. No going back.

It was too early to go to bed and too late to ring a girlfriend and go to a film or have supper. From having been glad that Jeremy and Ned were out, she now found herself craving their company. She wanted to share a beer with a mate, sit at the kitchen table and listen to some gossip, hear the boys cracking jokes, watch them cook a messy meal, feel part of something, anything rather than be alone like this, facing the enormity of what she had just done.

I've got to get used to loneliness, she thought. That's one of the things her father had told her, that she'd never stand the lack of company. Farming's a bloody lonely occupation, Josh had said, hour after hour trudging about on your own. He said she'd miss the office social life, the companionship of sharing a flat, but he didn't know how lonely London could be, she thought sadly, and anyway, isn't loneliness an emptiness that you carry around inside you wherever you are?

She wondered who she could telephone. None of her girlfriends would understand her passion about the farm because none of them shared her background. They would think she was mad to give up Rich and she didn't want to be told that now. She wished that her mother was at home. She could have telephoned her, made sure that she could talk without her father overhearing, and then she could have poured her heart out. She could rely on her to be an ally.

Grandpa. She could telephone her grandfather. Of all people, he would be the one to understand how she felt about Dancing Hill. She looked at her watch. Half past nine. She would catch him before he went to bed.

When the telephone rang, George was asleep in the armchair with the television on. It was a miracle he heard it ring at all, he told himself, as he struggled to his feet to answer. Who on earth would be telephoning him at this time of night? He picked up the receiver and when he heard the female voice he thought it was Kate.

'Kate? Kate?' he said. 'Where are you?' There was something in the voice that alarmed him.

'No, Grandpa. It's me, Anna. Mum's still in France.'

'Anna? Are you all right?'

'Yes, Grandpa. I'm all right. Don't worry, there's nothing wrong. I just wanted to talk to you.'

'You did?' George was nonplussed. As you got older, he thought, there were fewer and fewer people who wanted to do that.

'I wanted your advice, Grandpa. Have you got time?'

George harrumphed down the telephone. Had he got time? That was one thing he had got. What else did he have to do?

'You weren't going to bed?'

'Anna, love, even if I was, I'd rather talk to you.'

'Grandpa, here goes then. It's about Dancing Hill and everything . . .'

As she talked George pulled a chair out from beside the telephone table so that he could sit down. He concentrated hard, breathing heavily, and as Anna unfolded her plans, his mind began to race, to grasp the implications of what she was saying. At last, she paused.

'Grandpa? Are you still there?'

'Of course I am.'

'What do you think?'

George searched for the words he needed. 'Anna,' he said eventually, 'Dancing Hill has been Butler land for more than three hundred and fifty years, you know that. Eight generations have farmed here. You grew up with all the old stories of your great-grandfather and your great-great-grandfather. It was a sadness to me that the line would end with your mother and father, but it had to be faced, with your brothers not being interested and Tom not having children.'

'Yeah, Grandpa, I know all that . . .' Anna was impatient to get to his real reaction.

'I always knew that you loved farming. As a little girl you were the one who followed me about the farm, always wanting to help, to be given a job to do. Remember lambing up on the hill in the snowstorm? Remember bottle-rearing the orphans that your grandmother used to tuck up in the Aga plate oven down at the old farm?'

'Yes, I do.' Damn, thought Anna, it's now I'm going to cry.

'I never dared to hope that you would want to carry on with it, not with your university degree and your job in London. I thought you'd want to marry a city man and maybe end up with a house in the country, a second home like you see plenty of round here.'

Anna snorted. 'Some chance! He'd have to be a millionaire.'

'I didn't think you would want to take on the whole lot – to lead the life of a small farmer. I thought it was a thing of the past, young people wanting to do that. It was all I ever wanted to do and even when I came out of the army as a trained engineer, I never had a second thought about coming home and starting where I'd left off. It was all I could think about in the desert. Tony and I used to lie under the desert stars at night and talk about hunting – he knew the Vale as well as I did, and we'd describe a six-mile point to each other, imagine where we'd find the fox and where he'd run and which fences we'd jump on the way. It was what kept us going. I'd close my eyes and imagine I was walking on Dancing Hill, feeling the turf under my feet, hearing the birds sing.'

Anna burst in, 'That's what I do. I do that all the time in London, imagine I'm at home.'

'So if you really do want to do it, and I reckon you're a lass who knows her own mind, you should go ahead. It would make me a very happy old man.'

Anna swallowed hard. It was the longest speech she had ever heard her grandfather make. 'What about me being a woman and all that?'

'What about it?'

'Well, Dad went on and on about farming being unsuitable for a girl. It was his chief objection.'

'Then he's more pig-headed than I thought!' retorted George. 'Listen, Anna, when my grandfather and his brothers were away fighting in France, do you know who ran the farm then? My grandmother. Almost single-handed, with only a couple of men too old to fight. She did everything – running the dairy, hedging, ditching, turned her hand to ploughing with Granddad's old hunter, and it was hard, far harder, manual work than it is today. She did the lot and the place never looked better. Same happened in the last war. My father was an invalid, see. He'd been gassed the first time round and when my brothers and I went to fight, my mother took the place on and ran it with the help of two land girls. It was hard for my father to accept and he used to pretend that he was still in command, but it was my mother who did the work. Let me tell you, I've got great respect for women farmers.'

Anna's heart began to sing. 'You have? You really think I can do it?'

'Of course you can, if you put your mind to it. And I'll tell you something else. Women are often better around stock than men. They're quieter, calmer. They don't turn everything into a battle.'

Anna felt this was particular praise coming from George. His encouragement had given her the strength to tell him what had happened that evening. He would be the first person to know.

'There's one really sad thing, though, Grandpa. I'm afraid Rich and I are going to split up. He doesn't want to carry on with me if I take up farming. He told me so this evening.'

There was a long silence before George said, 'Then he's a silly young bugger.'

That morning Elspeth announced that her painting was finished.

'I don't want to do any more, Patrice. I feel it's time to stop.'

They were sitting at breakfast under the vine as usual,

enjoying the filtered sunshine and the little breeze that was skittering dried leaves across the terrace.

Patrice helped himself to a length of warm bread and dunked the end into his coffee.

'I think so too,' he said. 'You have put in it what you wanted to capture, and part of painting is knowing when to stop. I will prepare the canvas for you to take home with you on the train. For the rest of the time here, what would interest you? Would you like to visit the studio of Robert and be introduced by him to sculpture? He works in many mediums and I think you would enjoy it.'

'I would like that very much indeed,' said Elspeth. 'I thought he and Brigitte were charming. Do they live far from here?'

'Just over the hill. I will telephone Robert to make the arrangements and then I will take you there after breakfast. We will all meet later for dinner as usual.' He turned to Kate. 'And you, Mistress Kate, what would you like to do today?'

'I haven't finished my painting,' she said. 'I'd like to go on with it, if that's all right.'

'Fine, that is fine. After I have taken Elspeth to Robert's studio, I will be back to see if you need any help from me.' A napkin fluttered off the table in the breeze and he squinted up at the sky and remarked, 'There comes a change in the weather. You notice the wind this morning? The uncomfortable hot wind? It will bring rain, I suspect, and maybe a big storm.'

Kate looked up into the glittering sky which remained as blue as a beach ball between the green leaves of the vine. 'Not a cloud to be seen, but the air smells different,' she said, sniffing. 'As if it's coming from a different quarter.'

'So.' Patrice got up and stubbed out his cigarette. 'We

must make the most of it while it is still fine. Elspeth, I go to telephone Robert to give him time to prepare and then we leave when you are ready.'

'Lovely,' said Elspeth, who was getting more used to these unspecific arrangements. 'I'll just finish my coffee and then I will get my things together.'

Julie appeared at the kitchen door wearing a loose kaftan dress in a brightly coloured fabric. She nodded to Elspeth and Kate and then spoke to Patrice in a stream of French. He shrugged, pulled a face, looked at his watch and Kate gathered that she was asking him to do something and he was saying that he did not have time. Jean-Luc came to stand beside her and what followed sounded like low-intensity family warfare.

Kate and Elspeth talked quietly about the day ahead, but both with more than half an ear on what was going on behind them. Eventually, Kate saw Julie make an angry gesture with her hands and then turn to go inside. She looked as if she would have liked to slam the door. Patrice and Jean-Luc continued in lower voices and finally Patrice came back to where they were sitting and said, 'I am sorry, ladies, we have a small problem. Julie needs some shopping done and Jean-Luc has an appointment with Bernard to go and look at the old farmhouse which is being knocked down about thirty kilometres from here. They are hoping to salvage some materials for the guest accommodation we are building. This means that after I have taken you to Robert, I will have to go into town to shop.'

'Don't worry about that,' said Kate cheerfully. 'In fact, I wonder if I could go with you to town? I want to buy some little presents to take home, and I would like the chance to look around.'

'Of course, of course. That is wonderful, killing birds

323

with one stone. Elspeth, you do not want to change your mind and come with us?'

'Didn't you say that we would go to the town tomorrow evening? All the shops will be open then, won't they? That will be good enough for me. No, I would rather go and try my hand at sculpture.'

'Excellent. That, then, is settled. So, ladies, when you are ready.'

As they went upstairs to collect hats and suncream, Elspeth wondered briefly at Kate's intentions. She had quite deliberately decided not to accompany her and Patrice. Give them a bit of time together, she thought. Poor Kate. Her anxieties about her had proved quite unfounded and now the holiday was nearly over and then she would be back to her dreary old husband. It would give Patrice the opportunity to exercise his charm and would do Kate nothing but good. Poor Julie, but she couldn't do much about her. She was miserable whatever the situation and the route she had chosen for herself was never going to be a happy one.

She thought of one of Archie's sayings: 'As I totter towards the tomb, I care less and less who is sleeping with whom!' Glancing in the mirror in her bedroom, she squirted on some scent and then retied her scarf. She liked Brigitte and Robert and looked forward to a day in their company.

As Kate combed her hair and put on some lipgloss, she told herself that her motives were entirely honourable. It was ridiculous *not* to do what she genuinely wanted because she had dreamed up this *situation*, this schoolgirl thing about Patrice. No, she would go with him and enjoy an hour or so looking round the town. She loved French markets and produce stalls and would enjoy looking at the beautiful cakes and pastries, quiches and tarts from a professional point of view. She would take her notebook and jot down anything that she thought might work at home. She had perfectly valid reasons for wanting to go with Patrice and that was that.

She thought of home and her usual day spent baking for her weekend deliveries. She always quite enjoyed clearing the kitchen, putting on Radio 4 and getting down to work. Moving between the Aga and the sink she would look out of the window over the valley, down the drive to George's bungalow and beyond and feel she was at the heart of the farm. The landscape was usually calm and peaceful with only the cattle moving about the lower fields and the black and white dairy cows trooping out to grass. From the open kitchen window she could hear the farm traffic coming and going as she worked and at half past ten George would appear at the back door, hang up his cap and come in for a cup of coffee and a chat. He liked to know that he could always catch her on a Thursday morning, know for certain that she would be in. Sometimes she was too busy to stop and make his coffee, but he never made a cup for himself, even though it involved nothing more than a jar and a teaspoon of instant granules. He just sat at the table and watched her rolling pastry or beating egg whites for meringues. It was the company he enjoyed.

She hoped he hadn't missed her too much. Of course, Anna and Tom were right, they could all manage perfectly well without her, but no doubt it had seemed a long week. As far as she was concerned it had flown past and she could not believe that tomorrow was their last day. She imagined a second week, a third, a whole life lived as they apparently did at Arc en Ciel. She thought of becoming part of the place, of spending the whole year up here in the hills, painting and living in the sunshine, eating with local friends at the long table under the vine. She imagined her French improving, becoming fluent. She imagined herself in the kitchen, cooking for guests, getting the vegetable garden into shape, driving into the village for bread. She imagined living with Patrice, but not as Julie, in that martyred and suffering way, but as a proper equal, a partner in the enterprise.

It was only a dream, of course, but just *say* she wasn't married to Josh, wasn't tied by her responsibilities to Dancing Hill Farm, what a different life she might have led, what a different person she might have been. For a very brief moment, a fraction before she picked up her bag and checked her purse before hurrying downstairs to join Patrice and Elspeth, she imagined what it would take to make a fresh start, to have a second chance, to leave all that familiar world behind.

As Patrice drove down from the hills after dropping off Elspeth and they turned onto the busy main road, the calm and peace of the farm was left behind. Traffic hurled down towards the sea, nose to tail, only to clog the narrow coastal road in a glittering metal snake, the sun blinding, the fumes stifling and the wind blowing clouds of dust and sand into mini tornadoes along the scuffed roadside. The beautiful, secluded villas in the foothills gave way to smaller, shabbier houses and the road was lined with fast food outlets and restaurants and stalls selling gaudy beach toys which, tethered by strings, were tossed about by the wind. Beyond the narrow strip of trampled beach the sea, as blue as the sky, was choppy and unsettled, breaking here and there into white frills of surf.

'This, I am afraid, is the summer. Always this traffic. But

soon we will arrive in the old town. First I have to go to the fish market in the Vieux Port and after we will visit the food market in the Republic Square. Then I suggest you look around the centre of the old town where there are many shops selling typical products of the area, and the beautiful Eglise Notre Dame de la Victoire de Lépante, opposite the Centre Culturel. All the streets of the old town are for pedestrians only, so you can wander at ease.'

Patrice looked sideways at Kate and smiled before concentrating again on the stop-start procession in front of them.

'That all sounds lovely,' said Kate, just enjoying being alone with him, watching his brown forearms and his beautiful hands holding the wheel. Her feeling of being suspended from normal life was more acute than ever. It came from being driven into a strange town with no responsibilities to map-read or help find somewhere to park, to go shopping but not to have to make a list or plan a meal and not to have to hurry, with one eye always on the time in the usual race to get everything done in a day with not enough hours. It came from being with this easy, handsome man, free of the nagging little familiarities and irritations that dogged any time she spent with Josh. Only one more day, she thought, and then all this will be just a memory.

'Here is the start of Santa Lucia Port,' said Patrice as the beach gave way to a forest of yachts, bobbing and bucking at their moorings in the gusts of wind, their rigging clinking against metal masts. 'One of the largest on the Côte d'Azur.' What a different world, thought Kate, looking at the glossy hulls, the complicated radar masts, a group of sleek, bronzed people opening a bottle of champagne in the cockpit of a motor launch. Palm trees lined the quayside, their branches tossing in the air like plumes and little eddies of litter twirling about their trunks. Above, climbing the hillside, the white town rose like a wedding cake.

Patrice turned off towards the fish market. 'Parking is impossible,' he said, throwing both hands off the wheel in a gesture of despair, 'but I have here an old friend, an artist, who allows me to park outside his house.' He suddenly dived across the line of traffic and pulled up outside a peeling gate behind which Kate could just see the top of a ramshackle house. She bent to collect her belongings from the floor and to undo her seat belt, while Patrice raised himself out of his seat to search in the pockets of his jeans for Julie's shopping list.

'Ready?' he asked, turning towards her.

'Ready,' she said.

Together they got out and then stood by the car waiting for an opportunity to dash across the road. Patrice, with a round basket over one arm, watched the traffic while Kate stood looking over at the crowded seafront, letting him make the decision about when to launch themselves between the oncoming cars. It seemed quite natural, quite normal that he should reach for her hand and when they got to the other side, that she should slip her arm through his.

Elspeth was enjoying her day with Brigitte and Robert. Their farmhouse, higher into the hills than Arc en Ciel, was stripped bare to stone and timber, whitewashed throughout and the open spaces furnished with simple, architectural shapes. She sat drinking wine on their terrace, chatting with Brigitte while Robert, who had given her a tour of his workshop and studio and shown her the wire sculpture he was working on, disappeared to finish some welding.

'This is charming,' she said appreciatively, looking around. 'And you also have land?'

'Ah, yes. The goat scheme. Now we let the grazing to the ladies from the cheese farm and they take care of our goats. It makes us only a very little money, but it is better than when we started and we dealt with the animals ourselves.' She shuddered. 'No, the farming life is not for us. We do not pretend.'

'I'm with you there,' said Elspeth, 'but Kate is a farmer's wife. Did you know? And a farmer's daughter. She is very keen on animal husbandry, but not me. I'm a Londoner to the core. I like police horses and the Household Cavalry and those lovely great shires which deliver beer, but that's all.'

'How is your friend Kate? She has enjoyed it here? I did not talk to her so much the other day.'

'Oh yes, she has loved it. It's such a contrast to life in the English countryside where she is always up to her knees in mud, I gather. And of course,' Elspeth added mischievously, 'Arc en Ciel has its particular charms.'

'Patrice, you mean?'

Elspeth smiled knowingly and raised her eyebrows.

'Patrice,' said Brigitte, leaning forward confidentially, 'may have the appearance of being a man who, I do not know how to say this, who *enjoys* women, but really he is also a good man, a kind man. He will do no harm to your friend.'

'Julie seems to occupy an unenviable position.'

'He is honest with Julie. He has always been honest.'

Elspeth gave a little laugh, not really wanting to discuss Kate and trying to lighten the conversation. 'I would say it was more to do with whether Kate can cope with his attentions. I don't think she's used to it. I don't know her husband, but farmers are great ones for thinking a slap on the rump passes as a sign of affection. Patrice's charm is fairly potent by contrast.'

'But she is a woman,' said Brigitte, sitting back and taking a cigarette from a packet on the table. 'Not a girl.'

'Yes. Well,' said Elspeth in a final sort of tone. 'She has certainly enjoyed her stay.'

'And you?'

'Oh yes. I wouldn't want to go home at all, I can tell you, were it not for a dear old friend who needs me.'

Brigitte drew on her cigarette and looked at her through narrowed eyes. 'Come back,' she said simply. 'Come back and stay. As a friend.'

Elspeth was moved by this generous remark, whether it was a genuine invitation or not.

'We enjoy your company,' Brigitte went on, 'and we are far enough away from the rest of the world to look forward to our visitors. Ah, look. Here comes Robert.'

Her tall husband came in to join them, wearing an old stained vest with a scattering of burnt holes across the front and a pair of plastic goggles dangling round his neck.

Brigitte poured him a glass of wine. 'Excuse him,' she said to Elspeth. 'These are his clothes for welding.'

'Of course,' said Elspeth, laughing. In fact, Robert's lean, bony, aesthetic face made him look like a distinguished professor of an Oxbridge college with an eccentric disregard for appearances.

'Now, I will leave you,' said Brigitte, getting up and collecting her cigarettes from the table. 'Jean-Luc and Bernard are going to join us for lunch and I must busy myself in the kitchen.'

On Dancing Hill

★ ★ ★

The first drops of rain hit the hot pavements and exploded with a hiss of steam.

Patrice looked up at the sky which had suddenly darkened and filled with racing grey clouds. He and Kate were sitting having a beer at a pavement café and now he hurried her to get up and move under the shelter of the awning. Taking her bags containing lavender and dried herbs and the Provençal tablecloth she had bought for Susie and the cheese for Josh, he shepherded her out of the rain which, accompanied by a clap of thunder, began to sheet down in a slanting grey curtain. It pinged off the steaming pavements and almost at once the gutters were full and swirling with water, while the café awnings flapped and banged in the wind.

Passers-by hurried to take cover, holding bags and newspapers over their heads, and Kate found herself crowded against Patrice, so close that she could see the bobbly white strands in the weave of his blue linen shirt. She had enjoyed the morning more than she could have believed possible and felt light-headed with happiness. They had done the shopping together and after taking the bags back to the car had wandered about the market and the charming winding streets of the old town, often arm in arm, stopping to choose her presents or to try a delicacy from a pâtisserie stall, or a sliver of cheese from the épicier.

Patrice seemed as happy as she was, enthusiastically showing her the town, insisting that she tried local specialities, often putting a hand on her shoulder or guiding her by a touch in the small of her back. Now pressed together, laughing and ducking their heads out of the line of persistent drips from the awning, it seemed right that he

331

should put his arm round her and that she should lean her head against him.

Later, they made a dash back to the car through the rain, dodging from shelter to shelter down the street. When they arrived, panting and laughing, the legs of their jeans were dark with wet and Kate's shirt clung to her. Patrice opened the doors and they scrambled in and turned to one another, still laughing, and Kate shook the water from her hair which was flattened against her head. It seemed entirely appropriate that, twisting in his seat, Patrice should take her gently in his arms and begin to kiss her mouth, sweetly, expertly, while gusts of wind rocked the old car and the knob of the gear lever dug painfully into her ribs. Outside, a small stream of rushing water carried a little flotilla of leaves and litter down to the sea while the palm trees tossed their clattering fronds at the grey sky.

Elspeth had to admit she made very little progress with her efforts at sculpture, but she enjoyed her day enormously. The spectacular electric storm provided a great diversion. The electricity was cut off, and the sky became almost as dark as night, so that Brigitte lit candles in the kitchen and they went up onto the roof to watch the daggers of lightning strike across the hills. Then the rain came in a great flap of grey torn from the sky, bouncing off the stones of the terrace and flattening the grass on the hillside which was soon running in streams of ochre-coloured water.

When Bernard and Jean-Luc appeared in Bernard's pick-up, they dashed across the courtyard for the shelter of the house but still arrived with their shirts clinging to their backs and their hair drenched. Bernard looked very hand-some, thought Elspeth, like someone out of a dramatic

scene from an opera, with raindrops trembling on his silver
curls and his big chest displayed to advantage. The noise
and fervour of the storm had excited them all and they
laughed and talked loudly and the men slapped one
another on the back, enjoying some joke related to the
deal they had just made for five hundred roof tiles from
the demolished house.

Lunch went on for ever with delicious plates of cold
meats and salads and a warm onion tart and several bottles
of Bernard's own wine, of which he had a crate in the back
of his truck. It got so dark and chilly that Robert lit the fire
in the vast old fireplace and soon flickers of flame made
the white walls leap golden and rain falling down the huge
chimney hissed on the burning logs.

This is all too good to be true, thought Elspeth, trying
not to think of her flat in London to which she would
soon be returning. Robert produced a wooden bowl full
of walnuts which Bernard cracked on the table with his
fist and handed the delicious kernels to Elspeth to nibble,
which although not quite in the same class as Patrice's
peach-peeling performance, was still delightfully
attentive.

Later, they had brandies by the fire. Outside, the
sky cleared and by late afternoon the rain stopped
and the sun came out, tentatively at first, and then
blazing, so that the whole world trembled with tiny
explosions of glittering colour as every drop of water
caught its rays.

They took their brandy glasses and went to stand on
the terrace and watch the valley steam in the sunlight.
The air had the raw smell of fresh, wet earth and
vegetation and suddenly the cicadas started up with
renewed clamour. 'It's like the start of a new world!' said

Elspeth happily, turning to her hosts and taking care not to slip on the glistening paving stones, although from all she read in the newspapers a broken leg would be a much happier experience here in France than under the NHS.

Later Bernard took her and Jean-Luc back to Arc en Ciel, squashed into the cab of his truck, and every time they went round a corner, which was very often on the twisting hill road, Elspeth, who was sitting between them, leaned against Bernard's stout body and, apologising as it did so, his broad hand brushed against her thigh as he changed gear.

Sweeping into the courtyard of the farmhouse, where water still lay in pools, she saw that Patrice's car was back. As they were getting out of the truck he appeared at the door of the house, cigarette in mouth, and came over to greet them.

'You have had a good day?' he asked her.

'A lovely day, thank you, Patrice. You, too, I hope. Where is Kate? She can't have got much painting done today!'

'No, it is not a good day for being outdoors, but I think she enjoyed her trip to town.'

'Where is she?'

'She is walking back.' He indicated down the hillside. 'She asked me to leave her at the bottom of the mountain. She enjoys the cooler weather to take some exercise.'

'Ah,' said Elspeth, giving him a shrewd look. What, she wondered, had gone on between them? Patrice was as easy and relaxed as ever, talking and laughing with Bernard and Jean-Luc, inquiring about the roof tiles and then the three men trooped off to assess the progress being made with the barn conversion. Elspeth could hear them

334

as she went inside to go up to her room. Through the open kitchen door she saw Julie busy at the stove. She looked up as Elspeth passed and gave her a reluctant smile.

'Good afternoon, Julie,' said Elspeth cheerily. She believed in good manners and subscribed to the old-fashioned view that graciousness was a virtue. '*Bon soir*, rather. *As tu un bon jour?*'

This was the first proper exercise Kate had had since arriving in France and she walked fast, swinging her arms and striding out. Her damp jeans steamed faintly in the sunshine and with one hand she lifted her wet hair from the back of her neck. As she walked she noticed very little of her surroundings although, with her eyes on the path, she was aware of the glitter of the wet stones and the squelch of the slippery wet earth in between. She could think of nothing but what had happened in the car and was shocked to discover how much she had enjoyed Patrice's lovemaking and how easy it had been to reciprocate. I'm over fifty! she thought. It's ridiculous. Absurd. What has happened to me? It's only been six days away from home and yet I seem to have become a different person.

What was wrong with her marriage, she thought, that at the first opportunity she behaved like this? There was a residue there, a lingering flavour of what it had been like when they were younger and had desired one another. Josh, less bowed under so much work and worry, had been a good lover. But remembering this, what it had been like to feel wanted, made Patrice's attentions all the more wonderful. She felt sexually exhilarated for the first time for years and years and she smiled now as she walked, remembering his words, telling her how desirable she was.

It was like a whole forgotten part of herself stirring and coming to life again.

It made her panic to realise that he had aroused something which she was not sure how to control. Infidelity and adultery were horrible words. Condemning words. Shagging, knocking up, having it off, getting a leg over; all ugly words. It was frightening to think of what had been started between her and Patrice and where it might lead.

She walked on, the going harder now as the path wound upwards more steeply. She stopped to catch her breath. Josh neglected her, that was the cause of all this. If he was more concerned about her, more willing to put a bit of effort into their marriage, then she would not be here in France on her own in the first place and would not find herself so vulnerable to Patrice's attentions. It was Josh's fault. Nobody could blame her.

Suddenly, looking down at her loafers which were rimmed with thick yellow mud, she realised how dishonest she was being, not so much because she had already been technically unfaithful to the husband whom she loved, but because she was seeking to blame him for her behaviour. I can't do that, she told herself. If I am going to sleep with Patrice, I am going to do it because I want to, because it seems the right thing for me and not because of some peevish reaction to poor old Josh. If I do it, knowing the hurt it could cause the people I love, it must be because I reckon it's worth it. It's absolutely my last chance for this sort of adventure; I will never be in a place like this again.

She started to walk on as new clouds began to gather overhead and thunder rumbled in the distance. It had been a good idea to walk. She didn't care if she got wet again and she wasn't frightened of thunder and lightning. It had given her time to think and avoided arriving back with Patrice and having to meet Julie's watchful eye. Julie she chose not to think about. Julie was not her problem.

Chapter Fourteen

On Friday morning the weather broke and the sky was a uniform grey over Dancing Hill. It was damp and mild, the air heavy and still as Susie once again looked for George. It was past eleven o'clock so he would have finished with the sheep, but there was no sign of him at the bungalow and his cap and stick were gone.

As she drove slowly up to the farmhouse she saw him out in the field at the back, where Kate had her chicken house, and realised that the younger man with him was Mike Gledhill, who had promised to replace Kate's hens.

She pulled over into the gateway and got out and leaned over the gate. The two men were unloading birds out of cardboard boxes from the back of a pick-up, carrying them by their legs, upside down, one in each hand, and setting them down in the henrun.

'George!' she called and waved. He did not hear her and continued with what he was doing but Mike glanced over and must have said something because George stopped and turned in her direction and then lifted a hand in salute.

Susie looked to see if she could open the gate, but it was tied with binder twine and so, awkwardly, trying not to get her clean jeans dirty, she climbed over and hopped down and began to pick her way across the wet grass.

'George!' she called again, as she got nearer. 'I've come to thank you!' She saw the old man raise a dismissive hand and go back to collect two more hens from the truck.

He's embarrassed, she thought, but I'm determined to thank him. I won't let him get away with it, with going back to how things used to be. The events of the past days had made a difference and she intended to keep it that way.

When she reached the truck she could see that the old grocery boxes were tied with bright binder twine and inside them beady eyes looked out through the gaps. She intercepted her father-in-law on the return trip from the henhouse, and blocked his path and then on tiptoes reached up to kiss his cheek.

'The flowers were lovely, George. Absolutely lovely. It was a very sweet thought.'

George looked thoroughly uncomfortable. He'd never been accused of having a sweet thought before.

'Ah,' he said, glancing over at Mike Gledhill who, grinning to himself, the bugger, was busy with unloading.

'So I wanted to thank you. Roses and freesias and stocks – absolutely lovely!'

'Well, I didn't know what you'd like,' he said shortly. 'The shop chose them.' He wanted to distance himself from the gift, pretend it meant nothing to him, but Susie wouldn't let go. She's like a bloomin' terrier, he thought.

'And the lovely card,' she went on. 'I was just as thrilled with that. With what you said.'

'Look,' he said, desperate to change the subject, 'here are the fowl you wanted. In these last three boxes. You can lift them out, if you like.'

It was Susie's turn to look horrified. She had never

picked up a hen in her life. She very nearly said so, but stopped herself, thinking, he wants to make me look silly.

'Show me how,' she said.

George cut the string on the top of the nearest box and opened the flap a little. Inside, three reddish-brown birds crouched, their beaks sharp and curved, their eyes expressionless as glass. Terrified, Susie watched as George put his hand into the box and the hens flapped and beat their wings against the cardboard. He lifted out a bird by one leg and then swiftly caught hold of the other. The bird hung down, suddenly motionless.

'Like that,' he said.

'Why can't I hold it the other way up?' asked Susie. 'In my arms?'

'You can if you want.' George righted the hen and held it out to Susie who, trying not to grimace, came close enough to take it. If it flaps, she thought, I'll scream and drop it.

'Tuck her under your arm,' said George, 'that way she won't struggle.'

Gingerly, Susie took the bird from George and held her as instructed. She could feel the terror pulsing in the frail body. Poor little thing, she thought, examining the glossy golden-brown neck feathers and the bright yellow legs.

'What sort is she?' she asked.

'Welsummer,' said Mike, passing with another two hens. 'Lay a lovely brown egg, they do. Specialist bird, that is.'

With one finger Susie stroked her neck and walking very carefully followed Mike to the henhouse where she set her down on the straw. The hen remained crouching for a moment before scooting off to join the other newcomers in a frightened flock in the corner.

'How many have I got?' she asked.

'Six, like you asked for,' said George. 'But I told you they won't be laying for a few weeks yet.'

'Here,' said Susie, following him to the truck. 'Let me take another one.'

'This is the last,' said Mike, handing her a bright brown hen out of the box. 'That's it then, George. Twenty in all.'

'Right you are, Mike. What do I owe you, you thieving so-and-so? Eight pounds each? Daylight robbery.' He started to count out notes from his trouser pocket.

Mike laughed good-naturedly. 'It's a special price for you as it is, Mr Butler. Ten pounds a head I could get in the market.'

Susie came back from setting down her hen. 'Kate's are different,' she observed. 'What sort has she got?'

'They're hybrids,' said Mike. 'They're hardy and lay well, better than your lot, but not the deep brown egg.'

'What's a hybrid?' Susie asked, not caring now if she seemed ignorant.

'Cross-bred,' explained Mike. 'All the good characteristics of one breed are crossed with those of another.'

'I'll know mine by their yellow legs, won't I? They look as if they're wearing rubber globes.'

'I'll be on my way,' said Mike. 'Say hello to Kate from me.' He hopped into the truck and set off across the field to where the gate by the farmhouse stood open.

'We'll keep them shut in for a day or two until they settle,' said George, closing the henhouse door. 'The other hens won't bother them because there are more new ones than old. Fowl can be terrible for picking on the newcomers.'

'Hen-pecked,' said Susie. 'That must be where it comes from. I owe you forty-eight pounds, George. I'll drop it in this afternoon.'

'No you don't,' said George gruffly. 'Not after . . .' His voice trailed off. He looked at his watch. 'It's time I got home,' he said. 'Wilf will be round any moment. It's our day for the pub.'

Together they walked back across the field. Susie said nothing. She could see that it was better that way. She knew George would prefer it.

From up at the farmhouse Josh watched them from the kitchen window. He had come in for a late breakfast and to swallow some painkillers and make a few telephone calls. If anything, his ribs were more painful than ever, catching him with nearly every movement. He knew he had over-done it the first few days. There had been no alternative, he told himself. The hay and the silage had to be made and when the barns and the clamps were full he could take it a bit easier.

Then, this morning, he and Len had a difficult cow to calve and he found that he was of little use, it was too painful to use any strength, and in the end the calf was born dead and they had lost the cow, too. It was a terrible thing to happen and he felt miserable and upset. He had come in to call the hunt kennels to collect the carcass and then to ring for a relief milker. It was too much for Len to manage on his own and Tom was no effing use at all. He had telephoned him to come and help but he said that he was busy down at his end, that they had three sets of visitors arriving and Susie needed him. It made Josh fume with exasperation and he had put down the telephone with a bang. Then what does he see but Susie wandering about in the field with George, thick as thieves, the pair of them, and about as much use as . . . He couldn't think of anything contemptuous enough.

343

He gulped at his coffee and crammed the slice of bread and marmalade he was eating into his mouth. Thank God Kate would be back tomorrow and they could get things back to normal. The house for a start. Joyce had left another message to say that Kylie was still in bed and that she wouldn't be coming in on Thursday, and Josh had given up then. He couldn't be expected to cope with everything, and he let the kitchen pile up with debris and the heap of dirty clothes by the washing machine grew. Kate could sort it out when she got back. He had too much else to worry about.

The postman had dumped the morning letters inside the back door and painfully Josh bent to pick them up. He loathed the post. It was always bad news, as far as he was concerned. Bills, or some bloody directive from Defra, and since he never corresponded with anyone he never got a postcard or a hand-written letter to leaven the gloom.

He shuffled through the pile and shoved them on the counter, unopened. There was only one which had attracted his attention, a large square brown envelope, addressed in type to him and Kate but with URGENT written across the top in handwriting. He looked at it for a moment and then went to lower himself painfully into the armchair. Impatiently he ripped open the envelope, dropping it onto the floor beside him, and began to read.

At Arc en Ciel Kate was finishing her painting. The storms of the previous day had cleared the atmosphere and the day was bright and warm as ever, hotter if anything. The insect life seemed to thrum louder than usual, vibrating in her head as she concentrated, and she could hear the mewing of a pair of buzzards circling above her head.

She frowned as she painted and finally put down her

brush and stepped back, surveying her canvas. It had to be completed this morning in order to dry and be ready to pack the next day and the truth was that it really wasn't very good. This was not a question of false modesty on her part: she had sufficient objective judgement to know that it was a very mediocre effort and that the finished product had not lived up to the promising start she felt she had made.

She found a place to sit under a cork oak, glad of the shade, and took off her hat. This was the first time she had been able to paint with any concentration since she had been a student and she realised that she had allowed herself, in the intervening years, to believe that she had been deprived of the opportunity to develop into a pass- able painter. What occurred to her now, with a shock, was that this was not the case at all. She really had very little talent out of the ordinary, and despite Patrice's encourage- ment, she had produced a very dull painting. It was OK, quite carefully done, technically adequate, but that was all. Art schools must produce hundreds, thousands, of students each year with more promise.

This revelation came as a surprise and threw an awk- ward light over the past. It meant that she had not been denied anything very much, except the opportunity to discover that her skill was nothing special, but it wasn't only that, it also meant that she had been deluded into feeling that she had made a sacrifice. This had become part of how she thought about herself – Kate, talented student, who had given up a career to be a wife and mother. Kate, who could have been a success in a satisfying and reward- ing, creative job. And it wasn't true. Josh, the children, the farm, had not stood in her way.

She sighed and ran a hand through her hair which was

hot on the back of her neck. It was Elspeth's painting which had sharpened her critical faculties and made her assess her own work with a fresh eye. Elspeth's painting, which Patrice had stretched over a frame and was now preparing to pack, was totally wonderful – original and full of energy. The sensual, vibrant colour and dramatic intensity made it glow from the corner of the studio and they had all gathered round to admire it. Kate knew that Patrice meant every word when he said, 'But Elspeth, this is marvellous. This is very exciting work. You have a unique style. I like it very, very much.' Jean-Luc and Bernard were called from their work on the barn and Monique and Julie from the kitchen and they had stood round the little painting and exclaimed, while Elspeth shrugged and said, 'Come on, it's not that bloody marvellous. In the end I just slapped on the paint because I wanted to finish it!' It was easy, however, to see how thrilled she was by their praise.

Patrice disappeared and came back with a bottle of champagne and Monique brought glasses and they toasted Elspeth's achievement and Kate had felt both happy for her new friend and regretful that her own work had been so eclipsed.

Looking at it now, she could see why. Ordinary, that's what it was. Utterly commonplace and ordinary. Swiftly she began to put away her paints. Soon, Patrice would be coming down the hill to see how she was getting on and she could not face his kind and encouraging remarks, not when she knew the truth. She would pack up now, while there was still time to avoid him, and go for a walk instead.

She wanted to think about the other surprise that had occurred at the breakfast table. Patrice had told them that Julie was leaving after lunch, returning to Paris to attend a four-day refresher course in primary teaching. He would be taking her to the station to catch the train.

'Oh dear,' said Elspeth generously. 'We had wanted to buy her a little thank you present in town this evening, and now it will be too late.'

'She will be back,' said Patrice. 'She will return next week when her course is finished. She stays here until September.' He spoke about Julie so naturally in front of Kate that she felt needled. How could he, after yesterday? It was as if nothing had happened between them. She felt herself turn inward, grow quiet and still, so that Patrice glanced at her and said, 'Kate? You are well this morning?'

'Yes, yes, fine,' she said, trying to arrange a bright look on her face, to give nothing away.

There had been no time for any further talk between them. There was the delight and fuss over Elspeth's painting, and then she had collected her things and come down the hill to her painting spot where she could be alone and think.

Julie going away, she realised as she walked down the hill, following a steep little path made by the goats, would put a different complexion on their trip into town in the evening. The promised dinner, the fireworks, the sense of celebrating the end of their holiday would be quite different with Julie out of the way. Would it mean that Patrice would become openly loving towards her as he had been on their earlier trip into town? She did not know and felt uneasy at the prospect. Julie's absence would be like taking the brake off the situation – she couldn't call it an affair, because it wasn't – and she did not feel at all confident of how she would handle it, or even what she wanted.

Muddled, hot, disturbed by the revised version of herself she had discovered this morning, she thought with longing of the cool green valley at home, the view from her kitchen window, the ticking over of her uneventful life. I am much better off in my old rut, she thought. Comfortable and settled. I don't want these upheavals and churned-up feelings.

Faintly, from up the hill, she could hear Patrice calling her name. He must have arrived at her easel and found her gone. She stood for a moment, considering, and then continued down the stony path between the pine trees. She would not answer.

Anna watched the rain hit her office window and slide down the glass. Her days in the sun at Dancing Hill seemed like a dream and only the rosy brown of her arms leaning on her desk and the split in the inside of her lip, which her tongue kept seeking, were reminders of all that had happened. That and her heavy heart.

Despite her keenness to get the research done on Dancing Hill and the figures prepared for next weekend, it was only when she was immersed in work that she could ignore the downward drag on her spirits. Whenever she stopped to look out of the window or to take a break for a cup of coffee, or dash out for a sandwich lunch, the state of her heart made her feel miserable, lonely, sad. She seemed to be surrounded by reminders of happier days: the cinema showing a film that she and Rich had both loved; the travel agent with a window devoted to holidays in a country they had promised themselves they would visit; a bookshop offering signed copies of a new novel by his favourite author. Anna had to stop herself from going in to buy him a copy as she would normally have done. Most of all she missed his telephone calls which normally punctuated the working day, and the emails which flew between their offices.

Because she could not bear the impasse between them she had telephoned twice on Thursday evening and both times he was out. She would have expected him to telephone her back when he got her message but he had not done so and now pride forbade her from making further calls or sending him an email.

Perhaps it is best like this, she thought. Perhaps Rich thinks a clean break is the answer and less painful in the long run. Maybe, later on, when they had both got used to the break-up, they would be able to be friends again.

In her bag by her feet was her letter of resignation which she was going to put on the desk of her line manager as she left the office this evening. When she discussed her future with her parents next weekend she wanted to be able to say that she had already resigned. It was important, she felt, to show her father just how serious she was about a career change. It would shock and worry them, she knew that, and they would try everything they could to make her reconsider, which was why it was important that she should present them with a fait accompli. For her it was the easy part; she knew she would never regret leaving her job. That was one of the few things of which she was absolutely certain.

After she had checked her contract and realised that she had to work out three months' notice, she began to form an idea of the year ahead. If her parents and Tom and Grandpa would not accept her on the farm then she would still not regret leaving her London life. Although she hoped she would not have to implement it, she had another plan to put into action. She would go abroad. Take a year out. Work for Aid to Africa on an alternative technology project amongst nomadic communities in the southern Sahara. She had all the papers in her briefcase. If it did not go well at home then she would start to fill in the application forms.

Meanwhile she had already posted a draft outline of her ideas to members of the family, including her brothers, and she was now working through her plans for the farm in greater detail. She kept returning to an astonishing find that she had come across the last time she was shopping in her local branch of Waitrose. She had noticed, with amazement, a special French sourdough loaf selling for nearly ten pounds. She had since discovered a trailer load of wheat was worth fifty-two pounds per ton, and farmers got six pence for a standard-sized loaf. A ton of wheat produced upwards of a thousand standard loaves. There was a message here.

Her father got sixteen pence a litre for his milk and for that price he chilled it to 37°F and paid for transport to the processor. For all the hard work of a dairy herd, he was at the worst times making a loss, and at the best only a tiny return.

Anna pored over the figures and read report after report. She looked at farm conservation schemes and government subsidies. She downloaded information from one website after another, and gradually a picture emerged. Long after her colleagues had gone home, she was still at her desk. Just after eight o'clock, she printed out six copies of her findings and closed down her computer.

Collecting her belongings and putting them in her bag, she stretched and stood up and immediately Richard was back in her idling mind. The moment she stopped concentrating on something else, it seemed her consciousness played mean tricks on her. Damn it, she thought, and picking up her telephone she rang his mobile. It was switched off. Then, regretting it almost as soon as she had done so, she punched in the number of his flat and waited while it rang and then heard Steve, his flatmate answer.

'Is Rich there?' she asked. 'It's Anna.'

'Sorry, Anna.' Steve's voice was cold. 'He's gone away for the weekend.'

'Oh.'

'Yeah. He's pretty gutted, you know.'

'Is he?'

'What do you expect? Fucking him about like you have.'

Anna was shocked into silence.

'Do you know where he is?' she asked eventually. She was not going to justify herself to Steve, whom she hardly knew. He had only been sharing with Richard for two months and she had never particularly liked him.

'Yeah, I do. He's gone to stay with Mimi.'

Anna put down the telephone without another word.

Picking up her bag in one hand and her letter in the other, she crossed the room and propped the envelope on her boss's keyboard before letting herself out of the office and taking the lift down to street level.

'Have you read this?' asked Tom when he and Susie at last sat together over supper in the kitchen. Their guests were comfortable in the sitting room with their after-dinner coffee and homemade mints. The blowing squalls of wind and rain made the conservatory, where Susie would normally suggest her visitors sit after dinner, feel unwelcoming, and she had even made Tom light the fire although, despite the rain, it was a warm night.

'Yes, I have,' she said. 'Briefly.'

'What do you think? It's a bit of a bombshell, isn't it?' He passed the sheets of paper over the table to her and she cast her eyes down the first page.

351

'Hmm,' she said thoughtfully. 'You never suspected, then, that Anna would want to come into the farm?'

'No, never. I thought that she was set on a career in London. Didn't you?'

'I sometimes wondered. She always seems happy here.'

'There's a bit of difference between seeming happy here and wanting to farm.'

'I know that. I'm just saying that the life seems to suit her.'

'So what do you think?'

Susie hesitated. 'You know what I think about the farm. I tell you often enough. I think it's a hiding to nothing. Look at the work you and Josh put in and look at the returns. It doesn't make sense.'

'So you wouldn't support her? Look at these initials here on the bottom. She's sent a copy of this to us all, outlining her plans and asking if we can meet next Sunday morning. George as well. One thing I can tell you is that it will set the cat amongst the pigeons. I wonder what Josh makes of it, but come to think of it he was very short with me this morning on the telephone, so I'd guess he's none too pleased.'

Susie interrupted him. 'I didn't say I wouldn't support her. This paragraph is really interesting, I think. I don't know where she's got the figures from but she says here that seventy-five per cent of visitors to Dorset indicated that the environmental quality of the area was a determining factor in their decision to visit it. Particular growth sectors are in the number of visitors taking niche holidays, second and third holidays and short breaks.

'Niche holidays? What the hell is a niche holiday? It sounds like something garden gnomes might have on their time off from fishing!'

Susie ignored him. 'Look at this,' she said, ' "After the core farming business, the second priority should be to maximise other income sources which might include diverse business activity on the farm and maximising on the available environmental payments." '

'That's nothing new,' said Tom. 'We've been told that for years. That's what you're doing with your B&B and Kate with her cooking.'

'I know *that*!' said Susie crossly. 'It's *maximising* that I'm interested in. When have we ever talked about *maximising*? When have we ever sat round a table and discussed possibilities across both farms?'

'Often,' retorted Tom. 'That's what we do all the time, me and Josh. We run the two farms to complement one another, dairy and beef and sheep and fodder crops.'

'Yes, of course you do, but that's the core farming business. What about maximising the other opportunities? It only occurred to me the other day, for instance, that I should get eggs from Dancing Hill. I always assumed that Kate used all that her hens produced because she has never offered me any.'

'I expect she does use them all. She must get through a fair number.'

'So, George has got me six pullets to run with her flock. They arrived today and when Kate gets back I'll offer to share looking after them.'

Tom looked at his wife in surprise. It was not like her to want to get involved with a project like that, not with something to do with the farm.

'And there's vegetables. Why aren't we growing vegetables for our guests here and selling what's left in a sort of farm shop? We could do that, Tom. We've got the room and Kate is a fantastic gardener. Those beans we had for dinner came from her garden. I got George to pick some the other day. She's got every kind of thing growing there.'

'How have we got time for all of this? We can only just get round all we have to do as it is. Josh has had to get a relief milker in today, for instance. It only takes a little thing like his accident to throw us out completely.'

'Exactly,' said Susie. She tapped the paper in front of her. 'That's where Anna comes in.'

After lunch of delicious grilled lamb with garlic, rosemary and tomatoes followed by a warm apricot flan, Kate and Elspeth said goodbye to Julie. She came to shake their hands in a stiff and formal farewell but Elspeth leaned forward and kissed her and Kate followed her example. As she brushed her lips against Julie's cheek she had a close-up view of orange make-up clogged in the pores and the furry surface loaded with powder. She tried not to recoil, to be generous and sincere in her thanks.

'I don't know how to say it in French, but it's been such a treat for me to enjoy your delicious food. I've really appreciated it.'

Julie looked pleased as Patrice translated and when she smiled she looked younger and prettier. She said something in French and Patrice leaned forward and kissed her affectionately before picking up her bag and ushering her off to the car.

Elspeth and Kate went out into the courtyard to wave her off and stood for a moment in silence as the noise of the car faded in the distance and the heat of the afternoon sun bounced off the walls of the farmhouse.

'Phew,' said Elspeth. 'I'm going to lie down for a bit. It's too hot for anything else. Poor Julie, with that journey to do! I don't envy her.'

Kate said nothing. She did not know whether she envied Julie or not. She did not know what she thought. Her head had started to ache and she felt fat and heavy after lunch. The cool of her white-painted room with the shutters closed against the sun was the most inviting thing she could think of.

She woke after the heat had gone out of the afternoon and the light which flooded in when she opened the shutters was golden rather than a blinding glare. She drank a glass of water and wondered whether she could be bothered to have a shower.

She could not decide what to wear for the evening in the town. She had one clean pair of jeans which she had kept for travelling home and a couple of T-shirts and that was it, so the choice was not great, but she wanted to look as if she had made an effort. She thought of Elspeth's cleverly tied scarves, her unusual belts and jewellery, and knew that she would never achieve that sort of effortless chic. I don't have her sense of style, she thought, and frankly, she wasn't particularly interested in clothes. Her jeans came from a market stall and everything else from agricultural shows or standard high street stores. She didn't have to look good. It wasn't required of her, and Josh, certainly, never noticed what she wore.

This holiday, among these people, had made her see herself slightly differently. She found that she wanted to look more interesting, more individual, but God knows how, given the small heap of clothes spread about her bed.

'Kate?' Elspeth appeared at her door. 'May I come in? I've had the most wonderful sleep. Did you sleep well? Goodness, are you packing already?'

'No. I'm thinking about what to wear tonight. I don't have much choice, actually.'

Elspeth came into the room, wrapped in a cotton sarong, and stood looking at Kate's clothes with a thoughtful expression.

'You look at your best in this sort of thing, I think,' she said. 'Very understated clothes suit you.'

'What, you mean boring?' laughed Kate.

'Not at all. With your figure and your natural look, they suit you. I would be positively frightening if I went without make-up like you do. I have never been out of the door without eyeliner and lipstick since I was fourteen.'

'You'd look fine without it. You've got lovely bones. That's what counts, isn't it?'

'No, it's not. Make-up becomes essential after a bit. I couldn't function without it. I can't even answer the telephone before I've put my face on in the morning.'

Kate laughed. 'I suppose I've never led the sort of life that requires me to have "a face". On the farm there's nobody to care what I look like.'

Elspeth looked at her reflectively. 'It's always been enough just to be you.'

'That's too flattering. Anyone can haul buckets of calf nuts or make a hundredweight of Christmas puddings. Me-ness doesn't come into it.'

'All my life I've worked in areas where it matters to be smart, well-turned-out, but it's always mattered in my personal life too. I don't think I've ever gone out with a man who I haven't had to dress to the nines for.'

Kate made a face. 'How exhausting,' she said. 'I suppose it's different if you're a wife. I complain that it would take Josh several days to notice if I went round with a paper bag over my head.'

Elspeth did not smile. 'After Archie, I don't know. When one is over sixty the effort seems hardly worth it.' A tiny moment of quiet hung between them and Kate glimpsed a bleakness and sadness in Elspeth's face before she went on in a new, more buoyant tone. 'If you wear that pink T-shirt I could lend you my pink cotton scarf. It's Hermès – very special. I'll show you how to tie it.'

Josh went to get himself another bottle of beer and started to poke about in the kitchen, looking for something to eat. He'd left the bread on the counter top and it had gone hard and now he would have to give it to the dogs. There was an elbow of cheese in the fridge, yellow and cracked and unappetising, and the fatty end of the piece of cooked ham Kate had left. He knew that there were plenty of ready-made meals in the deep freeze but he couldn't be bothered to go through all the palaver of warming one up. He wanted food now, in his hand, which he could walk about with and eat without any fuss.

He poked at the bread with a knife. If he hacked off the top slice it might be all right underneath. An empty jar of pickled onions reminded him of something else he had finished. He couldn't remember where Kate kept things like that – at the back of the shelf where she stored jam, he thought, but although he looked he couldn't find another jar.

He sat down with the hunk of bread spread with butter and the lump of cheese which managed to be both greasy and desiccated, the bottle of beer in the other hand. He felt very, very tired. Balancing the cheese on the arm of the chair, he reached underneath him to fish out something that he had sat on and saw that it was the papers Anna had sent him. Frowning, he started to read through them again, irritation and indignation mounting. When the telephone rang a few minutes later, he got up to answer it and his voice was abrupt. It was George.

'That you, Josh?' Who did he *think* it was it for goodness sake? 'I've had this letter from Anna. What does she call it? A draft.'

'Oh yes. That.' Josh didn't want to talk about it. Not now, not with his father-in-law.

'Do you fancy coming down for a whisky? Susie left me some cold meat and I've done a few potatoes. I expect it's seemed a long week, without Kate.'

Josh started to refuse and then thought, why not? He heard himself say, 'That's kind of you. I've run out of things a bit up here. I was just gnawing on some stale bread.'

George laughed. 'Stale bread? Can't have that! Get on down here, I can give you something better than that.'

Ten minutes later he was sitting opposite George with a large whisky at his elbow and a plate of cold lamb and new potatoes and thick brown bread and butter on his knees. As soon as he started to eat he realised how hungry he was.

'This is good, George. Thank you for suggesting it.' He looked about him. He didn't think he had been in George's sitting room more than half a dozen times. It was always the other way round, George coming up to the farm, Kate coming down here to see her father. It was a pleasant room, he thought, comfortable, with a lovely view down across the valley, but despite the photographs and the one or two knick-knacks and ornaments, it was strangely impersonal. It did not feel as if any life ebbed and flowed through it. It was too tidy, too undisturbed. He thought of the muddle in which he had left the farm, the kitchen a mess, the stack of post on the counter, the pinboard inside the door cluttered with notes and notices, the telephone list overwritten with added numbers. There was no mistaking the relentless current of life, whereas this room had the sluggish feel of a backwater. Through the open door to the kitchen he could see George's stick and cap resting against a chair, his newspaper neatly folded on the table and next to it the brown envelope which had arrived in the post that morning.

This is what life comes to, thought Josh, this gradual reduction until only a few things still matter. It would have been different if Pat had been alive. It was surprising that without her, a gentle, quiet, undemanding woman, George was diminished, seeming to occupy less than half the life they had shared, which now hung emptily around him like an oversized set of clothes.

Josh found it a bleak and comfortless prospect. Approaching old age, perhaps life without Kate, who knew? He stared gloomily into his glass and George, watching him, thought, Moody bugger, what's wrong now? 'Here,' he said. 'Let me top that up. Give me your plate if you've finished.' He pulled himself out of his chair and shuffled off into the kitchen and came back with the whisky bottle and the jug of water. 'Same again?' he asked.

Josh stirred himself. He didn't know why he suddenly felt so cast down. Really, looking at George, whisky bottle in hand, in rude good health and still able to make a nuisance of himself, there was not too much to worry about.

'Thanks,' he said, taking his refilled glass.

'So Kate's back tomorrow,' said George, settling down again. 'It seems longer than a week that she's been away.'

'Yes, it does,' agreed Josh. 'But a lot has happened, one way and another. And then we've got to deal with this hornets' nest that Anna's stirred up. I don't know what Kate will think, really I don't.'

'You'll give the maid a chance, if you've got any sense,' said George quietly.

'It would be a terrible waste of everything – her education, her degree, everything, if she came back here. There's no future in small family farms, George. The writing's on the wall.'

'So you say. Seems she thinks otherwise.'

'It's no life for a girl. How can she farm here and hope to get married and have a family?'

'Kate did.'

'But she married me – a farmer! I was already working here and things were different then. Kate had no training like Anna has. She wasn't giving up anything to stay on the farm.'

The lapsed into silence and then George said, 'She's old enough to make up her own mind.'

Later, walking back up the house in the dark, the whisky making his feet feel slightly disconnected from the rest of him, Josh had another strange thought. Had Kate ever regretted the choice she had made when she was so young? The choice which he felt so adamant that Anna should not make? It had never occurred to him before that she might. She had never mentioned it, so he always supposed she hadn't.

Kate need not have worried about her last evening in France. The party from Arc en Ciel was joined by Bernard and Brigitte and Robert and in two cars they zigzagged out of the hills to the town, strung with lights which sparkled against the dark sea. Elspeth and Kate went with Jean-Luc and Patrice, the two women sitting together in the back, while Bernard and Monique travelled with Brigitte and Robert.

The seafood restaurant was noisy and lively and they had a delicious meal, sharing a platter of shellfish, sucking and probing for the delicate shreds of flesh, while Patrice cracked shells and opened oysters, his sleeves rolled up, displaying his strong brown arms and beautiful hands. Afterwards, they linked arms to stroll to the waterfront to watch the fireworks while a brass band played from the square. Patrice caught both Kate and Elspeth by the elbows and herded them along the crowded pavements, laughing and switching effortlessly between French and English. They oohed and aahed as the fountains and streams of light flooded the sky in explosions of colour and later they threaded their way back into the crowded streets and stopped at a bar to drink digestifs.

The fireworks, the music, the glittering town, the crush of people, the thick sweet drink which burned her throat made Kate feel loose-limbed and happy. It had been wonderful, she assured everybody. It had all been wonderful.

Patrice was uniformly charming, as attentive to Elspeth as he was to Kate, only once catching her hand and kissing her fingers, and resting a hand very gently on her waist as they watched the fireworks. As the evening passed, Kate became aware of time running out. Only a few more hours and she would be on the train home and all this would be over.

Driving home, she once again sat in the back of the car, this time next to Monique, with Jean-Luc and Patrice in the front, and when they got back, drowsy after the journey and so much to eat and drink, she declined the offer of a cognac and went straight to her room.

It was much later, when she got up to secure a shutter,

that she glanced down and saw Patrice sitting alone on the terrace, his cigarette glowing red in the dark, a bottle and glass in front of him.

Very quietly she let herself out of her room and went down to join him.

Chapter Fifteen

As the train from St Raphael sped north through the French countryside, Kate and Elspeth, sitting opposite one another at a table and hemmed in by a noisy family who spread the available space with crayons and colouring books, both closed their eyes and dozed. The sun was shut out by the filtered glass and half-drawn blinds and the train was smooth and noiseless.

Elspeth rested her head back and thought dreamily of Archie. When she got home she would telephone him, it wouldn't be too late, and arrange to go round the next day. They could take a gentle walk if the weather was nice, catching up on news, and then stop for lunch at Mario's. Archie would be full of the plans for his party and she would go over the guest list with him, and at some point or other she would show him her painting.

She felt quite shy about this, especially after the praise heaped on it by Patrice and the others. What if Archie didn't like it? He would be far too gentlemanly to say so, but she would know instantly. If he did like it, she would ask his advice about getting it framed and then she would give it to him for his birthday. It was almost impossible to think of something which he either wanted or needed. He was an old man, a rich man, but her painting was so personal, so much about them and what they meant to one another, and she would try to explain how she had felt on the day she had finished it.

It had been a lovely holiday, she would tell him, in a beautiful place. It had done her good and provided a wonderful rest after the dirt and noise of London. She thought fondly of the people she had left behind, especially kind, gentlemanly Patrice who turned out to be a much nicer man than she had first suspected, and of Bernard. She smiled faintly, thinking of his elaborate compliments and the reassuring sturdiness of his body and his square, workman's hands.

Vivid scenes from the last week flashed across her mind: the entertaining lunch in the hilltop town, the wily old Dolly and her frightful exhibition, the lovely meals eaten under the vine, the happy time she had spent with Robert and Brigitte. She had enjoyed every sun-drenched day and would be able to look back on them with the greatest pleasure.

Kate, yes, she would miss her, too. She had proved to be a good companion and for Elspeth, who chose her friends carefully, this was a significant accolade. She wondered if they would see one another again, if this chance connection between them would stand the pressure of ordinary lives back in England. She hoped so. They would certainly keep in touch. She imagined the odd weekend staying on the farm in Dorset, where she hoped she could admire the view through a sitting room window and manage to keep out of the mud and fields and any close proximity with animals.

She was ready to go home, but really only because of Archie. She had a couple of tours booked for September but August was always a flat sort of month. An ugly month in London when everywhere was teeming with package tour visitors and the freshness of the summer had worn off.

Before long, the restless child sitting next to her upset a carton of juice down its front and set up a wail and Elspeth turned her head firmly away. I have no grandmotherly instincts, she thought, thank God.

Opposite her, Kate also sat with eyes closed. The sun from the window struck halfway across her chest and slanted down onto her hands which were loosely clasped in her lap. Although she looked tranquil, dozing at peace, her body felt tender and bruised and she was aware of the places that ached sweetly. What she needed to do as she sat there in the railway carriage was go through everything that had happened, remember everything that was said, every touch, every look. Every single moment that she could recall she wanted to store away carefully, and it was hard work doing this because things kept jumping out of order, and she found herself remembering something after she had taken herself through that particular sequence and then she had to go back again to get it right.

Every single thing mattered, the feel of his skin, the softness of his inner arm, the flecks in his eyes. She remembered noticing the weave of the sheet, the snag of a fingernail, the touch of his bare foot on her leg. She must not let anything drift away before she had stored it safely somewhere in her memory so that she could always go back and visit it as she knew she would for as long as she lived.

As long as she could keep doing this she could hold on to how he had made her feel, remind herself of the person she had been with him, how, for the first time in her life she had felt beautiful, desirable and driven by wonderful, life-giving lust. She knew it wouldn't last, that she wasn't really like that, that day in day out in her ordinary life she would revert to her old self, but for a short time she had been transformed by the enchanting coincidence of man and place.

She tried to work out what had passed between them. She couldn't call it love, because clearly it wasn't, not in any useable form, anyway. It had no potential to grow or develop into anything deeper or lasting, it was complete in itself, just as it was, with no future and no past. She wanted to catch the essence of it and store it somewhere and seal it off, like a rich dark vein, a thick underground trickle, that would enrich all the ordinariness that she knew was going to be the rest of her life.

He was like a gift to me, a reward, she thought dreamily, but a weight too, a responsibility I will have to carry carefully from now on. I can't let what happened spill over and spoil or stain anything else or anybody else's life. For the moment she could not think of Josh, but he would need protecting from the inevitable and terrible hurt of discovery.

She knew that she would never see Patrice again and it was this that would save them. It was her cautiousness, her sense of being ordinary, that would stop her veering off and behaving wildly or recklessly. She supposed she should feel it as guilt, but it wasn't. It didn't feel like that at all. The ugly words like adultery and sin, infidelity, betrayal, she could not consider, because what she had done had felt so right and stripped-to-the-bone true. That was who she was, the woman in the hot, tossed bed, and it was like a discovery, a revelation, to think of herself in this new way, to have gained this secret knowledge before it was too late.

When they had said goodbye, properly goodbye, as the dawn turned the sky a pale milky lemon and she had wept from lack of sleep and happiness, Patrice had kissed her wet cheeks and said something to her in French which she did not understand and she tried now to recall. He had got up then, stood with his back, his beautiful long back, to her as he searched for his cigarettes in the pocket of his jeans which had been discarded on the floor. He sat down again, still with his back to her, and lit a cigarette and drew on it and then, looking over his shoulder at her, shrugged sadly.

It was a funny little eloquent gesture, a mixture of philosophical acceptance and resignation, not designed to comfort her but rather to suggest that her tears were pointless, which of course they were. It was a reminder of the terms of their relationship, that it was what it was and nothing more, and it introduced a note of self-preservation, a hint of toughness, as if the lovemaking had been so sumptuously good that a little balance had to be restored.

Kate could see, as she thought about it now, that it was perfectly judged because she had felt at once that it jolted them apart, introduced a sharp little necessary gap between them. She had wiped her eyes on the edge of the sheet and felt the first pangs of parting neatly pinched and squashed. It was not to be a dangerous, indulgent, lingering affair because Patrice had neatly brought it to its conclusion. If only she could remember what he had said in French. She felt that the words were important, that she needed them to complete her grasp of the scene. She would have to go through it all again and she realised that she did not have for ever. This journey, when she was suspended fleetingly between one place and another,

367

was the only chance she would have. As soon as she was home she would be reclaimed and reoccupied, and she recognised that the truth of how she had felt might be distorted by the familiar place, the people she loved, her old life. She wanted to make sure that she recorded exactly how it had been so that in the future she could guard against guilt or regret tarnishing what had been so perfect.

The warmth of the sun, the gentle buzz of conversation, the fat flank of the mother sitting next to her made her feel cocooned and comfortable and it was hard to make herself concentrate. She started off again from the beginning, thinking of how she went downstairs and let herself through the kitchen, the door to the terrace open, Patrice sitting smoking in the dark and looking over as he heard her come to join him. She wanted to get his expression exactly right, a mixture of surprise and pleasure, and then how he had simply held out his hand to her, his arm stretched towards her, drawing her to him. There was something else that she had forgotten. Had he kissed her then, or poured her a glass of cognac first? She must get it right.

At Dancing Hill Farm, Josh was surprised to see Joyce arrive to work on Saturday morning. He was busy in the dining room which doubled as an office, going through the piles of paperwork which made up such a large part of farming. He also wanted to check the figures that Anna had sent. He wanted to have an alternative financial forecast ready. She wasn't the only one who could blind with statistics.

Joyce, a thin, cheery girl with very short black hair, put her head round the door. 'Morning, Josh,' she said. 'I'll give you a couple of hours this morning, seeing as Bob's at home and can look after Kylie. I thought you'd have got into a right old state, and I can see I wasn't far wrong. Were you leaving it like this for Kate? She'd have walked straight back out if she had any sense!'

Josh grunted. He didn't welcome being interrupted and he hated being in the house when Joyce was there. He felt driven into the corner by her Hoover and mop and the fact that she took no notice of whatever mood he was in. She was what he supposed was a feminist, bullying her poor husband, who worked in a local bakery and was up at four every morning, into doing his share of childcare and even making him cook tea when she worked late. He also suspected that she and Kate laughed at him behind his back. He had caught them at it on occasions, having a 'Bloody men!' sort of conversation.

Now, as she worked in the kitchen, she kept shouting comments through the open door, putting him off what he was doing and yet he couldn't very well get up and close the door, it would seem too rude.

'You could have put these beer cans out!' she shouted. 'You know they go in the recycling box in the outhouse, don't you? Too far to walk, I suppose. What's this?' She appeared at the door, holding the leftover lump of bread.

'What's it look like?' mumbled Josh, hunched over his keyboard.

'Have you got another loaf out the freezer?' she demanded, ignoring his tone. She sighed theatrically and went out to the deep freeze, he supposed, because she then reappeared and said, 'I've got you another loaf out, and this lamb casserole. It will be ready to put in the oven for tonight. Kate won't want to cook when she gets back, but I don't expect that would occur to you!'

369

It didn't stop there. He heard her talking indignantly to herself as she loaded the washing machine and started it off, and then the dishwasher sprang to life, even though he knew it wasn't full.

'There was no need to put that on!' he yelled through the door, needled to respond. 'It was only half full. It's a waste, running it like that!'

'Too bad!' she shouted back. 'Kate doesn't want to get home to a load of dirty dishes! I'll empty it before I leave. Here,' and she put her head back round the door, 'if you're not doing anything you could get out there into the garden and pick some vegetables.'

'I *am* doing something. I am trying to do paperwork!' he cried indignantly. 'If you'd let me have a bit of peace!'

Joyce came to stand in the doorway. 'Here,' she said again, in a different, less hectoring tone. 'What's this about you getting knocked out? I forgot to ask you how you're feeling. No, don't bother to tell me. I can see for myself.'

'Bit late to ask me now,' muttered Josh. 'After the bollocking you've been giving me. Look at this,' and he rolled up his trouser leg to show her the livid bruises and puffy flesh of his leg.

'My word!' exclaimed Joyce, who loved a good injury. 'That's bad, that is! You'll have to watch out for blood clots, with a bruise like that. That's what killed Bob's uncle when he went under his milk float.'

'Yes, Joyce. Thank you for that,' said Josh sarcastically. 'Now if you'd let me get on, please.'

'Do you want a coffee?' she called through the door as she dragged the Hoover out of the cupboard under the stairs.

'Just leave me alone, will you?' groaned Josh.

Joyce laughed. 'Gladly,' she said, plugging it in and roaring over the carpet.

Josh looked out of the window and across the valley. It was a gloomy sort of summer day, the sun obscured by pearly grey clouds which pressed low on the hills. While not actually raining, the air was laden with moisture and the paving stones outside the window were dark with damp.

From where he was sitting he could see George's bungalow, which reminded him of the pleasant evening they had passed the night before. Despite the fact that they had worked together for so many years they had never grown companionably close. Josh had always felt that that was Tom's prerogative and that he was first and foremost a business partner and only secondly a son-in-law. They got on perfectly well and he was fond of the old boy, but he had never felt the need to exchange or invite confidences. It wasn't in either of their natures.

Last night had been a bit different. Perhaps Kate being away changed things. He wouldn't have gone down to George's in the first place, and they wouldn't have talked in quite the way they had, if she had been there. She and George were so thick that Josh never much bothered and because of that perhaps things which should have been said were left unsaid between them. It must have been Kate's absence and the effect of the whisky, and the meal and the comfortable chair, that had led him to confess, for the first time ever, what Dancing Hill meant to him. He felt embarrassed about it now. George had listened in silence and then said, 'You should understand how Anna feels, then, Josh. Why she wants to come back here to farm.'

Thinking about this and looking out of the window, Josh

371

noticed a car coming up the drive and realised that it was Susie.

God, he thought. Here comes another interfering woman. As if Joyce isn't bad enough. Resolutely, he turned back to the computer. It might put her off if she found him engrossed in work when she arrived. A few minutes later he heard her calling at the back door. He hoped that Joyce would go and greet her but he could hear her upstairs with the Hoover and so he had no option but to rise to his feet painfully and limp through to the kitchen.

'Hi,' said Susie brightly. She was wearing a white sweat-shirt and pale blue track pants and looked fragile and unmistakably urban. 'How are you, Josh? Still painful?'

'Yes,' he said shortly. 'Yes, it is.'

'I thought I'd just check that everything was OK for Kate coming back. I see that Joyce is here, thank goodness.'

'Yes,' said Josh, resenting the inference that he needed supervision.

Susie put a basket on the table. 'I've brought some sweet peas,' she said. 'For the kitchen table. I think flowers always make a place look more welcoming, don't you?'

The woman's mad, thought Josh, watching as she filled a pottery jug with water and arranged a bunch of paintbox-coloured flowers. It's Kate's home, for Christ's sake. It doesn't have to be made to look welcoming! Susie reached into the basket and drew out a postcard and propped it against the jug.

'There,' she said, standing back, satisfied.

She glanced at him, standing glowering in the doorway. 'So Anna's called a meeting for next Sunday,' she said.

'It appears so.'

Susie assumed a solemn face. 'I think, Josh, that we

should take her ideas very seriously. I think she has put her finger on a number of important points.'

'Really?' Josh felt increasingly irritated. What did Susie know about the farm, for goodness sake?

'Yes, George and I both think so.' Josh couldn't believe his ears. 'George and I' was it now?

'Really?' he said again, even more coldly.

'Yes. Changes are inevitable, we all know that. We can't go on losing money. Farming the way you and Tom do isn't viable any more. Anna is the future.' Susie could tell she had put his back up, but she didn't care. 'Righto,' she said cheerily. 'I'll be off. Love to Kate.'

When she had gone, Josh picked up the postcard. On the front was a painting of a cottage surrounded by a vast herbaceous border in full flower. At the door of the cottage stood a gnarled old countryman, peacefully smoking his pipe, while a small black cat rubbed against his gartered knees and a pair of doves nestled on the thatched roof. Josh snorted.

He turned the card over and read, 'Welcome Home!!! Hope you had a lovely holiday and a well-earned rest! Love, Susie.' Josh stared at the neat aquamarine handwriting. What the hell was this about? He thought you welcomed people home when they had been in hospital, or away at war or something, not on *holiday*, for goodness sake! Susie and Joyce, and Anna too, appeared to be in league over fostering this idea that Kate specially needed a break, which seemed to him to ignore the fact that he worked bloody hard too, and nobody was sending him postcards and good wishes. It was a female conspiracy, that's what it was.

Then he noticed that Susie had left a dish on the table, covered with clingfilm with a yellow sticker on the top in the same handwriting, saying, 'Warm in middle oven for twenty mins.' On inspection he found it was macaroni cheese, a favourite of his, and he felt uncomfortably caught out. Have I always been like this, he thought, so irritable and grudging? He didn't think so. It's the worry, he excused himself. The worry of running a failing business. It's enough to make anyone a bit short.

After the problems of the outward journey, the trip home from France went without a hitch. This time Elspeth and Kate were routed through Lille and they had half an hour to wander round the grey tubular steel station and drink a cup of coffee looking out at the side of a large building, a church maybe, covered in graffiti, and a scuffed area of park where young men lay on their backs on the grass in attitudes of despair, surrounded by plastic bags of belongings. 'Asylum seekers, do you think?' asked Elspeth, sharing a slice of lemon tart with Kate. 'They look Muslim, don't they, and look, the only girl is wearing a headscarf.'

Kate watched them through the window and felt infinitely sorry for these young people wrenched from their own countries and driven to consider a rootless life in a hostile place as preferable to home. Her own sense of home was growing now they were in more familiar-looking northern France and she thought more and more about what she was going back to. She thought of the week ahead, of getting back into the routine of work, and she looked forward to going round the farm with George on their Sunday afternoon walk. She must remember to take a chicken from the deep freeze because he would expect to come to lunch as usual and from then on life would be back to normal.

She thought of Josh and wondered how his week had been and whether he and Tom had got the hay and silage made and how many of the cows had calved. He would be glad to see her back, she could rely on that, and now she looked forward to seeing him, too. Treacherously, she wondered if later they might make love and found that she wanted to. She couldn't believe it of herself, not after last night, but it was true. She seemed to remember having read in one of Anna's magazines that extramarital sex could revive libido, and she felt some shame that this should apply to her. On the other hand, if it meant that she took a little more care of Josh, was more tender towards him, then that, surely, was a good thing.

She would telephone him when she got to Waterloo and had found a suitable train to catch out of London, and he would come to the station to meet her. When they got back to Dancing Hill it would be late but they could open one of the bottles of wine that Bernard had given her and eat the smelly cheese that she had chosen for him, and they would sit at the kitchen table and chat and she could tell him about Arc en Ciel and he would bring her up to date on the happenings at the farm. She imagined them sitting with their heads together under the circle of lamplight, the cheese on a pretty pottery plate and a loaf of crusty bread on the breadboard.

The dogs, too, she longed to see the dogs again. They would have missed her and would be overjoyed when they heard her voice. She would let them into the house for the evening and they would press against her legs and Bonnie would lay her greying head on her lap and whine with pleasure.

Yes, she was looking forward to getting home.

375

It was eight and a half hours after leaving St Raphael when Elspeth and Kate finally arrived at Waterloo and, feeling slightly zombified, stood together at the top of the slope from where Kate would turn right to the mainline station and Elspeth left, to join the taxi queue. It was a grey London evening and the high glass front of the terminal looked out onto a congested street, the red and white tape of roadworks, and a crawling line of black cabs. London looked tired and shabby in this dull half-light and the people hurrying and preoccupied.

They stood and looked at one another, both wanting to get away but caught for a moment by the necessity of making a proper ceremony of saying goodbye.

Elspeth clasped Kate by the shoulders and they kissed cheeks awkwardly.

'Thank you,' they both said at once.

'It's been wonderful, hasn't it?' said Elspeth.

'Oh yes!' Kate agreed fervently. 'Wonderful.'

'We'll keep in touch. Please tell me if you're coming to London.'

'Come and see us on the farm. Come and meet Josh!'

'I will, I will. Now you must go and I must join the taxi queue. I'll telephone you next week. Goodbye, Kate. Goodbye!'

Elspeth had only ten minutes to wait before she got a cab and gratefully sat back on the seat and closed her eyes. She felt exhausted by the journey and longed to have a bath and a drink. She thought of unlocking her front door, of the pile of dull post, bills and junk mail, and the blinking eye of her answer machine. Before she did anything else, leaving her suitcase inside the door and the post on the mat, she would telephone Archie.

The Saturday evening traffic was heavy and the taxi seemed to make interminable stop-and-start progress but at last she sat forward, her door key already in her hand, and directed the driver where to pull over and asked him to carry her case up to her second-floor flat. He was surly about it but she tipped him well, and as he disappeared down the stairs she had the door open and was stepping over the expected pile on the doormat. The door swung shut behind her and she was aware of the stillness of the flat and the familiar shape of the furniture in the gloomy light as she went to the telephone.

She pressed Archie's number and heard the telephone ring. It rang and rang. As she stood there listening, she knew with a terrible certainty that something had happened. She swallowed hard, her heart beating noisily, and with a trembling hand dialled the code to listen to her messages.

The first was from a shop to tell her that a skirt she had taken to have altered was ready for collection. The second was a friend asking to meet her for lunch. The third was from Archie's housekeeper. Elspeth listened to the message and carefully replaced the receiver. She moved in the half-light to an uncomfortable upright chair where she would never normally choose to sit, but she did so now, with her hands in her lap, her ankles crossed. Her grief, she realised, was for herself, for her own loss, for her life without him. She had readied herself for this moment, had rehearsed it often in her mind, knowing it would come, knowing that she would one day have to face his leaving her, but nothing could have prepared her for the grief she felt. He was an old man, a tired old man, quite ready to die, as he often told her, but that made no difference and was no comfort. She had lost her dearest friend, her fondest lover and nothing could change that. The most painful part of all was that as far as she knew he had died alone, in the afternoon, when, had she not been away in France, she might well have been with him. Had he called for her? she wondered. Had he wanted her beside him at the moment when he must have known the journey into the unknown was beckoning. She wished so much that she had been there that the misery of it made her throat ache and her chest contract so painfully that she wondered if she too might have a heart attack.

I suppose, she thought, that I could empty the bathroom cupboard of pills, swill the whole cocktail down with some of Bernard's wine and call it a day, but as soon as the thought was formed, she knew that although the gesture would be romantic, she could not carry it through. It would be too horrid for Maria, who would have to deal with her body, for one thing. She wasn't sure whether there would be unpleasant leakage and secretions but she suspected there would and she could not possibly wish that on anybody, least of all poor Maria who had a bullying husband and a child with some disability or other. She could cast herself into the Thames but the thought of dirty cold water closing over her head was uninviting and really, she knew that she would not take her life. Archie would be thoroughly disapproving, for one thing.

No, she would have to go on, much as she didn't want to. She would have to go on. Just sitting there seemed hard enough. She wanted to lie on the floor but found it too uncomfortable and so went to her bedroom and lay, stiff and cold, on her bed. Later she got under the duvet, and stared, dry-eyed, into the darkness, thinking of nothing, feeling just the aching loss.

Dawn was breaking when she got up again to go to the

bathroom and dirty yellow light stained the dark squares of her window. Her hands smelled of trains and travelling and she washed them and cleaned the make-up from her face. In all her years she had never skipped this particular ritual.

Going back to bed, still wearing the clothes she had worn all the previous day, she suddenly thought of her painting and went to fetch it from where she had left it in the hall. Patrice had packed it into a cardboard tube and now she turned on the light and pulled it out and unrolled the canvas. She was frightened to look at it, to discover that perhaps it wasn't as she remembered, but as she held the little picture under the harsh light the joyful colours sang out and she was carried back to the time on the hill when she had felt her love for Archie so acutely. She knew now that that was the day he died, and for the first time she allowed herself to weep.

After all the hours of travelling Kate felt a great relief to get off the train and breathe the cool, damp Dorset air. She paused for a moment, reorganising her luggage on the platform, while the few other passengers made their way over the footbridge to the station. A young man in old jeans and wellington boots and with an excited collie on a piece of string bounded down the steps to meet a pretty girl with long blonde hair in a thick plait down her back. He lifted her off her feet while the dog barked round them. Kate smiled. Young love was so attractive and the girl could have been Anna, she thought. She glanced up at the bridge. Josh wouldn't come over to meet her. It wouldn't be his way. He would be sitting waiting for her outside the station. She was confident he would be there although she hadn't spoken to him, only left a message on the answering machine.

From the top of the bridge she stopped to get a gulp of the late evening air which was so fresh and clean and soft. After the dusty heat of the south of France and the baked earth and the strong colours, the gentle greens and browns of the hills she could see to the south, over towards Dancing Hill, were restful and familiar. The sound of twilight birdsong drowned the station announcement as the little train drew out towards Exeter and the west. It is so beautiful, she thought, remembering the poor young men lying on the grass in Lille, and I am so, so lucky that this is my home and where I belong.

Glancing down the other way, she could see the Land Rover in the station car park, with Josh's elbow stuck out of the driver's window. His profile as he consulted his wristwatch looked rather cross. Of course, the train was ten minutes late and that would have annoyed him. How is this going to be? she thought. Her feelings for Josh had not changed but she wondered whether the deep and lasting effect of having slept with Patrice would mark her out as being altered.

She hurried down the remaining steps and out of the old iron station gate. Josh spotted her coming and opened his door and as soon as she saw him getting out, she realised that there was something wrong. He moved like an old man, wincing as he levered himself out of the driver's seat.

'Josh! Whatever's happened to you?' she cried as he put an arm round her shoulders in greeting. They did not kiss and she was glad of that. It gave her a moment to compose herself, to get a hold on how she felt at seeing him again.

'Nothing. It's nothing,' he said in a dismissive tone. 'Don't start.' His face was reddened and peeling from the sun and wore his habitual look of mock disgruntlement.

'Don't start what? Tell me what's happened. What have you done?'

'Got knocked over by Frank, that's all. Cracked ribs and a bang on the leg. I had a night in hospital. Nothing to get excited about.'

'Hospital!' cried Kate in alarm. 'When? When did this happen? Why on earth didn't you tell me? No, for heaven's sake, don't take my case!' Kate felt a rush of concern and a degree of agitation that she was finding this out too late, that it was something she should have known about. She felt as if her position had been undermined.

'Last Sunday. Anna said we shouldn't tell you. We didn't want you worrying.'

'Worrying? Of course I would have worried. I'd have come straight back. This is awful, you poor old thing. However have you managed on your own?'

And so it all came out as they drove home through the last of the daylight. Bit by bit, Kate heard what had happened, how Anna had stayed on to help, how Susie and George had struck up an unholy alliance in Josh's view, how the fox had got her poor chickens, how Joyce hadn't been in to work until today, how they had lost a cow and a calf.

Kate sat with lowered eyes, watching as Josh changed gear. His arms were burnt and freckled by the sun and covered in coarse, wiry ginger hairs. She tried not to think of Patrice's smooth brown skin but even as Josh was unfolding the drama of the week she found herself suddenly transported back so vividly to the previous night that she hardly heard what he was saying. Although his news was compelling she had to wrench herself back to the present and she put a hand to her mouth as if to shut off the surge of tender memories. Even so, for a moment the familiar, untidy cab strewn with binder twine, stray tools and vet supplies seemed invaded by the foreign presence of Patrice.

She struggled to concentrate. 'I can't believe that all this has happened,' she protested. 'I don't know why you didn't telephone me.' She felt it was a subtle punishment, that Josh almost welcomed the string of calamities as a way of proving the error of her choosing to go away at all. She thought she detected a certain satisfied tone in his voice, which grated on her nerves.

'What about Dad? Is he all right?' she asked finally.

Josh indicated to turn right off the main road and then said, 'Well, Susie has been on about him, Tom said. I don't know what exactly, but some bee she got in her bonnet that he was upset about something. I went down to have supper with him last night and he seemed perfectly all right to me.'

'He got to his doctor's appointment, did he?'

'No, I think he missed it.'

'What? How could he have done! Susie said she would make sure he went! Really, it's too bad!' Kate felt thoroughly upset now. How much more could have gone wrong?

'She found him up with the sheep. It was too late by then, apparently. I haven't told you about Anna yet,' he went on as he pulled over to let a car go by. It was driven by someone they knew from the village and they each lifted a hand in recognition and a smile was also necessary.

'What about Anna?' said Kate at the same time, in a tense voice. 'What about her, for goodness sake, Josh?'

'She says she wants to give up her job and come into the farm as a working partner.'

'What? I don't believe it. What about her job? Her career? When? When did she say this?' Kate was incredulous.

'While she was here this week.'

'Well, she's not serious. It must have been just spur-of-the-moment. She can't really mean it!'

'I think you'll find she does. I reacted like you, and we argued all through it. She's very determined. She's coming down next weekend. She wants to present us with a business plan.'

Kate stared out of the window, not knowing what to think. She felt very, very tired and as if all the exhilaration of her holiday had drained away. The reality of ordinary life felt as if it was pressing down on her, forcing out the oxygen of all that had happened to her, like air out of a punctured balloon.

Josh looked across at her.

'I haven't asked you,' he said, 'but you had a good time, obviously. You look very well.'

'I do?' said Kate wearily. 'Actually, I feel a bit banjaxed by everything you've just told me. I can't take it all in. How could so much have happened in a week?'

Now she was sounding suitably deflated, Josh felt he could afford to be kind. He patted her knee.

'How was the painting? Done anything good? Where's the masterpiece?'

As soon as he said the words, Kate remembered that she had left her canvas on the luggage rack in the train, and that by now it would be well on its way to Exeter. She realised that she did not care if she never saw it again.

George saw the Land Rover pull up outside his gate. He'd got the front door open ready and went to stand on the path while Kate got out. She looked tired, he thought, and older. Her tanned face made the lines more obvious. She turned to wave a hand at Josh, who nodded to him through the window and then drove off. George realised that she must be intending to walk on up to the farmhouse after she had said hello.

'It's grand to have you back!' he said, kissing her cheek. 'What a week it's been!'

'It's lovely to be back, Dad,' she said, wondering now if this was true, though it was good to see her father looking quite hale and hearty. She had feared that if there were a casualty while she was away, it would most likely be him. She took his arm and together they went into the bungalow.

Everything looked the same, shipshape and tidy, his supper things washed and on the rack by the sink.

'Come and sit down a minute, lass,' he said. 'You look tired out.'

She followed him into the sitting room and he went to the sideboard and poured them both a whisky. 'Here. This'll perk you up. Better than any of that French nonsense, a drop of whisky!' Kate smiled and went back to the kitchen to fill the little glass jug he used for water.

'It was a very long train journey,' she called through the door. 'Twelve hours of travelling, more or less.'

She went back and sat beside his armchair. Outside, the valley had filled with a navy blue light and the sky was dark except for a line of clotted yellow light in the west. George switched on the table lamp beside his chair.

'So you enjoyed yourself, did you? Had a good rest?'

'Yes, thank you, Dad. It was wonderful. A beautiful place.' How many times would she go through this rigmarole, she thought, making light of her week away, reducing it to the words of a postcard?

'That's good,' he said, satisfied. His imagination didn't run to asking any other questions. 'We've had quite a time of it, I can tell you,' he said, sighing and shaking his head. 'One thing after another, it's been. It was a terrible fright to find Josh like that. I thought he was dead, Kate, I really did. Josh told you about your fowl? I knew there was a fox about. I'd seen him a couple of evenings running. A big light-coloured dog fox. It was my fault, you know. I'd told Josh I'd shut them up. I don't know how I forgot.'

'Don't worry, Dad, it can't be helped,' said Kate wearily. 'It's easy to forget something that's out of routine. Poor things, I'll miss them. Josh tells me you've got me some pullets. Thank you for that. I'll have to buy eggs for a while, but they'll soon be laying. Now what's this about your doctor's appointment?'

George's face stiffened. 'Ah,' he said, looking uncomfortable. It was a long story and he did not know where to begin.

It was quite dark when Kate kissed him goodbye and started to walk up to the farmhouse. He had wanted to lend her a torch but she said she preferred the dark, that she knew every step of the way. As she walked she thought about what he had just told her. It was not hard to imagine his anguish and anxiety over the sheep. Poor old Dad, she thought. He had lived through all of that, looked over that dreadful precipice and faced the possibility of the terrible disease stalking Dancing Hill, and all without her. She felt grateful that Susie had proved to be an ally and that she had had the good sense not to tell Tom or Josh. She also recognised a stab of possessive jealousy, a feeling that it should have been her, not Susie, who had been there to share it with him and this made her feel ashamed.

She was more worried by what he had told her about Anna. Poor Anna, torn between the farm and Rich. She could imagine the misery and drama of the past few days and wondered how her daughter had decided to give up one for the other. What was it about Dancing Hill that was more powerful than the love of the man she might have married? Farming these days was almost written off as a miserable, bloody occupation. Why did Anna want to give up all the freedom of her present life to tie herself down here, and at what personal cost? George had said he understood, that Anna had a sense of where she belonged, just as he had, and that farming ran thick in her blood, but Kate felt uneasy. Did she really know what she was doing, what possibilities she was signing away?

The warm, damp evening smelled of grass and honey-suckle and she found herself thinking of the scented nights at Arc en Ciel. The memory worked like a soothing balm and she felt less troubled, less anxious. She stopped to lean against a fence post. What a muddle it all was, and yet she knew that things would be resolved as they always were eventually, and that what seemed to have been thrown like a handful of shredded paper into the air, her marriage, Anna, the future of the farm, would float down to settle safely on the ground again.

The dogs started to bark up at the yard and she whistled for them. Hesitant at first, they stood at the top of the drive, whining and alert. She called again and on hearing her voice they fled down towards her in a joyful stream of black and white. As she patted and stroked their squirming bodies she looked up at the house and saw Josh standing in a square of light at the kitchen window, staring out at the dark. He's looking for me, she thought. Poor Josh. He's waiting for me. Full of tenderness, she hurried on.

The back door stood open and as she went in she saw at once that the kitchen and washroom were tidy and clean and that a casserole dish stood on the top of the Aga. Josh had even set the table by the look of it and there was a jug of sweet peas in the centre. Kate stood taking in the familiar surroundings, seeing them with a fresh, appreciative eye. Josh had turned from the window and stood leaning with his back to the sink, watching her.

'There's food ready. Joyce made a fuss about getting something out of the deep freeze.'

'I've brought you some wine from France,' she said, trying not to think of that other kitchen. 'Would you like some now?' She searched for the bottles in her bag which Josh had left in the washroom and put them on the table.

She picked up the card propped against the jug and read Susie's words. 'This was very kind of her,' she said, waving it at Josh. 'Thoughtful.'

Josh was busy with a bottle and corkscrew. He looked up. 'Oh, that,' he said, shaking his head in mock disbelief.

Slowly Kate put the card back against the jug. Out of nowhere, as she stared at the sugary-coloured card and the jewel-like flowers, she had remembered what Patrice had said to her, and his words made all the difference.

Later, lying beside Josh, too tired to sleep, she went over them in her head. '*Je suis comme un homme marié,*' he had said. 'I am like a married man.' She remembered his sad shrug, his reminder of the limitations of their relationship and how it had put a check on her emotions as she lay, cheeks wet with tears and suffused with tenderness. Now a tiny barb of pride and indignation snagged at her. She would go on treasuring her memory of him, she knew that, but the now remembered remark made her feel defensive towards Josh lying beside her. It seemed to underestimate how important her husband and her family were to her and as if Patrice felt it necessary to remind her of his own obligations without appreciating the strength of her own ties. She could not expect Patrice to understand the deep pull of the unspectacular, durable love which grew like moss on a stone in a long marriage.

Through the open window she could hear her father's sheep up on Dancing Hill and a fox barked its unearthly, sinking call from Hanging Wood. Josh, propped up on his pillows, began to snore, and for once Kate lay and listened without irritation.

Chapter Sixteen

Susie was surprised when Anna asked them to meet at George's bungalow and not at Dancing Hill. 'It's more like neutral territory,' she explained on the telephone. 'If it's at home, I know that Dad won't be able to resist taking over, and I want to do this my way. So, if that's all right with you and Tom? About eleven? That'll give time to get jobs done on the farm first. I'm coming down on Saturday evening. I'm longing to see Mum and hear about her holiday. So much seems to have happened since she went away.'

Susie made sure that she and Tom were ready for the meeting in good time, with Anna's envelope in her hand, together with one or two other leaflets and brochures of her own. She had not told Tom what she was intending to say and she felt nervous at the thought of speaking out in front of them all, but she had rehearsed it over and over again and was as sure of her ground as she would ever be. She wondered where she had got this new-found resolution. Partly, it was that she felt a change between herself and George since the foot and mouth scare. Seeing him so upset and vulnerable had altered her view of him. She didn't care any more if for years he had treated her as an outsider. She saw now that she had earned a place in his affections, and earned a say in the future of the farm. She was no longer going to be treated as inconsequential and she was determined that the whole lot of them would hear her out.

She was more unsure of Kate's reaction than anyone else's. She knew what to expect from Josh. She had heard him talking to Tom and knew he was opposed to Anna's plans and thought that the whole thing was pie in the sky. Kate seemed torn, sometimes appearing to support Josh, saying that she didn't think farming had a future for young people and that Anna was throwing away opportunities to make a prosperous, happy life doing something else, and then arguing that Anna should be given a chance.

Altogether, thought Susie, Kate seemed unsettled since arriving back from holiday. She had observed as much to Tom and he had told her that it was most likely the shock of walking back into everything that had happened while she had been away. Then she shouldn't have gone, thought Susie. Not if she wasn't prepared for the possible consequences of leaving everything and everybody to get on without her.

Kate looked brown and well and said she had enjoyed her holiday very much but she had nothing to show for it except a book of sketches, some of them done by her teacher, and a story about leaving a painting on the train. Susie would have expected her to be more upset about that, seeing that the whole point of going away was to be able to paint.

She had made a funny remark, too. One that had puzzled Susie at the time. She said she had forgotten something, a delivery or an order, and that since coming home she had felt like a horse turned out in a strange field for the first time.

'What do you mean?' Susie had asked. She didn't pretend to know anything about horses.

'Oh,' laughed Kate, 'completely unsettled. Galloping about with my head in the air. Rushing up to the rails as if to jump out and swerving at the last moment.'

'I see,' said Susie, though she didn't. Whatever had Kate meant? That coming home was like being fenced in, was that it? But why in a strange field? There couldn't be anything more familiar than home, surely. Either way, it had made her sound dissatisfied to be back and as if she would rather be elsewhere, which had surprised her, when she was always on about Dancing Hill being the best place on earth. Susie had been going to mention it to Tom, but thought better of it. He would tell her she was reading too much into things as usual.

Kate had brought her a pretty Provençal tablecloth as a present and also a bar of homemade soap, rather misshapen and grubby in colour, which she said was made on the farm next door to where she was staying. Susie had put it in the old washroom where Tom could use it. It wasn't the sort of thing her guests would appreciate, although Tom did say it smelled nicely of lavender. Kate had thanked her at once for her card and the sweet peas and for all the help she had given everybody while she was away. Susie was pleased with that. It wasn't often that Kate was put in a position to thank her for anything.

She had been a little nervous about mentioning the hens, worried that Kate might be annoyed to find that she had taken the initiative and introduced her own birds into the flock while she was away, but Kate seemed quite happy about the arrangements and even more so when Susie suggested that they shared looking after them on a week on, week off basis. 'That's fine, Susie,' she had said. 'I don't know why we didn't think of it before.'

Susie checked her watch. 'Come on, Tom,' she called, 'it's ten to. We don't want to be late.'

Tom appeared from the farm office, dressed in the tidy check shirt and cord trousers she had put out for him to wear. 'Oh,' he said, seeing the envelope in Susie's hand. 'You've got the paper Anna sent. I was just looking for it. What's that other stuff you've got there?'

'Just some ideas of mine,' said Susie mysteriously. 'I'm not going to tell you now. You'll have to wait.'

Tom nudged her as he went past. 'Planning a rival takeover, are you?' he joked.

They were the first to arrive at the bungalow. George had pulled the leaves out of the dining room table and was fussing around, arranging chairs. Tom went to help him.

'Shall I do coffee?' Susie asked. 'I'm sure everyone would like a cup.'

'Kate said she'd do it,' said George. 'She's bringing some shortbread biscuits.'

'Fine,' said Susie pleasantly, adding, 'Saves me the bother!' under her breath. She sat down in an armchair and picked up the Sunday paper.

Kate and Josh and Anna arrived in the Land Rover. Through the window, Susie saw them pull into George's parking space and Kate help Josh out of the passenger seat. He was still moving painfully, even after two weeks. Anna had an important-looking folder with her, and was carrying something in a supermarket bag. As she followed her parents inside she was already flicking through some papers as if checking that she had everything she needed.

Susie got up to say hello and to kiss Anna and give her hand a little squeeze of encouragement.

'I would have got the mugs out, but George said you

would do the coffee,' she told Kate. 'He said you were bringing biscuits.'

Kate pulled a face. 'Did I? I've clean forgotten. Oh dear.'

'In that case, I'll get on with it, shall I?' said Susie, going out to the kitchen and filling the kettle. She couldn't help but hope that George would notice.

Susie was impressed by what Anna had to say. She had expected a rebuttal of Josh's gloomy outlook and wasn't surprised that Anna passionately argued the case for the survival of small family farms. What made the difference in their case, she said, was that in the south-west the beauty of the environment was the single most important asset and the small farmer was crucial to the survival of the landscape. Josh looked impatient and tapped his foot and then interrupted.

'Anna, we've heard all this. You're not telling us anything we don't already know. We've had all this from every bloody agency going. What it doesn't change is the fact that farm gate prices are at nineteen seventy-seven levels. That's like going into a pub and asking for a twenty-eight pence pint. Or that we've been working on average sixty hours a week for an income that hasn't topped ten thousand pounds for the last five years. Those are the facts I think you should be addressing.'

'Shut up, Dad, and listen. I haven't finished,' she insisted. 'What I'm saying is that because we're small we shouldn't try to compete with the agri-business boys. We've got something completely different going for us here. We should seize on this growing idea of small is beautiful, of the quality of our naturally reared products, of the integrity of our farming systems. People will pay more, much more, for carefully produced, specialist foods. I've got something to show you,' and she drew a large round object out of a plastic bag at her feet and banged it on the table in front of Josh. 'A loaf of bread, Dad. Now tell me how much that cost me? You can't guess? Let me tell you, then. Nearly ten pounds! Look, here's the label. I bought it in the super-market just up the road from where I live. The loaves are made in France, I grant you, but I asked the bakery manager and he says that they can't get enough and that they walk off the shelves. Now compare that shelf price with the price farmers get for wheat and you will see what I'm getting at. There's money being made in specialist food production, but not by the primary producers.' That shut them up for a bit. It silenced even Josh. Susie saw George eyeing the loaf suspiciously. She could imagine him think-ing, 'Bloody French. Daylight robbery. They'd get away with anything.'

Slowly Susie heard Anna's plan begin to unfold. She told them that the only two areas of the present system that were making any money were the two sideline businesses, her bed and breakfast and Kate's catering, and that they should be re-thinking the farming and land management strategy around this undeniable fact. Susie sat up at that. Wasn't it what she had been telling Tom for the last few years? There was more to come. Anna thought that the farm, as a company, should help Susie expand her busi-ness, converting the empty cowsheds down at Lower Holton to holiday cottages and opening a farm shop. 'Susie's visitors would be attracted to staying on a proper farm with hens and ducks and sheep and cows. They could have a hands-on experience with the animals and be encouraged to explore and find out what goes on here.'

Kate, she said, could supply both the shop and Susie's guests with homemade specialist food and home-grown vegetables and maybe start a mail order business as well. 'Your cakes and Christmas puds, for instance, Mum. People round here fight to get them and you can't make anything like enough to meet demand because you're too busy with the farm. With only Joyce to help you, you never will have time to expand. You'll always earn only pocket money unless you start to run it as a proper, developing business. If I'm here I can take over from you on the farm and you can concentrate on expanding the food and catering.' Susie glanced at Kate, who was chewing the end of her biro and looking thoughtful. She couldn't tell what she was thinking, although surely it had crossed her mind that she could be making more of a go of things.

As for the core business of farming, Anna suggested that they should move to finishing their own beef and lamb, whatever that meant, slaughtering it locally and selling the meat direct to the consumer. 'Look at lamb and beef prices,' she said, 'and compare them with what we get for the best quality cattle and sheep. It's not us that's making a profit, is it? We're receiving a declining proportion of the final price. The profit goes into the pockets of everybody else in between,' and as she talked Susie felt more and more excited. It seemed that she and Kate were key members of this plan and that their contributions were properly recognised at last.

'As for the dairy, Dad,' Anna said, turning to Josh, 'I think we should look to a more humane method of milk production. I'd like to see the calves left with their mothers for longer – less milk yield, I know, but we're hardly making any money on the milk as it is, and I believe that people would pay more for milk produced in the old-fashioned way.'

Josh made a gesture of impatience and Anna went on. 'You're quite right, Dad, in saying that farming isn't something young people want to go into. The average age of a farmer in this country is now fifty-eight. It is a declining industry and farms will continue to go out of business. I know all that, but I also think it is a time of new opportunity and I want to come in now, if you'll let me. I'm young and enthusiastic and I've got a business background and I'm convinced that with a different way of looking at things, we can make Dancing Hill viable again. Here.' She spread some brochures on the table. 'Take a look at these. These are ways enterprising farmers have devised of staying in business and holding on to the land they love. Equine hydrotherapy, specialist ice cream, on-line underwear for larger ladies, a mail order wedding boutique run from a barn, a maize maze. These are just a few.'

She passed the brochures and pamphlets round and Susie saw George fumbling for his glasses while Josh leaned back in his chair with an unconvinced look on his face. She could imagine what he was thinking. That he was being turned into a theme park manager. She had heard him say it often enough. Now, she thought, I must do it now, before Josh starts, and while I am lit up by Anna's fighting talk. She cleared her throat but the others took no notice. She heard Josh say something about bloody Disneyland and Kate answering him sharply. How could she get them to stop talking? She picked up her coffee spoon and rapped it smartly on the rim of her mug. Everyone round the table turned to look at her.

'I've got something to say,' she announced. She saw the look of surprise on Tom's face but she ploughed on. She agreed wholeheartedly with everything that had been suggested, she said, and trying not to gloat that her little business had been identified as central to success, went on with her piece about needing to work together rather than against each other, of stopping all the defeatist talk and recognising how lucky they were and to maximise the potential of living in such a beautiful place.

'You might think I'm the one who doesn't understand farming,' she said, 'and that I'm always complaining and telling Tom that we can't go on like this. Well, Anna has just supported me on that. We can't. It's head in the sand to think that something will happen to save us while not doing anything to change what we are already doing. Don't look at me like that, Josh. It's not a criticism. I don't need to be told how efficient you and Tom are as farmers. I know that, but it still doesn't mean that we're making a living, does it? Let me tell you, I've been married to a farmer long enough to know something of what goes on and to understand how you feel about this place. I know that you probably think a townie like me doesn't feel the same, but I do. I love it, I love Dancing Hill and every single day I thank God that I married Tom and that I came to live here.' She had to bite her lip then, to stop it trembling, and was aware of a silence deepening round the table. She could tell that they hadn't expected this outburst from her of all people, and that it made them uncomfortable, but she hadn't finished yet.

'What I can't put up with is this readiness to say everything is going to pot and blame it on the government, the weather, the EU or whatever. If you want to save Dancing Hill, keep it in the family, you should accept Anna with open arms. She's our salvation and without her I think we're lost. But there's something else. I want you to look at this,' she said, emptying an envelope on the table.

'You all know how much Tom and I would have loved to have children. It has been the one thing missing in our lives.' She could feel her face reddening and prickles of sweat on her forehead. She had never spoken like this to any of them before. 'I would like you to consider doing something for these children.' She picked up a leaflet and waved it in the air. 'For me and Tom it would be a way of making up for not having a family of our own, and for the rest of you it would be an opportunity to share what we have here with kids who wouldn't know a cow from a sheep. What we take for granted.' She passed round some of the leaflets she had fanned out in front of her. 'Grumbling and complaints is all I ever hear from you farmers,' she glared at George and Josh, 'and I think that's part of what's going wrong. You're always sorry for yourselves, always worried about losing money, about the government not caring. I know there's plenty of awful hard luck cases but we're the lucky ones. We may be short of cash but we're not really poor, any of us. The bank might own the farm, but we're all right. We'll survive, and look where we live. Every single minute, we should be thankful for living here with all this . . .' she couldn't think how to express it and waved her hand towards the window, 'all this around us!'

Open-mouthed, the family sat on as she opened the booklets and explained the scheme that brought disadvantaged inner city children to spend time on farms. She hadn't any idea what they thought of it all, thought she was quite mad, probably, but she wasn't going to let that stop her now. She had hoped Kate might give her support, or Tom, but it was Josh, unexpectedly, who came round the table and patted her on the back and said, 'Susie, that's the best idea I've heard today!'

The meeting broke up then. They all started to talk at once and Tom put his arm round her and said, 'You're a dark horse, you are. That was quite a bollocking you gave us!' and everybody laughed.

George pottered about getting them all drinks, beer for the men and sherry for the ladies, and when they all had a glass in their hands he coughed and asked for a moment's quiet while he toasted Anna and wished her luck for her future at Dancing Hill. That looked as if they'd accepted her, thought Susie, and she said, 'Hear Hear!' loudly.

Anna came over and kissed her on the cheek and said, 'Thanks, Aunt Suze, and thanks for what you said earlier. That's a fantastically cool idea about the city kids. It's exactly what I'd like to see here. We can't be the traditional closed community we used to be.'

After that Susie had a second sherry and then a third and by the time Tom drove her home she was seeing double.

Up at the farmhouse Josh carved the chicken and Kate dished up the vegetables while George and Anna talked about the farm. It was lovely to hear them, thought Kate, Anna full of ideas, her face shining with excitement, and George just as enthusiastic. Of course he would be happy because Anna's plans gave them all a future and something to work for.

She wasn't so sure about Josh. He would be outvoted if it came to it and so he had no option but to accept that the proposals for change should be adopted, in principle anyway. It was obvious to Kate that he was struggling to come to terms with the future, while George, who should have been more traditional and fixed in outlook, seemed to embrace the new ideas. Of course he had lost his grip on the farm anyway. Change meant less to him than it did to Josh.

She watched his face as he concentrated on carving the chicken and thought she saw hurt and disappointment. Everything he had worked so hard for, transforming an old-fashioned farm into a modern, efficient business, now seemed like no achievement at all. In fact, a lot of what Anna suggested sounded suspiciously like turning the clock back. It was hard for Josh, Kate could see that, and she was moved to put down the oven cloth and go to put her arms round him. He accepted her embrace stiffly, holding the carving knife and fork aloft in each hand. 'Hey, steady on,' he said. 'What's all this about?'

'Nothing,' she said, then added with a smile, 'maybe because you are so good at carving.'

'At least I'm good at something,' he said, his voice thin with resentment.

'Oh Josh.'

The telephone rang and when no one moved to answer it, Kate went to pick it up.

'Elspeth? Hello! How nice to hear from you. I've been wondering how you are.' She said all this before being struck by the frozen quality of Elspeth's voice. 'What's happened? Is everything all right?'

'No, not really, as a matter of fact,' said Elspeth evenly. 'Archie's dead, Kate. He died while we were away. I found out when I got back.'

'Oh, Elspeth! I'm so sorry. I'm so, so sorry.' Behind her, Kate was aware that the others had stopped talking.

'I just thought I would let you know. The funeral was on Tuesday. A small family funeral. There will be a memorial service later on.'

'The family, his daughters, are they . . .?' Kate did not know how to put it.

'They've been surprisingly kind. I think that when they heard the contents of his will they were so relieved that they can now afford to be generous. They asked me to join them at the funeral, sit with them as family, for which I was pathetically grateful. I suppose they could always explain me away as his devoted PA of many years.' There was a bleakness in her voice that Kate found agonising.

'Elspeth, would you like to come here? Come to Dancing Hill? I hate to think of you on your own.'

'It's very kind of you, but actually I prefer to be alone just now. Later on, perhaps. May I let you know?'

'Of course. Please come whenever you feel like it.' She hesitated, knowing that the others were listening. 'I've thought about you a lot since I've got back. Thought about our holiday.'

'Yes. Of course this rather spoiled things.'

'Yes. Elspeth, I'm so sorry.'

'Thank you. I thought you would like to know. We have become friends, I think.'

'Yes, yes. We have. We are.'

They said goodbye and sadly Kate replaced the receiver.

'Who was that?' asked Josh while Anna and George searched her face for clues.

'It was the woman I was with on holiday. Elspeth. A very dear friend of hers died while she was away. She only found out when she got back.'

'Oh,' said Josh, sitting down with a plate of chicken. 'Only a friend. I thought from your conversation that her husband, or someone close, had died. Extraordinary to telephone at lunchtime. She might have guessed it would be inconvenient.'

★ ★ ★

After the washing up was done, George, Anna and Kate went for the usual walk round the farm, leaving Josh to rest. They ended their circuit at George's bungalow, where they left him to go and have forty winks, as he called it, and walked together up to the farmhouse. It was the first time that they had been alone since Kate got back.

'The accident seems to have taken a lot out of Dad, poor old thing,' said Kate. 'He's still in quite a lot of pain and seems to get easily tired.'

'The doctor told him he would,' said Anna. 'He said that he could expect to feel a bit low for a few weeks. Of course Dad would ignore that advice, wouldn't he? He would be dismissive of any caution like that. He's so convinced he's bloody superman. He was all right, though, wasn't he, about me joining the farm? I thought he might put up more of a fight. I didn't expect him to just roll over like that.'

'I'd hardly call it rolling over,' said Kate defensively. 'We all need time to think about things, to mull over what you suggest. We've talked about it a lot this week and Dad and I think that you should start here on a probationary footing and see how things work out. We think that would be better for both sides.'

'That's fine by me,' said Anna. 'I've got three months' notice to work off, so we've got plenty of time to thrash things out. I can't start until November, but I can do quite a lot of the groundwork meanwhile. Get on to the various agencies, get estimates and grant applications, all the stuff that Dad has no time to do.'

Kate glanced at her face. For Anna, like her father, work was a good way to bury pain.

'Is it going to be hard without Rich?'

'I'd rather not talk about it, Mum. There's no use going over it all the time. It wasn't going to work out and it's better to have ended it now. I'm determined to farm and he is just as determined that he doesn't want me to. It's as simple as that.'

'It's not really so simple, though, is it? Feelings are more complicated than that. I worry that you'll throw yourself into these projects of yours and get stuck into life down here and that your personal, your emotional life, will suffer. It will be hard coming back, Anna. Have you thought about that? Hard to be an employee and a daughter at the same time.'

'Of course. I know how bloody-minded Dad can be, but I still want to do it. I won't live at home, though. I realise that that wouldn't work and I will make a real effort to keep in touch with friends and have a bit of a social life too. I'm not stupid, Mum. It's fairly obvious that I could bury myself down here if I'm not careful, and I don't intend to do that.'

'What about London life? Won't you miss the buzz of it all? The freedom, the possibilities?'

'Mum! You have a rosy view of my life. It's pretty soul-destroying, beating yourself up in a job you couldn't care tuppence about. OK, there are more opportunities to go out, go drinking, see the latest films, but frankly I won't miss any of it. I'm not a particular culture vulture, as you know. I've been twice to Tate Modern and got no further than the restaurant and I haven't been to the theatre once since I moved to London.'

Kate sighed. This wasn't really what she meant, but she didn't know how to say it, to suggest to her daughter that to come home, to accept the life of the farm with all its limitations, might one day be a cause of regret.

403

It was Anna's turn to look at her mother shrewdly. 'I do get your drift, you know, Mum. I do understand what you're getting at, but you must see that for me it will be different. It's not like it was for you, marrying so young and coming back to where you were born to follow in Grandma's wake in the traditional role of farmer's wife. I come back as a proper working partner, not as an unpaid supporter. And there's another thing you might not have considered with all this concern about me breaking up with Rich. I quite *want* to be on my own for a bit. I've had a boyfriend since I was at university and I'm actually looking forward to just being myself. Seeing how I shape up on my own. What I turn out to be.'

They walked on in silence, Kate considering what Anna had said. She could see the truth in it but she also wondered if the self was always there within, waiting to be revealed, coaxed out like a shy animal. She preferred to think that self-knowledge came in rare glimpses, like a blessing. It came, unexpectedly, like a chink of light through clouds parting or curtains being drawn back from a window to reveal a new landscape. But only after a lot of plodding along in a fog, she thought, just bloody getting on with it, the rough with the smooth, the ups and the downs. These sudden illuminations were painfully earned.

Anna took Kate's arm as they got to the farmhouse. 'Don't worry about me, Mum. I'm sure I'm doing the right thing. I've never been more sure. I need to come back here. I can't ignore what's in the blood.'

Kate smiled at her fondly. 'I don't have to tell you how much I will love having you here. You, me, Susie. We'll be quite a team.'

Back in the kitchen, Kate put the kettle on to make a cup of tea, while Anna went out to look at her calf. There was no sign of Josh. Kate took two mugs and went quietly upstairs to their bedroom. Josh was still asleep and Kate put the mugs on his bedside table. She closed the bedroom door and unzipped her skirt and pulled her T-shirt over her head. Without waking him she slipped into bed beside him and very gently took him in her arms.

It wasn't until September that Elspeth came to stay and she and Kate walked with the dogs up the track above the farm.

'So this is Dancing Hill. You told me how lovely it was,' exclaimed Elspeth, 'but I imagined endless mud and sort of potato field greyness, not all this beautiful grass and a sense of being on top of the world.'

She stopped halfway up the hill on a little rutted path made by the sheep and looked over the Vale where the gold of harvest chequered the green, and a touch of yellow and red fingered the deep woodlands so that they looked as if they were licked by fire. Big puffy white clouds banked along the horizon but the sky was high and blue and the gathering swallows dived and swooped above their heads.

The grass on the hill was short and dry, no longer freshly green but scattered with the bright crowns of knapweed and thistles. The lambs were big now, stocky and round, kneeling to butt greedily at their mothers who impatiently knocked them away.

'Yes, it is beautiful,' agreed Kate. 'We always knew it was, but it's been Anna who has got the official recognition. We just thought of it as our place, where my family have farmed for hundreds of years, and worried about losing it. It's now been classified as an environmentally sensitive area and we have a grant to look after it. That means just doing what we have always done. No plough-ing, no spraying, no over-grazing.'

'So Josh has accepted Anna coming into farming, has he? I hardly liked to mention it in front of him. You thought there would be a problem, didn't you?'

'It's been hard for him because he prided himself on being a top-class farmer, which he is, but he'd be the first to admit he's not imaginative. What it took was Anna's fresh vision to see the potential of this place and to be quite bold about moving away from traditional farming. He didn't like it and things were difficult to begin with. He keeps saying he never wanted to go into tourism and we have to keep him away from Susie's visitors when they want to ask inane questions about the stock, but on the whole he has had to accept it.'

'And you? You must love the prospect of having her here.'

'I don't know,' said Kate. 'In theory, yes, but I'm not so sure that she's done the right thing. The farm isn't every-thing, is it? There's her personal happiness to consider.'

'The boyfriend, you mean?'

'Partly. She thought she loved him. I think she probably did, but the farm separated them. If she hadn't been so dead set on coming back home I think they would be engaged by now.'

'Don't you think if they loved one another enough they could have overcome their differences?'

'I expect so. It's too late now. He's getting married in December to one of her friends. I think that's been quite hard to bear.'

'Oh, the bastard!' cried Elspeth. 'But she'll find herself a lovely farmer, won't she? A sort of Gabriel Oak type, who would be much more suitable in the long run. Anyone as pretty as she is won't last five minutes in the country where every man must be longing to look at something more attractive than a cow's backside!'

'I hope so. But there aren't so many men to choose from down here and who will she meet when she's working flat out on the farm? She's moving into a cottage on the estate next door. It's terribly pretty but very isolated. I worry about her being there on her own. She should be having fun, at her age. Seeing a bit of life.'

They walked in silence for a while, Kate feeling anxious that what she had said about Anna might have reminded Elspeth of her own solitary state and Elspeth wondering whether Kate was not thinking more about her own past when she expressed concern about her daughter's future. They stopped by the fence at the top of the field, where the brambles grew in thickets, their branches bowed down with the weight of glossy blackberries.

Kate passed Elspeth a plastic ice cream box and they started to pick. Side by side they moved along the fence, avoiding the stinging nettles, brushing away lazy flies which circled their heads, and picked until their fingers were stained deep red.

'I'm going back, you know,' said Elspeth suddenly.

'Going back?'

'To France. I'm going back after the memorial service. Brigitte and Robert have invited me.'

Kate looked at her, surprised. 'You are? I never thought . . .'

'I'm going back to stay until after Christmas, as a sort of paying guest. I want to try my hand at painting more seriously and Bernard is a bit of an attraction. He lives with his old mother, you know. He's a widower and lonely, and I'm, well, you know how things are with me.'

Kate said nothing, surprised by Elspeth's news and alarmed by the sudden rush of feeling which she thought she had safely sent underground and sealed over. Going back. She thought of the winding road, the pine-covered hills, the farmhouse and the sunshine. Acutely, she remembered being with Patrice, the texture of his skin, the feel of his hair, the taste of his mouth. She swallowed hard, trying to stop the dangerous lump from rising in her throat and the tears which were pricking at her eyes.

'I wondered, actually,' said Elspeth, innocently enough, 'whether you would come out again, if I was there? Knowing how much you enjoyed it last time.'

Kate knew what her friend was asking.

She continued to pick, concentrating on seeking the ripest, juiciest fruits which were hidden deep amongst the thorny branches. She could feel Elspeth waiting for her answer and when she was ready she turned to her and smiled.

'No,' she said. 'Lovely though it was, I won't be going back.'

The author would like to draw her readers'
attention to the following charity.

Farms For City Children
Nethercott House
Iddesleigh
Winkleigh
Devon
EX19 8BG

'For some children, it is the first time they
have seen a sky full of stars or a horizon that is
not man made.'

You can buy any of these other **Review** titles
from your bookshop or *direct from the publisher*.

Green Grass	Raffaella Barker	£6.99
Cuban Heels	Emily Barr	£6.99
Jaded	Lucy Hawking	£6.99
Pure Fiction	Julie Highmore	£6.99
The World Unseen	Shamim Sarif	£6.99
Blackthorn Winter	Sarah Challis	£6.99
Spit Against the Wind	Anna Smith	£6.99
Dancing In a Distant Place	Isla Dewar	£6.99
Dad's Life	Dave Hill	£6.99
Magpie Bridge	Liu Hong	£6.99
My Lover's Lover	Maggie O'Farrell	£6.99
Ghost Music	Candida Clark	£6.99
The Water's Edge	Louise Tondeur	£6.99